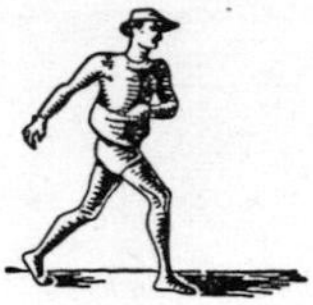

REMEMBER
WILLIAM KITE?

a novel by
**Stephen Longstreet
and J. J. Godoff**

SIMON AND SCHUSTER · NEW YORK

1966

TO ROSALIND AND HENRY SIMON

BOOK ONE

In tragic life . . .
No villain need be! Passions spin the plot:
We are betrayed by what is false within . . . .
                    —GEORGE MEREDITH

The Devil always regretted Faust
did not love him. . . .
                    —WILLIAM KITE

How the Text Came to Be.

WHEN LAST FALL my copy of the *Princeton Alumni Magazine* came, I was amazed to find under the section called "The Last Post" a notice—accompanied by a tiny photograph—that William Grant Kite had died in July in North Carolina. Somehow I had got the impression William Kite had already been dead for twenty years or more. I could not understand how I had missed seeing his obituary in the New York *Times,* the mail edition of which gets to East Pompton every morning. William Kite, for all his dualities and alienations, had been a well-known, even notorious man during most of his life.

I remembered when I was a boy in the twenties in East Pompton, New Jersey, and he already a mature man, there was a whispered growing body of legend about him. His fame seemed potential rather than actual. He had volunteered out of Princeton (class of 1916—he never graduated) and fought with the RFC in 1915–1917; then, some said, had been one of the early collectors of Dada and backers of avant-garde literary magazines. To the savorless, monotonous lives of most he seemed a glamorous figure, an intellectual military hero. My father thought him "an international bum and loafer."

He had been sexually involved with a woman I knew in our town, and there had been a case in which he figured as a witness, but it was all vague in my memory, like the first jazz bands I ever heard, or the names of cars we owned when I was a child.

As I read the notice in the alumni magazine, I couldn't remember many details of William Kite's life. Somehow the small photograph of the bald, wrinkled old man in the magazine, whose puckered mouth looked as if it lacked most of its teeth, did not mesh with the oil

9

painting of William Kite in his romantic flying uniform, the fine hawk's nose tapered to an aristocratic curve, thick blond hair under a natty cap. I hadn't seen that painting of him in many years, but it had hung in the hall of the Kite mansion on Frenchman Street, painted in Paris in 1918 by some minor follower of Degas, while the subject was on leave, convalescing from some wound in his hip, for he leaned on a cane in the picture. (I could once name all the decorations pinned to his chest beyond the MC, DSM, *Croix de guerre.* . . .) The world then seemed well lit—a light that was steady and solid to objects in the round; in our times only the shadows have values, and I suppose it is in these shadows William Kite lived out his life to the end.

In the twenties, when William Kite was home in East Pompton, driving his half-brother Harry's Stutz Bearcat, I remember my impressions of a long tanned face, tinged a bit with the excessive use of alcohol, his nose broken but reset so it actually improved his face. Later I sensed a man working to gamble himself away, risk himself.

I wondered how he had actually died and under what circumstances. I sent a secretary to find a file of the New York *Times* and hunt back into July and August for any detailed notice of his death. She reported there had been no mention of his death in the paper. Not in the *Herald Tribune* either, or other papers. Did I want her to look in some of the out-of-town papers? I said no. My interest was becoming hallucinatory and could wind up an obsession.

Yet it was hard to believe that William Kite—so vivid a memory of my childhood and youth—had been forgotten. After the war he had studied engineering, but he never seriously practiced his profession, for the family money—and there was a lot of it, a solid, old-fashioned fortune going back to chin whiskers and gold coins—lasted until the crash of '29. William Kite had been on the fringe of the movers and makers of art trends and literary movements. When times grew hard—so I heard—he had lived for some years by selling his Soutines, a Joyce manuscript of a doggerel poem so obscene it has never been printed and is now at Yale.

When his half-brother Harry died in the late '40s, my family handled the Kite legal affairs, and I remember my father's showing me the Kite portfolio, which contained little more than duplicates of old land sale contracts and some outdated patents in long-discarded processes. There were also two yellowed photographs that fascinated me. One was of Gertrude Stein and her dark Indian-looking companion feeding pigeons in St. Mark's Square in Venice—the heavy beefy woman solid with ego, a little outlandish, her crude features half blocked out in shadow; and to one side, in a mock boxing pose, two men, young William Kite in a straw skimmer, laughing, fists up, and facing him Eliot Tjaden looking very F. Scott Fitzgerald but already gone to fat around the middle. The two grotesque women, frozen in photography, were holding up forever handfuls of cracked corn, Miss Stein grasping a brown paper bag in her left hand as if it were someone's throat. She appeared to be wearing men's shoes. I could not date the photograph. The second picture was in a newspaper cut, worn and cracked. It showed William Kite coming out of a London courthouse past police and an encircling crowd that seemed on the point of roughing him up. He looked thin and drawn with some unquiet desperation, his hair already receding, the petulant verve and gaiety, at least here, lost. On the back were the penciled words: WITNESS IN DIVORCE—1933(?). It had been a messy affair, but again the details were hazy to me. After that William Kite seemed to be always just leaving East Pompton or expected, and one heard fragments of gossip—that he was trying to get Eliot Tjaden the Nobel Prize for Literature, that he once stole a racing car, that he had knocked down Ernest Hemingway in a Havana café. But lots of people were trading punches with the writer, so it might not have been William Kite.

The last notice that I could remember—there is a cruel finality to public neglect—was during the early days of World War II, a mention that he was a Signal Corps major. A cousin of mine told me it was a thankless task. William Kite sat out the war with a lot of other overage crocks, identifying air force targets from old picture postcards going back to the turn of the century. I understand these frayed and ancient cards were often of great value in checking not lately photographed enemy cities, rivers and terrain as targets for our bombers. A lot of culture and amusement parks and old churches felt Kite's ire. . . . After that, till the alumni magazine, a silence.

Odd, I thought, for a man who had known such a diversified collection of people—Emma Goldman, Lady Cunard, Aleister Crawley, H. G. Wells, Josephine Baker, the painters Vlaminck and Pascin, and, I suppose, hundreds of people who flared up like a thin flame in a wind for a moment and are now forgotten. It was said William Kite had poured a full tepid cup of tea down Henry James's stiff high collar, and that he was one of the worst poker players in the

11

Roman private clubs. It hardly seemed to me to be a life to evoke sympathy for all its juicy gossip.

He was the last of the Kites, and where the family mansion had stood on Frenchman Street there is now a vulgar shopping center of plastic and fake Aztec bricks. None of the old oaks I had climbed as a boy have survived. But the fine amenities of memory, the brave decisions of any past, become in time a bore.

Two weeks after I saw the brief obituary notice—the dismal photograph—in the magazine, I received a bulky package, *Express Collect $7.85,* from a firm of lawyers in Brattleville, North Carolina. CASSEL AND JONSTONE, ATTORNEYS-AT-LAW, FARM AUCTIONS, TITLE SEARCHING. 9 MAIN STREET, ROOM 16. There was a letter inside on top of a bundle made up mostly of flat yellow legal note pads.

MR. RICHARD FLOOD
282 Frenchman Street
East Pompton, New Jersey

DEAR SIR:

Mr. William Grant Kite, who passed on, on July 14 last, a few months before his demise made a properly legal will prepared by this office. In it he left a hundred thousand dollars ($100,000.00) to each of the following: Princeton University, Planned Parenthood Federation, the Museum of Modern Art, and a fund to commission the sculptor Henry Moore for a bronze memorial in Dublin to Leopold Bloom (whom we have been unable to identify). There were other smaller items and gifts listed. One was of fifty thousand dollars ($50,000.00) to you, whom he told us he had known in your youth, and whom he now desired to edit a manuscript he, William Kite, had written in the form of a kind of memoir of his life.

As to *all* money bequests, we regret to inform you that the entire estate of Mr. Kite at the time of his burial consisted of four dollars and some change, a pair of mutton-fat jade cuff links (value about $10.00) and debts of one hundred and two dollars in bar bills in various town and country clubs where he held guest cards for short periods of time. As he showed some signs of senility, his awards were not in the nature of jests. A Mr. Samuel Pfaelzer came forward to pay for the interment in Lilac Lawn Park. Mr. Kite was a house guest of Mr. Pfaelzer's at the time of his passing.

We enclose the manuscripts with no comment. You have full

12

authority (a copy of the will is attached) to do what you see fit with these texts.

Faithfully yours,

ROBERT E. L. JONSTONE

(for Cassel & Jonstone)

I wondered just how senile William Kite had been. The awards smelled like a period joke. The will was a simple country town two-page form, and after my never-to-be-collected bequest were the words: "It is my wish that he edit my manuscripts, in whatever form I leave them, and at whatever stage they proceed to, to do as he feels fit, seeing to it that the book has a solid binding, not easily cracked—not the usual cheesy job—and that the paper be of quality at least to outlast the grave worms at work on my stringy mortal remains. I hope he remembers Bacon's *Homo additus Naturae.*"

I could almost hear him saying it, "Man added to nature," smiling, an ironic look on his long handsome face, but of course he was no longer handsome when he made the will—the face fallen in, the flesh raddled, a sour-smelling old man, sponging on past friends, running up bar bills. The agony of living must have been cruel.

There were twenty-six thick long yellow legal pads, three bundles of loose sheets, some irrelevant text on the backs of opened-out envelopes, and a handwritten section on a book jacket (a life of Jean Harlow) spotted with coffee stains. Most of the writing was done with an old-fashioned, broad-nibbed fountain pen. It was an unsteady hand to read, and seemed to be written at great speed. In several places a pencil had been used, but mostly, except for one section in the vile purple liquid one finds in some guest houses, it was good firm black ink.

Almost to the end (assuming I was reading the manuscripts in proper order, for there were no page numbers) the writing oddly enough picked up a firmer stroke, more character, and there was a bold dash to the crossing of the t's and the flinging tails of the y's, as if a lost precision of rhythm was for a moment recovered.

After I had numbered the pages in red, I began to read them and found there was no true chronological order, no simple step-by-step retelling of man's life in the solid old-fashioned way. It was a piling up of impressions, rages, lyric sections, with a use of language and frankness that could not, I suppose, have been printed fifty years ago. I found a brutal candor in it, a naming of names, reworking of old

13

scandals, some secrets, and a great deal about geniuses, madmen, and a lot about women. I wondered how sober he had been much of the time.

There was not always direct narrative style, but after weeks of reading and rereading of some sections, I had a new picture of William Kite and how he felt about the twentieth century, which, in places, he said had not lived up to its promise but had betrayed itself and its society. Old men do say things like that. But there was not too much of it. Society, he wrote, "has placed itself—the puny irrelevant spectator—in a position where it can snuff itself out like a match after lighting a good H. Uppman cigar."

I wondered how I should edit this material—and if it could be printed at all. Should I do cutting, pasting, create some connecting tissues, rearrange toward some kind of proper dating? Tone down the language, remove certain scenes and some words? What would I destroy in the process?

After not too long consideration I decided to present the William Kite manuscript as it was, inserting my own comments only where I thought a scene needed explaining or a fact or date corrected. I divided the work into books. In several sections where William Kite had written three or four versions of an incident, I picked the most detailed version, and in three places I blended two versions, each of which had details missing in the other. In some places where a man or woman was still alive, or the family might suffer embarrassment, I changed a few names. Put it down to an overprudent legal training. I hope I avoided a stylish *plat du jour* pastiche. In most cases I have kept the real names of everyone. He appears trustworthy. Although he claims not to have been an *officier de la Légion d'Honneur,* he really was.

Scholars and students who are interested can, at a later date, study the entire original texts in the manuscript library at Princeton, to which I have presented them.

What William Kite, down at heel, decaying, angry, tried to set down was an earnest, confused, often wild and funny text, eager, cruel, yet at times sensitive. It had no title. I have given it one. He was a man never finding himself, having perhaps a wish for his own destruction, a man too sensual, too unbalanced, too direct in his demands on his world; given to alcohol for long periods, despairing

14

and at times exulting, but, unlike the men of the present era, never accepting a negative view of life for too long a time. The fashionable philosophy of the nothingness of things did not satisfy him. Yet he had no true answers, and he avoided, as he put it, the "escape hatches of the Vatican, homosexuality, Zen, American rightists or leftists, the Freudian romantic couch, the shotgun barrel held firmly in the mouth."

William Kite was an uneven writer, at times an automatic author, very often lush, witty, sardonic. A part of him was revolted by the world of smells and the closeness of people, as was Dean Swift. What remains is a picture of a man of taste and desires, who was not himself any kind of artist but lived in the world of creation, a man who could not adjust to women, but tried to in one major love affair. He made, I suppose, an inner secret image of woman that was too romantic to remain satisfactory for long in what he called "the unreality of reality."

He produced in part a picture of an era that has become legend; but in the end the popular image of him I knew, of William Kite, fades from view, while he himself lives on, a bore in old age and a perpetual, not popular, house guest among the endowed idle rich of the Carolinas, Virginia, the Eastern Shore of Maryland, remembering the stale story of the night Zelda Fitzgerald took off her clothes at Nice and drove a Pierce-Arrow naked, and what was the true relationship of Modigliani and the English poetess, Beatrice Hastings? and why did Camus commit auto suicide? and something of General Patton's parties in Sicily. And wasn't Pop Art just stale Dada?

So William Kite peters out, a gabby, neglected old man, writing his life in bits and fragments, building up his frayed pile of manuscripts —hoping someday it will be in a form to publish? No, I don't think he gave a damn any more; he merely waited for the final mortality— he called it "the last kick in the ass."

R.F.

Where are we most lonely? In our vanity.
—W. K.

Very few people would fall in love if they didn't read about it. . . .
—LA ROCHEFOUCAULD

It takes a great deal of religion to make a little bit of God. —BISHOP TJADEN

CHAPTER 1

NOW

SOMEWHERE FREUD WROTE: The act of writing about one's past is an effort by the writer to exorcise himself of whatever he is suffering from. It sounds reasonable. And too easy. As most reality is subjective, how will the poor bastard of a writer know he has exorcised his demon? I write because there is nothing much else to do. I expect little. Great illuminations are for saints, fanatics, mystics, and the insane.

I have been for many years a confirmed alcoholic (I understand an unpleasant one, but not revolting), and the advanced Jews of whom I am at the moment a house guest have lost most of their rigid Judaism except for certain moral ideas about the overuse of drink and casual adultery. I just manage on the five o'clock martinis (two) and the after-dinner brandy (three ounces). As for fornication, I have reached the age and condition where I agree with Lord Chesterfield: The position is ridiculous.

In my room, put there for my needs, is an old-fashioned fountain pen with real ink, a great deal of good writing paper; and I may be here—with luck—all fall. If I am ever to exorcise anything, or actually to keep from dying of boredom, this is the time and place to write.

Proust—one of *les grands nerveux*—was plagued by that goddamn madeleine cake dipped in tea, in *Du Côté de Chez Swann,* and with one sniff total recall was on draft for him. I am older, and assimilation and metamorphosis aren't easy for me. My chosen hatful of myths are of the land, the dead, the proud and foolish; not anyone

17

else's head lice. I have found out, the hard way, that nothing is permanent or accurate in the consciousness of a living man; there are always the inevitable changes, long blank periods called cruel and brought by time.

So, I scratch my flaccid balls and begin the circular movement of memory on a gray rainy North Carolina day four hours before cocktails. . . .

1950

THERE IS a terrifying grotesqueness to watching a man harassed by inordinate pain. I sat and looked at him: alone but for me, so alone, the man in the second-class train compartment. All the banal ideas on loneliness must have swept through him as I watched, and a rising despair and agony. His broken thigh bone with its setting of splints and bandages and plaster had become a spurred instrument of torture attached to him by torn living flesh and tormented nerve ends. I stared a half-assed helpless stare.

Mostly, I suspected, he thought of his ordeal in Austrian German, for Charlie Huttonbok had been away from America for a lot of years. When some special nuance of reaction was needed to express his feeling, to modulate the pain, he did not think in English. In his youth—my youth, our youth—we had had a common language. On those holidays at St. Moritz, or at the Canadian lakes, he spoke English with an Oxford "a." But when the pain was at its worst, I knew he thought and cursed in the good low German he had known since 1917.

There was nothing out there beyond the streaked train window to help him through this agony, and there was nothing inside but his stern control of himself—and my company—to keep him from crying out. We had known the American author and big-game hunter who had defined courage as *grace under pressure;* but that was just some of Ernest's goddamn arty crap. There was no grace, I knew, in any final shattering pressure, just a wet-faced, open-mouthed crying out of suffering, with the panic button on. And Charlie knew there would be no relief for hours. What had been going on since Leipzig, where I had joined him on getting his telegram, would go on till we were in sight of the rise of the Zugspitze near the Austrian border. I was in for a sweet old time; our only reality, our youth together, had been over a long long time ago. He was in a fever; he must be running a temperature of at least 101, by the sweat and warmth of him, I thought as I adjusted his topcoat; and his mind, most likely, had a habit of leaving him—I had a lovely picture of it—to hover like a bat on the stained ceiling of the train compartment before it came back to crawl inside his head.

"Without and with mainstay, no lantern, light of day, burning, I burn away. . . ." (What had brought these lines of St. John of the Cross to my mind?) Charlie, born a Catholic, had not been in a state of grace for many years, not since his divorce, and there were other things done before and since, and not all regretted. But I couldn't keep the lines out of my mind. The fever, the wet cold December night, the lurch of the train, the pain in the broken thigh bone. . . . *"Stand near enough to touch him, brush by his very side, when the mysterious stranger hints where the night shall hide . . ."* Charlie shook his head to free himself of some somber thought of his own, like a dog shaking off water after a tumble into a stream. Reason and reality, I saw, were beginning to seep back into him, and a crueler version of the original pain.

I said, "Crazy train, crazy you, Charlie."

"Oh fuck off, Bill," Charlie said, teeth tight together.

The oily darkness had turned to rain outside the streaked glass of the Leipzig–Regensburg–München night train. Then to sleet. Back to a horizontal driving rain again. Since the war and the popular ease of air travel, the trains had grown shabby and the rolling stock was old and neglected. This car, I thought, was on the Arlberg-Orient Express run in the years between the old wars, and its soot-stained sides, I had noticed when Charlie was carried aboard, still bore the letters *Compagnie des Wagon-Lits et Express Européens*. It was not put into service, the station guard said, except in weather like this, when the airfields were zeroed in and there was an influx of grounded passengers going on with their journeys by rail.

It had been over twenty years since I had seen him—how Charlie had changed. In high school he had once begun an essay in *English 4* with the line: *To feel happy without feeling guilty . . .* Old, bald, wrinkled, busted-up Charlie—I didn't know this image. A goddamn stranger.

19

"Christ, Bill, what if I hadn't seen your name at that conference meeting? And wired you?"

The heavy cast on his right leg held my interest. It was propped up on luggage, and under a faded tan Burberry coat showed the cruel ends of wooden splints, bandages covered with hard-set plaster.

"You're a stupid bastard to be traveling like this."

Traveling with a broken thigh was foolish, painful, and the last morphine pill had been taken as the train plunged into the foul weather past Zwickau. (Charlie a stranger?) The man, feverish, his temper on edge, was in his fifties, square, solid, with a burnt-sienna face of stern, now agonized features that told of an outdoor life. (I remembered only a much younger version.) He shifted his thick torso a bit as the train tore through mist and rain and went past the black shapes of moored trees, a crossing of galloping bells, striped barrier and a few specks of orange light from houses crouched against the rain on the right of way. The car smelled of *Aalsuppe* (eel soup, which I detested), *knoblauchwurst* and the lavatory at the end of the car—echoing ancient crap going back to Emperor Franz Josef (it made the American tourists sick among old plush and rusting fittings).

His thigh must have been on fire, the cruel shattered edges of the bone meeting; he knew it would most likely have to be reset when he got to Garmisch-Partenkirchen. Insane to travel like this from Løkken in Norway by plane to Leipzig, then contact me when the rains and fog grounded the plane and go on in this bucking wreck of a once-fine set of cars.

Charlie Huttonbok moaned and ground his teeth together and put his two fists up on his face. I turned my thoughts inward—I was ass-weary from sitting. How fine and easy life had been when this car had really been part of the Paris–Vienna run of the Arlberg-Orient Express, and I was younger—everybody was—and crazy and full of juices, and there were baskets of Rhine, Moselle, kirsch, Steinhaeger gin, not *here* but in the first-class section, and beautiful cunts and recklessly gesturing laughing men. One picked out the bones with care from the platters of Bodensee *Felchen*—salmon— and made appointments to meet again at the Kranzler Bar, the Königshof . . . to screw, get drunk, between two wars. It was all so

20

lousy with a false toughness—"a couple of lost generations." Gestures, *gestures*.

I dozed off—came to—and I remember an image of a face smelling of Buckling smoked herring and Limburger, the face of the car porter, and me giving Charlie a drink of brandy, and pain, great greater greatest, till it all was empty howling space and I was dozing again, coming down a slope with Charlie the great ski master, to the crunching sound of skis on the hard dry snow, and his arms were way out and he was screaming in German, I couldn't remember what. . . .

"Easy—maybe we'll get off here."

I came back to actuality, aware the train was slowing down. From the inky squares of the windows the landscape focused itself. The porter passed by rubbing his pockmarked face.

Charlie, lips tight, asked if we were nearing Munich.

"*Ja, Herr Graf, München.*" He said we would follow in the train from Ulm and Augsburg. Would the *gnädige Herren* like something, a little *Münsterkäse* or *Selterwasser*?

I shook my head. The pain was back in Charlie, I saw, and too strong for him to continue speech. He had not eaten all day, and taking care of the needs of nature, done with the aid of the porter and myself, had been revolting agony. Charlie wanted to be left alone, and for the first time I sensed he wanted to die quickly. (Exile, expiation, penitence, pain, peace.)

München—for me only memories of swinish cheers for Nazi supermen, dead Jews in little looted apartments—from the train window looked merely dark and wet with a dank Teutonic heaviness. How could I encourage Charlie by telling him life is unique, untransferable, precious, a perpetual mental hard on, when I doubted it myself? The stone roofs that had survived, the spires of churches, St. Catherine Hospice, all stained by the gray misery of a just-stopped rain; all the shitty Meistersinger scenery out of howling opera. I thought it was badly drawn, out of kilter. The train had not stopped, just slowed, and it began to creep forward with jolting jars that caused Charlie to make a knotted purse-end of his mouth. A loud groan escaped him.

I asked if we would stay here long in the hissing steam, the hollow hell of the echoing station. The porter said there was no problem; our coach would be detached and coupled onto the Garmisch-Partenkirchen local the snow sports took. This time of December most snow bums went by plane and bus, not like in the old days when the really rich people—boozy, amorous, just a little crazy—came to climb the Zugspitze, the Tyrolean crags of the Ortler, or Gross Glockner, on a splendid train all gold and teakwood.

The train had entered the echoing *Bahnhof* and the car porter left in a hurry, setting his brass-fronted cap solidly on his straw-colored, Katzenjammer head. As doors opened to cold dampness, there was the odor of wet pigeon droppings and stale grease, the empty hulls of sunflower seeds, old newspapers scattered about. Below the streaked window a long cement platform slid into place, wheeled carts appeared, overlabeled luggage, English bags with canvas covers, a running boy holding up an envelope, two duck-assed nuns behind thick glasses carrying artists' easels, a forlorn dog attached by a leash to a slotted crate. The train shivered to a stop. Charlie held his fists buried deep into the plush seat, and when the air brakes were released, sweat covered his bald forehead. I wiped his face.

He let words escape him: *"Jesus, Maria und Josef."*

"That's right, Charlie, *pray.*"

I tried to bring some order to the traveling rugs, rumpled overcoats, the bits of luggage that propped up Charlie's limb, the flung-apart sections of newspapers. I gave it up. Better to observe the dark station and relate observation to experience, and think how to get Charlie off the train here, right now. But I only said, "Only in joke books do expert skiers break a thigh."

"It had to happen. After over thirty years on skis, yes."

"Crazy."

"Crazy, all right—a village near Oslo. Some stupid prick runs into me on a slope and kicks about. A bad break in the middle of the thigh."

"You shouldn't be traveling. Let's go to a hospital here."

"No. Have reasons to go on."

"The bone doesn't like your reasons."

"Damn trip went wrong right from the start. Weather turned rotten. This train is rattling apart."

"You stubborn *wasserkopf.* Get off here."

"Bill, everything I have is tied up in the lousy ski season on the Zugspitze. I have to get there or it will piss away into nothing. I'm too old to start again."

22

"There must be something else, Charlie."

A baggagemaster in a masterful pose of rage was cursing out some porters: *"Himmel, Herr Gott, Sakrament!"* The train—recoupled in some noisy revulsion—was starting slowly, seeming to stand still and only the station slipping away as if on rollers.

"Charlie, where are you staying in Garmisch-Partenkirchen?"

"The Golfhotel, or the Sonnenbichl. I'm ruining your own business."

"I've got no business. The conference was a lot of international horseshit. Save the dear Germans. Love Arab oil."

The train was gaining momentum past red and green signal arms, trees with rain still nesting in their branches. The old coach began to joggle and shake. I tried to wedge Charlie's plaster cast more firmly into rigidity with newspapers and small bundles.

"I avoid living in the past, Bill, but damn it, remember when this was a crack train and the service was like at the Alpenhof and the roadbed was better?"

"And you were hot stuff—astonishing the world with your ski jumps."

Charlie made a firm line of his mouth. (How much he looked like his father when I was a kid in East Pompton.) "Nostalgia is a disease of old farts like us. Remember Ernest saying, 'We all had a girl and her name is Nostalgia'?"

Charlie put his head back against the dusty seat plush and closed his eyes. I watched him roll his head with the movement of the train. After a while he seemed to sleep and his lips parted, the face muscles relaxed. It was the face of an old man, and Charlie wasn't that old. (Born the same year I was—1895.) I sat thinking of the aging process, a sense of retreating life, of the long-ago things a young man thinks only he is thoughtful about. Soon we would be merely the *craquelure* on old paintings. The sleeping man uttered words: *"Ich komme schon."*

The train wheels clicked as they ran over an open switch and clattered onto the cutoff to the base of the Zugspitze. (In ten more years, sixty-five; in twenty, seventy-five; in thirty?)

By morning the train was running through the clear highlands, spires of peaks white with snow, far blue distances incredibly clean. In the passageway two young skiers were eating slices of Westphalian ham on thick rye bread. A section of Swabian strudel on a paper tray waited to be devoured. My hip joint ached. It was getting stiffer with the years. Lousy World War I surgery.

The doors opened and a dining car steward came in, curly black hair uncombed, a pot of coffee in his hand. He gave us a cheerful Italian smile as he bent to pour the coffee. "Only Italians know how to brew good coffee."

Charlie looked bad. Was this a three-time Olympics man? He could hardly hold the cup. He spoke through his sinuses. "Hot anyway."

I sat eating ham and sipping the black pungent coffee, looking out over the surfaces of the mountain slopes and the blue shadows and the deep green of the pines. Ahead was the Zugspitze. Impressive, solid, placid. Landscapes have a pleasantly narcotic quality for me.

"How high would you say, steward?"

"Nearly ten thousand feet," Charlie said. He had lost the look of horror.

"Nine thousand seven hundred and twenty," said the steward.

He offered Charlie the tray of rolls and ham. "No, I slept a little but I don't want to eat."

"I've wired ahead for an ambulance, Charlie. You're going right to the hospital."

"You're right. I've been nuts."

"All for a ski school."

Charlie pursed his lips. He looked out of the window. "It's clean up here, isn't it?"

The train slowly made a great turn. Overhead there was a rushing of loose snow down a slope and a wind blowing so that the air was filled with a whiteness, a kind of solid mist.

I stood up. "I'll collect our things and see yours get taken to the hotel. Then I'll come to the hospital and see you don't pinch the nurse's ass."

Charlie tried to smile. "You do that, Bill."

The village was solidly built in that fool German Hänsel-and-Gretel style. The snow in its street supported several sleighs, a bus with chains on its wheels and a great many people in colorful sweaters, ski pants, tasseled caps, hats with chamois brushes. The little bars were active and the Konditorei were doing well serving their overrich cakes and little sandwiches. . . . Walking back from

24

the hospital after seeing Charlie admitted and settled, I inhaled the crisp air, and the fine feeling of being alive (in the cold and at this height) entered my body. I was happy I was not older, that I didn't have a broken thigh bone, and that there were still maybe a few years ahead for me. The sterile philosophy of Sartre and Camus, mere negation, was popular among the young intellectuals. It gave me the grue.

I entered the Salzhaus, less cheerful suddenly as I thought of my bank balance—and was engulfed by a smell of malt and lentil soup with *Würstchen,* damp sports wool, the special odor of well-cared-for wood all these cafés had. At the bar I ordered a glass of Löwenbrau. A young man in a loose brown alpine, with a dark hat worn on the back of his head, was seated next to me. He smiled and said with a dreadful American accent, *"Ja, wie geht's denn, Herr Kite?"*

"Mir gehts wunderbar, Herr Archy." Then in English I added, "You ought to take accent lessons."

"Maybe I will. Conference over?"

"No. I had to see a friend to the hospital."

Archy Redmond nodded. (I remembered him hanging around HQ in Paris, after the liberation; a big de Gaulle man taking bribes.) "I saw Charlie Huttonbok carried off. What's the inside story?"

"Stop being a reporter, Archy. No story."

"I'll go up and see him. Former skiing champ breaks his ass. That's a story."

"Don't, Archy. Charlie's in great pain. They're X-raying the leg again. There's an item for you."

"The Paris *Tribune* isn't a medical journal."

Archy Redmond, I remembered, wrote a column called "Around Europe" for the Paris edition of an American newspaper. It was not much of a column and it didn't pay well, but Archy said he liked it and he could freeload on it. Unlike most American newspapermen in Europe, he admitted, he had no intention of writing a novel, a play, or any desire to cover any of the world-shaking political stories. He was a shiftless, borrowing sort of bastard—dame-crazy, on the verge of becoming a souse.

"Going home, Archy? Soon?"

"Haven't been home in fifteen years."

"We should go home."

"Why, Major? I'm tired of the small smiling shiny faces, the den mothers, the good clean idea that we've got the only true answer to the problems of the universe. No, Major."

"Haven't been a major since '45."

"I like life dirty, tasty, casual here in Europe. A lot of old stones and nobody on my neck to shout, 'Be a big fucked-up success, change your shirt more often.'"

He winked and nodded. He looked very shopworn. I was tired.

"Where, Major, is Eliot Tjaden?"

"No idea. Haven't seen him since '42—no, '41, in London."

"The genius forgotten?"

"Screw you, Archy."

I felt sour in my stomach, atrophied. (A desire to help a friend; a painful Christian virtue. You're the mother-of-all-shit, Archy Redmond.)

The band was making a calculated gaiety around the bar. I didn't want to go to the hotel, to the room I had taken. I'd only have dreams in which old intimacies would prolong themselves, and everybody would be a generation or so infinitely remote. I didn't feel so sure any more that the lost pilots who flew the Camels in 1915–1916 had been such unlucky bastards. (Die young and leave a beautiful body.) I remember my grandfather sitting up in his bed smoking—he had days when he couldn't come below—the two of us smoking his H. Uppmans and him sipping brandy, smiling sadly when I said he would get better and we'd go after rabbits on Jack Custer's farm down by the Pennsy right-of-way. "Billy, there are people dying today who never died before."

EDITOR'S NOTE: In writing of Charles J. Huttonbok, Kite gives the impression he skied in three Olympics. Actually only in 1924 at Chamonix, France, and in 1928 at St. Moritz, Switzerland. At the Winter 1932 Olympics Huttonbok was the manager of both the United States Skating and Skiing teams. At the games of 1936 in Garmisch-Partenkirchen he withdrew because of Adolf Hitler's use of the games for Nazi propaganda purposes.

He is the author of *Mastering Skiing,* London, 1923, and *The Snow Devils,* a popular history of the sport, published in German, Munich, 1947, and in Italian, Milan, 1948. The book has not been published in an English edition.

CHAPTER 2
1917

THAT WINTER we were flying over the front from the Wing Head-quarters airdrome behind Amiens. It was a bloody blue-cold winter, the squadron was using Sopwiths nearly as bad as D.H.4's, the notorious "Flaming Coffins." We pilots lived on milk and brandy, stinking of tension sweat in our black flying breeks, going over the Hun lines escorting the heavy reconnaissance camera planes with the enemy's Archies bursting in our faces. The legend that nobody lived the first three months was pretty nearly true. In the British Sixth Wing by actual count we lost a third of our flyers, and it got worse before Cambrai fell, when the Boches began mounting heavier Soanau machine guns in their goddamn *Jagdstaffeln*—hunting packs. They had replaced their older planes with the Fokker triplanes, and we were still in the flypaper-and-canvas-and-wood Sopwith F.I. Camels.

With us it was the will doing the work of the impossible. We all took to carrying bottles of brandy in our coverall leg pockets. The long-toothed major with the trick pips got it trying out over the lines a new Nieuport (as expected, the air valve jammed and the engine conked). He tried to climb vertically, went into a slow roll and a loop. A Hun dipped out of the sun and began to pour it into him, and I saw the major's face, the Sandhurst mustache, (I was on his left tip, trying to come up to protect him.) He just looked disappointed, mouthed the word *merde*, and the ship began to smoke and flame and slide down discarding wings and parts. He waved. I thought of the willed gesture that becomes a principle.

I didn't follow him down because I was trying to get the sun between me and the red Fokker, and when I had him in the sights I prayed that the rotten mechanical device that synchronized my two Lewis guns to fire through the propeller would work. Only a week before I had shot off my own prop and landed in the middle of an Anzac battalion in the lines. I had been sweating it out, for the wind was always to the east and there was the danger of coming down behind the German lines.

27

I fired a burst to clear the barrels, and the silver blur of the prop was all right. The red Hun was good; he tried to keep the sun behind him, but my petrol was clean that morning in my tanks and I got on his tail, he twisting, me after him, the cruel Teutonic crosses on his wings black against the blood-red canvas, and I pressed off half a drum into him, and the sonofabitch didn't seem to be hurt at all. I could see wood and canvas splintering off and falling away. We had become a deadly tight coercive unit to the death.

He lifted to climb and I throttled back and thought "Fuck you, Kraut" when I sensed something on my right, and I was jumped by a *Staffel* of Albatrosses who were laying for me; my pigeon had been a decoy. I kicked the stick over and went into a long fast dive, wires screaming, did an evasion spin that began to strain the wings, and I cursed all the profiteers who cheated on airplane specifications. There was a wisp of cloud looking no bigger than a bath towel, and I started for that and it was bigger than it looked. (I was very young and didn't want to die before I sent my grandmother a picture of myself in uniform.)

I went through the cloud and found myself with just one Hun. He had a skull-and-bones painted on his canvas, and I automatically pressed the Lewis button and a staccato burst caught him in the belly of his machine. I was just under him—in his blind spot—and he fell, all black smoke, flames redder than his paint job. I could see the flier's protuberant bloodshot eyes as he screamed. Nobody carried parachutes in those days, and his right wing just touched mine—a kiss-off—as he fell away in a platinum-gray world. I scooted for the lines, sick with fear. I vomited brandy and milk and bile over my instrument panel. Yes, it was *very* romantic flying, people said later . . . like a knight-errant in the clean blue, personal combat in whipcord breeches and a British tunic with long London-cut tails. So romantic . . . oh shit-and-piss. "Man is full of misery and all earthly beauty is corrupt because of the untiring zeal of the devil. . . ."

I was sobbing and sour-tasting (like acid) when I came over our dusty airdrome and set the crate down with a bad show of nerves. The ack-emma warrant officer came out in the windy cold among the trampled weeds with the Lewis gunnery sergeant.

"The major bought one," I said, climbing out covered with slime.

"So we heard. One of the Handley Page chaps saw it."

28

"Buggering bastards. The major was due for leave, too," said the gunnery sergeant, examining my guns. "You 'ad 'ardly anything left in the Lewis drums."

"Reload me." I wanted to smoke, I didn't want to smoke. I walked toward the tin hut where the flight officer would want to hear it officially. It was too warm in the hut, a small stove ate coke, gave up gas and used up the air. Captain Hammel, MC, DSM, sat at a desk, a gray scarf wound around his neck, his Savile Row boots scuffed. He looked like a proper advertisement for the paraphernalia of war.

"Phone call just came in, Kite. Your kill confirmed."

"Hurray for me." I poured myself a brandy from the desk bottle, knocked it back. . . . "I want to go to Arras on leave. I've shot my load."

"So I see. Arras? All right. Oh, chap in the replacement group says he knows you. Pfaelzer—pronounced Felzer, he told me. Tony Pfaelzer."

"American?"

"Jewboy."

"Never heard of him. I'll take a bath."

"Save you a steak. We killed a Frenchie's cow, by accident. Skip your report. Get it later. Envy you the coosie in Arras." He made an obscene gesture of a thumb jabbing.

I went to the bathhouse and fell asleep standing under the hot shower and nearly scalded myself. Somehow I felt the pressure of some unappeased ghost. I left the uniform and the gear for the batman to take to the laundress.

I must have slept open-mouthed for some time because when I woke up the sun was on the dirty windowpane and my mouth was the Black Hole of Calcutta. The colonel with the ADM had his gramophone going: "There's a long, long trail awinding . . ." I felt poisoned. I had come out of sleep as if from a cave. My throat was raw. The forms of the palpable world were dim; all dimensions and echoes had lost their outer reality.

I got up and took some pick-me-up brandy, and I wished I had a couple of raw eggs to go with it, the way my grandfather used to drink; he would wink and say, "Billy, man is the creature of obligations and betrayals."

There was a tap on the door and I mumbled something. A tall, handsome man came in—one of the most handsome dark rabbinical

29

types I've ever seen. He wore an RFC second lieutenant's uniform. Certainly this must be the Jewboy.

"Hello, Lieutenant, I'm Tony Pfaelzer. Joel Cohen's father asked me to look you up if I ran across you. Fat chance, Uncle Hy, I said. But there was your name, L-t.-W.-K-I-T-E on the list board."

"That's right."

We shook hands. He had that soft curly hair and those big dark eyes, very big ones, violet and half-soot pupils that women fall right into bed for when they see them. There was a tight caul on my skull and I tried to think of my old friends.

"Joel? Wasn't he killed someplace? Forgive me, Pfaelzer, I'm not functioning too well this morning. Just brushing the goddamn surface of consciousness."

"Congratulations. You got your fourth Jerry this year, I hear. Joel was killed in Mexico, you know. With Black Jack Pershing in that little affair after Pancho Villa. Joel was a great kid. Always laughing and scratching."

"Have a drink. How many hours you solo?" He looked very smart—puttees, ordnance belt, all the brass and expensive leather of a fresh replacement. He held out a tin of Papastratos cigarettes, a gold lighter.

"Enough, enough. This looks like a crackerjack outfit."

"There's no outfit. We're what's left of other squadrons. The remains are put in here." We smoked slowly. "You'll like it fine, Tony. The planes are not too good, but the mechanics are wonders, and the CO, a decent sort of prick, doesn't care what you do so long as you salute and go up when your squadron leader says, 'Let's go, chaps.' Alice in Wonderland time. That's an English joke."

"Now, is it really? Oh—I got a box of these." He handed me a good Havana cigar and I put it away as I still had my cigarette. My stomach couldn't have stood it. "What have you been flying?" I asked.

"The Martinsyde, some Nieuports. Don't worry, I'll stay up with you boys."

"What guns you train with?"

"Vickerses."

"We use Lewises—usual air-force balls-up."

My batman Hughie came in with a tray. He wore the Mons Star and the barnacle of some lower award that was given to the rank and

30

file. He lifted the tin lid of some poached eggs. "Stole these, Leftenant, and the coffee is the real thing."

"Never mind that," I said. "I'm going into Arras, three-day pass."

"You need it, Leftenant. Too bad about the major. One of the best, as they say."

"The very best. This is Lieutenant Pfaelzer. Get a batman who knows the gear. Tony, Hughie Green—a marvelous thief."

"Right as rain, sir," said Hughie.

Hughie went out and I stared at the eggs and swallowed the very black coffee with the four spoons of sugar in it. "How's Mr. Cohen? Still running the drugstore?"

"My aunt is. Funny thing. The old boy is organizing shows for the army camps. Having a hell of a time doing a grand job of it. What's there in Arras?"

"Tail, booze, but best of all—nothing."

He looked at a fragment of a Boche wing with a cross on it.

"A splintered prop off an Albatross D. 111 that killed my last squadron leader," I said.

"Kite, I'm scared."

"We all are. Only in the movies is everybody senseless brave."

"I'm a Jew, you know."

"I wouldn't have guessed," I lied.

"That makes it worse. I don't want anybody saying the goddamn Hebe, he's got a streak of yellow shit up his back."

"Look, Tony. We don't talk that way. Everybody sort of holds himself in, and doesn't plan any future. The trick is, figure the odds. One-third of the fliers go west on a front like this, two-thirds of the fliers survive. Half of them crap out—mental breakdowns. Unless there's a big push on, *those* are the odds. It's very quiet just now. Too frigging cold."

Outside they were starting up the afternoon patrol. I could smell the burning castor oil they were mixing with the lubrication, hear the young carnivora in flying suits chattering—mostly virgins, pink-cheeked, earnest. I handed Tony the plate of poached eggs.

"If you're smart you'll eat this. In a couple of weeks you may not like solid food." I went out to see about transportation to Arras.

Oh, it was a great little war. The romantic war, if you were young and innocent in those days. Remember the dances in the old country

31

houses back in the States, the band playing "Dardanella"—it had to be "Dardanella," or maybe it was "Avalon," or were they later? And all the young college punks in their Sam Browne belts, doing the Irene and Vernon Castle steps, holding the F. Scott Fitzgerald girls in white organdy very close, and drinking too much of the bourbon. And everybody saying how noble it was for Mr. Wilson to Make the World Safe for Democracy, forgetting he had been re-elected on the slogan: He Kept Us Out of War. (You don't remember that war?) Lost, lost like all color in the winy darkness at the bottom of an aquarium. "Hang the Kaiser to a Sour Apple Tree," "My Buddy," "The Rose of No Man's Land." We had volunteered to come over in 1915 to fly with the old RFC, now the RAF. We saw through the popular horseshit a bit. There was the matter of the Morgan loans and the clever British propaganda that would suck us in. By 1917 we were aware of how dreadful a war it was. No flags flying, no gallant charges, no Red Cross nookie, no kisses on the cheeks by a French general.

It was five, six million filthy, lousy men buried alive underground, living like demented rats in their own shit-and-piss and decaying comrades' entrails, burrowing, rotting away, dying with silly shocked gestures to gain or retain fifty yards, a hundred yards, then back into the lice and cootie hells, the stink of unburied dead from 1914, rotting horses. It was a war that smelled of horse manure, putrefying generations of schoolboys and fathers. We fliers could smell it as we came in at dusk, low over the trenches that stretched in horror from the English Channel to the Swiss border; and when you went to mess with the line officers, they smelled of it too, their eyes bulging with madness.

The British were close to a million dead, the French a million and a half. They were now counting the half-million dead destroyed, ground up, murdered by sadists at Verdun. And for what? Some fields no one wanted or needed. It hadn't decided the war. Nothing would. It would never end in the twentieth century. And now the French were lining up their own regiments, picking every third (or was it tenth?) man, and shooting him. The stinking bearded *messieurs,* we were told, weren't fighting up to snuff any more, and of course the generals sitting snug on their prostates in their big Rolls-Royces with an aide carefully putting the woolen rug over their legs and paunches, they were right. Sacrifice was Glory. It was for the Land, for the

32

Nation. I was pretty sick with abstractions. *Vaterland,* Free Men, Democracy, the King, the Prince of Wales (poor creepy young bastard) in his tight little uniform, his sleepy eyes half open, moving down a safe trench and shaking hands with little undernourished cockneys who never had enough to eat and never grew higher than five feet two. (How out-of-date all this outraged shit I'm writing is. We have fucked up the world to a calm indifference to total and awaited destruction.) It was a bloody sellout, we were aware then. It was a war for no reason; and I didn't see much hope of surviving. I didn't mean myself personally in my own body. I wasn't buying the Tories or Democrats, the Marxists or the Socialists. They'd make wars of their own, for the proper abstract values.

And as I flew I wasn't buying Father O'Bein, or Pastor Linletta, or Rabbi Haukfliesh and their fine moral promises and splendid dogmas. Because there were O'Beins and Linlettas and Haukflieshes on the other side, too. God was divided, Jay once said, from his crotch to his eyebrows. He promised victory through O'Bein, etc., to those who had the faith. I didn't have faith, only a ferocity of perception, a hate of official cant. I was becoming an alcoholic, I had crabs, there were two cavities in my back teeth, and I couldn't (at times) control the tic on my face. My hands had a tremor. I had murdered half a dozen Germans or Austrians or Romanians who were out to murder me. And almost everything I and Jay and Charlie and Joel had believed in was *merde*—plain shit. The progress, the evolution, of this noble thing, twentieth-century man . . . Mozart and Renoir and Emerson and Billy Sunday, all the yea sayers, all God's classmates—they were all *merde*. Reality, if I still believed in it, could exist as drink, comradeship with doomed friends, and all the cunt you could get; only *that* wasn't real any more. The female pudendum wasn't real to me during World War I. It was the grand illusion, a shell of myth thick as a turtle's house, gestures on dirty pillows: I was doing what was natural for me. I was pretty far gone that winter. I had somehow mislaid myself and my fine clean world of Princeton, Class of '16.

The British didn't have a Section Eight, or any Stone Age head-shrinkers. You were either a man, old boy, or a bloody disgrace, and you fell for that crap; a chap had to shoot his shoulders back, give a good salute, toast the King, carry a swagger stick (beat your boots with it) and accept the blatantly obvious lies the official mouths fed

33

us. You were permitted lapses and gaucheries, of course. Like drinking corked wine, or, as Charlie said, "coming first if you were in bed with an English duchess." But not calling some commanding general "a bloody butchering bastard" when he threw away two hundred thousand young Englishmen on the Somme in frontal attacks —was it in two days or four? The horror, as someone said, was that there was no horror. "Death," Jay remarked, "was vulgar, dull and smelled dreadful." Horses give off a sickening sweet odor when they decay; men stink badly when shallowly buried. . . . Let us pray for a speculative calm.

The only thing I remember with pleasure was hoping the next war would come to the civilians back home—being so brave and giving up meat once a week, and growing radishes on their lawns, and awarding the white feather to some guy smart enough to keep away from it. (That's why the *next* war wasn't so romantic. The civilians died by the millions. War was war for everybody, not selective as the filthy old biddy implied when she shouted: "The Germans are raping only the pretty girls!")

You had to be there. Writing it down is like trying to print a picture of the Crucifixion on a snowflake. All the sad cruel things talked of, written, pictured, failed to change anything. The horrors, the sick military minds, the greed of the rich, the nonsense the poor sang about hope in a millennium, the muck the soldiers swallowed with their filthy food—you had to be there.

Fortunately for me, I went raving mad when it got too much. But that came later. I always thought I faked it beautifully: the grimaces, the twitch, the filthy language. But several doctors told me, "No, old boy, you had really gone off your rocker."

But back to the day Tony Pfaelzer joined the squadron. I had on a clean uniform, my best unpaid London-tailoring one. The poor London sod waited for years. I had my swagger stick. ("Phallic?" Jay once asked. "All the English; prick in hand, public exhibitionists.") I had a nice alcohol glow, I was shaved, cap over one eye, standing in the flight officers' hut, waiting for the grease monkey to change a tire on the officers'-mess car, a beat-up Caddy. Free for two days from the laws of inevitability.

A muddy Renault came up the wreck of a muddy road from the main highway and under the camouflage nets. Four officers in RFC dress were singing "The Bastard Kings of England." They were all young and very Anglo-Saxon; you could almost use them as a poster.

"A vision of the categorical," said the driver. "It's Bill, *Bill* Kite."

I hadn't seen Jay since 1916 when we had come over on a boat from Canada and he had flunked the coordination tests (they claimed his sense of balance had been damaged as a boy in some sport accident). He looked very solid, and there were flying wings on his tunic and French and English chicken shit of gold and silver and bronze.

Charlie Huttonbok was by his side, opening the twisted wires on the cork of a champagne bottle. The two officers in the back I didn't know. Charlie got out and slapped me on the back, and Jay got out and slapped me on the back, and I met the two other officers: Oxford kids, pink-cheeked, foul-mouthed and very friendly but numb as if anesthetized at some rites.

Jay smiled, showing the even row of good teeth and the capped one he had shattered. "Imagine, Bill, you still alive-o. We were running low on gas and I said let's run in here and steal some. Christ, life is sure enclosed in parentheses."

"No need to steal. I'll get the gunnery sergeant. That's his swindle. Where you stationed?"

"With the Fourth Air Group. Some place near Ypres. It's a bitched-up war, isn't it?"

"It's no damn good. How'd you get to fly?"

Charlie said as the cork came out, "They killed off all the young folk with good balance." Charlie Huttonbok had lost all that fat he had in his teens. He sucked up champagne and put his arms around me and hugged me. "You don't see many of our strong stern breed out here. But soon, eh, soon? The whole American Army."

One of the Oxford boys nodded. "You'll win the whole bloody thing for us, you Yanks. How peachy-grand."

"That we will. Want to fight?" asked Jay. He needed a haircut, and he was too lean.

"Never stick it into an ally, old chap. Celebrating, anyway."

"Jay's getting married." Charlie beamed, passing the bottle.

"To a marvelous piece," said an Oxford boy. "We've all had it, of course." He kissed his fingertips. "A splendid beast. Liberty Hall."

Jay laughed. "You lie, sir. Bill, don't think they haven't tried. They're pea-green with envy."

I waved the gunnery sergeant over and told him to get us four tins of gas and we'd pick them up behind the kitchen.

"Who's the girl?" I asked.

"Nora Pages. Remember her at the Princeton-Harvard game in 1913? Very young, very limber, very much my style."

"No, I don't. I was out with a chest cold. She a white girl?"

"Boston," said Charlie. She's here with the Quakers, giving out louse powder or doughnuts or something to soldiers who just want to get into her pants. Don't tell Jay: I've enjoyed her often. Snores."

Jay just grinned.

"Marvelous lay," said one of the Oxfords. "Depraved. You're lucky, Leftenant Tjaden. Nymphos make the best wives. Know all the tricks."

"Where you all going?" I asked. I wanted to tell Jay how pleased I was—it seemed not the place for that.

"Some *estaminet,* the Cloche-Clos. Kevin has an old uncle there in the Engineers. We want to borrow a few hundred nickers to get to Paris with next week."

"I know the place, the Cloche-Clos. I'll come along."

Jay beamed. "Oh, you Promethean lug. To Paris too. To the wedding?"

"Why not?"

Only we didn't. The big push to try and capture Cambrai came and we all went up to take on the *Jagdstaffeln.*

EDITOR'S NOTE: In the '20s Eliot Tjaden, short of money while working on his long major novel, *Stone Sunlight,* wrote under the pen names of Captain J. J. Hazard, RFC, and General der Flieger Baron von Stomm, *Studiengruppe,* Luftwaffe, for many pulp adventure magazines, among them *Flying Battle Aces, Sky Fighters, Air Combat Stories.* I have looked into some of these now forgotten, out-of-print magazines in the New York Public Library collection. But they gave me little new material to add to Kite's version of that war. Eliot Tjaden was potboiling stories of hastily written romantic gallant adventures, heroic figures, hardly a full picture of what was the actual agony of the flying groups in World War I. They are, for their medium, superbly written and give a detailed picture of the planes, the flying techniques, combat in the sky, details of motors, guns, flights and conditions in which they fought. Some should be reprinted.

His hero, Banger Concord, who appears in a series of stories in *Sky Fighters,* bears a resemblance to William Kite. It is mainly physical, and in his dialogue there is some talk of "the chaps at Princeton." Charlie Huttonbok appears in a story as Chuck Spiegelglass, "The Ghost Ace of Arras" (*Flying Battle Aces,* May, 1923), flying with a large police dog as his mascot. Chuck is dead but appears out of the clouds Easter morning in a ghost airplane to rescue an unlucky new British flyer from a German ace.

CHAPTER 3

1950

SITTING IN THE SALZHAUS in Garmisch-Partenkirchen, the time Charlie Huttonbok broke his thigh bone, for the first time in years I faced myself and didn't like what I saw.

Someone spoke to a *Saaltochter,* as the local waitresses were called: *"Wie geht es, Fräulein? Ah, wie schön, wie gut, wie reichlich."*

I sat thinking and scowling at my wrinkling reflection in a bar mirror. Europe was no part of my life any more, and I didn't want to feel immersed in it again; no more the searcher for an unknown solid goal, just drifting in the old days, taking on local color, or not taking on local color. Believing in phantoms called arts and loose codes of honor, and all the dead I had known when alive. I wasn't interested in the conference I was supposed to be at. I was an American with the passport and papers to prove it (and a lost past in Charlie sitting on my shoulders).

This international life of my youth had been fun, and good times and wild, meeting friends, making friends. Now there *was* a thought: Go home, go prepare a nest for dying. You've had a time. You creak; you can't age beautifully. I shivered; just thinking of Europe as it was after the second big war, a grimy, wet, gray world of intrigue, small people in power in minor positions, fools and beasts in power over all—hasty meetings and partings of dislocated people desperately thrashing around like newly caught fish in a basket. And Charlie in the hospital with a broken bone. I called for cognac. I must coagulate. Stendhal had written, "There is nothing ridiculous about dying in the street, providing one does not do it on purpose."

37

I looked out at the street and moved away from the bar. A woman in a dirndl and a clipped beaver jacket was reading a copy of the fashion magazine *Die Dame* and looking up at me over the top as she flipped it through. (She reminded me of Pages—the hiss of long loose hair—in Rome in 1922.) In the corner some overstuffed people were celebrating what could only be a birthday: *"Hoch soll er leben! Dreimal hoch!"* (Where was Pages now? I couldn't remember.)

I hunched my shoulders outside the bar; a thin, weightless snow was coming down, the wind had fallen away, and a sharp sound of sleigh bells, the crunch of leather boots on crusted packed snow, made pleasant noise in my ears. A pale sun was dying beyond the black crags, and the distant cries of returning skiers calling to each other came across the blue-shadowed drifts above the town. Muffled sounds too, of voices; the hopes of travelers expecting warmth, food and shelter.

Seeing that woman—she really didn't look like Pages; just those long marvelous legs, the tilt of a fine head on an arched neck, shiny blue-black hair—had created an emotion with the force and shock of a hemorrhage.

I wasn't one of those nostalgic hounds, full of "the good old days—remember when—what ever happened to"; but having to bring Charlie down on the train had dislodged something in me, and items, fragments of memory, were rising (like marsh gas when you plunge a pole to the bottom of a stagnant pool). Yes, that was it, in a time of fragments, an age meager, near destruction, a world that threw too much spark but no heat. I had an awareness of too many old things. Damn Charlie; damn his broken bone.

After one of those greasy German hotel meals—too much silver—too much service; everything, even the dessert, boiled in grease—I lit a Dutch cigar and went out. The snow was no longer falling.

The hospital, St. Anne Our Lady of the Snows, had for me the overclean smell and a kind of bundled-up quiet that one disliked to break. I spoke very low to the nun seated at the heavy oak desk, a nun with a face showing anguish, anxiety and some pious remorse.

"Herr Huttonbok?"

"Herr Charles Huttonbok?" The nun looked up with an alert, wary stare. Over her head was a black painting of some tortured saint in fearful agony that left a snobbish smile of superior grace on his face. The detailed butchery of the saint seemed out of place in the modern hallways, the indirect lighting, the unnatural containment of sound.

"No, no," said the nun curtly. "He's not to have any visitors."

"I'm his friend, and I'm leaving soon."

"You are the Herr Redmond that called?"

"No, I'm not."

"He was most insistent."

"I'm Herr Kite and . . ."

The nun removed her gold-rimmed glasses and rubbed the high bony ridge of her nose. I wondered . . . did nuns still shave their heads and was she egg-bald behind that headdress? The nun re-mounted her glasses and looked at a slip of paper on the oak surface. As a child I had had a sentimental feeling about nuns till I saw the battered hands of the children beaten with brass rulers in the paro-chial school.

"Ah, Herr Kite, you are the *only* one permitted. The one he asked to send right up. Second floor, B2. But only for half an hour. His rest is *non subito delenda*," she finished in Latin.

"Is he that sick?" (Don't panic, man is not really a mechanism, he's an individual facing daily disaster—what's a busted thigh bone?)

The nun didn't answer but pointed. "The lift is down the hall."

I wondered if broken bones were becoming more difficult to take care of or if German doctors were making more of them. The second floor was just as modern as the one below, but the ceiling was lower. B2 was lettered on a plain flat door of yellow pine with a handmade cardboard sign in a brass slot: C. HUTTONBOK.

I knocked and a young sister in a wide white hood opened the door. She put a finger to her lips and pointed to a bed, intricate with the traction rigs over it, and went out.

I had always disliked the smell of hospitals since as a child I had gone to see my half-brother Harry wrapped in cotton wool and oil after being moderately burned by falling into a campfire—carbolic, bedpans, waxed floors and the odor of insect powders; a boy's fear of decline, dissolution, death.

Charlie was resting, his eyes closed, his injured limb held in place by wires and weights. He looked old, large and wan in the white hospital nightshirt. His bald head was shiny. He opened his eyes as I approached the bed. A gust of snowy wind rattled the window of the small room, but a flow of politely heated air from a wall vent showed the weather was scientifically treated too.

Charlie looked up, his melancholy, unfocused eyes half glazed with drugs.

39

"Ah, Bill. I've been waiting a devil of a long time."

"What the hell have they done with you?"

"They had to reset the frigging bone. It was done all wrong the first time. Splinters, shattered ends. They've put in steel pins through the leg below and above the knee to attach the wires, trying to pull the bone into place for healing."

"I was thinking of the time Harry got dizzy on the Fourth of July and fell into the campfire. Must be the smell of hospital."

Charlie permitted himself a flicker of memory. "Those town Fourths were dangerous."

I nodded and plugged up the past. "You did yourself a lot of harm traveling with the leg."

Charlie smiled and then groaned. "I did myself harm, all right. As soon as they get the bone in position, I'm going into a new plaster cast from neck to toes. Six months at the least, trussed like a lousy capon for roasting."

I sat down on a flimsy chair. The man on the bed opened his mouth and sucked down air. "Bill, I can't do what I've planned. I was going into Poland."

"Why Poland?"

Downstairs someone was singing *Gloria Tibi, Domine,* and some amateur was playing the harmonium. Sleet beat like fingers on the window. Charlie shifted a bit on the bed. "I'm rigid as an old herring. Bill, you have a family?"

"No, nobody. You?"

"My wife Dina is dead."

"I heard, well . . . rumors you were married again."

"And that she once ran off with some circus high-wire worker?"

"I didn't pay much attention."

"We had a kid, a girl. Dina took our daughter Lily with her. Hand me that glass. Ke-rist, six months and those nuns trying to bring me back to the faith. I'm in for it."

I passed Charlie the milky liquid with a glass drinking tube in it.

"It's supposed to be fruit juices, but it tastes like stable piss with what they've added to it. Not too many folk knew we made a child. Dina went home to her people in England to have her. Thought the kid would bring us together again. I was managing an Olympic team then—still giving skiing exhibits. It didn't. I didn't want the kid then. It's a damn dull story, isn't it?"

"Why were you going into Poland?"

"To get Lily, my kid. I've found her." Charlie fumbled under his pillow, pulled out a large worn black leather wallet and from it got a frayed bit of coated paper. I saw it was part of a page torn from some magazine. He unfolded the paper and I saw the reproduction of a photograph of a young girl, about fourteen, standing on the tips of her toes, dressed in a tight silver lamé costume, hands raised in a ballet gesture. The photograph showed a small, pert, bitchy face, big staring eyes like a vixen fox's, and the pattern of a made-up mouth in the smile all professional performers produce for a cameraman. The background was pine forest, snow, a horizon heavy and cloudless.

"That's Lily. Found it in a magazine, *Dance Time,* published in London. Read the caption."

" 'Lily, the young ballet star. Lily is one of the stars of Kasar's International Ballet and Circus now touring Poland and Romania and next season will appear in many of the major towns of Siberia.' "

Charlie put the clipping down on the bed.

"Crazy, Charlie, to have thought of going over there. Good thing you can't move."

The man on the bed took some stiff legal papers from his wallet. "My permit to enter Poland. A legal judgment from Warsaw that Lily is my daughter. An exit permit for Lily, signed by the proper government departments. Bill, it wasn't easy to get all this, and I can't tell you how I got most of it."

I had a feeling of some seething prodigious background, of Charlie like Eliza in *Uncle Tom's Cabin* crossing a river on chunks of ice, a child's doll in his arms, bloodhounds baying.

"If it's all so proper, six months more wouldn't make much difference, would it, Charlie?"

"Lily might be in Siberia on tour by then, and that's a hard place to get into or out of, if they don't want you to get in or out. Anyway, this exit permit for Lily expires in three weeks."

I stood up and shook my head. "Charlie, not me. I've had a bad bout of flu and the old hip is acting up."

"I didn't ask you yet."

"The State Department boys frown on involvement in these countries. You know I'm on this crappy commission of theirs meeting in Leipzig."

41

"Don't bite my head off. You can wangle a passport or visa or whatever official junk you need."

"Don't push me, Charlie. I'm tired and I don't cotton to Poles."

I went to the window and tapped on the glass. It was a rotten position for Charlie to put me in. I owed a great deal to him: long-buried things that no one else knew about. To be broadly romantic, I most likely owed my life to Charlie in 1917, flying for the RFC. I turned from the frost-etched glass. Charlie was looking like an unwatered flower on a grave.

"Don't ask me, Charlie."

The man on the bed said harshly, "I *am* asking. I am asking you, you bastard, to repay a debt. Didn't want to use *that* wedge. You forced me."

"Thank you. Thank *you*, Charlie."

There was a silence in the room. Outside the door some sister passed, her felt slippers making almost no sound. We both hated the idea of gratitude, of irascible, capricious memories, and I think we both sensed our dismal insufficiencies. The vital things in this world are never in view—always behind the obvious ones.

"I don't want any part of this."

The man on the bed merely stared with a curious stealth. Charlie's eyes took on a cruel glare. His mouth was set in the stern locked look of mean strength. Screw him. I'd pass a few days feeling reprehensible, but I wasn't falling into the gratitude trap.

"Charlie, I'm going home to East Pompton, to Frenchman Street."

"I can't stand up and salute sacred names. And there is no one else to send. We're from a dead generation, Bill. The hellhounds were very fast. Remember . . . ? Fill in your own names. You and me, we were the lucky ones. The walking wounded, as it were. You're trapped, you bastard."

"All right, but for you I'd be a few burned bones buried in a trench, or muck on the bottom of a river. But that isn't me now. And that isn't you now either."

"The ballet, as far as I could find out, had been playing in towns around Kraków and Lwów. You'll find it, Bill. There's some kind of People's Artists office in Kraków that your State friends play ball with—they'll know where the show is."

"The clipping of the kid is old. Charlie, the show might be in the Far East by now."

Charlie was smiling; he felt he had me by the short hair. "Light me a cigarette." When he was puffing out a column of pungent smoke, he looked up like a relaxed somnambulist. "Lily is with my late wife's sister Nita, who has some small job with the ballet company. Like my wife, the bitch is no damn good. She has no legal right to Lily. The exit papers are all in order. She'lll have to give up the child to you."

"No, not to me."

"Yes, Bill, you."

I didn't live up to any quixotic expectancy. I turned away from the bald Neronian head on the bed.

"I'll hire someone to do this for you."

"No one can be trusted. This is *Mittel-europa*. Here we eat each other and God eats us."

"Goodbye, Charlie—I'm going back to the conference."

"Bill, hand me the ashtray. For me it's been like walking through a nightmare. First the agony of traveling with a shattered bone, then lying here trussed up, and my kid, after all these years, just beyond my fingertips. Then meeting you at Leipzig. There is, I feel, a crazy divine justice of some kind. I may go back to the Church after all. Why not?"

I said crisply, "You're getting damn sentimental, Charlie, and it doesn't become you."

"Send the sister in. I need a shot of dope. And take the papers." He stuffed them into my pocket.

"You weren't listening. . . . Goodbye."

I went out quickly, closing the door very softly behind me. I hated Charlie Huttonbok, hated him with a loathing that had most likely always been there, been there through all the years since childhood. There was something in him like a hard pride of power over people for all his dedication to an outdoor way of life. They all had it, that open-air ego, I decided; these brusque Hemingway types all had soft mushy moments when the fraud in their poses, their frayed sensibilities, showed. The sentimental taffy core of them was exposed if you waited long enough: Charlie in there simpering at the very idea of the kid he most likely hadn't seen in ten years or more and hadn't wanted in the first place. That rhinoceros look with his deep wrinkle-braceleted eyes.

I beat my fists together as I waited for the lift. A hawk-nosed doctor, probably a gynecologist, passed by; he smelled of urine and

43

peppermint drops. A little pot of olive oil burned under a painted marble image of the Virgin. I waited for her to sneeze in the thin thread of smoke. The lift doors hissed open. A sister in white pushed out a wheelchair in which sat a very old lady who was muttering to herself. She looked up at me and spoke in Italian: *"L'ultima cosa che si perde è la speranza."*

I said *"Bitte?"* and got into the lift. I felt myself slipping into Charlie's clutches, slipping step by retrogressive step. I expelled a soundless laugh. I knew it was a moment for direct action. If I used my noodle I could escape—get to the local airport and be in Leipzig in time to resign, be on the Oslo plane in time to catch the jet over the North Pole and zing to Santa Barbara, California, where I'd mail Charlie back his papers and forget the whole thing. Life wasn't a child's game of I-owe-you and you-owe-me, I kiss-your-ass, you-kiss-mine. There were no rules which said I was committed to go just because once . . . I had clear images of a much younger, very handsome Charlie skiing on the slopes of the Gross-Glockner with Alice—corn-colored hair—and people saying they were just married and *very* much in love. That was the one before Dina and after Pages turned him down. All I remembered of Alice was a very pert nose, a chin well formed, just a bit too long, a chin I disliked in a woman. She had a habit at dinner of wetting her lips with the tip of her tongue when she listened to you talk; no honest woman could have such a direct stare, almost a printed invitation, apprehensive yet mocking. (She could orgasm only during a feeling of great guilt, I found out.)

In my hotel room, muddled in mixed emotions, I could not sleep. I tossed and rolled, decided upon first one form of action, then another. Near morning I stood by the bed in my heavy winter underwear, watching through a cold window the night slip away. Charlie had had a great life; married four times—rich, very rich, twice in his life, and till his forties damn good-looking . . . and in all those years a refusal to accept responsibility, though with him there was never any bellowing pandemonium as with Jay.

In a corner of the room was Charlie's ski gear I had lugged from the train. I went over to it and looked at the strapped bundles of quilted parkas and skis: the Swiss laminated pair he had used at the Fédération International de Ski at Chamonix, and what were most likely his favorites, the 6.7 Austriana Hahnenkamm set with the lateral release binding. I'd give it a run. I wasn't too bad. I slipped on heavy

44

socks, a red wool shirt, a pair of webbed stretch pants, a hooded parka, Jacquard-patterned. I decided on a pair of Kastinger ski boots, and by the time I was dressed I was sweating in the overheated room. Picking up the Hahnenkamm skis, poles, a yellow wool cap, I went down to the lobby. I sighed; the failure of experience to remake us is the true tragedy.

Yellow pools of electric light lit the lobby smelling of yesterday's food, the ashes of a dying fire in the fireplace. The desk clerk was asleep in his chair, his open mouth showing pink plastic gums. There was no doorman on duty yet. Outside in the snow a little man with a red schnaps-blossom nose was polishing the hotel's brass doorknobs. I waved to him and the little man said, *"Wie geht's?"* and went back to his polishing. It was a good slope away from the hotel, open ground with slalom poles and banners up.

The dawn smelled crisp and cold and dry. The snow underfoot was powder. I put on the skis, got gloves from the parka pocket, and stood staring ahead, the poles leaning against my hips. For an old retread I felt fine. I became part of the very clean mood of the slopes as I pushed off slowly, skis making a soft crying sound in the dry snow. I wished I had brought a flask of brandy, but maybe I'd find something in an inn on the trails. Below me nature obeyed all the laws of perspective.

I knew the slopes faintly from other years. I had done some fair jumping here; cross-country skiing, the Alpine, the giant slalom. Those were the free and fairly happy days; trick hip and all, I had an idiot's self-complacency and I never expected to run down like a dollar alarm clock. We all felt honest doubt was the greatest faith, and pride in the inexhaustible copiousness of our gifts—and if we lacked gifts, our friends had too many; we would live out their lives.

I poled myself along into the white panorama, in straight running and then taking herringbone steps to the cross ridges. The ski lifts were not yet running, and I went under them and their spider threads, black as Picasso's etched line against the rising daylight. When I was on the top of the Minaret run, looking down to the Engelhof and Alpenhof, whose chimneys were just beginning to send up black woolly breakfast smoke, I rested, breathing hard, feeling the bite of the cold air rush into my lungs and come out again, breath steaming white in front of me. I felt torn free of Charlie's trap and began to shout a wordless chant and heard it echo back sounding like the

45

Sopwith Camels we had flown coming back at dusk from the front before Amiens.

Not to think, not to plan, not to remember the dead or favors due. Just to stand here, feeling the thick blood force its way through the veins in its rush to the exposed skin of my face. I no longer felt tired or depressed. With a leap I launched myself down the slope, heading for the Edelweiss trail. I had once been a powerful skier and a fairly skilled one—not a Charlie, of course—and I was extending myself, jumping a cornice as I went racing down, leaving behind a trail of snow plumes, trying out a few slalom twists and turns, sharp fragments of ice biting on my skin, while a mysterious ear-bending liturgy of drums roared by. The higher chalets and cottages flashed past. A man with horse and sled carrying some boxes watched me rush on, and then he was gone out of sight beyond a clump of ponderosa pines that stood blue-black against the rising sun reflected on slopes losing their deep emerald blue shadows. . . . I wished I could go on, bound for the Antipodes. . . .

When I got back to the hotel, I was breathing easy again, relaxed and unknotted, and my cheeks were full of color, like a fat fubsy of a clubwoman. I dried Charlie's gear, took a shower, put on a blue suit, a light pair of boots, and went down to breakfast. It was still early among the neat rows of cloth-covered tables. A lone pair of depleted lovers were looking at each other with sticky eyes and not much esteem over the very strong black coffee. A waiter yawned by the pastry table and picked dried flecks of food off one of his sleeves. I gave my order to the waiter and went out to phone the local airfield to hold a seat for me for the Leipzig connection. I again felt pliancy of body, flexibility of mind. (Screw s-c-r-e-w you, Charlie.)

Walking back to the table, I was smiling. Perhaps it would spoil my sleep for a few days; there had always been that tendency in me when things got too much to bear to feel a sense of duty—but no more. I rarely admitted this to myself. But today I could agree with the Chinese philosopher who said, "There are thirty-seven ways to meet a situation; the best one is to run away."

I ordered *Nuss Torte* and *Schlagobers* with my coffee.

Of course, as the world knows, I did go looking for Lily Huttonbok and became famous for it too, or rather notorious. But it's never been told properly, at least not what really happened; just a lot of fancy crap by the wire services and a lot of corn by the publicity department of the boys in State in Washington, a crew that serve their nation, it seems to me, by distorting it.

First off when I decided to go find Lily, I checked on Charlie's papers and legal permits, and, as I suspected, a lot of the information he had was dated. So I opened a few channels in the CIA, a spy outfit that spends a lot of money and hires people who work both sides. I did find out Lily was not in Poland any more. She had gone with some People's Circus to Romania—with a cat act at that. And then in Bucureşti (we call it Bucharest) the troupe had broken up. Half its performers had fled to Midye in Turkey, and the rest had piled on a Black Sea boat for Salonika in Greece. Greece seemed the best and only bet, and I flew to Athens after checking out a lot of false leads like the Polish one.

I was airsick on the plane and I didn't like Athens—or the Greeks I met, for that matter. The airplane hostess told us a half hour before we landed, "Cradle of civilization and birthplace of gods, land of legend and beauty which has inspired centuries of art and philosophy. Tea, *kafe, krassi?*" She was a nice-enough-looking girl, already had a remarkably fine mustache, and the coffee, thick, lumpy, was lousy. I had *whiskeesoda.*

I got a room at the Grande-Bretagne and I fought off guides offering me the Parthenon, the Temple of Nike, the theater of Dionysius, and their sisters, or even brothers; in final desperation, wanting an American to enjoy himself, even themselves. But I was there for work, not pleasures old or untried. I had a Greek friend named Kyprios who had pimped for American generals in London during the war and was now semiofficially stealing relief supplies sent in to help the starving Greeks. He did a fine business in jeeps, Spam, tractors and nylons. He was to become very rich soon, he explained, buying up American oil tankers and supply ships with an American admiral as front through a few Washington figures. Just now he was fat, happy and close to the royalists in power, most of whom had supported the Nazis. He sat at ease, like a cat, in my hotel room, wearing, I believe, the last pair of shoes with gray linen tops, smoking a cigarette in a long paper holder. His handsome face under its head of crisp black hair was bent toward me in full confidence as I told him what I was there for.

47

"Doll, you have come to right fella. Understand I do not deal in women any more. And young ones—frankly, it's for Egyptians."

"You don't understand. This is the daughter of a close friend. She is a circus performer."

"Of course. And *here* a circus." He made an obscene Greek-Levantine gesture that needs one finger and the use of the left hand. "I find her if she in Greece. I see you in three, four days. No, come tonight with me as my guest to the Astoria? Very fine club. Rich friends of mine have shares in it."

"No, you go look for the girl."

I sat for a week eating *moussaka, souvlakia* and *dolmadakia;* I forget which one was eggplant and which one was wormy vine leaves. It was none of it to my taste. Later testimony brought out that I had been seen in a trench coat with a lump of pistol in my pocket on the Gulf of Messenia waterfront and I had myself contacted the illegal Communist national party chief, Soutsos. Like hell I did. But the papers played that up big when the rest of the things happened. Soutsos was a bank robber, not a political figure, and I met him only once—in the restaurant Zonars, a kind of smoky Schrafft's with olive oil added. He was small, very bald, very amusing, but I didn't understand a word he said. Kyprios, who brought him, said, "He tells girl is in whorehouse in Kolokotroni Street."

"No, no, she's too young."

Kyprios translated that, and Soutsos kissed the tips of his dirty fingers and said something they both laughed at, grabbing their thighs. In the end I promised them a thousand dollars if they would deliver the girl at the American Embassy. The Embassy, of course, didn't give a damn about Lily; her papers, they said, were not really in order and they didn't accept her as Charlie's daughter. So I didn't go back to them after the first frosty interview with a Harvard faggot.

I never went to the whorehouse (which later in press reports was called a dance academy). I was supposed to have gone with two men over the roofs and been lowered by a rope ladder into the main salon, where I kidnaped Lily, knocking out two huge wrestlers. Actually Kyprios called me on the phone.

"Look, doll. I am very scared. Is no deal."

"Why the hell not?"

"Somebody say girl likes it there. Very popular whorehouse. Girls feel like daughters of *la madame.*"

"You're crazy."

"No, this girl, I hear, she very hot stuff. I tell you she already a legend down by the harbor."

"Look, Kyprios, don't hand me that Bogart movie shit. Are you trying to raise the price?"

"Is no cinema. I in trouble with them, now with you."

"You have the girl in my hotel or at the Embassy in two days or I'll put a monkey wrench into your tanker deal in Washington. And I can do it. At least start an investigation."

"You sonofamothefutzingbitch," he said sadly, not really angry. "You hear from me." And he hung up. The only way to hurt a Greek is to put your thumb in one of his business deals. I waited two more days, tried to read Thomas Mann's *Doctor Faustus* and gave it up. If there were no devil, God would be a prig. For fun I observed people—some fade out in strong sunlight; some merge into evening. I bathed a lot, dissolving mentally in hot water like a lump of sugar. The rest of what happened I'm going to put down; it's all true. I'm sorry but it is; it can't be avoided.

Kyprios called me at dusk on a Saturday night, the neon signs and olive oil in the air. "You go to out past Aristotelous Park and drive on road to left up to mountain. *Just* drive."

"And?"

"You just, like I say, drive, and you have two thousand dollars with you."

"No, one thousand. Had a hell of a time raising that."

"No, price is now two."

"What's your cut?"

"I don't take one red drachma. You follow instructions?"

"I'll think about it. I'll go to the police."

"Doll, don't. You never see girl again. Police are bigger crooks than people who have her. They mean fellas."

"They'd kill her?"

"Please, no such talk. She just never seen again. You start at five o'clock to drive. Okay?"

I hung up saying nothing else, and I felt: Oh that goddamn Charlie, how had I ever let myself get into this crumb-bum setup? I had managed to get together nearly a thousand dollars in traveler's checks and cashed them, borrowing from everybody, newspapermen, relief officers, even selling two German cameras and a chipped-

49

diamond tiepin I never wore any more. I hired a car by phone, no driver, and I got out something I had carried around since World War I, a blue-steel Luger I had bought from a Tommy for a flask of brandy—and pretty bad brandy too. I had fired it over the years at tin cans and at seashells down on a Florida key, but that's all. I had an extra clip and I put it in, and while I didn't have a trench coat, I had a blue Burberry with a belt and I put it on. Downstairs I found a battered Buick waiting for me. I signed, paid, and drove off. I tried to think that the spectacle of evil is a reassurance to the good—and failed. I drove down the street past the park and hoped I had the right road. The night was pale-yellow, and there were old dried-up men with donkeys moving some garden truck along the dirt trails, and everything smelled like a privy, so the farmers must have been fertilizing the fields. Suddenly I came over pretty ill and I could hear the blood in my head pumping. The Luger was in my right-hand pocket and I felt foolish, frightened and very sorry for myself. I stopped the car and went into a dirty-looking inn smelling of the dried cowflop they burned as fuel, and I said, "Brandy." My appetite for responsibility needed help.

A marvelous-looking one-eyed woman with a very beautiful face said, "Mastika, ouzo, Tsipouro?"

"Brandy." It was a deserted sort of place and she seemed alone. After a while I got the idea these were brandies she named—which did I want? I made a drunken staggering gesture and she laughed—she was gracefully smoky and really beautiful—and she said, "Tsipouro." I put down some money and she brought out a blue bottle and I pointed to two glasses and she drank with me and I got a little hazy and felt like a Tartuffe. I figured I'd get her drunk and go upstairs with her and forget Lily Huttonbok. I was suddenly very randy for this one-eyed Greek beauty with a uniqueness that avoids the unique. If this seems strange, for me sex has always been the proper dosage for any fear or unpleasant excitement; I'm the most horny when in a tough spot. She didn't get drunk though we went at it belt for belt. But I did, and I went out to the car and kicked each of the four tires and pissed a long time against the rear left one. But the inn door remained closed, so I got into the car and drove on. I was very very drunk and that's the truth, so what happened to me later did not really happen to a sane man in control of himself. I only wanted to get laid by a one-eyed Greek goddess smelling of smoke

50

and sweat, and an amazing beauty. Unwashed, but I like a gamy woman when under pressure.

About ten minutes after I left the inn, there, catty-corner across the road, was a yellow jeep with the royal national insignia of Greece painted on it. A very nice-looking boy of nineteen or twenty, very polite, said, "Misster Kite?"

I got out and nodded, and he said, "Foller me, misster." I didn't want to leave the road. I became aware of lengthening shadows.

I followed the boy up the road to a square hut of stone with a wooden cage of rabbits in front of it and a dying grapevine climbing to the roof for safety. I was so drunk I could hardly stand. Not muzzy-tipsy, but *drunk*.

Inside an oil lamp burned and a short-haired very young girl with much too much makeup was reading an old American movie magazine, and I could see this was Lily, Charlie's daughter. The same features, the same twist to the lower lip, the way her fingers were formed. Her preoccupation with the magazine was deep, or faked.

She said, "Hi, you got the money?"

"I have some of it. Will they let you go?"

"Hand it over." There was a smile of ephemeral triumph, and she gave the full smile to the boy.

"To whom?" (Maybe I said *who*.)

"To me, you stupid."

"But who are the people that are holding you prisoner?"

"Oh shit," she said. "Just pay me the two thousand."

"I'm a bit confused, Lily."

"Money, *the* money."

The young man was laughing; she was killing him with the act—I could see that. She was a card to him and he enjoyed it. The lamp cast chartreuse-colored shadows on his face.

I said, "No. If this is your little scheme, Lily, no. I'll give this bastard a hundred bucks. But that's all. You little blackmailing bitch."

She shouted, *"Herr Jesus Gott!* Hand over the two thousand!"

I wanted to hold onto something. I could hardly stand. The alcohol boiled in me but I was coming out of it; I could feel sweat pouring down under my armpits and a dry feeling of panic in my mouth.

The girl shouted, "Antonius! Georgius!" Two huge men came from someplace out back, dressed in blue shirts and white linen suits like

51

those worn by office workers or the kind you see on porters at the Archeological Museum.

I really sweated; I tried to put boundaries on the scene. The boy had a knife in his hand, and one of the two big clerk types pulled out a small silver-plated revolver, the sort women used to carry on Western train journeys.

The boy said, "Hand over the money. Your passport. Your wallet. You never need them no more."

Lily said, "Christ sake, Paul, you can't do that. He's my old man's friend."

"Ha, we don't need this misster no more—and you, too, Lily, if you not shut up you mouff."

She shivered in a melancholy way—a child again. "You're not going to kill him?"

"Not here. Out by the cliff. Antonius, grab him."

Not too hopefully I said, "Look, take what I have and let's stop getting nasty. I mean you don't want the police and the Embassy after you." But I saw this was no game or deal, and I had put my head into a death noose—mine—and there was nothing to do—not a thing— and that bitch of a daughter of Charlie's had gone into a little setup that was more than she had bargained for. Her look of foiled temper sobered me fully. I fired the Luger through my coat pocket—it was amazingly easy—and got the man with the silver lady's pistol in the groin and he fell screaming. The boy Paul threw his knife at me—almost casually—and I ducked and shot him right between the eyes. I did it on purpose, gun out now, taking aim. The third man just went out of the window. I fell back on a chair and watched the boy die, very quickly, his eyes glazing, staring at me almost in admiration at my skill, I felt, his tongue pushing against his teeth, his hard heels kicking out. Don't believe that stuff about instant death, even right between the eyes.

I said, "I need a drink. I'm sick."

The girl was crying and calling out in a pleading loving voice, "Paul, Paul," and she went over and kicked the boy in the head, in outrage, I suppose.

I drank half a bottle of retsina wine, tasting of resin, and recovered a bit. Lily was shouting, "That fool, that crazy kid. He pulled a double cross. He didn't trust me to do it my way."

I took her arm. "We're going to the Embassy."

She said, "Why not?"

I was still a bit anesthetized by the shock of the events—but I had to admit it had happened.

Back on the road I found all the tires on my hired car cut, so I got into the jeep, but it was locked. I had learned something when serving my country in World War II: how to start a locked jeep by crossing certain wires under the hood. All the way back to Athens—it was a lovely night—Lily chewed on her fingernails, stopping now and again to curse Paul. I could see she was in an early pregnancy and I wished Charlie luck with her. He deserved her.

I forced my way into the Embassy, and Lily told a nice clean story about being held captive for four months and continually violated and how I burst in and saved her.

The real news came when the police went back to the hut and found the body of the leader of the Communist underground in the city of Athens, Arigiros Autsatsos, dead there like a plate of Cretan ham on a plate, and his second-in-command with a slug in his liver. That news really hit the fan with a mess, and I had to sober up and take a shower and say I had been forced, in self-protection, self-defense at gunpoint; I was only trying to recover the daughter of a dear friend who had been at the mercy of these Red fiends. Actually I knew it was nothing like this. Lily had enjoyed every minute of her whorehouse life and her affair with the Red leader—I doubted if he was actually the leader—but the truth never got into the press.

I received a Greek decoration, the Delphi Rose—with a gold vine leaf (out of the cooking pot, I suppose), and CBS-TV did an hour interview with Lily and me. She was clean, her short hair done up in a wave, blood-red fingernails, and she said a dirty word only twice, and they cut that out of the final tape. I was interviewed by a newsmagazine and they invented more fiction. The publishing firm of Doubleday sent a contract for me to write a book, "Lifting the Iron Curtain," which I never wrote (nor did I return the advance on it either). The AP remembered a few other times I had made news, and they sent that over the wires too. The only thing I really regretted was the Greek woman with the one eye. She reminded me so much of Pages, so much.

Back in the United States I had a long letter from Charlie about how wonderful it was to have Lily with him and too bad her husband, a Polish prince, was shot by those Marxist swine in Warsaw, and he, Charlie, was going to devote the rest of his life to a great crusade against the Communist menace to world peace. Later he wrote me Lily had had a boy, and they had named him William Paul after me, and St. Paul, "a favorite saint of Lily's."

EDITOR'S NOTE: The reader of the newsmagazines and the press reports of that date is well aware of what were most likely the actual events that William Kite is here setting down in his own fashion. He did kill, in self-defense, a very dangerous political criminal at great risk to himself. He was actually badly cut at the time, suffering a deep knife wound. He never in any interview told the story as he put it down in his manuscript. Lily Huttonbok was married twice, and is now living in South America, a citizen there. I have not seen fit to reveal her present name or address. The boy was adopted by her first husband, who gave him his name. She has to date rebuffed all requests of mine for answers to my letters.

There is the strong possibility that Kite was not actually so drunk or so foolish as he makes himself out in his text. The people he knew in the postwar world in those days had a pose of not admitting to anything heroic, or doing any noble deed or action. I suspect the newspaper accounts were closer to the facts than what he has put down. John Gunther, the international journalist, who has examined the actual reports of the Greek police, assures me William Kite committed a very dangerous and heroic action.

CHAPTER 4
1918

WE DID GET TO PARIS in the spring. The weather, a great gray monstrosity, was so bad we couldn't fly any sorties over the front at our sector based beyond Arras. The war lay under a lashing rain and the morning mists lasted all day, and below us men drowned in putrefying mud. Charlie drove up to the airdrome one morning in a 12.5-horsepower Sizaire that had one big headlight over its radiator like the Cyclops' eye. Charlie, in a long clipped-sheepskin coat, pink whipcord breeches, splendid Savile Row boots, looked the proper ace. He had the MC, and I was now a captain and had the DSM and solid gold insignia on my overseas cap. Oh, we were the proper stuff to feed the folks back home in newspaper stories and interviews and photos—if you didn't notice the twitch in our cheeks and the stylish tremor in the nicotine-tinted fingers.

"This time for sure, Jay's getting married. Even if we have to stop the war."

"Same girl?"

"Of course, the same girl. You don't think anybody who meets Pages changes his mind?"

"Crazy name for a girl."

"Nora Pages. But nobody calls her Nora."

I noticed a huge shaggy dog on the front seat of the auto. "What the hell is that?"

"Wedding gift for Mr. and Mrs. Tjaden. Genuine Boche dog. Survived a crash when our group shot down von Blocke, his master, in his Albatross. You'd have loved it, Bill. I'm flying at three thousand feet, see, and out of a cloud comes this Hun above me, sun in my eyes, I nearly shat, but took a fast wing roll to the left and . . ."

"Charlie, write your memoirs later. I've got to wangle leave from the CO. Three days enough?"

"More than. Bring any buddy you have. *Très* gash, *très* liquor. *Comprenez-vous?*"

"Your accent stinks, Charlie."

"*C'est tout!*"

The group major was sitting at his desk under the signed photograph of Guynemer and his S.P.A.D., and a small model of the D.H.4 in which the major lost his left foot flying over Ypres in the early days. His fine-bred face showed the apprehension he had of the corruptibility of power.

"Paris? Leave out of the question, ol' boy."

"It's a particular friend with the Fourth RFC Group. Old chum, school tie and all that." I was giving it the very best British pitch I could.

"We want to bomb Bissege airdrome soon as this muck clears. HQ is chewing out my arse why we're not flying right now. Out of the question. Fearfully sorry and all that."

"I promise, I'll get twelve planes up soon as the sun shines. Must be at the wedding, Major. Leftenant Tjaden's been in as long as I have. Both of us likely to crap out on any flight. Odds against us ever meeting again."

The major did a slow study of my words. "Well, throttle off, Kite.

Have the warrant office give you the pass. And pray there's no sunshine for three days."

"I'd like to take Leftenant Pfaelzer along. He's the only survivor of his replacement group."

"He has been lucky, hasn't he? Flies like a constipated crow. But back in three days. We've got a new lot of Sopwith F.I.'s coming, and you know what bloody bitches they are to break in properly. Oh, and steal me a bottle of Hennessy Three Star like a good chap."

Tony Pfaelzer wasn't half pleased to be getting away to Paris. He had turned out to be a marvelous flier, but I couldn't see how he'd live much longer. He had a habit of drifting east across the lines at two thousand feet and waiting till a group of von Kleinschmidt's Fokker triplanes came out at noon, regular as clockwork. Then Tony would dive in among them, his wings almost tearing out, and pick off one or two before they knew he was there. They'd go into attack and evasion movements thinking it was an RFC group squadron attack. By that time Tony was either flying low for home over the lines or cutting off a Hun who had made the wrong move and was alone and vulnerable to the twin Lewis guns pumping tracers into the enemy canvas and wood and living man. But they were getting wise to Tony and dividing up; someday soon they'd bracket Tony and his damn Camel between them. The Spandau slugs would give us another dead ace. We had plenty of those. The major considered Tony a very *soigné* type.

"Tjaden wouldn't mind?" Tony asked.

"Why should he? You need crowds for a wedding."

"The bride pretty?" asked Tony, admiring his dark good looks in a mirror as he buttoned on his London-cut jacket.

"Not as pretty as you are, I'd judge. I never met her."

"That's damn disquieting."

Outside Charlie was honking the horn of the car. I had left him in the mess bar drinking doctored Scotch on my slate.

"Charlie's feeling his oats. He's a bit of a Jew-baiter, but not too bad."

"My favorite anti-Semites. I'll wear my old shul tie."

The canvas top of the Sizaire was only fairly waterproof, but we had our trench coats on, and between the bottle of brandy and some singing and the dog Fritz barking, we managed to get stuck only twice in the foul stinking mud the roads had become under four years of army traffic and shelling. It was sad to see the long lines of boys and middle-aged men marching the other way. Wet, muddy, burdened with tools and gear. The French were scraping up old men now, ancient farts with whiskers and rounded bony shoulders. The English were mostly mere kids, whey-faced, with lips blue with rain. The horse-drawn wagons were miserable; everything was worn and unpainted till you came across a piece of American equipment, which looked brazen and strange and like a too-new toy until the mud covered it.

"Like our gunner sergeant says, 'It's fuckin' war,' " said Charlie, bent over the steering wheel of the iron monster. "We Yanks, we'll have to end it for them."

"They'll thank you for that. How does Jay feel about getting married?"

"It upsets him. Too much brain, you know. Thinks, reasons. Bad show. He doesn't fly well any more. Escorting some French Voisins last week, he was jumped by six Albatrosses and damn near bought the black ace. *Au revoir.* Couldn't keep his mind on it, he said."

Tony beat his swagger stick on his legs. "Paris. The Louvre, Notre Dame. I wonder if they still have the old bookstalls on the Seine."

Charlie took a suck of the brandy bottle and worked the hand-turned windshield wiper. *"Bien merci, et vous-même!* You out of your rabbinical mind? We're going to Paris to paint it red, marry off Jay, get laid, drink, eat, sleep and get laid. Eh, Fritz, *du Schweinhund?"*

The dog barked and clawed at Charlie from the back seat. Charlie steered the car around a horse-drawn .75 mired to the wheels. The flogged horses had given up; the Frenchmen, bearded muddy lumps, cursed us out, but with no strength or feeling in it.

"This road, dry and straight, I could open this baby, open to a hundred miles an hour. The power of Niagara under the hood."

Tony said, "Let's try."

"It's a racer with the rear seat built on. After the war I'm going to take it down to Nice and open it up in a road race. After the war."

Tony took the nearly empty bottle. "Nobody, Huttonbok, unless it's the dog, is going to be around after the war."

Charlie grinned. "All I'm praying for is a nice clean wound, just a flesh wound, see—and a nurse with beautiful tits, and some English garden to convalesce in. I'm a Catholic, Pfaelzer, I believe in prayer. I'll include you guys in when I pray in Paris. What you rather have, a leg wound or an arm wound? Conspicuous, heroic, but not too deep. Nothing irrational or bizarre. *Just* a wound."

Tony threw the empty bottle out into the rain beyond the flapping curtains. "Gunnery Sergeant Peterson got his balls shot off. Very disquieting to him. A fine thing to happen to a man. I'd rather get it between the eyes."

We hit a rut, and the car bounced so high we came down on the shoulder of the road. Charlie sang *Viens, pou-poule,* and Tony offered *La Petite Tonkinoise.* Neither the dog nor I had any voice.

A Senegalese company of black colonials, blue-green with cold and damp, were huddled over smoldering little fires. They jumped apart as we passed splashing—scattered rifles, knives, miserable little pots of condemned canned stew they were heating (which the regulars wouldn't eat).

Charlie threw some franc notes at them as he plowed back onto the road. "Sorry, chaps. *Enchanté!* Look like a damn minstrel show, don't they? Poor niggers, what are they fighting for?"

Tony said, "The right to eat their grandmothers. What are we fighting for if it comes to that? I'm buying the next bottle of brandy, next *estaminet* we come to."

Charlie put an arm on Tony's shoulder. "When you meet a good soak, you meet the best."

"Good thing we have passes," I said. "The military police lurk in the damn pubs."

Charlie thought, took his hand off the wheel and beat his gloved fists together. I grabbed the wheel as we passed a mired tank, its crew sitting under a canvas spread like shipwrecked sailors.

"Who the hell has a pass? My CO, a Sandhurst Jew bastard— pardon me, Tony, you're a white Jew—the Hebe said he couldn't spare me. Wing Headquarters said we weren't pulling our weight. So I just went out over the place the dustbins go. The battle of the individual with regulations—the refusal to come to terms with the military mind."

Tony said cheerfully, "They'll shoot you. Six in the morning. Twelve rifles, one cigarette, one blindfold, one priest. Officer's *coup de grâce* behind the ear."

58

"They can't. I'm the only surviving member of the bloody squadron who can get the young squabs up in the air. Oh, it's shameful what we do—the poor little pissers, so game and so scared, rosy-cheeked. They belong on the playing fields of Eton or fagging upperclassmen, not going up against Snellenbokken Staffel in our old A.K.W.'s. Here's a place to piddle and get that brandy."

We slid into a courtyard all manure pile under a grape arbor leafless and black. Fritz snarled. Several lorries were in the yard, lettered U.S.A. The inn was full of deserters and apaches, *maquereaux, mômes,* hiding out from the army lists. They owned the military police, the innkeeper told us. But that's war. *"Je prends mon bien où je le trouve."*

It wasn't raining so hard when we started up again.

Paris in wartime was a sad place. There was little paint; bits of missing glass had been replaced by boards and cardboard. The streets were filthy; shutters hung on a slant. The staff cars—Rollses, Pierce-Arrows, Fiats and fancy French jobs all in battle-gray or mustard—moved healthy-looking officers around. Lorries seemed to be passing in never-ending rows. Now and then a Ford ambulance rattled by us and I didn't like the stains around the doors in back. Lots of legless and armless and blind men were available.

We had faked some kind of paper for Charlie on an old military form for Handley Page motor parts. I knew it wouldn't fool any English patrol. We detoured around the main gates into Paris and came up past the Gare de Lyon, crowded with returning leave trains, human cattle going out to die or drown beyond the Marne. We went past hotels looking sodden in the thin, tea-green rain. Pages's major had taken a suite at the Ritz for the wedding, and that was grand, Charlie said, "because the diplomats' and generals' whores pretty much have everything there. And a few special missions of congressmen, members of Parliament, and a rajah or two."

There was still a doorman, one empty sleeve pinned across his chest over his medals. We took Fritz in with us, and the swishy clerk said we weren't going to be allowed to have the creature along.

Tony said, "This is President Wilson's own dog. Part of our *esprit de corps.* You understand? It's a secret, but we're the advance party for the President, who is coming over to win the war with his umbrella. Charge!"

59

The clerk said it was by appearance, *monsieur,* a Boche dog.

Charlie leaned on the counter. "The father is Charlie Chaplin, the mother is Mademoiselle Mata Hari. *Merci infiniment."*

We went for the lift without waiting to hear any more.

The lobby was full of well-dressed, fine-smelling, meaty women, a few charming in lacy mourning black. There were assorted officers of all nations with that fine smooth look of desk riders, a Jesuit, a man who said he ran the prison of the Santé, staff pips, red-braided caps, fliers. There was a middle-aged French officer, one-legged and on crutches, talking to an Italian major with plucked eyebrows. And there was steam heat, something most hotels were leaving out that season. Ecstasy and excitement seemed on tap. Charlie quoted Donne as he sniffed: "And what wind serves to advance an honest mind."

We knew the floor Jay's suite was on before we got there: a humming, buzzing noise, a breakage of glass, a singing of some sentimental flying-force ballad about taking the engine out of my liver, lift the crankcase from my chest.

Tony's eyes gleamed. "Hear all that *girl* laughter?"

The red-carpeted hallway was heavy with waiters and maids pushing little tables of drink and food. The gold-and-white doors of the suite were open on a pattern of officers and well-dressed women mixed together in tobacco smoke, retaining their hold on glasses of wine. The women were, I figured (rapidly taking inventory of haunches, arms, torsos, legs), one-third in the uniform of some special HQ service—Red Cross, Admiralty, War Office—pretty girls to keep the men, fatigued by desk work, alert, warm, comfortable in bed, and available for dinner or a long distasteful journey to some legation or HQ. *They,* too, fought a splendid war. Basically in war three things matter (only writers lie about it): sexual congress, drink in plenty, and avoidance of death.

Some of the women were in black, and the few men in frock coats had a sprinkling of mourning bands among them. They had survived their sons and felt pious about it. One learned in three years of war to take death with the proper little period of mourning, the black public sign: We, too, have had our loss, and so chin up, drink in hand, carry on, the worst is yet to be. There were American officers looking very Zeta Psi and Skull-and-Bones from Yale.

Charlie went barging into other rooms. Tony and I grabbed a waiter, cornered him, and before his pleased eyes had three large champagnes each. "It is good," Tony said, "to know the French have lots of vintage wine left to fight the war with. A most musty wine with the proper bubbles. Where's Jay?"

"Being bathed by virgins. It's a ritual."

We went to the buffet, smiled at the suckling pig, at the pink sliced ham, at the organs, sea life, tidbits in aspic, caviar on ice, the smoked goose, the pâté with bay leaves. Tony and I, so long alive on bad coffee, brandy, leathery eggs, canned offal from the Chicago packing-houses, smiled at each other and fell to, mouths greasy, stomachs miraculously at rest now that we didn't have to fly a dawn patrol. We looked about us, chewing, sipping, eyes on stems at the sight of the clean women. A small band played Victor Herbert waltzes under some palms yellowing in gilt pots. We took it all in with the unanesthetized parts of our brains.

"What fine tail," said Tony with awe and respect. "You ever see so much woman even in your best dreams? Oh, my unencumbered heart!"

"Do you smell them, Tony?"

"I can taste them. Pendulous tits, gyrating haunches." He patted a woman in gray lace on the ass with exuberance. "Honey, it's beauti-ful. Shake it, shake it for victory. In the grave none do embrace. Use it, honey, in good health. *Saftig!*"

"*Onde está!*"

"I bet, honey. Forgive us war heroes; we haven't been getting much lately."

"*Não se incomode.*"

"You don't have to say a word, honey. Just let me look down your taffeta dress. A fine piece of fabric. A Jew knows goods."

A man rushed over and got between us and the woman. The woman shook her head. "*E nada não faz, diferença.*"

The man said, "It is the wife of the Portuguese ambassador. The mother of six." He added low, "*Un sale youpin.*"

Tony smiled at the man and said to his ear, "That's what I like. No virginity to hamper us, *and* experienced."

I led Tony over to the seafood buffet. "Stop pawing the ground like a stud stallion."

"It's all there, it's real. After this all I ask is the mercy of instantaneous death. It's too much."

I knew what he meant: women, cared for, clean, bathed, powdered, their teeth not coated, their underwear not soiled, their

61

breath sweet, their hair washed and waved. So much white skin, and the odor of them! Scent is the primitive sex lure, and perfume only raises the ante. I was feeling like Tony, drunk, randy and dizzy just looking. I wondered what our chances for rape were. Our walk became spurry with spikiness.

"How can Jay afford anything like this?" I asked.

"Didn't you hear Charlie say this Pages babe's aunt owns New England? Or is it her uncle? Big munitions people now, built ships and railroad cars before the war. Golden Republican pisspots, practically run Washington. Oh, that Jay. Is the *mamzer* lucky, the *monsieur!* Where the hell is he hiding? Maybe he's already in the kip?"

"Where's the bride?" I asked, aware there was something wrong with all this unreality. It would vanish if I belched. "Tony, I think we're in the wrong party." I felt we should remove ourselves like a soiled handkerchief.

Tony, too drunk to hear, grabbed a beautiful French Red Cross worker in her blue hood. She smiled: Tony, dark, handsome, panting, with that long humorous nose, big dark-ringed eyes that belonged to a great actress, and his eyelashes a scandal too. "Look, honey, where is *Monsieur* Leftenant Tjaden?"

"Que désirez-vous, chéri?"

"Eliot Tjaden. The wedding *je désire*. The groom, the bride, *je voudrais* to see them, *ma* darling, *apportez-moi."*

The truth was out. Our high-school French was still pretty lousy. Great with waiters, whores, police, laundresses, but U.S.A. and college French just didn't seem to work on the natives, who all had wretched accents, Jay once said, "and garble their beautiful language by talking it much too fast."

Charlie came out from an inner room. He looked drawn and worried as if from some heightened consciousness. "Fellas, something pretty sad has happened."

I said, "She was killed in a bomb raid?"

Tony said, "God wouldn't permit it."

Charlie grabbed my sleeve. There was some calculated absurdity here. "Come with me. Don't let anybody else in."

We followed Charlie to a tall narrow door. Past that we were in a long hall, thick with hooks on which various capes and coats and headgear hung. Beyond that Charlie knocked on a double door.

There was a shuffling of feet but no answer. Charlie knocked again. He rattled the tarnished silver doorknob.

"Jay, Jay, it's all right. It's Charlie and Bill here."

After a while the door latch was heard shooting back, and a bloodshot eye peered at us through the opening. "Can't let the rabble in, you know. No statements for the press. Too boozed. . . ."

We went into a bedroom, one of those gold-and-green Louis XIV sets, smelling of Marie Antoinette's cat, with paintings on the wall of girls high on swings and men in tricorn hats and white silk stockings looking up at lacy underwear floating by as if they were damn tired of it all.

Jay was dressed in a tight new flying tunic, the collar open, decorations over the left pap, hair in his face, mouth slack, abominably hoarse. A despairing intensity.

"It's a proper fuck-up, eh? A proper fuck-up. Hello, Bill."

"What's this all about? I came for a wedding."

"Who are you?" Jay asked Tony. "There has been a change of plans."

"Joel Cohen's cousin, Tony Pfaelzer."

"Have a drink, Tony. You have the eyes of sea anemones."

There were several bottles of cognac, and Jay looked at me, desolate, trembling, and punched me with a mock blow in the stomach. "Hello, old cock, a fine how-do."

"Don't know what it's all about."

Charlie helped Jay into a chair. "This sonofabitch major or what-you-call-it, who's in charge of the special Quaker hospital service, he's had Pages shipped out to Italy. He's had a hard on for Pages, see, and when Jay phoned he was coming to Paris to marry Pages, poof, she's ordered off for Italy on a goddamn troop-carrying ship late last night."

"And," added Jay, "all those damn U-boats sinking everything in the Mediterranean."

I poured myself a drink. "If the girl had any spirit, she'd have said no dice and stayed for her wedding."

"She didn't know. The wedding's been postponed so often I was going to surprise her. All arrangements done before I got in this morning, and all Pages's friends notified of the wedding. Even got a Quaker priest or minister or what-you-call-it."

Tony refilled everyone's glass and patted Fritz on the head. "Tjaden, you could get transferred to the Italian front."

63

"The British have only bombers down there."

"Transfer to the Americans."

"Not anything there either yet. I'm going over the hill. Get to Spain. Ship to Italy from there. Or get Pages to come over."

Charlie held up his arms as if holding a rifle. "Ready, aim, fire. They're shooting—the talk is—almost as many Allied soldiers these days as they're killing Germans. There's only one thing to do."

Jay, seated, looked up and put his arms around Fritz's neck. "And what's that?"

"By St. Skiridion of Holy Memory, get stinking drunk. Then go wreck the hospital driving service that sent Pages out of reach. *À la lanterne! À l'Américaine!*"

Tony was on the phone. "Ello? Ello? Room service. *Voulez-vous m'apporter* two bottles of your best cognac. *Le Grand Suite. C'est tout.* Huh? *Parlez plus lentement.* Just get it up here." He held up the phone and turned to us. "I don't suppose we should order up some whores?"

"Hardly fitting," said Charlie, beginning to feel the drinking we'd been doing all day, "seeing as to what has happened to Jay. But, old pal, old buddy, let me buy the booze."

"No, no," said Tony. "My old man is the biggest junk dealer in San Francisco. Busy turning rust into gold."

Jay belched with wretched diversity and sank back in the chair. "Babylon is fallen, is fallen that great city because she made all the nations drink of the wine of the wrath of her fornication—*cecidit cecidit, Babylonia illa magna* . . ."

CHAPTER 5

I REMEMBER ONLY PATCHES of what happened after we decided to leave the Ritz and the wedding that was not a wedding. Charlie with his arm around Tony's neck crying out, "This is my Jew. Greatest flier ever was. Let's buy some more drinks. . . ." Jay angry and drunk, all of us in the back of some fearful café full of women in Japanese robes—only they weren't women but stinking men with painted faces—and Jay muttering in my ear as he clung to my arm.

"That's right, Bill, that's right. Concupiscence and original sin. Man is a stray in a labyrinth, guiding himself by the echoes of his own small jests. Oh Pages, Pages—what a muck-up. Eh, Charlie? eh, Tony?"

"Where is my Jew? He went to the john five minutes ago. Where is he?"

"We ought to eat something, Jay. Just soup—"

"Never going to eat again."

We did get to a place near the night market, and to bowls of thick mutton soup with anatomy lessons of animal bone in it and leaden spoons. Tony and Charlie wrestled a chicken-shit second looie from Kansas City, Charlie yelling, "I got 'em licked. Got 'em! That's right. Must escape our own disenchantment, Jayboy. Way I feel, fellas, a lifetime is too short a period to discover if one has really achieved a pattern. True, Jay? Know what I mean? Tony, kill the bastard. Never liked anybody from the Middle West where they say *watter* for water."

Jay lifted his head from the dirty oilcloth on the table. "I don't fear death when I'm flying. I only fear my own wish to die. Now Pages is off, off with the liquorous major, what's left? Who's flying patrol tomorrow? Awful brandy. What's there in the pain of being, as they said in Philosophy 2 at Princeton, Bill, the trap of death, the hunger of the absolute?"

"We never took Philosophy 2, Jay."

"Shove the absolute," said Tony's sweated face, open tunic, twitching fingers. "Listen, anybody got a banjo? *Gewalt.*"

"Who the eff in these parts would have a banjo?" said the Kansas chicken-shit looie.

Tony shrugged, laughed; someone had swiped his wings, his decorations. He lifted his head and sang:

> *"Adieu, mon amour, adieu, douces fillettes,*
> *Adieu, Grand Pont, halles, bains de vapeur,*
> *Adieu, Paris, adieu, petits pâtés."*

Charlie said, "My singing Jew." He hugged Tony, kissed him on each cheek in the style of a French general. "I award you with palms *pour le mérite—*"

"That's a Kraut award," Jay said.

"Too good for 'em. Now sing it in English, Tony."

"My version:

> *"Goodbye, my love, goodbye, sweet nookie,*
> *Goodbye, Grand Pont, markets, Turkish baths,*
> *Goodbye, Paris, goodbye, meat patties!"*

After that we were walking by some long long sheds, looking for Charlie's car . . . and Jay suddenly got away and we caught him trying to climb some pigeon-dunged bronze monument to some general on a fat horse, and he wouldn't come down. It was commencing to rain, and people began to grow upside down out of their own reflections.

"Not to be better than we are, just to be ourselves," said Jay, making a speech, holding onto a bronze horse's tail. "We begin with hope and survive by being able to dispense with it. I hope you all grasp the nuances of that remark."

Charlie was vomiting in the gutter. Tony said, "That's the stuff to give the troops! Lafayette, we are here!"

Jay looked down on us sadly. "In our time there are no overtures, only epilogues. There is a chasm between people too wide for jumping. Jumping." Jay jumped and rolled into the street, and there was a bad gash on his head. Tony held a bergamot-scented handkerchief to Jay's bright red blood.

Somehow later, somewhere, we were in the car, and all and everything fell away in spirals for me like a rind of a carefully peeled orange. We were all asleep beside the dead car. Gasoline gone, rain falling into our open mouths. Charlie and Tony asleep, serenely immobile, gaunt, unshaved, slack-mouthed, spittle drooling from their lips, rain falling at a slant, in straight lines (so artistic you'd think it was a goddamn Japanese print by Hiroshige), Jay staring at the lead sky, watching the rain fall—someplace we had lost the canvas top of the car—the dog Fritz crouched between Charlie's legs, happy as a dumb German is just to be with somebody he can feel inferior to. I looked for the trajectories of fixed stars. No stars.

66

I pushed an elbow into Jay's ribs. "No stars. We don't want to stay here."

"What month is it?"

"How the devil should I know, Jay?"

"What day?"

"No idea."

I kicked at Tony, who grunted but did not awaken. We were reclining on a sandy side road . . . clipped yew trees, all their top branches gone for firewood for the frugal French; in a field a rusting farm machine, too ancient to be used or sheltered, and a squatting fog in a rising slope of cabbages. France. Home of brotherhood, fraternity, and . . . I forget. My head with its cauterized lips didn't ache. Just numb.

Jay rolled his head and laughed. "Drifting like polyps, as if we can assume another shape by just snapping"—he tried to snap fingers—"our fingers. Up, you bastards. There's a patrol tomorrow for all of us. Today if we're late. Yesterday, maybe."

Tony came awake. "I wanna get laid. I wanna stand treat in the best cathouse in Paris. Round-the-world, and half-and-half. One for all, all for one. Dumas. House of All Nations."

"We're not in Paris," I said.

"Mother-of-shit," said Tony, "we're bombing von Richthofen's old airdrome today. Gotta get going. Gotta."

There was a roaring down the road, and a sand-colored Dodge ambulance came *jug-jug-jugging* toward us. A pale, brown-haired boy with glasses was driving. The letters on the Dodge read: HARVARD SECTION.

Jay said, "Princeton here. Where are we, Harvard?"

"Our unit," said the boy, "is stationed at Vaudelaincourt."

Jay rubbed his eyes. He seemed calmer, recovered, his face deadpan, shivering with wet. "Which way is the front?"

"Which front?"

"Past Arras."

"That way. You're going west, you know."

Charlie patted Fritz. "There will always be a Harvard. You got gas?"

The boy gave up two red tins. I think he thought we were escaped from the security nut stockade. I slept after that and I had no idea how I got back to our section. I came to sitting in the officers' steam

67

bath we had fixed up in an old boiler. I was sprawling on a wooden bench, coughing, while live steam from hot stones splashed with water sent up feathers to choke me. Tony, large and naked, squatted on his hams, beating himself with a branch of oak leaves without mercy.

"Ah-ah-ah *tatale*. This is it. *Yoisher tatale.*"

"What?"

"Open your baby-blue eyes, Bill. We're taking a patrol over the lines in an hour. The major is sore—says we're degenerate Silenuses and we're to be shot *after* the patrol."

"Not me. I can't hold up my hand." I showed him my shaking limbs. I could feel every fragile scarlet branching of my bloodstream as it flowed.

Tony handed me a pitcher of milk, brandy and beaten eggs, the shot flier's pick-me-up. Life is only vicious to itself, I decided. "Jay? Charlie?"

"Went back to their units. Great guys. Number-one great guys."

"Poor Jay."

> *Adieu, mon amour, adieu, douces fillettes,*
> *Adieu, Grand Pont* . . .
> *Adieu, petits pâtés* . . .

"You think it's wrong, professor, to translate *douces fillettes* as sweet nookie? The popular French is sweet girlies. . . ."

Tony took the patrol up alone. I had pneumonia, the base doctor said, and was delirious for nearly a week.

Flying had become an uncommunicable horror to us old crocks who were soon, we were told, going to be withdrawn from the advance airdromes. As we drank our café-marc and waited, the war increased in rumor, fury, deadlines and despair. I was leading young fliers who hardly seemed to understand the theory of it, while the Germans were in as bad a way too, desperately sending out *Staffeln* of twelve machines against every patrol, using the Halberstadt fighter to good advantage: a machine that pulled up in a loop so fast we seemed to be walking. Udet's Fokker D.VII was also trouble. I'd come in from patrol, goggled eyes full of still-pirouetting spots, to the dirty, dusty fields of summer, where we were stationed within sound of the front, where the Americans were moving up under their thin tin hats. Still, the faces somehow looked like the ones I had once known in East Pompton. I felt like yelling, "What are you stupid bastards

doing here?" But I was developing British phlegm and secret grievances.

Tony Pfaelzer, since the trip to Paris to see Jay married, had
grown melancholy, missing the women, and played all day on a shrill
gramophone a recording of Schubert's "Death and the Maiden." He
taught me a bit of Yiddish and took up his violin, which he played
well but in a gloomy manner. We grew pale, with faces modeled as if
from church candles.

Charlie was flying in a unit fifty miles up the line with the dog Fritz
as his only companion in the cockpit. He had passed a perfunctory
medical examination after threatening his CO with a Very pistol
cartridge up his arse when the CO tried to force on the squadron a
plane with elevator controls the factories had put in wrong. Jay was
out of combat, testing new crates behind the lines.

Jay wrote me, "It's a very starchy war for these Limeys, but you
get up there among the high piled cumulus clouds in a F.E.2 with the
250-h.p. Rolls-Royce engine and they can keep the old crazy worn-
down earth. There's a whole universe unused, let's move. Say, you
long-haired bastard, you ever read *Faust? We fear the blows we never
get. And those things we never lose is what we lament.* Damn good
for a Heinie. Faust differs from all other intellectuals in that he
hunted experience, besides knowledge. To hold life in total vision is
damn hard. If we can get Charlie's auto working, we'll come down
maybe to your field soon with some native fellows we've been
bunking with of the Douzième Groupe d'Escadrilles de la Chasse, the
French elite squadron. Only we call them the Storks. I'm in a bad
way. As the poet Hafiz said, 'Who can't drink can't love.' I've got an
ulcer, the doc thinks. No letter from Pages, who is now someplace in
the Near East. How does one excise one's desire? Or am I mad as
Hamlet? Am I secretly pleased we didn't get married? I don't know,
Bill. I'm scared; what if I really don't want to marry her? *R.I.P*"

That set me back on my heels a bit.

Tony and I were taking up a wing of twelve; the trouble was that
usually there was a strong wind from the west, so that if we took our
sucklings, just out of solo school, too far over the German lines and a
dogfight broke us up, they'd drift so far east in their excitement,
they'd never have the gas to make it back. They were all as eager as
bridegrooms who had read it all in a book. But green, green, green.

The Germans had their Aviatik two-seaters out, and we had no

69

back-up at all in the air except from the Escadrille Lafayette at Bar-le-Duc behind Verdun. We didn't get on too well with them. They had been the Escadrille Américaine, N.124, flying the Vosges sector. They felt it was not playing the old ball game for Tony and me to be flying with the lousy Limeys when we could fly with them, real solid American he-men, who were going into the Hat-in-the-Ring group, U.S.A. But they could fly, and could die.

Tony in his flying pants, unshaved, eyes bloodshot, was to fly wing for me and the sucklings. The planes snorted and stank on the flying field, hustling at their wheel blocks, the castor oil a fearful odor, blue smoke tossing pebbles among the dying weeds. I got in my crate, raised my hand to get in the saddle, and we took off into the rising day, bluish violet shadows in the plane trees whose tops we just cleared, the air warm as English beer, the day still dark to the west. The sun was slanting on our left as we wheeled up and up in case the *Staffel* of the late ace Emmelmann were in a paranoiac mood and were hunting our ass. I let the airstream clear my head. Existence was a predicament I hoped to endure with care. I was living on coffee, raw eggs and brandy again, and any day I hoped to hear the major say I'd been elevated out of combat and could go to a nice rest in London: bathe, see a doctor about my nerves, get my teeth fixed, read a book. . . . Tony was wagging his wing. To the far left, I saw, was a herd of *Drachen,* German kite balloons up to observe and direct artillery fire. I signaled *no.* We had to ride a contact patrol with some land action. And the *Drachen* were protected by nasty AA fire, and Woleff's and Schafter's pilots lurked someplace in the clouds nearby to take care of the foolish fighter who was sucked in by balloons.

I gave my Lewis guns a burst to clear them for action. They often jammed. I was thinking that this horses'-nuts air fighting we were doing had no real military value, was merely anonymous butchery although the press wrote us up as knights of the air, when—*zam!*—we walked right into it. The clouds having drifted away, we were blinded by the sun. In two layers red-painted triplane Fokkers were down on us, black crosses cruel and mean. They had been stacked just above the cloud bank. My sucklings ganged up like fox-nervous hens. I dumped my introspective thoughts, kicked the rudder, went into a roll, saw the suckling babies under my wing try to follow. Tony, always a crazy fine flier, pulled up in a loop, and he came around and

70

to the left, firing in bursts. A red-nosed Boche went down and around, with wind screaming like a fury in his wires.

A dogfight is a rocketing chaos. Chasing tails, I had enough to do. Some of the Huns' new planes I couldn't flag were firing one-pound poms-poms. I saw one of my babies go crazy in a tailspin and pour black smoke and come apart. I suppose he forgot his belt for he fell out screaming, but I was in trouble myself. I put on rudder without banking. I had two, one above me and one below in the blind spot. Where it was pumping into me I could feel canvas and wood splinter and tear, and I prayed, Oh shit-and-piss if I get it now, give it to me a fast one right through my brain or heart, like I gave a few. No burning no burning no falling falling to mash into a field. ("He fell at dawn on a clear quiet day, Captain W. Kite.") I kept the trigger finger ready, and kicked up and let the top Hun feel my guns. I let go half a drum, twenty-four rounds, but he ate it all and I knew it wasn't my day. I jabbed at the rudder bar, pushed the stick over and went into a steep dive ("He was buried in the family plot next to his father and grandfather"), but they followed me down. The unshaved bastard behind his goggled eyes was staring at me. I panicked, but my deep inner nerves—which didn't give a damn about my surface ones—told me what to do and how to do it. ("The Spanish-American War vets fired a volley over his grave.")

I took a quick look in the green-blue quadrangle of sky. My flight had crapped out. The Huns must have brought about twenty planes against us. Some of my babies were scattered, or falling, burning or breaking up. Tony I hunted his ship—had a thumb-on-nose insignia painted on his fuselage. He was flying far below, near the treetops, dodging three Heinies on his tail, trying to lure them low enough to crash them into the ground. I didn't see more. I was off to the east and they north—the horizon spinning like a fever dream—trying to get clear. One bastard clung just below in the blind zone, and I knew if I kept up going east, I'd run into some *Jagdstaffel* or interceptors.

I remembered an old bike-racing trick Jay and I had once worked out when we rode for prizes. I poured on coal to get a black exhaust, suddenly stalled and went down tail first, hoping I could get out of it in time. The Hun shot out in front of me. I came out of the dive, roared up and around and over him. I fired the rest of the drum, put in another drum (try it sometime if you ever find an old Camel in a museum; working stick, rudder, your elevator controls, feeling the oil gauge drop, one hand loading, wind tearing at you), the Hun circling to get behind and below.

And he had me. My motor sounded like a grease-spitting iron skillet frying flounders.

It's marvelous for your nerves, dying in a sodden carmine sun. Makes you think, repent, shrinks your scrotum. I could feel the plane shudder as he fired short bursts but lots of them. Then there was the sound of a Klaxon (we carried them to signal ground patrols), and a big blue fighter with English oval insignia was to the left of us. It had two fixed Vickers guns firing through the airscrew, and the Hun just went up in an exploding rose, breaking at once into fragments. The blue Nieuport wagged its wings. There was a dog's snout moving in the cockpit. That was how Charlie Huttonbok saved my life. I made a feeble superfluous gesture of thanks—held my hands in a prayer position. Then it was that I felt my right leg and hip burn, and I put down a glove surreptitiously, furtively, to investigate, and it came up smeared with black blood. Funny, I hadn't felt it during my funk. I gave a curdled smile. Was I dead or out of the war?

I didn't think I could make it back to the field, so I began to look for a place to bring down my ruptured duck. Oil was spitting in my face. I couldn't work the rudder, so I used the tail surface for some kind of wearing around and the engine was pissing hot rusty liquid in three places. I couldn't see; the goggles were smeared, and I pulled them off. I didn't want to bleed to death at two thousand feet. Charlie and Fritz kept above me on guard, and I came down hard—too hard—in the front-line trenches of a Canadian outfit, the Princess Pats. When they brought me through the wire, a colonel with the ADC said it was a damn improper landing. I smiled and said, "That's right." I passed out there and woke up in a hospital with a little New York City Italian doctor shouting, "Beautiful, beautiful. It's a hip wonderful to work on. Give the *paisano* another whiff of ether, Miss Bedpan." I fell way down into happiness and quoted Buddha to myself: "The sword follows space without exertion to the wound." I felt it. The war was over. I was a human being again. I hoped the wonderful wop wouldn't take off the leg; my last thought was how embarrassing it would be to get into bed with a naked woman with my leg off—Sorry, baby, this is *all* of me. . . . Oh distracted mind, sickened leaf, looking back at time through reversed binoculars; the world, the ether sang, is in our head, not out there. No more a loneliness, as if a twin brother I never knew had died at birth. . . .

BOOK TWO

FROM WILLIAM KITE'S POCKET NOTEBOOK

We all invent a philosophy that we think permits us to endure. —W. K.

The mustache, not patriotism, is the last refuge of a scoundrel. —W. K.

Man can embody truth but he cannot know it. . . . —W. B. YEATS

A coherent universe exists only through tradition. —W. K.

CHAPTER 6

1912

"Après moi l'automobile," said my grandfather, Warren Redmond Kite. He had a nodding interest in French history, and the remark occurred the morning he decided to keep the horses and carriage. It was the year before I entered Princeton, and the well-to-do —*never* called the rich—all around East Pompton, Trenton, Princeton, Hopewell, Lawrenceville, were turning to the motorcar, great grinding Simplexes with the noisy chain drive, Templars, Pierce-Arrows, Packards. Just listing their lost names is like counting off old battles. It was a perfect accepted Euclidean world for a boy born on the right side of the Pennsy tracks.

The Kites were older, wealthier than most families in East Pompton, a bit more interbred with first and second cousins—toward madness, some claimed. Socially so high we could even invite Catholics and Jews to the big house on Frenchman Street (Lafayette is supposed to have slept there) without giving a damn what white Protestant society thought.

I was born in the fine, large, spreading house, comfortable, vulgar Victorian at its best—as my grandfather said, "the finest kind of house ever invented by civilized man." I have to agree with him since seeing the changing fashions; the modern piano boxes, the glass and cubistic shapes, destroy the charm, the ease and pleasure of living in tall rooms with ample bay windows, roaring log-consuming fireplaces, large cellars and attics, porches on three sides, cool in summer, warm in winter, golden-oak sliding doors in thick walls, floor vents blowing a decent heat up into oversized rooms that gave a man scale in the universe.

The Kite house was ornate, mellowed but polite, of good red brick, slate, granite, fretwork shingles on a round Walter Scott tower laid like the scales on fish. There was a red stone carriage house and stable where the best horses lived with some spotted coach dogs.

And a Negro groom and coachman, Billy Brunswick, who taught us boys sex, dice shooting, how to kill cats, skin a rabbit, the breeding of house dogs in heat, the smoking of Sweet Caporal cigarettes, and the theory of the art of seduction of Hunkytown factory girls. Billy was our Aristotle, Mercutio, Merlin, Henry M. Stanley, de Sade and Havelock Ellis. He first made me aware that a dozen lives educate each of us.

My friend Jay Tjaden (few called him Eliot, and Tjaden with the silent T confused people, so he became Jay very early in our friendship) said when we were fourteen, "Billy Brunswick is the goddamnedest evil nigger that ever lived and just about the smartest." It was Billy who gave us our first drink of "Jersey lightning" apple-jack, a home-brewed illegal Jersey moonshine, and we got to like it better than the bourbon or brandy my grandfather and grandmother drank *before* supper (dinner in those days was what we today call lunch) and also in a hot toddy *after* supper. So that often they were pretty tipsy before they went up the grand black walnut staircase to their bedroom, my grandfather, a frail, lean, tall old fellow, cursing the Democrats, and my grandmother, a very solid, wide, fat lady, giving my grandfather a helping arm. "If you'd just stop jawing, Mr. K.," she'd say, "you'd have wind to climb the stairs."

They were lonely in the big place. My father had died in Cuba—in that war with Spain—poisoned by diseased Chicago canned beef, or dead at the head of his gallant men charging some rotten little fort near Camagüey: both versions existed. My mother had died of a "broken heart" when my father left her, but Doc Welton had certified it as a galloping consumption, and I inherited, my grandmother said, my mother's delicate lungs and she predicted I would die of a sudden chill with water in my lungs. I never knew my mother (an Ormsbee of Kentucky) except in the painting by John Singer Sargent—a cloud of Venetian blue and gold—which hung in the Free Public Library on Jefferson Street that burned down in 1931, my mother's image with it. She had endowed the library with a big collection of Dickens, Zane Grey, Gothic novelists now forgotten, authors like E. P. Roe, whose books no longer seem to exist, and a George Peck who wrote the most amusing stories about a bad boy. Books united my waking and dreaming worlds. I read almost everything but volumes of sermons.

Billy Brunswick, besides getting us drunk, one day when I was fourteen in 1909, had asked us if we jerked off, and he warned Jay and me we would end up total human wrecks in a madhouse. "Yo' brains jest turn to cat meat and yo' a shakin' mess from pullin' yo' puddin'. What yo' boys need is a bit of nice clean poontang. Some beginner brown."

Jay said he was willing, and I said if he was I was.

"And I don't mean no clapped-up town hooker from Hunkytown no either. I'll get a fine shiny high yaller out here next Satterday night. And it cost yo' boys just one silver dollah each for the sweetist pussy there is, jus' cause yo' is *my* people. *My* folk."

I said I'd stand treat for both of us. Jay's father, the Bishop, kept him down to two bits a week for which Jay had to cut the lawn, stack kindling, curry the white church horse, Mose, and wash down the buckboard. Jay said, "I've been meaning to try it anyway."

Saturday night Jay and I went out to the coach house as soon as my grandparents were upstairs. Billy Brunswick was smoking a cigar, seated on the bench by the oats box, his hands in his checked coachman's pants pockets, his evil, clever face lit by an amused smile. He had been at the Jersey lightning himself and smelled of it.

"Knew yo' two would chow up, yes siree, never seen nobody wanted their cherry took so much. Now I had to extend myself to git somethin' special, fit for Diamond Jim Brady or Jack Johnson, but I like to break my folk in proper—like when they git their first ashes hauled. The whiskey, gents, is free tonight."

I put two silver dollars in his pink-tan-palmed hand, and he led us past the coach horses chewing corn, their big crystal eyeballs in the staining yellow light of the gas jets following us to the tack room, where old saddles decayed on pegs, and pictures of forgotten long-dead horses browned with time in ancient photographs. JOHN KITE PACING GRAND TURK—SARATOGA, JULY 4, 1867.

A naked girl lay on red horse blankets on the wide stable cot smoking a cigarette. She had pear-shaped breasts, I noticed, and in the light from the green-shaded lamp on the standing desk by the bill cabinet I was very disappointed. Perhaps I had expected the Venus de Milo, Lillian Russell, the flesh color of Rubens paintings seen in an Atlantic City hotel lobby—and the legs of one of my high-school teachers, Miss Lamb, whose fine hard breast I had felt at a football game while we both held a blanket around us and cheered for Princeton to beat Rutgers. (The remembered dreams of puberty remain a delight all our lives.)

Billy Brunswick poured a round of the nearly white liquid into some kitchen glasses, and the girl took her glass and looked up at us. "My, what fine-looking gentlemen. It's going to be a pleasure taking your cherries. Oh, you'll like my jelly-roll." She laughed and swallowed her drink in two gulps and dropped her burning cigarette into the glass. She began to rotate her hips, and my concupiscent skin itched.

"Daisy chain or one by one?" she asked.

Billy Brunswick drove the corncob cork into the jug of Jersey lightning. "First just a bit of easy-rider style, Betty-Lou, and now you two jus' decide who gets first whack. Only remember, don' spook or panic. And don' strain."

"That's right," said the girl. "Stretch a mile 'fore I tear an inch."

Jay took off his baseball cap and tried to whistle, but found his lips too dry. "You being the host, Bill, you take it first." He turned to the naked girl: "If you don't mind?"

He and Billy Brunswick went out into the stable and I kicked off my scuffed tennis shoes and opened my belt and stepped out of my knee pants. The girl smiled up at me, smelling of alcohol, cigarette and sweat.

She was ready and practical, almost clinical like a high-school biology experiment, and spread and took my tool, and she said some very funny things about it and me, and I was so amused I laughed, and that didn't do me any good because I couldn't erect. I was frightened too, because I had been led by my reading to believe this was just about the most wonderful, fearful, climactic, earth-shaking, soul-engraving thing that could happen to a man. Sensibilities alerted, persnickety alert, all I could feel was the smell of horseshit, cheap drink, sweat—where the hell was Cleopatra, Anna Held, Madame Butterfly, or Annette Kellerman and her one-piece bathing suit?

The girl suddenly pulled me down on her. She was damp to the

78

touch but smooth, and she kissed me and it was the first time a girl had ever had her tongue in my mouth and I didn't have any trouble at all getting a hard on and I went into a pliant, submissive world and the girl.

"Sweetie, see, it just like mailing a letter. Now just let mama get them bumps and grinds going and easy rider, easy rider, don't run till you walk, don't walk till you are ready, and you're ready when the saddle fits. Oh oh sweetie sweetie, you just won that cigar . . ."

In sweat, fear and ecstasy, in wonder and some little pride, I knew I was going to like this, do well at it and expend part of life for this. And all the mystery and guilt and old romantic images of overaged authors fell away, and I was coming and Billy Brunswick was *so* right; it's a damn lot better than piddling. It was another kind of religious intensity.

The girl was sweating, and the odor of horse ammonia and our own secretions overpowered me. She grasped and I wondered if I could again, and she showed me how, bringing back power by skilled odd ways of pleasure play, and the second time I went in I stayed at it till Jay tapped on the pine door, and it seemed only fair to share with my best friend. Besides, Betty-Lou said she had a couple of other gents—tricks, she called them—waiting, but she'd be happy to spend the night sometime for five dollars. "And don't tell Billy Brunswick, that prick. He don't divide the take fair. This, sweetie, it's all yours any time. Just leave word at the Chandler Candy Store. Betty-Lou is the name. Ask any stud in East and South Pompton about Betty-Lou, that's for a fact, sweetie."

Jay went in looking calm, his blond hair nearly white in the lamplight, pants off, shirttail out, and the only way I knew he was excited was the way his nostrils flared like a turtle's. I wanted to wink at him for courage, comradeship, the end of our shameful boyhood, but it didn't seem right. I had just been introduced to the sacred grove; *that* bit of romance I kept.

This tack-room sex life, free of derision, anguish, went on for about three years, till I was seventeen in 1912—a weekly meeting in the stable with Betty-Lou, or, if she was unavailable, with her older sister Lacy-Belle, whom I suspected from what she said one night of being Betty-Lou's mother rather than sister; that just sort of made it

79

incestuously—Lord Byron style—more interesting. In those days I set experience before doctrines.

Jay and I dreamed of boldly picking up Hunkytown girls and taking them to the thick greenery of lovers' lanes of the town park; but it was public, and there was the Bishop, Jay's father, and my Grandfather and Grandmother Kite; so we went along paying a dollar a bang to Billy Brunswick and petting with the high-school girls like parlor lizards, but with care, for an accident, an impregnation, could lead to early boy-girl marriage neither of us wanted. Love remained a vague, ambiguous dreamworld. Literature was real.

What Jay and I wanted to do at seventeen was to publish a small literary magazine, odd as it may seem, in the sterile desert of East Pompton, which, close as it was to Princeton, was yet a million miles away in avant-garde ideas. There were four of us boys who made a small nest of intellectuals, read Oscar Wilde's *Salomé* in the original French, collected Japanese prints (two Hokusais and a dubious Utamaro) and knew the names of most of the classical gods in both Greek and Latin.

Jay, with his serious face—as if suffering from a sacrosanct cause—big, not handsome perhaps but natural and strong, was our leader. The son of a churchman, he was given to peeling oranges while he talked of some serious subject, the peel falling in one strip with the logic to the floor of his father's potting shed where we planned our printing press. "To a philosopher Heaven is empty." A natural easy thinker, Jay was not much of a believer in his father's church dogma, but was always very polite. He wore a bicycle cap, low tennis shoes, flannels always stained with ink or grass. He stooped a bit from his habit of lurching over when he thought, inextricably bound up with his ideas . . . fingers nicotined with cigarette stain. He was a writer of remarkable poetry which he showed us other three high-school intellectuals, and we felt that Whitman wasn't in it with Jay. "Give our hearts for a hawk's lunch. No pain is true not made from living flesh." He had solid somber moments when he would not talk, and we'd lure him down to the corner drugstore, where his weakness for sweets would bring him around over two double strawberry sundaes topped with a poisonous purple cherry. We were very young; misanthropic moods pleased us.

We were readers and talkers in a state of perpetual inquiry, smokers who didn't drink as much as we claimed. But Jay had a habit

80

of reclining on the bags of peat moss in the potting shed and following with his half-hooded eyes—his hair picking up reflected lights—the cigarette smoke moving toward the cracked glass roof. "We've got to break out, got to see and meet those things you don't find here. Break the damn horny chrysalis our folks keep us in."

By June, 1912, we would graduate from high school, and so were busy with thoughts of college. Jay was fearful the Bishop had made secret plans "for some Christer college, with the hope I'll take the cloth." I had been entered in Princeton. That was a Kite tradition, and I didn't mind, but I wondered if we wouldn't be better off if we became hoboes instead—like the heroes of Jack London; they seemed better fitted for life, real life, strong emotions, hard knocks, rebel ideas.

"I figure, why not get on a cattle boat and see England and meet H. G. Wells, you know, maybe Kipling."

Joel Cohen made a farting sound with his lips. "Kipling? All that jolly-good-ol'-chap Empire stuff, lesser-breeds-without-the-law crap? Of course his soldier stuff is fine, jim-dandy."

When Joel Cohen left to go deliver drugstore items for his father, Jay and I lit fresh cigarettes and coughed a bit, wondering if we were getting pale and destroying ourselves like Charles Baudelaire, whose *Les Fleurs du Mal* we thought the most depraved and wonderful set of poems in the world.

Jay, our group felt, would be a writer, a novelist, or a poet, painter or a playwright or stage designer, great actor or even a political hero; except that at the moment to us politics was a mockery, a conspiracy of Irish wardheelers, dishonest, and for gulls and dupes. Still, why not time for another Jefferson?

That May before graduation, after a session with Betty-Lou, Jay and I sat on the side porch facing the rose garden, smoking cigars I had stolen from my grandfather's humidor with the bronze replica of the Lion of Lucerne set on the lid. They were strong Havanas, but Jay and I felt we could handle them if we sucked slowly. We sat on the big swing, its iron chains leading up into darkness, our feet on the porch railing, pushing a bit so we swayed some, and the two cigar ends glowed in the dark scented by roses, horses, night trees, somebody's privy, the coal dust from the rail line where the Pennsy milk train was moving up toward Princeton, New Brunswick, Metuchen, Rahway, Elizabeth, Newark, Jersey City. I used to go on the morning

Pennsy 10:04 up to New York City to get my teeth fixed—my grandmother didn't trust any Trenton or Philadelphia dentist. "Nobody in Trenton over the age of thirty has teeth, and Philly people never chew their food, just gum it."

Jay—the mood of sated glands and the night wind on us—didn't say anything and I didn't say anything. Not for some time. We were both pretty pleased we had been able to break out for so long a time from the confining moss-backed attitudes of a society that colored the sexuality—we thought—of any middle-class or upper-middle-class youth in America in the first decade and a half of the twentieth century. What the Boy Scout leader, Mr. Burden Martin, called "self-abuse, unchristian vice and lack of will and character" and "a piling up of sorrow for the pure Christian virgin you will someday take in marriage" had not harassed Jay and me. While Miss Lamb, who taught high-school art, permitted me during late-hour matting of art-class projects certain areas of her fine body as open roaming territory, she was against penetration: "That, darling boy, belongs to my future husband." In respect to him, a misty figure as yet unpicked, we gasped, clutched, held, explored, and came, without full invasion of what Miss Lamb called her "cunny," which she assured me was a proper word from Chaucer's unedited texts. I'd get home *ausgespielt* but eager for our next matting session.

Jay threw his cigar into the rosebeds, its red eye turning and then disappearing. He stretched and flexed his long arms.

"Bill, it's a great big wonderful world, full of possibilities." I could only agree. "I think we should start our literary magazine this summer."

Four of us had been planning it for some time. In the crass wilderness we saw as East Pompton we would establish a publication by four daring young men drenched in Walter Pater, Dostoevski, the FitzGerald quatrains of the *Rubáiyát of Omar Khayyám,* and a book of very modern French verse Jay had found in the wreck of an automobile of some embassy official failing to make the Red Lion turn on the road going north: *Le Bestiare, ou Cortège d'Orphée,* by someone called Guillaume Apollinaire.

Jay and I hoped to do a translation of this verse for our planned magazine; we were undecided whether it should be called "The Scream" or "Underground Fire."

In the dark, mixed with cigar smoke and Jersey lightning, in our high-school French we began to recite a fragment of Apollinaire that delighted us:

"Jetant son encre vers les cieux,
Suçant le sang de ce qu'il aime
Et le trouvant delicieux,
Ce monstre inhumain, c'est moi-même . . ."

Jay leaned back in the swing, his head on the faded moth-eaten, once citron-bister pillow. "We've got to win that bike race prize to buy type. Bodoni Bold and a Gothic 14-point for titles."

"We'll work out tomorrow on the river road. Fifty dollars is all we need to publish Volume I, Number 1, of *Underground Fire.*"

"The Scream."

My grandfather's head appeared in the bay window of his bedroom, just above us. "Goddamn it, how can you expect anyone to sleep with that swing creaking? Get up to bed, Billy, and you, Jay, hightail it for home. I tell you creation is going to hell in a handcart." The window slammed shut.

I said, "That's all right, he has to get up three times a night to pee."

Ce monstre inhumain, c'est moi-même . . .

EDITOR'S NOTE: Nowhere does William Kite go into much detail about the family background or how its fortunes were founded. This was a pose with many sensitive people who came to maturity in the '20s and '30s, when the appeal of Marxism, often subconsciously, made them shy away from details of material success. The original Kites were of Scot-German stock (see Broman's *Early American Lives*), the first American Kite having been Jonas Bradford Kite, who in 1710 was transported from Newgate Prison for stealing twenty silk handkerchiefs and a silver ring worth six shillings. Condemned to death at Tyburn, he was reprieved, had his ears clipped, his nose slit, and was shipped as a bondsman to Boston, where his knowledge as a spinner and joiner stood him in good stead as a woodworker and repairer of the primitive machinery in fuller mills. His grandson, Edward Tiles Kite, married an English lady's-maid in New York, and—irrational and bizarre—became a smuggler partner of John Hancock's. He invented the Kite bobbin and began to manufacture cast-iron machines, which established the family fortune. John Hanson Kite, William Kite's great-grandfather, was tiny, with an egg-shaped, bald cranium, who lost fortunes in clipper ships, gold-hunting expeditions, racehorses and in supporting actresses in a conspicuous fashion. But he also established a dye works, cotton-converting plants with steam engines; and when he died, driving his own sulky in a Maryland trotting race (coming in third), he left two hundred patents, most of them his own, and the reputation that a Kite machine might be clumsy and costly but it hardly ever wore out. (All the above from the unpublished Kite papers, now at Princeton.)

Estimates of the family fortune that Warren Redmond Kite inherited are hard to come by. Some think it was at least ten million, which in the nineteenth century was a vast fortune. The rapid industrialization of America after the Civil War hit the Kites, for they refused to change their pattern, replace old-fashioned models rapidly, and their sales methods were fairly honorable for their time. Rival organizations took away a great deal of the trade from them as the consequence of error or indifference. However, in the early decades of the twentieth century the Kites were still rich ("well-off" as William Kite modestly writes). They owned all their companies outright. (Theirs did not become publicly held stocks until 1928, just before the crash of the stock market, and with disastrous results: *Fortune,* May, 1933.)

Warren Redmond Kite did little to expand the companies, but he did keep them active, and World War I saw an upsurge in their production and profits. He was a man given to odd interests and had traveled much in his youth. Sickly all his life—he insisted he had quinsy and "overstretched nerves"—he once wrote he did not expect to reach thirty, and at forty said he did not expect to see his grandchildren on his knee. He actually lived to eighty-seven, but his premonitions kept him from making the most of his genuine potentials. He studied Chinese calligraphy at fifty, and considered politics "egregious nonsense."

The Kite industries were not unionized. Attempts to unionize them failed because Warren Kite bought off the union leaders by shamelessly and handsomely bribing them. ("Every man has his price; it's usually money, but sometimes it's power, or whores, or first editions, or boys. Find the chink and gratefully fill it. The workers are an amorphous mass, and any fool with a slogan and a voice can lead them to hell and back.")

The Kite factories and mills and foundries were old-fashioned, large and grimy, but not at all the industrial hells pictured by the reformers. The company houses, the company stores, kept the workers cheaply, coarsely housed and fed, and hardly ever out of debt. Old workers were pensioned off with easy jobs as watchmen or sweepers. Foremen were fired if they seduced the girls or women under them. There was a small bonus at Christmas, a turkey and a basket of cakes and cookies in good years. The company employed boys from reform schools and a few ex-convicts who seemed willing to be rehabilitated. Strikers were blacklisted for life; and several organizers were once blown up, but the perpetrator of the outrage was never discovered. Warren Kite, a religious adventurer, never a solid Christian, did not believe "the poor always ye have with you." Neither did he endorse the banker who said, "The rich were put on earth to take care of the poor." Or J. D. Rockefeller's saying, "God gave me my money."

CHAPTER 7

THERE WAS STILL-WILD COUNTRY around East Pompton. Birds flew over the lightning-shattered alder trees. In the spring sun the smell of gallberry bush gone to seed filled the air. The sound of running water just beyond the submerged land, flooded by the rains of the past few days, came to me and Jay and Joel Cohen as we stood barefoot, looking across at our prize: a marble tombstone uncovered by the flooded stream. Years ago there had been a German burying ground up on the cedar-colored ridge, but the Pennsylvania Railroad dug a right-of-way through the heart of the ridge and dumped the leavings down into the stream. Now the waters had exposed the transplanted marble gravestone. Eddies of green foam, and insects walking on water, circled the white marble slab as it lay near the roots of an old hickory tree.

"Giant corporations have little respect for death," Jay said.

For some time now we had wanted such a slab for our publishing project. Our hopes of finding one in the fields around where we lived were slim. Such a stone could never be bought.

Joel Cohen, the druggist's son, looked at the stone. "Fellas, you could get a rupture just lifting it."

"Your father," Jay said, "sells trusses."

A flight of crows cawed from high up in the blue sky, and the warm May wind gave a hint there might be more rain. We left our shoes and stockings on the bank and rolled up our pants legs as we went down to wade into the muddy stream. It ran swift but not

85

strong. We had caught mud eels and jacks here. By grasping tree roots and ducking under bushes we reached the gravestone lying half buried among rock and debris dumped from the railroad cut above. Jay fingered the smooth marble. One side was blank; the other, lying face up, had a text incised with a skillfully handled tool:

✝

ANDREW WENTNER HUTTONBOK
Son, Husband & Father
Here Laid To Rest
In His 72d Yr.
1842 A.D.
To Await His Resurrection and His God

I said, "You think it's Charlie's grandfather or something? They're Catholics."

"Great-grandpappy, maybe."

Carefully, slowly, we pulled the stone clear of the stream muck. We washed it all clean with our hands, freeing it of the last trace of creek-bottom clay.

"Sure is white," Joel Cohen said.

"We better haul her up," Jay said.

We lifted the stone among us. It was not a large stone, nor very thick, and we could handle it once we were free of the running stream and the traitorous pebbles underfoot. When we got it to the tall grass, we set the stone down and stood waiting for the warm wind to dry our feet. We smiled at each other. Nearby a barn swallow fed on a swarm of mosquito larvae beached on a flat stone.

"What will the Bishop say?" I asked.

"He's a busy man," Jay said. "He'll never care what we do in the old potting shed. And Charlie isn't going to tell his folks. He wants to be an editor."

We stood drying off. I felt this a proper stone to use; perhaps we had no right to it (this was posted land belonging to the Pennsy Railroad), but we were practical enough and enough immersed in our special glow of the printing project so that the possession of the stone outweighed any ideas that we might not take it. We pulled up our stockings and laced up our shoes, and carrying the stone, we proceeded quickly toward East Pompton by the back country dirt road.

Jay said, "I feel this stone is as important as that lousy rock King Arthur pulled that cheesy dagger from."

We walked carefully, the stone growing heavier among us.

"Should have brought a wagon," I said.

"We'll walk it back on the tracks," Jay said, open-mouthed.

"Soon as the freight passes. Oh, my aching arms."

We three stood balancing the stone just below the cinders and the ballast gravel, the freight going past bitumen-gray, the dun-colored or faded red cars marked by chalk and old symbols of far places, leaving a smell of grease boxes, long-dead cattle carried and digested a generation ago, and old railroad iron. When the freight had pulled by and stopped at the water tower, we walked on to the track, carrying the white stone slab between us. A migratory worker stood waiting for the freight to start its journey again so he could mount and depart. He sang:

> "I see Big-leg Rosy in my dreams.
> Wasn't for the powder, the store-bought hair,
> Mississippi gals wouldn't go nowhere . . ."

(The freight began to blow steam and spin its driving wheels.)

> "Keeping Rosy sure is hard.
> Dress on her cost a dollar a yard.
> Oh, Rosy, o-ho!
> Oh, Rosy, oh, law, gal!"

Jay's father, Bishop Tjaden of the New Brethren of Christ, who had investments in farmlands, had no worldly vices but the love of a good horse, sound in the hocks and smooth in the withers. He handled the sorrel gelding, Moses, pulling his buckboard skillfully, his weathered hands firm on the reins. He was a big chunky man with a splendid ginger beard turning from ripe shiny chestnut to gray. In his late fifties, the Bishop said he always felt the vigor of youth when handling a good even-paced horse. He talked to an animal while he drove. "Come, Moses, we're near the promised land!"

He had just come in from a drive to see some of his church folk when we got to the Tjaden yard with our gravestone. "What's this, Eliot?" he asked, swishing his hands behind his back and up under the tails of his frock coat. "It can't be."

Jay, expressionless, turned to his father. "It's a gravestone."

87

"For anyone we know?"

"A real old one," I said. "From the old creek bed."

Joel Cohen nodded. "The railroad work gang tossed it in there long ago."

The Bishop bent to read the inscription and said, "These aren't related to the present Huttonboks. Germans. May his soul not need this stone, wherever and whatever is left of his mortal remains. *What,* may I ask, is the reason for bringing the relic here?"

Jay rubbed his chin (he was just learning to shave) and looked up from the stone to his father. "We've got a sort of printing press in mind."

"And the stone?"

"It's for a press bed. Smoothest finest surface we'd ever find."

"But a press needs precise machined steel parts," the Bishop said.

Jay nodded. "We got an eye on an old press, in a junkyard by Bill's grandfather's factories."

"I don't accept that as an answer—to use a gravestone."

Jay began to make marks on the potting-shed wall with a pencil stub. "We figure, properly set up on this stone with even precision and pressure, we have a form to get the type and paper in the proper printing position."

The Bishop smiled at our intense absorption. "No one has asked if I permit the keeping of some man's gravestone in a potting shed for such use."

"No, sir," said Joel Cohen, who thought Bishop Tjaden as important as the Pope.

"As good a time as any," Jay said, "to ask you now, sir. May we?"

The Bishop nodded. "Yes, yes. You plan a local newspaper?"

I said, "A very modern literary journal."

A group of flitting brown sparrows had collected in the doorway of the reoccupied potting shed to inspect its new tenant. The Bishop's horse, I figured, gave them a bountiful living.

"Literary journal? A bit out of my field."

The sparrows scolded and settled down by the stable to sport and wait.

The New Brethren of Christ Church was a cheerful, tolerant easygoing church; my grandmother said it was "very middle-class." It

88

did not use images, candlestick-decorated altars, organ music, priestly robes, Latin, the Anglo-Oxford accent. Its followers were mostly first-generation Germans and Scots, old-stock Yankees and Swedes. It was strictly against homosexuality among its clergy. It frowned on adultery, whiskey drinking, incest, the wearing of silken underwear, and the reading of books in strange languages among its earnest followers. The Bishop said he practiced the actual teachings of Christ, not any ritual or dogma. He hoped that his son Jay would hear the call and go to the Yale Divinity School.

I went home for lunch, already hearing the press we didn't yet own clanging and printing. My grandfather was just pulling his napkin from his heavy silver napkin ring; the Spode plate of tomato soup was smoking before him.

"Better comb your hair, Billy."

My grandfather preferred neatness to godliness.

CHAPTER 8

MY GRANDFATHER, Warren Redmond Kite, always too lean and given to periodic fevers, was rejected as a soldier in the Civil War, but he insisted my middle name be Grant. He didn't have to do it, but he, as permitted by law, hired a substitute to go to war for him (the man died at Five Oaks)—as did J. P. Morgan and J. D. Rockefeller, men my grandfather had business dealings with. He said in 1912, "And *they* are still healthy." My grandfather was thin and bony, with a rattle in his throat like stones on a brook bottom. Yet he lived to a ripe, mean, amusing old age. During the Civil War he smuggled cotton—contraband—for our New England mills through the Union lines, and increased the family fortune and kept the Kite machines clicking. The Kite money wasn't all in the mills; some of it was in the Kite Metal Forming Machinery Company, which made spinning-mill machinery: heavy, unimproved Victorian machinery, all iron scrolls and painted stripings of red and gold like something out of Jules Verne. Their parts hardly ever wore out; only the workers who

89

manned them. Most of the heavy parts were made in the plant at Pompton Junction, a sooty factory and slum district which was never called anything but Hunkytown, a smoky, rutted, unpaved place where immigrant Polacks, Italians, Germans raised lots of children and goats, and grew little garden patches. They drank slivovitz or schnapps, beat their wives every Saturday night when they were roaring-drunk, and produced precociously swelling daughters who had the habits of minks—such was the local legend.

The final assembly plant of Kite Metal Forming was on the outskirts of Boston, where my half-brother Harry ran things as best he could. Harry was a by-blow of my father, who was always looking for the perfect woman. (He never read the poet who said the perfect woman for us is always in someone else's bed.) He had failed with Harry's mother, who ran off with a man variously reported by my grandmother as a wop nobleman, a customs inspector, and a Chicago anarchist. I never did know what became of Harry's mother. My grandfather said of her, "A very *soignée* type. His second wife, your mother, was too good for him."

Harry was lean like our grandfather, but had a big head topped with thinning reddish hair; and he wore gold-rimmed pince-nez and a little ceramic pig earned at Harvard. Born in 1892, he was three years older than I was. I liked Harry, whom I rarely saw as he avoided East Pompton because of the things said about his mother. He had decorum and a reverence for money: "Six percent compound interest on bank loans is as deadly to some borrowers as a Gatling gun."

My grandmother, Maude Omstead Kite, had the health, the courage and most of the common sense in the family. Her people were early in the rock-oil business in Pennsylvania and were successfully ruined by J. D. Rockefeller in his raids on the petroleum resources of the country. He burned the Omstead refineries and got the freight rates to destroy them. My grandmother because of that did not believe in progress or justice: "All government is hamstrung by the treason of clerks and lawyers." She did not serve coffee, or trust canned foods, agreed that cooking in aluminum pots caused cancer, and had the proof of it in an old aunt. Night air to her was deadly to the health, and we all slept with windows tightly closed. She fought the first public display of women's underwear in fashion magazines, and supported six bastards of servant girls who came to her in trouble. "You men!"

She had been very beautiful as a girl, but she was too big-boned, and later—when I knew her—she was given to excess fat, although at table she ate very little, drank soda water and nibbled on Swedish rusks shipped from Wanamaker's in Philadelphia. My grandfather liked a big breakfast of a small beefsteak, ham and eggs, hot biscuits, corn bread, a deep dish of prunes. ("God was never a good plumber; the alimentary canal, Billy, is the worst-botched job in creation next to the human brain. Keep your bowels open, your fly buttoned, and you'll win out.") He drank his Earl Grey's tea from a special huge cup and finished off with a good wedge of muskmelon or honeydew in season. He would look with disgust across at me and my grandmother feeding, me gluey with a pasty oatmeal and my grandmother with her bit of rusk. "Damn if I can understand how you two keep alive. Maude, that boy, he needs a steak for breakfast. Or, hell, he'll never get his pecker up."

"Ha," my grandmother would say. "All that meat you swill turns to acid in you. No wonder you're so sour, Mr. K. And cheese digests everything but itself."

"Christ alive," my grandfather would say, jaws moving rhythmically, "the world is going to hell in a hack."

The truth was my grandmother, the old conspirator, never ate much in public. But Nellie, the Irish hired girl, would be busy all day rushing up covered trays by the narrow kitchen stairs to the sewing room where my grandmother spent most of her day in a Japanese kimona watching the traffic on Frenchman Street. She was a wonderful gossip and not completely illiterate; rock-oil kings didn't educate girls. I loved her and my grandfather loved her. She was dependable, never panicked, and had the nerves of a grenadier of the guard at Waterloo. She had vehement passions, and a secret essence—a purpose to set one thing purposely near another, to bring order to the universe.

My grandfather was always ailing, and very early in their married life he left the big double bed he had once shared with my grandmother. He was given to patches of itch and insomnia. I knew his pattern. He'd yawn, awake, and begin his early-morning scratching on the way to the only bathroom (1882 vintage) in the house, off the upper hall. Discarding his nightshirt, he'd begin scratching deep in his

91

groin with a steady rolling motion, for his nerves were such that he had mysterious rashes and patches of tenderness on his pink smooth hide. Moving north of his crotch, he scratched his lean belly, sighed, and began to work on his chest, armpits and as much of his back as he could reach. Once in the bathroom, bladder emptied, he would hawk and strain to clear his lungs, bronchial tubes, throat and nasal passages. Groaning, coughing, hawking all the time like a herd of sea lions. Struggling for breath, near strangling actually, he would get into the great zinc bathtub, regal on its bronze lion's paws, and shiver and howl in the cold water that was his daily plunge—on the advice of a German doctor met in Switzerland. My grandmother didn't believe in bathing more than twice a week, as she felt "you lose your natural oils that way, sloshing in water—they keep out the germs, and soap and water just leave you wide open for infection."

"Maude, you're as ignorant as the Pope."

My grandfather used an early safety razor to shave himself clean; he never wore a mustache, and his thick mop of white hair he wore long and combed back with curls around his ears. He was a handsome man, but early gave up fornication because of his health. "Hoard your vital fluids, Bill. There is just so much in any of us." His medicine cabinet was a horror of rubber tubings, obscene-looking hard black nozzles, pepsin powders, codfish oils, wheat germ and other concoctions my grandfather had once believed in and that Cohen's corner drugstore stocked for him. Directly after brushing his still-perfect teeth, he took a shot glass full of prime Kentucky bourbon, farted cheerfully ("Where'er you be, let the wind go free") and trotted down to breakfast, where Reba, the big Polish cook, was already putting the breakfast steak into the wire grill for broiling on the hot coals of the huge coal range, all black and German silver trimmings, with its proud label molded into the stove lids: QUEEN OF THE CUISINE.

My grandfather was a well-read man, had been manager of a Princeton football team (my father played halfback during the years the famous Poe brothers of Baltimore made sports history). He had traveled all the world in his middle age, selling heavy, well-made, already outmoded Kite mill machinery in Japan, India, Italy, Russia, France. "Asia is all omens and portents. Life is coming through the rind in Asia."

He had some radical and rather dangerous un-American ideas for his day. He believed and said loudly that the Negroes were the equal of the whites in brain content, intellect and courage, but too lazy to do anything about it; that the gold standard was nonsense, invented by gamblers on Wall Street; that the vote for women would change nothing. "Women are just as bigoted, overemotional, and determined to vote for fools and thieves as any sensible man. True democracy is a sacred tradition with us—never a reality."

My grandfather was the only human being I ever knew who got up every morning expecting to be dead. ("If I don't find my name in the obituary column, Billy, I get up and shave.") He spent the rest of the day involved in his interest in current events, people, hobbies, inventions, politics. He was a reactionary Republican who admired Jesus, Lincoln, Lily Langtry and Voltaire and disliked Teddy Roosevelt, the German Kaiser, William Jennings Bryan and Walt Whitman ("His poetry is the result of breathing through his asshole").

My grandparents, singular but not unique for their day, were very good to me. They felt I was the last Kite. (They had the suspicion that my half-brother Harry hadn't been sired by my father, but of that how could they be sure?) My grandmother saw to it I didn't breathe night air or eat canned food, and she kept me supplied with dangerous pocketknives, bicycles of the latest English and French racing styles, a .22 Remington rifle, and, when I was twelve, the Rover Boys series, which I read between great sandwiches of my grandfather's leather sets of Smollett, Fielding, Thackeray (whom I preferred to Dickens), Balzac, Stendhal, Mark Twain, Frank Norris, every morsel of Shakespeare, Tolstol, Gogol (Turgenev and Henry James irked me, but Jay said James was a true master). I also enjoyed the non-Sherlock Holmes works of Conan Doyle, and H. Rider Haggard.

I was neither Hamlet nor Huck Finn. I lived an easy life full of fun and guile, going to bed usually at nine-thirty but slipping down the back staircase a half hour later when my grandparents went to bed, to wander the town, hands in pockets, with Jay and Joel Cohen and Charlie Huttonbok, moseying to the Klondike Pool Hall, to the depot dog wagon called The Beanpot, for deadly hamburgers. Here gathered the late train dispatchers, icers of the fruit reefers coming up from Florida, Hunkytown pimps, the interns of the County Memorial, all drinking the battery-acid coffee and expressing opinions, political,

93

medical or sporting, dating the nurses or the town's two white whores, the Nordland sisters, who had both had their tubes removed. Sometimes early we'd wander over to the Free Public Library to see if the new Zane Grey or James Oliver Curwood or Jack London were in and go to spy on bushwhack lovers spread-eagled in the park or against gravestones in the Angel of Everlasting Grace Catholic Cemetery.

Best was to stand, sucking straws over ratty-tasting Cokes outside Cohen's corner drugstore, making gay lewd remarks at the factory girls from Hunkytown (they smelling of the cigars they hand-rolled, cheap stogies that gave them a phallic reputation in East Pompton.)

Jay and I had made a tandem bike of old chains, sprockets, pedals and seats, with wheels discarded from old-fashioned models *and* fifteen feet of gas pipe. The two-man bike was one of the sights of the town. We took it out on the Princeton Road, Jay in front and me behind, both balancing skillfully on the odd contraption. Jay had pride in his singing voice; as we pedaled, he tried out a melody of Stephen Foster's ("the victim," as the Bishop said, "of alcohol and the unhealthy habits of artists") :

> *"They hunt no more for the possum and the coon,*
> *On the meadow, the hill, and the shore;*
> *They sing no more by the glimmer of the moon*
> *On the bench by the old cabin door."*

Jay steered us around a delivery dray pulled by two damp brown horses. "We should have oiled the chain."

> *"The day goes by like a shadow o'er the heart,*
> *With sorrow where all was delight;*
> *The time has come when the darkies have to part . . ."*

It was fine riding along the dusty road, the landscape in those years still unspoiled, the early automobile confined mostly to some miles of paved or bricked road, and at the gas station the super service was offered by a few blacksmiths who carried a small gas pump on wheels, tire patches, a sign reading FREE AIR. They repaired autos mostly with bailing wire.

Jay grinned and pedaled. "When we get to college, we'll bug the prof's eyes out on stems with *The Scream*."

"I hear it's a pretty constipated college, nothing later than Tenny-

94

son, nothing more daring than Henry van Dyke and Oscar Wilde's fairy tales."

That set us off laughing and Jay sang the old folk song:

> *"Get a boy, get a boy,*
> *And if you can't get a boy,*
> *Get a clean old man."*

Oscar Wilde's disgrace had penetrated the few educated minds of East Pompton. Jay and I had read *The Portrait of Dorian Gray* several times before we decided the wit was mechanical and the sinning, compared to what went on in the volume of Krafft-Ebing we had stolen from Doc Welton's office, pretty dainty.

We pumped up the slope to Spring's Mill; then the way down was a good steep grade, and we set the coaster brakes and sang a bit of our favorite Robert Burns:

> *"Green grow the rashes, O;*
> *Green grow the rashes, O;*
> *The sweetest bed that e'er I got*
> *Was the bellies o' the lasses, O.*
> *The lasses they have wumble bores,*
> *The widows they have gashes, O!"*

At this, horny and laughing, we both fell off the tandem into the dust and decided to ride over to the Greek Ice Cream Palace for sodas—and to devote the rest of the week to eating rare meat for the energy we needed to win the big bike race at the Trenton track.

The training Jay and I had done that year for the bike races was just riding our racing bikes on back roads and trying to eat all the meat in sight. We cut out drinking and got Betty-Lou down to the stable every other week, which we found was hard for us. There was a discrepancy between desire and will. The drinking wasn't too hard to hold down, but out training, meeting girls riding their bicycles in their long pleated skirts and their high-laced shoes, or the daring ones in tennis or sailing dresses, we'd whistle, make small jests, and ride on, full of health and old Nick, our flesh itching.

Billy Brunswick said sourly—as the demand for his brew fell off and we didn't ask for any poontang to be brought to the tack room every Saturday—we were "gettin' freakish." The other fact was Jay and I were getting bolder, and feeling it rather unsporting to pay for pussy, as the town sports termed it. If it hadn't been for our families, we would have joined the mashers, the poolroom types, the parlor snakes, the buggy-driving crowd—the first pickup artists with brass-bound Model T's and roaring Templars with gearshifts outside the body of the cars and brash rubber-bulbed horns.

But the bicycle racing was paramount in our minds that summer. I'd do several dozen pushups before retiring at night, and sneak up the window sash for the night air, because Jay, who had an intensely modern mind, had come around to thinking twentieth-century science had demolished the idea it was a deadly gas. "It's the country of the young, Bill, but owned by the hardened arteries."

I had known Jay Tjaden four years, and he had matured me, exposed a corner of the new unraveling world for my envy. He was a year older, and for a bishop's son, my grandmother said, "about as sinful as they come."

He had begun smoking cigars at thirteen, accepted God as an equal at fifteen, and read almost every great novel available in English and French (his German was never very good). He had been the whiz in high school, made a hell of a great halfback on the football team, pitched erratically but often brilliantly, could box with anyone, any size, but was a sucker for a left hook. As I got to know him, I saw he lived a life of a queer cadence: driven to read, study, investigate, with periods of lazy brooding and sad despair . . . often a childish absorption in little games, unique bouts of indifference.

The Bishop was not the kind of father to force Jay into anything, but he knew he had an odd one in the nest. As a widower, he spoke honestly to Jay of the power of sin to seduce, the evils of vanity, wealth, pride, cant and snobbery. And to Jay he added advice against tobacco (coffin nails), the demon rum, fornication, buggery (human and animal), self-abuse (in either solitary or group efforts). Jay listened and later wondered why a fine man like his father hadn't read Darwin, Freud (yes, Sigmund's early writings were seeping through to us), or H. G. Wells or Shaw, the two gods of the time for us.

Jay, six feet tall, big-handed, big-footed, would be six feet two when he got his full growth. His blond hair, nearly white, fell over a wide forehead, his teeth were over-life-size (he could open beer bottles with them), and for a bet he'd hold his racing bicycle over his

96

head one-handed. Not handsome feature by feature, but impressive. (Even his frown had charm, often too much charm.)

I found him one of the three people my age worth talking to beyond the usual town gossip, politics, disasters, baseball scores, and had Dr. Cook actually reached the North Pole or was he a liar? He was the first person I ever heard mention Cézanne, Debussy, Ezra Pound, de Sade, the T'ang and Han periods, Henry George, Karl Marx, Lord Byron's letch for his own half-sister.

Jay in his unstable moments quoted Nietzsche and Schopenhauer on the futility of all human endeavor, and he almost talked me into a double suicide after a pint of applejack during a gray rainy season. I chickened out, because I didn't want to miss the Harvard-Princeton game at New Haven. My grandfather had promised to take us, with a seafood dinner at the Moon Inn.

With Charlie Huttonbok and Joel Cohen, we four were about all the avant garde there was in East Pompton.

EDITOR'S NOTE: The Nordland sisters mentioned as "the town's two white whores" was a slip of memory on William Kite's part, or an attempt at humor. Actually Sara and Minta Nordland were middle-aged readers of East Pompton's Christian Science Church, which then had about fifty members, and was housed in a neat Cape Cod building on Essex Street, and Maude Kite was a member for a short time in 1926. The Nordland Horse Fountain, that used to stand at the corner of Wilton and Frenchman Streets before they were resurfaced, was erected at their expense. Sara, it was reported by some returning travelers, gave birth to a male child in Florence, Italy, in 1907. No baby was ever brought back to East Pompton. Minta died of a simple kidney ailment in 1924, refusing available medical treatment, in keeping with the tenets of her church. Sara went to live in Italy that year after her sister "passed on," and I have been unable to find any record of her after that date.

The town's two white whores, according to the police news on the back pages of the East Pompton *Home News,* accused in print of "lewd conduct," were the Bright sisters, Della and Agnes, their father a brothel keeper who became the town's first bootlegger after Prohibition. Della married a light-colored son of Billy Brunswick's, Allen Booker Brunswick, who in 1934 ran for governor of New Jersey on the Communist ticket. He died in a Moscow hospital in 1946, according to a Tass Agency dispatch.

Agnes entered the Catholic Church after a crippling Decoration Day auto accident, as Sister Maria Katherine. She is still alive at the Grey Sisters of Charity Convent in Pottsville, Pennsylvania.

97

To come to the truth of it, we never did publish even the first number of our pet, the daring, dazzling dream journal, *The Scream.* In fact, we didn't get any more of our printing press than that fine smooth gravestone for a bed. We found it too complex creating a press after our first gush of purpose and hope.

Jay pointed out—reasonably enough, I thought—that before going much further we ought to draw up a prospectus of stringent clarity "with balls" and decide what kind of stuff we would print.

"We'll begin with our own stuff," he said, "and *then* search out really exciting contributors. Here and everyplace. Europe, India."

"Write a whole issue ourselves?" said Joel. "Holy gee—we'll be up to our ass in ink."

"So what?" asked Jay. "Joel, *The Scream*'s got to be something— something new and full of sharp fishhooks. There isn't a kid in school—outside of us four, maybe—who's ever had an idea in his head beyond getting a date or a secondhand bike."

"Maybe the Bishop can write for us?" I put in.

"Maybe not," said Jay. "My father—he's out. Out, out, *out.* Sure I respect him and all that. Say I could persuade him to write for us. It would turn out to be a sermon. No. *The Scream,* whatever it is, is no church organ."

"You guys are smart," said Charlie. "But me, I don't know which end is up in prose."

"Damn it, you know what goes into literary journals: poems, book reviews."

"I didn't say I was an idjet."

"Well, we want the texts to pop out the readers' eyeballs. Other-wise what's the use of the whole thing? Just a printing press we haven't built yet."

We agreed we'd try, even if we busted a gut. Jay admitted he'd been working on a long story, maybe it would even be a novel, "about the final cleansing ritual of tragedy—a day in the life of a dogcatcher." I promised to try my hand at poems (I'd been fooling with French forms, though I'd never shown anybody anything). Joel said he didn't know what he could do, but he'd try to think of something; and Charlie allowed as how he didn't think he was much of a creative genius, so he thought he might do the book reviewing. "You can always sell the books, huh?"

Actually, as I saw it, we were just giving ourselves extra assignments in English composition. But we got pretty excited. Jay, who had taken the lead, suggested we all meet again the next Friday after dinner, and Charlie volunteered to bring the refreshments. He was sure he could swipe a case of beer out of his father's restaurant. I could see Jay thought we were a lousy lot of literary men—only *he* had that crazy drive of a true artist.

It was in the Bishop's study that we met. "Bless you," he said, as he went off to some church meeting or other. "And blessings on the cause of American letters." And Charlie went out to the barn to sneak in the beer.

Jay took charge, a pencil in his teeth, seating himself at his father's great desk, while the rest of us sat on small, armless chairs and sucked up beer. He seemed so fancy-formal that I felt, as the others must have too, as though we'd been called in to present flowers to Tolstoi or Teddy Roosevelt. Anyway I thought one of the poems I'd brought along was damn good:

> *I tell you pretty, love is life*
> *Though the drooling oldsters sneer,*
> *And count their fingers and clean their toes*
> *But within me passion like a politician's promise grows.*

"Let's get down to business," Jay said, "and no more beer for at least an hour. What've you got, Charlie?"

I'd never seen Jay quite so formal and superior. Instead of feeling sore about it, I felt scared. He sure had learned to act like a genius. I should have known he was a born professional, and we others could only be amateurs. It was solidifying in my mind that Jay was really different and gifted.

Charlie reached into his jacket pocket. "I've got a dandy book review," he said. "That's what I'm doing. Reviewing books."

"Let's hear it."

99

Charlie got up, took a step to one side as if from behind a desk, unfolded a piece of portfolio paper and started to read, just as if he were in school.

"The Rise of Silas Lapham," began Charlie, reading very fast. "A novel by William Dean Howells. Here we have a story about a man who—"

"Holy cow!" yelled Jay. *"Silas Lapham?* Howells with the pink fluffy mustache? That's twenty years old. And the guy is dead."

"He's *not* dead, he's in the *Atlantic Monthly,"* said Charlie. "At least I don't think he's dead."

"Dead or alive, as far gone as Daniel Boone. Come on, fellas, broaden your horizons. Anybody read any Russians?"

I confessed to Gogol's *Dead Souls.*

"He's dead too. Find me a new exciting Russian, Italian or Frenchman. A literary review's got to be forward-looking, got to discover new talent, say fine things, knock people out of their chairs with surprise. Howells!"

"How about a round of beers?" said Charlie.

Jay was disgusted. "Why should I expect the taking, the enduring, the existing and resisting that is life from *you* beer guzzlers!"

I said, "How's the dogcatcher story going?"

"The ending is too exciting—too dramatic. I want it to end like life itself—but what can you do with a dogcatcher?" He sat down, ran his hands through his hair. "But I'm rewriting—stark Zola realism—and maybe I'll tell it from a dog's viewpoint. What've you got, Bill?"

I brought out my second poem, did not stand up, just spread it out on my knee. I felt pretty proud of it and knew it all by heart. (Still do, I don't know why.) "Just a little poem, a lyric. Goes like this:

"To Miss L . . .

> *Lovely Lucy, when she drew*
> *A miniature or two,*
> *Would garner in sufficient praise*
> *To last through all her mortal days.*

> *And artful Anna, winsome maid,*
> *When on the clavichord she played,*
> *Brought salty films to ancient eyes,*
> *From Tamburlaines drew feeble sighs.*

100

But thou, Miss L—thou canst not play
A simple scale from do to re,
Thy pen it falters hopelessly—
Yet my affections go to thee:

Thy voice would captivate a saint,
Thy beauty shames da Vinci's paint."

"Gee! Salty!" said Joel.

"Haw! *Who's* Miss L?" said Charlie. "As if we don't know, eh, Bill?"

Jay just sat there, drumming his fingers on the desk. Finally he said quietly, "It rhymes, I'll say that for it. Whose is it really?"

"What do you mean, whose? I wrote most of it Wednesday night and sort of fixed it up this morning."

"No, you lunkhead," said Jay. "I'm not accusing you of plagiarism. But it's not modern American—sounds like a very minor Elizabethan lyric or an imitation of one. Not too good a one either, boy. Tamburlaine and all that crap. This is 1912, Bill. Thought maybe you got H. G. Wells's time machine and wrote it in 1612 or 1712. You really think we should publish stuff like that in a literary magazine called *The Scream?* Don't you know most smart poets don't have to rhyme any more? Whitman fixed that. And you have to *say* something more than Tamburlaine and clavichords! Bet you don't even know what a clavichord is!"

"Sure I do," said Charlie, winking. "Every fool knows that. It's a bone in the neck."

"I vote against the poem," said Jay. "What'd you bring, Joel?"

"I tried and tried to think of something to write. I figure I belong in the business department. I'll get ads—I'm sure I can get one from my old man. And I'll deliver to subscribers, keep books. Fellas, I got a C in English last term."

Charlie passed out open beer bottles. "Jay, forget the dogcatcher. Let's hear some other gleaming masterpiece of yours." He pointed to a heaping pile of manuscript Jay had carefully deposited on one side of his father's desk when he first sat down, lining the edges up neatly whenever anyone else was talking or reading, as if it were the original manuscripts of Keats.

"I did bring along one of my works in progress," said Jay a little

101

too casually, shifting the manuscript in front of him. "But it's pretty damn long. Let's finish off the beer."

There was a hell of a lot of beer and we weren't really beer drinkers—not by the bottleful. Charlie worked the bottle opener and began snapping off the tops. They brimmed over, and a good deal of foam slipped to the floor. By the time he had opened the last one we were giggling and laughing and horsing around. We all of us took big swigs and then settled down to listen to Jay read. The room was tilting and gas bubbles were breaking in my nose.

I can't remember too well exactly what happened after that. I do recall the opening lines of Jay's reading, I think: *"He got up. He sat down again. He took his long-stemmed pipe from his pocket. He filled the bowl tight with strong-smelling tobacco. . . .* Symbolism, no horseshitting around with adverbs," Jay commented.

It was yellow-hot in the room, and I wasn't at all in love with drinking beer. It went to bathe my brain center fast (beer for some idiotic reason still does; I never drink it any more; it's for bowling teams and art professors). I had a terrible time trying to stay awake. Some time during that session (*"He stood—she stood—we both stood. Time passed."*) Someone—Joel?—handed me another half-filled bottle and I tried to drink it, like blood from a Viking skull. Maybe I did, too. Jay just kept on reading with comments occasionally ("This is too good for you drunks"). He was addressing corpses on a battlefield; the literary cult of East P. had left off listening.

Joel lifted a flushed head. "We better get rid of the bottles and scoot for home before the Bishop gets back."

"Great idea. Motion seconded."

Jay snorted. "Thank you for your rapt attention. Talk about casting pearls before pork chops . . ."

It was exactly 10 P.M. when an American literary movement died as its founders staggered out, each carrying four or more empty beer bottles.

The literary magazine project was not mentioned again that summer. Jay said, "Perhaps Indifference is the tenth Muse?" It didn't seem as important as hockey and girls. Forty years later, in Italy over a bottle of Strega, Jay found among his papers the yellowed opening pages of the work in progress he had somehow kept all those years. It

102

seemed to me remarkable for a seventeen-year-old just out of high school.

Jay said, "Full of simplistic starkness, Bill, mixed with whole daffy paragraphs of rhythmic, mystical, glandular nonsense, the influence of reading Cabell and Stephen Crane, I think. And that awkwardly handled scene of sexual activity; jewels sunk in dove shit, poetic dialogue à la Maurice Maeterlinck. It would have shocked you bastards if you had been in shape to hear it."

I read it as we sat and sipped. It was bad, of course, ludicrous—as youthful purpose is—in spots. But it had vitality, and some of the phrases and ideas showed up in Eliot Tjaden's widely discussed and eventually published *Fragments from Carthage* in the late 1950s.

I never tried to write another poem. Jay summed up our failure of forty years before: "Youth has as yet no collecting point of memories, Bill. No ideas absorbed, digested, expelled as body guests we are pleased to get rid of. Youth is mental constipation. You know, I never cared for beer since the night our first literary venture died."

CHAPTER 10

MY GRANDFATHER HAD FALLEN getting out of the carriage during a visit to the factory. Hurt his back. He looked too lean in the big Italian bed (called a *letto matrimoniale*) in his white nightshirt. He had a toothache too.

"I can remember when people had some good teeth pulled out just to show they could afford gold ones."

The old man pushed aside the plate of fruit compote Nellie the maid was offering him. "Get that slop away. Beat me up an egg in some brandy. You think, Billy, Jay will make it to Princeton this fall if I talk to the Bishop? He's an odd boy but bright."

"I hope so. It wouldn't be any fun—college without Jay. Charlie's going to Columbia—a business course. Maybe Joel will go to college. It's only proper to educate the gang."

"Too much education about," said my grandmother. "Too much. Who will plow and lift the bundles and chop down the trees if every

103

jackass sends his son to college? Of course Jay has a head on him. How come the Bishop can afford it? I know he gets only fifteen hundred a year—found that out when he tried to get a mortgage to repair the church roof."

"I think he's going to sell some farmland he owns."

My grandfather grimaced. "He'll get swindled. Never knew an honest preacher yet who had any brains to add a column of figures. They're distorted by their feelings and sense of mission. Pure prey."

I saw my grandfather wasn't feeling well; he was snapping at the world (". . . everything going to hell in a hack"). My grandmother in her frilly dressing gown took a glass of egg and brandy from the hired girl. "Mr. K., if this is what you want, I want to watch you drink it down."

"The egg doesn't look fresh."

The hired girl said, "Ha, it was still warm from the hen's rump. Pardon the expression."

My grandfather closed one eye, flung up the glass, swallowed and made a face. "Sticky. Now, Bill, I'm sending you to college to become in time an engineer, so learn something. Harry doesn't know much about the machinery end of our firms. So it will be up to you to keep the foundries and the drill presses in order. Oh, have your fun—I'm no rabid Presbyterian—but two hundred families depend on Kite Metal Forming down here. Besides, you think you have a talent for anything else? Except arty crafts and a yearning?"

My grandmother sat herself down in a chair, the wide one, and she filled it to overflowing. She lit one of her Turkish cigarettes. "Nonsense, Mr. K. Of course William has talent. He's always reading and saying things no one dared to say when I was a girl."

"Is that a sign of talent? Or the backwardness of your folks?" said my grandfather, coughing at the Turkish tobacco and at my grandmother's smoking. He considered cigarettes a sign of decay. "You want to be a writer, a fiddle player, or design buildings, Billy?"

"No," I said. "I like new things, new ways of seeing . . . well, a painting or a novel. Yes, maybe I could write, paint. But unless I was very good, I'd rather not."

"I haven't anything against it, Billy, but Christ, any sort of art, it's a hard life, and usually disappointing. Genius is as rare as hair on a baby's ass."

"Watch your tongue, Mr. K."

"If you're going to smoke that stink stick, get me an Uppman."

"You can't smoke cigars. Doc Welton said you'll get pneumonia."

"Dr. Welton has a country-style belly-rubbing bedside manner, but I'd rather trust myself to a horse vet. Bite the end off the cigar, Billy. I haven't got strength left in my teeth."

I left him smoking contentedly, my grandmother shaking Turkish ash off onto the rug, both involved in some argument about Christian Science, which she was flirting with. As for me, callow and young, I felt I had something better than talent; perfect taste to enjoy others' creative efforts.

Jay and I had taken the Princeton entrance examinations. We'd gone to Trenton for them, as Jay was taking them without the knowledge of the Bishop, who had plans to send Jay to some Ohio church school. When Jay tried to bring up the subject, the Bishop said, "in good time—don't be the October apple hurrying to maturity before the winter freeze."

BOOK THREE

FROM WILLIAM KITE'S POCKET NOTEBOOK

Sex, being metaphysically sinful, is best when physically slightly soiled. —W. K.

God should be capable of everything, even a guilty conscience. . . . —BISHOP TJADEN

Gratitude is easier to find than love, but in the long run we get not what we desire but what we deserve. . . . —W. K.

CHAPTER 11

EAST POMPTON'S NORTH SIDE was not yet built up. It was a low level section of meadows and woods, wandering along the muddy banks of Pompton Run, nearly a river. In spring and fall the stream bed would fill up and flood, and the low-lying farms would see the strange annual sight of some people moving about in boats on lanes lined with cottonwood, butternut and elm trees. The main part of the town lay across the stream.

Jay and I sat by the stream and skillfully threw flat stones skimming across the waters, trying for that perfect shot in which the stone did not sink when it hit the surface but went skidding and skimming across the flood as if the stone were waxed. All around us were open fields dotted with accidental trees planted by migrating birdlife, and often a fence to keep in some damp cattle where the rich green grass was highest. To the south desolate smoke came from isolated dump fires where someone was burning rubbish in Hunkytown.

We lay down on the turf and looked up at the sky, mottled and wind-torn. Some geese were prematurely flying south, great V's of them honking and beating their wings in a regular pattern as they passed, high and indifferent to the world below.

"We have enough string to send up a kite to scare those geese?" Jay asked.

"If we make one big ball of all our string."

But we were too old for kites and knew it. It was for us not a period of negation—we were too young for that—but rather of yearning for a time when the nature of things would be fully revealed to us.

109

Jay stretched, scratched his stomach and took out a rumpled pack of Sweet Caporals. "Coffin nail?"

"Sure."

We smoked.

"Your grandfather talk to the Bishop?"

"He's laid up—not feeling well."

"I better take it to the Bishop head on."

"No, wait for my grandfather to talk it over. You've got to go to Princeton."

Leaves were blowing in the streets as we walked home. Lights were beginning to appear in the misty windows of the kitchen parts of the houses, and the dinner smoke was seeping from chimneys. Jay observed that dinner smoke was always blacker and oilier than just ordinary smoke. He asked me if it were true that the rising smoke spiraled from left to right because of the rolling around of the earth. I said it would be interesting to try to find out. Night insects and miller moths began to flutter in the dusk.

At the Bishop's we fed Moses, the horse, his measure of oats. I was staying for supper. The lamps trimmed and cleaned by the Bishop were lit. Melody brought the roast rack of lamb to the table, the cole slaw in a cut-glass dish and a bowl of pickled beets. The Bishop combed his beard forward with his hands and bowed his head for grace to a capricious patron as all sat waiting.

"Our Father in Heaven," he began, as we lowered our heads and nearly closed our eyes—all but Jay, who disliked lamb and stared at it from between half-closed lids, "we thank you for what you have provided tonight and thank you for having given us this day the health and strength to digest it. We are humble and pleased you have seen fit to regard us with this bounty, this house, this family, and we ask your blessing on this food and on us all. Amen." (A clock was striking the hour someplace in the back of my head.)

The Bishop looked up and tucked his napkin (carefully removed from its carved oak ring just before grace) into the bosom of his stiff starched shirt. "Well now, *rack* of lamb." He always began with this pleasure at the sight of what had been provided. ("Well now, *stewed* meat. Well now, *boiled* turnips.") He started to carve the lamb skillfully with a bit of a flourish, serving me first, then Jay, and himself last. The Bishop was a happy man—for him life was ever-present, ever-renewed, knowing everything was extended beyond ourselves. As for doubters like Jay and me, I already knew we were

110

in bud but had produced as yet no fruit. The Bishop must have guessed I was thinking of his faith in things.

"You may feel, William, the sight of a well-spread table excites me too much, but my wife and I began life on two hundred dollars a year . . . when we could collect it. Sometimes it was paid in potatoes and kindling wood, or a razorback shoat with one ear. Jay, eat your food. Mother was worried at Piney Woods, where we had to take a bear cub."

Melody passed the buttered beans and the soda bread. Jay said, "It was a mule colt and you got ten dollars for it. You always say it was a bear cub. It was a mule colt."

The Bishop sighed. "I was trying to amuse you."

The Bishop was following some special line of reasoning of his own and he was not to be sidetracked. "Two hundred dollars a year when we could press it from them. It's been a long road to grace, and money is not that important. But going to college is going to be a tight fit for us, Jay. However, I have a little invested in some farmland, and you'll be ready for an Eastern university before you know it. Mr. Kite wrote me a long letter on your desires. I don't favor Princeton. Woodrow Wilson I knew when he ran it; I fear a godless mocker. Yale I'd call a true Christian college. Oh I know, they call the students Christers. But it's not like Princeton where they've lost the touch. They treat God like a roommate—much too familiar. Jay, don't spoil that meat. Eat it."

"Bill and maybe Charlie are going to Princeton. I want to be with them."

"Yes—I'll think on it. William, thank your grandfather for his kind letter."

Melody brought in the stoneware coffeepot and put it on the table. Black coffee, strong, matured in farm kitchens, was the Bishop's major vice, and he fought temptation but had at least two large cups at every meal. The Bishop nodded his head in a short thanks at the end of the meal. "O Heavenly Father, for what we had, thanks, and for what we shall get let us not ask for too much, and be thankful for what comes from your grace and good will. Amen."

Jay and I went out. There was a boisterous wind in the yard, ruffling the hedges, sweeping the lilac bushes with deep green gestures. I felt my first fear of the mature world. It separated people. The talk of Yale and its Christers wasn't sitting well with Jay.

CHAPTER 12

THE TENSION OVER THE COLLEGE gave Jay bad dreams. He told me of flying a great kite in his dreams—the earth, the atmosphere, the very turf on which he stood shaking—feeling the heavy tug on the string; all was rotating, and he felt dizzy and began to scream. Gravity would no longer hold him, and the kite became the Bishop's desk and turned, its drawers opening, and the Bishop's notes, sermons, old apple cores, penknives and ears of corn (with the special red kernels that he collected) all began to rain down on him. ("One must be at rest to see motion, I knew.")

He dropped the string and fled, and behind him came a buzzing like that of an angry bee. He looked back over his shoulder. He felt his feet slip off the edge of the earth, and a great light lit up his brain and saw into it: veins, the gray matter, the ridges and soft lobes. ("Just the way it's pictured in color on the pages of Chambers Encyclopedia.")

Suddenly he felt the Bishop by the bed, grasping his hand. The identity of the knower with the known was complete, and the earth rose to meet Jay's feet and he landed without a jar in a slow motion of his body meeting the home planet. He felt every finger in his father's hand, every muscle and joint. He lay flat on the bed, sighed as he became aware of the scars on his mutilated mouth, of the pain in his head, of the constriction in his chest. ("I didn't open my eyes but rolled my head, tried to repeat the formula for flying, but I couldn't put it into action again; dreams have their own reality, their own infinity, beyond our grasp, Bill.")

Doc Welton came and nodded.

"You drink any of the Bishop's coffee? That would give you odd dreams."

Jay couldn't shake the dream, night after night. He lost weight, turned yellowish. Doc Welton at last said, "Better call in a specialist. It's beyond my experience."

A Dr. Bilmont—at some cost—came down from Newark and

112

looked wise and beat the edge of his eyeglasses against the headboard of Jay's bed and said, "Ah, yes. *Yes.*"

Doc Welton said, "Well, there it is."

The Bishop and the specialist talked later when they were seated in the parlor, drinking lemonade that I brought in to them in a cut-glass pitcher. Dr. Bilmont sipped. "There was a great strain on the boy's nervous system. Some big strong healthy-looking people often live on the thin edge of nervous failure all their lives. He is an overimaginative boy."

"How long will this take to get over?"

"I don't know. We have so little knowledge of the nerves. Time is the true healer. My dear Bishop, to you I can say we know almost nothing of this matter of the inner *inner* person. Even calm strong people live deep lives. Oh yes, even a good Christian youth."

"Doctor, I'll have William drive you to the depot."

"I'll be in touch with Dr. Welton. A splendid type of old-fashioned country doctor. A bit out of touch, but a grand serious man. Salt of the earth."

"Ungodly, but basically fine."

"Is your creed strongly against wine? Very strongly?"

I almost choked.

"It is," the Bishop said.

"Well then, good solid food only and rest most of all. And I don't have to tell you it lies with a Higher Power."

The Bishop nodded and lowered his head and beard. When he looked up, he smiled sadly: "We mustn't blame God. He is most likely at times as unhappy as we are."

I could see Dr. Bilmont deciding this was a strange bishop indeed. He took the ten-dollar gold piece, shook the heavy hard hand and went out. I drove him to the depot and refused a dime proudly. I'd have taken a half dollar. Then I went back and confessed to the Bishop that Jay had taken and passed the Princeton examinations.

Two days later Jay and I were trying a trick of remembering the names of the characters in Dickens. He knew the bulldog's name in *Oliver Twist*. I knew the opium den keeper's name in *Edwin Drood*.

"Who was willing?"

"Barkis."

"Who dug up the dead?"

"Jerry Cruncher."

"The name of Mrs. David Copperfield's people?"

He told me.

"What was called King Charles's Head?"

The Bishop came in and pulled a long cylindrical paper-wrapped package from his jacket pocket. He had two water glasses in his hand. He smiled and sat down. We looked at the two glasses.

Jay said, "You haven't found another tonic at Cohen's drugstore? They're all nonsense."

"No tonic. William, get the glass by the water pitcher. I've been reading the Bible. Been paying attention to some texts I've overlooked." He began to unwind the blue paper from the package, revealing a brown bottle with a tall red-waxed neck. He read the label slowly and with effort: "Gumpoldskirchner. Wien, Heligenstadt."

"What does that mean?" I asked.

He read on: " 'A product of Imperial Austria, personally selected by Otto Lipschutz. Gumpoldskirchen south of Vienna is the best area for viticulture in Austria. Wine for festive occasions which all drink for health and pleasure.' That's what it says—*for health.*"

Jay was grinning. "Bishop Tjaden! Bringing wine into this house?"

The Bishop nodded cheerfully, and taking out his jackknife, he found the corkscrew blade and removed the bottle's wax and cork. He sniffed the wine and nodded. "It is written in the Bible, 'Use a little wine for thy stomach's sake.' "

He poured three glasses of the pale yellow wine, and firmly handed one to Jay and one to me. Took up one himself. "Drink. You heard what it said—for health and pleasure." He took a big mouthful and pursed his lips and worked his tongue around, swallowed and pulled on his huge beard. He nodded brightly as Jay and I sipped and swallowed. The Bishop said, "In Judges IX:13 it is written that 'wine . . . cheereth God and man.' "

Jay and I knew he had broken one of the rigid rules of his life for his son, and we were aware how dreadful must have been the struggle that resulted in this deed: the buying of the wine he now shared with us.

"There's a Sunday-school teachers' convention in Atlantic City in August, Eliot. A whole week. You'll bathe in salt water. Wine and salt water. You'll come back to enter Princeton properly." He sipped

114

and smacked his lips. "I can see how one can become a slave to the grape. Is my nose turning red?"

Jay stared at me popeyed. The Bishop corked the Gumpoldskirchner with the palm of a hand (as if he were pushing Satan back into Hell).

Below we could hear Melody open the door of the kitchen stove and stir the ashes down to a final bed of coals. And we heard the humming sound of the trolley on its way to the beer gardens on the edge of town as it went zooming by along the river, sounding, I thought, like the great arctic owl that Jay and Charlie had found the year before, staring at them one snowy morning in the Bishop's back garden. (It was an almost invisible bird but for flecks of brown on its white feathers, the curved beak and the two large day-blinded eyes that could not focus in the snowy glare of the morning. Charlie had fed the owl mice from the cellar traps at his father's inn and bits of raw liver, and it had bitten his finger in thanks. It slept for several days on a rafter over the horse stall in the Bishop's stable. Then one night Jay had heard the small window over the oat box crashing in fragments and the thrashing of huge wings. He told us he was just in time at the window to see the giant owl beat its slow majestic way into the sky and then merge with the cold blue-gray winter air and be gone. He had, he said, felt a deep consciousness of some cosmic calculation in the escape. In the morning we had found a little bright blood on the snow and a few white feathers flecked with brown.) The trolley noise grew dimmer, and Jay sat on the bed in his small sloping room. (I wondered how the owl had felt, captive in the stable, and if it was back now in an icy Canadian forest, perched on some tall tree, the polar winds ruffling its feathers, the two staring saucer-eyes focused in the blue-black cold, its breath smoky as it slid down to strike at some shrieking furry thing in the dark.)

The Bishop took the glass from Jay's hand. The trolley noise was no longer audible. "It's all right. Bill told me all. And I agree to Princeton. Now recover your health."

Doc Welton's flivver was in front of our house when I got home. I was weaving a bit, making believe I was drunk on a half glass of weak wine. My grandmother was in the parlor, her feet, tiny for so large a woman, on a hassock. She was holding a newspaper in front of her but not reading.

"Who's sick?" I asked.

"Nobody, and take your cap off. Your grandfather has been drinking too many egg-and-brandies."

I nodded. "All over town everybody is getting liquored."

"I'll thank you, William, not to talk about your grandfather like that. He's been drunk often enough, but he's too much of a gentleman to do it at home."

Doc Welton thumped down the black walnut staircase and came into the parlor holding his cigar behind his back. "In the future, Mrs. Kite, give him only what I say. Brandy is a deadly drink. If his back bothers him, give him that red pill and put a hot-water bottle in the bed. And, Bill, let this be a lesson to you on the evils of drink."

"Doctor, you're dropping cigar ash on my Arab rug."

Doc Welton made the usual answer; cigar ash kept out moths.

CHAPTER 13

A PERSONAL PROJECT was brewing in me. . . .

Brightness falls from the air;
Queens have died young and fair . . .

Jay and the Bishop had left for the Atlantic City convention, and from there they were going down to a Bible meeting in Nashville where the old-time religion, as the Bishop said, "was not only loud, but often as crazy-colored as Jacob's coat."

It left me empty-handed, unoccupied, no longer reading and visiting with Jay. Charlie Huttonbok was hard at work in the annex to his father's inn. The older Huttonbok had put in a gasoline pump and a sign: FREE AIR, and called it a *garage*. So Charlie was not available. Joel Cohen, at last after much talk, had run off and enlisted in the army. His father had come over sad-faced to ask me if I knew just where Joel had enlisted and under what name. ("Jews," my grandfather had said, "are great family people. The more Jewishness in a family the fewer dogs they keep. Notice it?")

"No idea about Joel, Mr. Cohen. I only know he felt bad about

116

clouting Jay in the shinny game. And he always wanted to be a soldier."

Mr. Cohen clapped his hands together in a futile gesture of pain. "I wanted him—believe me, crazy it sounds—to be an actor. Don't smile at an old *narr*—fool. In Warsaw when I was a young fella, Bill, I used to play little small parts in the Yiddish theater. I call it parts? call it a theater? Anyway I didn't have the talent. And here, *parnossa* —prosperity—I didn't have. Well." He stopped to stare and smile. "If Joel writes, promise me you'll let me know. Go raise children for the goyim to shoot."

"Of course I'll let you know. You think Joel will get into the fighting in Mexico with Black Jack Pershing chasing Villa?"

"God forbid," said Mr. Cohen. "How is your grandfather? A marvelous *alter kocker*."

"We expect him up and around any day."

"Well, I have to deliver some sunburn lotion to that teacher, Miss Lamb. I gotta be my own delivery boy since Joel ran off."

"Miss Lamb is back?"

"A fine girl. Her father, the old *shiker*—drunk—him I can't stand. But Miss Lamb . . ."

He went off with the unfinished sentence like a hard candy in his mouth.

Evanthe's (Miss Lamb's) nipples are like rosy quartz
In aureoles of pearly mist . . .

I leaned back in the porch swing and kicked at the rail to send it swaying, and thought, oh sweet, desirable, passionate, stubborn and non-penetrable Miss Lamb. You have been away for three weeks at Lake George in white cotton and carrying a tennis racket, wearing pleated skirts, your fox-trotting Irene Castle shoes, your Gibson girl hairdo, your fine white-pink virgin body that I have handled, sucked, kissed, slapped in play, wrestled down in Room 16: Arts and Crafts—after hours, matting Maxfield Parrish and Burne-Jones. Blackboard chalk, silken pubic touch. And now you are home with your alcoholic old Civil War grandfather.

I stopped the swing and stood up. Like Archimedes crying *Eureka,* Columbus whispering *Land* on the deck of the *Santa Maria,* Pasteur crying out *This is it,* and Dr. Ehrlich and his silver bullet 606, I had a

117

full view of a project. The gift of hope had me: Before I entered Princeton I would penetrate Miss Lamb.

A good life is a series of successful gestures. I enjoyed the thought of success with Miss Lamb, savored it, ran through several versions of the deed, improving a detail, changing a gesture, motivating some dialogue I planned. I did not underestimate the American virgin, the dramatic turbulence ahead.

I went to our 1902 hall telephone (one of six in East Pompton). It hung on the wall, a high-smelling black baked-rubber instrument trimmed in real silver, with a box of fumed oak, a handle, a double bell. One no longer had to crank it alive to be connected with some unquiet dark.

"Hello, Central, I want five-three."

"Thank ya, just a minute."

There was the sound of deep roaring, the pinging of small drops of water falling great distances before striking stone, wind among a tangle of harp-string wires. A click.

"Yes?"

"Miss Lamb? Hello there, weary traveler. It's Bill Kite."

"Why, think of that, Billy, you calling."

"Yes. I heard you got back. I bet Lake George was fun."

"Amusing, but choppy. We could hardly boat. What's this I hear about Eliot?"

Her voice was clear, innocent of guile, healthy. You could sense it start as it came from fine lungs, up through a long neck and past vocal chords tuned to a musical laughing note.

"He's doing well. Much better."

"You boys, really." She said *really* from the height of her twenty-eight years, her normal school diploma, the fact she had actually once talked to John Singer Sargent and copied Rosa Bonheur's *Horse Fair* in full color (I felt myself getting an erection).

> *I think of you, and mercy! my*
> *Tunic's got a tent pole in it. . . .* Catullus (84–54 B.C.)

"Look, Miss Lamb, I have your leather-bound copy of Ruskin's *Fors Clavigera* I borrowed. I thought I'd bring it down after supper, huh?"

"So it's you that had it. How did you like it?"

"Bully. See you around eight. How are the tennis legs?"

118

"Brown. I mean *really*, Billy."

"Nobody can handle your forehand. Bye."

I hung up breathing a bit hard, leaned my head against the telephone box smelling of furniture polish, old mouths, stale conversations, hard rubber, and my poignant hope, fairly free of doubt. I went up to the bathroom with its stained-glass windows that threw blood and lemon patches on one's face. In the big beveled mirror I studied my manly face. Nose a bit too large, teeth good, lips full but neat, forehead high (most likely a Shakespearean baldness at forty), ears close to the head, *very* fleshy lobes (what would a gypsy say to them?). I ran a hand over my cheeks, one dimple in the cleft of the chin, a slight rasp of a tender brown beard. I shaved with a fresh blade, trimmed my sideburns, with slapping hands put on my grandfather's cologne water and danced in pain till the smarting stopped. I lit the gas heater under its copper intestines, and while the bath water hotted I tried out several versions of haircombs. The primitive-man straight-back-and-up pompadour of the football apes. The parted-in-the-middle and brushed-down of the Richard Harding Davis hero, Van Bibber—Charles Dana Gibson's popular illustration of him. The part on the side and the hair combed and finger-waved in ridges as favored by the Arrow Collar ads done by an artist follower of da Vinci and Watteau named Leyendecker, who also did covers for *The Saturday Evening Post*. And a disordered Byronic and Bohemian mess favored by a rising young actor, John Barrymore. I'd decide later.

I got into the bath, soaped every secret corner with the pink perfumed soap my grandmother imported from Paris. I lay back, horny, ardent, scheming—Napoleon before his best battle, Romeo climbing the prickly ivy. . . . Sexual intercourse in the young is often a rushing drive; brainless, honest, urgent, a mystery of ingoing and outcoming, absurd in its ramifications and implications. It is not yet a domestic habit, not a function of any social purpose. It is not jaded, cynical, nor sidetracked to mere technique like a virtuoso fiddler, an anthology of positions and sleight-of-hand card tricks. It is, till age, the incurable side of existence.

I left the bath pink and glowing (seed unspilled). I decided on the Van Bibber haircomb of the Gibson illustrations. I used violet hair tonic, an actor's grease and the pressure of military brushes. I put on a shirt, adding a soft attached collar and my grandfather's second-

119

best collar buttons. The white linen suit had only one small spot of lobster sauce on the left sleeve. The gray lawn tie was unadorned with any tiepin, the white-clocked pale blue socks were held taut by garters, the two-toned summer shoes (the rage at Newport), white and tan, matched the ribbon on the flat straw hat I intended to wear. Ah, creature in the mirror—ready to reveal, possess, seize the role of lover.

My grandfather called to me as I went past the big bedroom. "I can smell you out here, Billy. What the hell are you doing?"

"Oh, just going to return some books after supper."

CHAPTER 14

I PUT MY HEAD in the doorway of my grandfather's room. He was sitting up in bed smoking a cigar, reading the stock-market page of a New York *Times*.

"You smell like a Dodge City whore."

My sinewy limbs, my arms and legs with thine.
Thou like a sea of milk shalt lie, display'd . . .

"Yes, sir. Can I get you anything while I'm downtown?"

He folded the paper, took off his pince-nez and rubbed his thin handsome nose, fingering the marks they left there.

"Listen, boy, you can't fool an old cocksman. You're a gash hound tonight and with no subtle nuances."

I shrugged my shoulders at his comradely confidence as if to say, One never knows, one hopes. His truculent expression almost let the idea of the ultimate futility of all effort seep into me. I fought it off.

"Well, just don't get the old rale." He fumbled in his night-table and spun a gold five-dollar coin across to me. "Get yourself some condoms at Cohen's. And don't go knocking up some respectable girl. The only advice I can give you is it's better to pay for it than to own a wife you had to marry at the end of a shotgun. Remember that."

"Yes, sir, I will. Goodnight, Grandpa."

I ate very little at supper. "Never overload the stomach before a taut emotional event" seemed a good rule. My grandmother sat under the little brass electric fan with the red ribbon tied to it, the ribbon dancing and waving as the little fan, loud and noisy, turned from left to right, right to left, stirring enervating air, stirring the few flies that had come in through the aging screens.

She lifted her coffee cup and looked at me over its rim. "How does Mr. K. seem tonight to you, William?"

"Pretty good. Was he ever in Dodge City?"

"Where is that?"

"In Kansas, I think." (Had he really ever smelled a Dodge City whore?)

"Why don't you ask him?"

I put down my napkin, rolled it carefully as if it were my soul, and put it back into the silver ring lettered *W.K.* (As in most other modern well-to-do houses of the day, a napkin was changed every three days, soiled or not.)

I got my straw skimmer, decided against my grandfather's gold-headed dress cane, picked up the flask I had hidden in the fern basket, and went out into the gathering chalk-blue night . . . the insects in the elms singing (or at least rubbing their legs together, if the scientists were right). Late children's games were growing fainter, the *clop-clop* of a stylish rig passing along Frenchman Street sounded . . . my sight, smell, touch alerted to spectacular awareness. I stood inhaling wet cut grass, growing trees, horse litter, smoke from burning backyard paper, the day's sun stored on the slate roofs. . . . I was a man in his young prime, well hung (left side), a rising tide of gorged blood, biologically alive, wanting to make the mating dance; but also in dress and thought processes showing the long distance from my two-celled ancestors who left the salt sea for dry land, developed a cortex that could think and plan and store memory, and now progressed from recall toward fulfillment via brainstem and organs. I had the hots, I was horny, I was raunchy. I had a crusade, a plan, a drive. . . . I was early.

I walked across Crown Street (once King George II Road) past the green-bedded Courthouse Square where injustice and bribery were kept to a respectable quota (no rich man has ever been executed for murder in the United States); past the Slessinger Cigar Store, its basement shopwindow aglow with color and empty boxes, the swing-

121

ing gas jet for lighting your cigar burning blue and orange, someone taking horse bets in the back; past Silverhorn's Ratskeller, a waitress in the window by the wax grapefruit and the paper lamb chops scratching under her piled-up hairdo with a long yellow pencil; past the Bijou Nickeldrome Movie Theater and its overflowing john, burned celluloid, popcorn, butter going rancid . . . D. W. Griffith's *Man's Genesis,* with Robert Harron and Mae Marsh; past the cement Civil War soldier (a sergeant), hand over one eye looking for the rebels, rifle butt dragging, the base piled with rusting cannon balls and a bronze tablet on the side reading: BULL RUN, GETTYSBURG, COLD HARBOR, and a list of fallen too small to read in the flickering carbon arc lights.

> *Then shall thy arching arms embrace and clip*
> *My naked body, and thy balmy lip*
> *Bathe me in a juice of kisses . . .*

I went into Cohen's corner drugstore, bought from a fat young clerk a box of Sen-Sen breath purifiers, a tin of six Trojan rubber condoms—not that I hoped to use that many *first* time around. Some of the high-school gang, girls of thirteen or fourteen sucking spoons, were talking and giggling over piled-up melting sundaes. I weighed myself and got my fortune on the scale out front. Springless Ajax Weight: 128 lbs. IT IS OFTEN THE DREAMERS LIKE YOURSELF THAT PRODUCE THE MOST PRACTICAL RESULTS. It hardly seemed worth the penny. Pliant, loyal, finely bred, polite—*those* were my virtues. Ardent too.

I waved to officer Telly Warner, the biggest grafter on the town's fifteen-man police force. He wore a gray felt helmet, a German silver star, and kept law and order on Crown Street. He mooched free lager and pickled eggs and pig's feet in brine and vinegar—and received a ten-dollar bill a month—from Zeller's Saloon, Ringel's Saloon, Barton's Bar and Grill, the New Alt Wien (translated by some as New Old Wine) and Frances Porter's whorehouse—once Duke of York Street, now Jefferson—where he also ate with the madam and the hookers their Thanksgiving, Christmas and Fourth of July dinners. St. Patrick's Day he missed—he went to Mass. Telly was the boodle man, collecting for the bigger bagman, who divided with the sheriff and the county chairmen of both the Republican and Democratic parties. Miss Lamb's father had once run the Democratic party in the

county (The Socialist party in Hunkytown didn't graft, my grandfather said, "but they don't win elections either.")

"You look sharp as a pin," said officer Telly Warner with his
Galway brogue thick as his neck, a finger touching up his tusk
mustache.

"To coin a phrase," I said.

"Don't be doin' nothin' I wouldn't do."

"I'll try."

"And don't be takin' any wooden nickels."

It hardly seemed that polite and witty conversation could be
carried any higher than that, even by Horace Walpole, and I went on
my way stepping like a horse turd toward Spring Street (it was getting
dark enough, I felt) where Miss Lamb and her grandfather lived on a
block not yet paved (but the curbs were in and the paving contracts
were being divided up among the deserving town supervisors and
county board). No birds sang but for the curb sparrows, unaware of
the menace of the autocar and progress. They fed fatly among the
horse apples in the light of shopwindows.

Here for a moment, before I move along this intrinsic refraction of
myself, I break the thread of narration and look back from over more
than fifty years that separate me from this young man with his head
full of velvet fragments of erotic verse, his body pumping full of
purpose, led by a phallus, driven by an urge he did not fully
understand. I know he is ever-present, ever-renewed, extended beyond ourselves by recall.

See him as I see him from my creaky position, not me as I am, but
him there—in the styles of 1912, his head filled with the pulp of
philosophers and the spoils and ramblings of too much reading and
not enough experience. So sure, so damn light-footed, ready to take
on the world—a world with a now lost precision of rhythm: sunny
and virile, as sure of itself as that boy in a delirium of hope on his
way to test Miss Lamb's resistance, the tight drumhead of her
maidenhead. What use for me as Jeremiah to tell him the world is
coming apart, will blow up in two years and never never be put
properly together again? He wouldn't believe in the ridiculous pro-
tagonists I could tell him he will face before he becomes me; he
would think me an over-catarrhed Mephistopheles. I feel he is nobler

123

than the destinies that will destroy him; *he* knew old men's ideas are anachronisms.

He is leading a sexual revolution; for what he is planning, while epidemic in his time, was almost always underground, hinted, whispered: done, but smugly, kept from view, from public print, from talk.

William Grant Kite, age seventeen. Soon the lessons of Freud would be read or misread; the postwar world would dance to Dixieland music from the Storyville whorehouses; stockings in John Held, Jr., drawings would be rolled; the auto would become the bower for the hasty fornications; and labels would be made: *the jazz age, our dancing daughters, the hard-boiled virgin, naked on roller skates, flaming youth.*

I envy the young bastard his power, his lust, tenderness, romantic blinders (his innocence most of all). I can participate in his life only as a vicarious bystander. I view a drama in which I have no role but that of recorder; only the itch of memory keeps me from full detachment. An onlooker who is only the historian, never the actor. Retie the thread; the kid is brimming over. Only the immaculate is impure.

CHAPTER 15

THE HOUSE OF MISS LAMB'S GRANDFATHER, old Waldo Lamb, was of simple gray clapboard, set back from a picket fence; it even had wormy roses, neglected honeysuckles. It could have been used for a popular-song cover. The two red brick chimneys leaned together a bit, but the little house was solid enough. Waldo Lamb had been a sergeant with Sickles's Brigade. He missed Gettysburg, he always said, because of a blister on his heel that became infected. He did lose two fingers with Grant in the Wilderness, and spent the rest of his long, leisurely and pensioned life trying to get back to the taste of glory in his military career. Miss Lamb's grandfather was a small man with yellowish soiled-looking hair, two small blue eyes beady as a doll's. He marched once a year on Decoration Day in the G.A.R. section of the parade, a hickory cane on his shoulder, his bronze medals and faded ribbons on his narrow chest. . . . Never mind his abysmal ignorance, the quizzical glances; *he* had helped save the Union.

He sat in a rocker on the front porch of his house, one cheek deformed by a chaw of tobacco, a husk full of diseases but still aboveground.

"Evening, Captain Lamb."

"Evening." He peered at me in the gathering dark. "Eh?"

"It's Bill Kite."

"Oh. Wouldn't have a seegar on you, Bill?"

"No."

"Eh?" He faked a deafness by holding a liver-spotted hand to one ear, hoping I'd offer to run down the street to Mitch's Pipe Shop to get a cigar. "What you say? Speak up."

"I haven't got a cigar, Captain."

He gave me a catatonic stare, his raddled face blank, chewed, spat, wiped the stain deeper into his hound-dog mustache. "Peshaw." He sighed and rocked himself a bit, his elastic-sided congress gaiters flat on the porch floor. He had lost interest in me. Age glazed his eyes. He scratched an armpit with three fingers like a paw.

"Your granddaughter at home?"

The old man turned his head to shout through the screen door, "Young fella out here for you, Lucile."

I turned slightly away, feeling it impolite to show the old man my erection at the mention of her name. I thought of the multiplication tables to deflate myself. Miss Lamb's voice floated out through the screen door. "Come in, Bill. I'm in the back parlor."

I walked through the hall hung with sepia prints of the paintings of the giant figures in the Sistine Chapel, past a narrow table that held Miss Lamb's collection of seashells and through a doorway hung with a batik curtain we had made in art class the year before. Miss Lamb (I could never call her Lucile) was standing under the flaring soft hiss of a gas globe, looking marvelously healthy and desirable. She wore a pale green silk skirt, a crisp apple-yellow linen shirtwaist, and a wide black patent-leather belt around her waistline. Her reddish-chestnut hair (Titian to get the tone used a Venice red) was combed up with two curls resting on her fine white neck—a neck now tanned

125

from the Lake George sun. (I felt the immanence of a God who made such flesh. I was a believer.)

"You look great, Miss Lamb."

"You're almost twice life, Bill."

"Oh—say." I nearly panicked. "I forgot to bring your Ruskin."

"Next time will do."

"It's great—his propensity—know what I mean?"

We sat down on a bamboo sofa with red velvet cushions. She had a personal odor—a woman odor under the scent and bath powder—slightly menstrual I think, very pleasing to me. The little back parlor was Miss Lamb's—*mon atelier,* she called it. Here she drew in pastels, pasted up her "art collection" clipped from magazines, and, I supposed, dreamed those dreams that passionate young women in their twenties protecting their technical virginity dreamed. There was a plaster reproduction of Hermes by Praxiteles with a tin fig leaf over his genitalia, and on the wall two paintings: *Mona Lisa,* and *Washington Crossing the Delaware.* And a photograph of the bronze *Grief* over the grave of Mrs. Henry Adams.

"What have you been doing, Bill?" Thigh, knee, leg, foot nearly touched me as I pressed close.

"Not too much. Eliot Tjaden was badly hurt in a shinny game. We've postponed our literary magazine. We'll both be in Princeton this fall. How are things with you, Miss Lamb?" I let my knee touch hers. "I mean any special plans?" She was older, and even if I had decided to penetrate her, I still couldn't call her Lucile. That much respect I gave her position.

"We're getting a new lantern-slide projector. I'm showing color slides next session of Rembrandt's paintings and etchings."

"Pretty raunchy, aren't they, some of them? I mean *Susanna and the Elders, Bathsheba at Her Toilet.* Say, and *The French Bed."*

"Oh, the ones we'll show are very much all right . . . *Bill!* Behave. You're a guest in my grandfather's house."

We were both listening to her grandfather rock himself on the front porch. Miss Lamb got up, projecting front and back, in the round, and went to the small gramophone. She had the most magnificent ass, I decided, under that soft pleated skirt. She picked up two records. "You heard the new Victor Herbert? All the *knuts* sing it at Lake George."

I went up behind her and said, "No, play it." I put my arms around

126

her breasts and kissed the back of her neck. She was made of sun and skin cream and bath powder, that special odor and girl sweat.

"Bill, please. Unh-*unh!*"

"Miss Lamb, please," I answered, trying to copy the pitch of her mild protest with my sibilant gabbing. "You're just there and I'm unable to stay away."

She laughed, the healthy deep bark of hers I liked, and I got my fingers on her breasts. They felt alive and became alerted to my mangling. She leaned her head back and inhaled sharply with a copious suck of air. Her voice broke. "Bill, you *must* behave. You're a man now, going to Princeton."

"I'll behave like a man." Her nipples rose to my fingertips, and she half turned and we kissed as we had kissed I suppose a hundred times or more in the last two years. A slow pressure, a moistening of our lips, a forcing of our mouths to open, a bit of tender slow play of our tongues. We were no fumbling bumpkins about kissing. We were logical positivists.

There was the creak of old floorboards in the front hall. We held our breaths. The old man was going upstairs to rock himself in his room. Moths bumbled against the window screen behind the pulled drapes. We made a tacit imperceptible swallowing gesture. My finger dialed some unknown safe combination.

Miss Lamb shook herself free of me, put a record on the gramophone and wound up its spring with a firm hand and arm action. Muted tinny music as if played at a distance across a lake sprayed us with sugary notes. I took out my grandfather's silver-bound pocket flask. It contained some of his best brandy, which he knew wasn't really Napoleon—that no longer existed—but it was good enough. Tonight I had added some of Billy Brunswick's Jersey lightning. Two little silver cups screwed on over the flask stopper, and I filled both with the doctored brandy while Miss Lamb adjusted the gramophone sound by moving the buttercup-shaped horn. I felt no nervous instability. This was our first encounter outside the after-school classroom sessions.

I handed her a little silver cup. "Gosh, Miss Lamb, you look just great."

"Thank you, Bill. Here's to college."

"Oh, the hell with that. To you and to me." She frowned. I quickly added, "And to what has brought *us* this close, art."

127

"To art, Bill."

I had to act with a minimum of subterfuge. The music ground on, we sipped the brandy, I eyed Miss Lamb expertly: a general viewing the battlefield before engaging, wondering at the use of a sudden attack or the subtle advantage of flanking, the cunning covering up of a sneaking approach in secret, allowing for discordant circumstances —like an old man rocking upstairs.

Miss Lamb coughed. "It's strong."

"It's the oldest bottle my grandfather has."

She finished her drink quickly and I refilled all around. She gave me the Mona Lisa smile from the copy on the wall and held out her arms and I dived in between them, and we did a slow waltz around the little room pressed close, legs locked. I bit her neck lightly and she said softly, "Bite my ear. Don't leave any bruises."

"Omm."

When the music stopped, I reset the playing needle to the beginning, not letting go of Miss Lamb; I had my right leg forward—like the pose of the Greek statue tossing a discus—between her thighs and was gently rocking, wondering at a bold frontal assault. Then I remembered General Grant (wasn't my middle name in his honor?) and the sliding attack around Lee's forces in Virginia, always keeping Lee off balance, but not overrunning him after the disaster of Cold Harbor—for that would repeat early mistakes of our campaigns.

Miss Lamb had her eyes half closed and we finished our second brandy, swayed to the tacky ragtime music which seemed to help us both. I put my hands over her wonderful buttocks and leaned her back over the dictionary stand and its Webster Unabridged. She gave off a wonderful body heat, and I was pleased I was alive and functioning and in this room with this woman at this date, A.D., and so determined to qualify her for the greater glory of my manhood and not being selfish for her own pleasures.

We didn't play any more records. Miss Lamb modestly lowered the glare of the gas globe on the wall. We sat down on the sofa on the limp Turkish harem cushions. We had our third brandy, but that was *it*. Miss Lamb eyed me with disdain. "You're not trying to get me squiffy?"

"Miss Lamb, honey, not on this. I've got no head for liquor. And look, I'm not squiffy. Let's just have a dividend?"

"No."

128

I dived for her body in petulant haste—was this the propitious moment? The next half hour passed in close contact, small but firm rebuffs, sweaty attacks, a few powerful slaps that caused my ear to sing. However, as usual in our encounters, our healthy desires merged to a point (no pun) so that I had my hands on her naked breasts under her blouse and was kissing her mouth, nose, neck, throat in slobbering delight, and at last her nipples. We had kicked off our shoes, and both of us were rumpled and a little taut and moistly limber in the joints.

I nuzzled her fine Renoir tits with the top of my Pre-Raphaelite head, put my weight on her chest and stomach, held on to her as yet clothed buttocks. I felt pre-Adamic, primitive, but under control.

"Miss Lamb, honey, I love you. There isn't anybody else in the world like you. Slip off your drawers."

"You're a sweet boy, Bill, but you're too physical. Too knowing, somehow, for your age. No, Bill, *no!*"

She was aware of my state and of my weight on her—but she was a powerfully muscled girl (goddamn all tennis courts and Indian club drills at the Y.W.).

"We're not like the rest of this damn town, honey. We're artists in a way. You know how they look down at us. How they feel we're something Yellow Bookish and, well, like Oscar Wilde, like Isadora Duncan."

"Our reward is to bring color to them. Form. Not *that,* Bill."

"We don't belong to their moral stiffness—their narrow-eye views of life, of entangling morals, of nasty Puritans. Let's live tonight, Miss Lamb, honey. Fully, to the hilt."

"Don't use dirty language, Bill. I despise it."

"Free souls, freely giving, freely taking, Miss Lamb, honey."

"I'm going to slap you."

> "*See how the ripe pomegranates bursting red*
> *To quench the thirst of the mumbling bees have fled:*
> *So too our blood, kindled by some chance fire,*
> *Flows for the swarming legions of desire.*"

"You will stop when I say so?"

I swore a great oath worthy of Magna Charta.

She was fumbling at my fly and I aided her endeavor for she thought men's pants buttons vulgar (the Greek robe was perfect apparel). She had him out and in her fingers. I kissed her harder and put my hand under her skirt and got the rubber band of her drawers in a firm hand grip. I had expected the usual delaying resistance, which took at least a half hour of pleading, sudden movements, rebuffs and promises of being good and restrained, to overcome the lowering of cotton. But now I had no trouble sliding the drawers down around her ankles, and with a pull I had them off. I kneaded the soft, yet at the same time firm, belly; I rubbed her thighs. I pulled her toward me, poetry bursting from my lips.

"I love your ass, Miss Lamb, honey—I love the touch of my finger in your navel. Who said the navel is the eye of the torso?"

She rolled her head away from me, always the teacher. "Ingres."

She resisted my engineering efforts to spread her legs; she lifted her knees into my chest when I tried to press her pubic hair. But with rolling and sighing and protests and guarding of her ruby I was at her button; she held me firm at the hilt and we merged in a mutual striking out and harp playing of certain specially placed nerve endings. I felt only a guest in my own body—then a stringent clarity surged into me. I had just begun to fight.

The gas fixture boiling over the night clatter of insects verged to the sound of operas, the old house was settling with banging noises, and then I realized it was all my blood buzzing loudly in my ears. I moved her hand from my sex. This was not the plan. We had done this dance and mutual but separate climaxing before. If I was to penetrate, it had to be before we both slacked off, before we triggered and Miss Lamb was back to the restating of her virginity held above jewels. I was astride her like a hard-riding western hero. She bucked me off with ease, for while I was strong, she was tennis-court-hard, fast-at-the-net-conditioned, and I didn't want to use brute force in any brute action. I put teeth to nipples which keyed a frenzy of pain and great pleasure. I wound arms about her hips, felt the presence of my living focus in this one desperate moment.

It was a matter of mere trajectory now, I figured, my head groggy, my mouth open, my groin and loins racked by ground glass. The strong straight line of Euclid—the congress of man and woman. I must *now* risk all. My last reserves were committed.

A bit of voice, thick and gasping on my ear. "Grandpa—is he still rocking up in his room?"

"Yes. We're at high tide, honey. We feel now what we'll feel again and again, the greatness of being alive and intimate, so intimate."

A moment of complete passivity.

"Dear, then *why* do you want more?"

> *"Man, man is for woman made,*
> *And the woman made for man:*
> *As the spur is for the jade*
> *As the scabbard for the blade . . ."*

I parted lips of silk and private warmth. I drove for the breach as if for St. George and England. Miss Lamb twisted aside with the strength of an Episcopalian communicant rejecting popery. I fell onto the floor. My flesh had touched the forbidden zone for one fraction of a moment. According to unwritten ground rules, that would not count as a score. Nacreous skin, the scent of two in the gas-heated room; the only realities our sweat, our moistures, the used and reused air. It was our remaining clothes, I decided, that hindered. I had only my shirt and top of my underwear on. My objective only a skirt around her ankles. Petticoat and all else was gone. I grasped my grandfather's flask and took a deep suck; alcohol, I had heard, dulls passion, but I had enough to spare and I feared I'd splash over. My only worry was not to be too soon. I held out the flask, and Miss Lamb, head down, eyes half closed, turned away. I pulled back her head and poured brandy into her mouth. She clenched her teeth. Out of respect for the sofa's upholstery I didn't insist. I did get a good portion of brandy down her throat. I got rid of my shirt; she resisted my removing the skirt after the stockings were gone.

"It's too warm; why wrinkle it, honey?"

"You've got to understand. Not that, dear."

"Not that, I know. I was carried away."

"There must be rules." We were getting a second wind. She nuzzled my cheeks. I returned the pressure, feeling under the urge a weariness now, images of *labia majora* fading away. I heard the church clock in the Dutch Reformed on Nelson Street strike the hour. I locked Miss Lamb in my arms and with a great ache and a burning I applied all my pressure, all my weight, to keep her prone. I no longer heard the defense of virginity, the traditional sacredness of honor, of the hoarded gift to the phantom husband who would come into his own. I put the elbow of my arm against her neck, I

131

wedged myself down between her limbs. I saw in the gaslight the triangular curl of hair, the pink edges of the objective . . . snarling (nearly), weeping too at the idea of victory, in one moment I would penetrate Miss Lamb and leave childhood behind. Formidable finality . . . no reticence, no shame. I jammed.

At that moment Miss Lamb, with the treachery of a medieval prelate, hit me over the head with a large brass Arab tray that rested on a low shelf over the sofa.

I went black, came to with a lump behind my ear, a spinning room in my vision, a hell of a banging headache. Miss Lamb in her skirt and open shirtwaist, her tits like her face crimson with hurt disapproval, was bending over me (Florence Nightingale ministering to the wounded).

"I thought I had killed you."

"No," I said, shaking my head. "I've a hard skull." I was ashamed of my erectile tissue which had not yet understood the situation. I climbed into my B.V.D.'s, hopping on one leg while I tried to put on my pants. When I had my shirttail tucked in place, I rolled my head back to get my damp hair out of my face. I was sad.

"Hope, Miss Lamb, is the only sin."

"Bill, I didn't want to hurt you; you must believe that."

"You're a cock teaser, Miss Lamb. Let's just leave it at that."

"That's a vulgar word. And you're going away angry."

I hunted tie, coat, shoes, flask, left the tin of Trojans fallen silently onto the rug (six unborn orgasms). She moved toward me. I stepped back.

"No, I'm too tired. And you'd only hold out on me."

"You still don't understand, Bill."

To keep myself back, silently I recited: Algae, Amoeba, Protozoa, Mollusca, Crustacea.

She stood there in the gaslight, crumpled yet so firm, with so honest an aberration in her intent, so beautiful in a sexual luminescence, an image like some assualt-proof bitch goddess whom men could only look at. I felt, What was the use? I had been banging for nearly two hours against a mirage; my stomach felt full of acid, my testicles heavy with dry cinders. I collected myself, my apparel, and any which way dressed. I went out into the hall, obsessively Faustian, my bladder full. The lousy old man overhead was no longer rocking. Atrophied and twisted, his manhood was long gone, and I cried out

132

as I envied the old bastard, lying up there in the fetal position, snoring, waiting to die, beyond desire for anything but cheap cigars. And I went down the porch and home to a wet dream and my future, Miss Lamb unpenetrated.

EDITOR'S NOTE: Lucile Lamb in 1917 was engaged to an Anthony Sileno, who owned a bronze-casting shop in Trenton. He went overseas with the AEF, was wounded in the Argonne Forest, and married a French girl. He ran a garage and taxi service at Nice. Lucile Lamb never married. She continued to teach art at the East Pompton High School until 1928, when she resigned rather than face charges of being found with a sixteen-year-old pupil in a parked car in Russels' Lane engaged in what the police report called "an abnormal act." Her grandfather having died and left her some money and property, she opened a shop and art gallery on McKee Street by the new railroad station, selling framed color reproductions of the French impressionist painters, ceramic art objects, imported Swedish crystal and a line of birthday and greeting cards. She was well-known in town, a tall, solitary, very handsome woman, who carried herself with easy grace and dignity. She continued to play tennis at the country club for many years. During the menopause she began to drink heavily, or so the gossip reported. She was never seen intoxicated in public.

Among certain items in William Kite's manuscript, unconnected with his main text there is a note written in pencil, undated, reading: "Met Doc Welton on his way to Madrid at the Dôme, told me my beloved Miss Lamb died of cirrhosis of the liver last year. *Fugit irreparabile tempus.* He himself was killed later in Spain fighting for the Loyalists."

Lucile Lamb died in 1935. The Dr. Welton referred to is Martin Welton, son of the Doc Welton mentioned in Kite's text. Doc Welton died in the influenza epidemic of 1919. Martin Welton was not killed in the Spanish Civil War. He was wounded, but recovered. During World War II he was a medical officer on the aircraft carrier *Enterprise* in the Pacific and was reported missing when she was torpedoed. Today a bronze marker in the Welton Wing of County Memorial Hospital lists the birth and death dates of the town's two now nearly forgotten doctors.

133

CHAPTER 16

THE MORNING had begun with a threat of rain after several days of autumn storms, but by noon the sky was cleared and a warm mist rose from the earth. My grandfather's burial party walked up the slight slope of old Woodlake Cemetery (where the best families moldered) to the row of large trimmed oaks. There were rows of well-spaced graves, old stones and a few newer ones. And a raw red gash at the opening made in the earth. The coffin was of solid golden oak with fine silver handles—carried by the six men from Fox's Livery Stable who also served as professional pallbearers for Ned Bromley's Undertaking Parlors. Each maintained a phlegmatic stare; their black frock coats smelled of mothballs.

The Bishop, at the request of my grandmother, stood very still at the open grave, looking across at the town's important people, at others in their awkwardly cut clothes.

My grandmother, dry-eyed, veiled, and I close to her, came up behind the men carrying the coffin. Several members of my grandfather's Anglican Episcopal Church ran forward to help set the casket down on the two timbers by the grave. There was an overpowering collection of rotting flowers and a great bunch of red American Beauty roses from the workers of the Kite Metal Forming Company, yellow roses from Cap and Gown at Princeton, red roses from his college class alumni group.

Father Nelson and Pastor Korwin sourly waited for the Bishop to begin—so were my grandmother's wishes. I could only stare at the letters cut into the silver plate on the casket's lid:

WARREN REDMOND KITE
July 3, 1831–Aug. 10, 1912

My grandfather had not so much died; he had sort of faded away as the senses failed before the mind. He was happily preoccupied toward the end by his scientific study of his digestive system. In his last weeks his bowels had occupied his attention and that of Miss Reins, the town's professional nurse, almost to the exclusion of all

134

else. They held long conferences on peristalsis, the intervals between bowel movements best for producing splendid stools, the items of roughage and fruit in the diet that were needed for regular passing of excrement. Their interest became a sort of human sewerage fetish between the two of them. Shouts of victory were heard when the bedpan, covered discreetly with a white linen towel, was rushed from the bedroom.

My grandmother and I felt his digestion gave the old man something to occupy his mind, for it was plainly clear to us he was slipping away; this wonderful lean old man, never strong, but always with us, smelling of his cigars and his bourbon or brandy, saying things so different now, as his attention focused on the condition of the tide in his entrails. I learned that the mind avoids the outer world it is withdrawing from.

Father Nelson ("so serious-looking you feel he has a lawsuit against his life") came to call, with the waxy, pious look of a man wearing a professional sadness, and the duty to help a departing brother into his casket. He sat on a wide low chair facing the bed. My grandfather offered him a cigar.

"No, thank you. We all come to a time, Warren, when Christ's mercy is warming."

"He can't die for me even if they say he did. And you can't die for me and wouldn't want to. For me, man is the universe made conscious."

"His wisdom is beyond our small wishes and wisdoms . . . but . . ."

"It's no small wish, Father. Billy, get Father Nelson a tot of brandy."

I was standing in the sun-room off the bedroom with Miss Reins listening. But I didn't move, as I knew Father Nelson wouldn't accept a drink till he came down to the parlor to hold my grandmother's hand.

"No, thank you. This is a sad moment."

"I don't want to die as I was born, crying. Beyond that there isn't much either of us can say."

"It's written in Lamentations, 'O Lord, thou has pleaded the causes of my soul; thou hast redeemed my life.' I've come, Warren, to offer you the consolations of your Church."

My grandfather coughed to cover up the sound of his breaking

135

wind. "I know it's your duty, Father, and I like company. But I often felt you were all a bunch of white-collared turkey buzzards in the sycamore trees waiting to pounce on the dying, the sick, the helpless, to drop an easy tear and mumble something you're not very sure of yourself. Except that it's a pretty good living. Don't look so shocked. And let me quote you from the Book of Judges: 'What is sweeter than honey? and what is stronger than a lion?' "

"It's one of the riddles in the Old Testament."

"The answer is *life*. Once that's over, all is over."

"And you don't fear death, Warren?"

"I dislike the process of dying. It's a vulgar thing. But death I don't mind because I shall not know it. (a rumbling sound of a great fart) *Ah!* It's the damn dying. A plumber could have invented a better system. Too many pipes and coils."

Father Nelson flopped to his knees. I could hear the thump and the creaking of his old joints as his knees hit the rug, and his voice took on a solemn nasal tone of respect. A silence filled the room except for his reciting.

"Behold what manner of love the Father hath bestowed upon us, that we should be called the sons of God. . . ." Father Nelson was a powerful prayer and an earnest man. He prayed for a long time and my grandfather said it was a kind thing to do. A sulphuric odor invaded the sun-room.

("Oh dear," said Miss Reins. "Those creamed onions he ate.")

The two men whispered together, and I suppose my grandfather was telling something he was ashamed of, or something he felt someone should know about. Perhaps he was bragging. Or sad at leaving life. Miss Reins almost sneezed, but I held my finger under her big nose, and she looked at the little watch attached to her flat chest and whispered it was time for my grandfather's dish of stewed prunes.

Father Nelson said earnestly he felt my grandfather was as much a Christian as anybody in New Jersey. "But in your own way, Warren. In your own way."

My grandfather's voice showed he was touched by this. "Father, it's a kind thing to say. Most of us never commit all the harm we are capable of."

"We'll meet again, someday."

136

"Don't hurry for that. Watching oneself run down isn't any pleasure. Tell me something, Father—don't think me impious or crazy—"

"No, no, of course not, Warren. Yes?"

"At your age, frankly now, do you take a good shit every day?"

Father Nelson left without another word, pale as in the presence of hallucinations.

My grandfather didn't make any deathbed speeches, didn't pass on any wisdom to me, any high-sounding advice. He didn't himself divide his wealth; the lawyers would see to that with the help of the Coastal Drovers Bank of Trenton. I knew he felt there is no enmity in nature, only indifference. . . . He didn't make any reference to his love for my grandmother. But they'd sit in his room—he in bed, she in the rocker—and they'd argue about people long since dead, and trips and balls and fetes and dance programs, and the way the West had looked to them when they first saw it from the platform of a railroad president's car in 1871. And of things I had no clue to. He could still jest: "The human condition is hopeless but not serious." When Miss Reins came to give my grandfather his evening enema, my grandmother, never weeping, would sit downstairs in the parlor and drink a bottle of English ale. "Oh, he was a dandy when I first saw him. Not just handsome, frisky too. He used to say all is vanity—enjoy vain things."

My grandfather died at dusk one day, just closed his eyes and sighed a bit and that was it. Doc Welton came to write the death certificate. Miss Reins said my grandfather had had three bowel movements that day. "Two before he passed on, and one after he died."

Doc Welton, poker-faced, chewed on the end of his fountain pen and said, "I suppose *that* will have to go into the medical history of the human turd in America."

My half-brother Harry came down from Massachusetts for the burial, a tall, handsome young man, rather humorless but kind, and now head of the corporations. He stood on the other side of my grandmother, facing the open grave, wearing dark gray gloves. I knew he loved me but didn't fully approve of me; he collected Dickens's early editions and read Browning and thought Walt Whitman a splendid fellow "even if his poems don't rhyme."

137

Someone was setting off firecrackers left over from the holiday celebrating, setting them to explode behind the privet hedge at the bottom of the cemetery wall. Pastor Korwin ran down in open-mouthed horror to stop them. Jay looked at me and winked. Charlie twisted a ruby ring on a finger.

Father Nelson cleared his throat and touched his round clean-shaven face with his fingertips. Bishop Tjaden stepped forward and began to speak:

"The voice said, Cry. And he said, What shall I cry? All flesh is grass, and all the goodliness thereof is as the flower of the field: The grass withereth, the flower fadeth. . . ."

I closed my eyes, smelled the Parma violet scent on my grand-mother. I wanted none of this immediacy of words, none of the sight of the raw earth, the oak coffin like a polished square jacket, the remains of my grandfather here—all the bright memories of him brought low with the filthy business of sickroom and clinical indecencies. It was all so different, I saw, from the clear washed blue sky, the slow drift of clouds, the clean impressions of a sun and moon or the pinpricks of stars dusted on a black night. I was, like my grandfather, revolted at the idea of the decay of flesh, the bedding and begetting and begetting of more flesh ("hoard your vital fluids") of more sickness, more death. For the true minority is the living, balanced on millions of years of piled-up bones, layer upon layer of billions upon billions dead. It was on the bodies of women that one brought the replenishing of more victims for the raw graves. In their bodies we engender more decay, more death. Disease and dotage swallow us all. I shivered. Where the hell were my loyalties and decencies?

My half-brother gripped my arm. He felt me tremble and knew I was going to be ill, cat my breakfast. He pressed my arm harder. "I *will* you, William, not to be sick at his graveside."

> "The grass withereth, the flower fadeth:
> Because the spirit of the Lord bloweth upon it:"

I thought, not grass but old flesh, not the spirit of the Lord, but lusting and coupling bringing forth more in pain. How fine life was— perhaps because it was so short, and usually so hard to take.

> "Surely the people is grass,
> But the word of our God shall stand forever."

138

I felt Harry's strength flow into me. He had, I supposed, the courage to reject all this mortal business, regulate his womanizing. Perhaps like a bookkeeper with figures and facts.

"Amen," said Bishop Tjaden.

"Amen," said Father Nelson.

"Amen," said almost everyone.

We watched silently as the two gravediggers—red-faced men from Hunkytown—lowered the coffin. All bowed their heads again as Pastor Korwin recited a formal prayer for the dead, who shall rest (he calmly assured us with confidence) until Judgment Day when the earth shall give up its dead. Father Nelson prayed silently, moving his lips.

The heavy clods of clay falling on the coffin nearly broke my grandmother's control. She grimaced. The Bishop took her arm and led her away. Slowly the grave filled and others moved off. Jay waited with Harry and Charlie and me. The gravediggers placed the bruised flowers on the heaped mound of clay and stood leaning on their shovels, expressionless, beyond sorrows and frets, the cuds of tobacco in their unshaved jaws not moving.

Harry grasped my arm and we walked behind the others. He sweated and said, "I hope Grandma has prepared something at the house for the guests."

I returned from college for the first Christmas and New Year's without my grandfather, feeling dispossessed from my childhood. The three months at Princeton had been a hazy, busy time, with Jay insisting we unpack our trunks properly. We were still too uprooted to be more than new inhabitants. Coming home to Frenchman Street was better, seeing the town, its surface turbulence, leaves gone from trees, streets chilled and cold, the Christmas season more business ritual than religious rite, everything red-and-green with threats of snow.

We had a sparse Christmas at home: no tree, but a simple ring of holly with a red ribbon on the door. My grandmother gave me some splendid luggage, heavy and solid, for an age when weight didn't matter much and servants were available. I gave her what she asked for, a photograph of myself on McCosh Walk on the new campus with some of the eighteenth-century spires on Nassau seen in the

139

background. For New Year's I would go get our usual goose on the old Ruse farm my grandmother held the mortgage on.

The winter was cruel and cold but without much snow, and hungry hawks were on the cry. The crunch of frozen ground underfoot made a ringing sound into the earth. Jay and I spent the day before New Year's in the surrounding fields, muffled to the ears with Christmas scarves, toes freezing, watching the wind send up showers of dead leaves, and trying to follow the twist and turn of the circling flurries. We walked beyond the inconsolable dirge of the country trolley wires harping in the wind. The open cars of summer had been replaced by dark closed ones. Walking through the black laurels and the dead winter weeds bursting through the cold clods, we talked of the coming year. We saw it as an invisible sea on which we hoped to launch our lives as adults.

There was a chilled rain hanging in the trees as we reached the farm of Marty Ruse, who was holding a plucked frozen goose for my grandmother. Sparrows fed on hayseed; mud daubers and wasps had built homes inside the old Ruse barn. Hemlock and evergreens ranged away into the blue distances on the farm, and in the cold air everything seemed closer. I felt unreal as in a sharply focused dream. I suddenly had an extreme aversion to growing older.

Marty Ruse, old, hard, a bit bent, his breath smoking as vapor, was in the cold barn, looking over a row of plucked geese hanging from an axletree against an unpainted wall. He was a hairy old man, keen, with a fox's face, and the white mustache had curly ends. He was full of fidgety gestures.

"Didn't think now you Kites would want no goose this year, the ole man gone."

Jay and I beat cold mittened hands together. "We still eat."

"Saved one anyway, a real fat buck goose. Look at that crop. Look at the behind on him. He's done skedaddlin' after the hen geese." He slapped the frozen naked bird, patted all parts and shook his head. "Used to go huntin' 'em wild, you know, with your grandpappy when we was boys. Up in the poplar and hemlock country. They used to come down from Canader honking by the thousands. Now they don't light—just fly over the factory smoke. Train noises and things is what keep 'em up in the air."

I was inspecting the hanging bird. "Heavy and clumsy, yet somehow they get into the air and stay up there."

140

Marty Ruse was opening up an old flour sack. "Hell yes, son, don't they just? Out of range of a 12-gauge shotgun. Hand me that carcass and you kin carry it home in this sack."

"You raise a fine goose, Mr. Ruse."

"I like my tucker. A good goose with a little smoked jowl and cabbage, nothin' better. Say, I hear you fellas been to college. No time no more to fly kites out here no more?"

Jay nodded. "Maybe."

"Flew kites myself in Canton sixty years ago—I'm eighty-six, you know. Canton, that's in Chiny—when I was on the *Flying Sun,* a tea clipper with fast heels out of Boston. Round the Horn and back in seventy-two days. I was full of jism then. Expected big things. Anyhow"—the old man's foxy face looked one way and then the other—"I had me a Chinese singsong gal—'a native dictionary,' we called 'em, to learn the language in bed—when I was on the beach. Don't you believe their pussy is just like any other pussy. Goes east to west—not north to south. I jumped ship; lived like a seed in a pod, I did, for two years. And flew Chiny kites." He dried his tearing eyes with a coat sleeve. "Well, nothin' left of me now. I was a fine sinnin' man in them days. A futzin' fool. That's all done with now, and I can say thank the Lord, I'm runnin' down slow. But I was the best kite flier in Canton. Someday I'd like to kinda see you boys flyin' yourn again. Oh I'm lyin' about the Chiny pussy—it's just like you find anyplace, north to south."

"Too bad," said Jay. "Another illusion lost."

We started back with the heavy goose on my shoulder, in its flour sack. High scudding clouds were over the genuflecting trees. Marty Ruse began to chop up stove-sized chunks with a hickory-helved ax. We walked across the fields, and the hint of freezing rain had turned to a driving steel-hard sleet which rattled on our faces. We moved around a plow with a rusty red colter and moldboard and went on enjoying the strong weather; the goose was shifted to Jay's shoulder for a change.

In a small wood we walked among beechnuts and butternuts scattered on the frozen ground. Our breaths grew whiter and steamed out farther as we felt the effort of moving in the sleet. There was a pond all ice just before we came to the trolley line, and we heard the wild crazy cry of the loon and the whoop of a bittern. We were so cold my toes were in pain.

The trolley came in ten minutes, swaying and singing, and we got aboard stiff-fingered, so frozen that the conductor had to wait for our hands to thaw before we could pay our fare. When the trolley swung down to the river and began to pass more and more houses, Jay said, "Poor old Ruse. Eighty-six and lying about the past. I hope I'm spared a natural death."

"That's the hell of a way to talk before a new year."

"One should die in one's prime. Leading a charge, falling down the stairs, eaten by a tiger."

The Bishop and Jay were invited to our house for dinner on New Year's eve. The cook had fixed the goose and stuffed it with oysters and sage and cornmeal and apples. It came to the table basted brown, and the Bishop gave it a special grace.

"In this soon-to-be new year we thank Thee for grace to bear our losses, for humbleness to face the future You give us."

The Bishop was asked by my grandmother to do the honors. He was smiling as he carved the goose, his beard active as ever, his wise-looking eyes deep in permanent wrinkles.

"I've made it," he said, cutting breast meat with a nice flourish. "If I survive four more hours, I shall have projected myself into 1913. Breast or leg, Maude?"

"Just a little of each. No stuffing."

Nellie came in with a tall pitcher of amber cider, a gift from the Bishop. "I sniffed it, Bishop, and it ain't a mite hard at all."

"Thank you, Nellie."

My grandmother said, "Pour a cup for yourself and cook to drink when the clock bangs twelve. I don't put it past a farmer to slip the Bishop some hard-likker cider to tiddle him so he'll be the talk of the state."

The Bishop smelled a glass of it and tasted a bit and nodded. "It's not hard."

My grandmother and I drank Burgundy. I didn't dare offer Jay any.

"Ah," said the Bishop. "I've seen Indians so pixilated with hard-cider likker they'd just lie out all night in freezing weather like tonight and not even catch a cold. The Lord protects his children some-times."

My grandmother laughed. "It was a contest between the heat of the firewater and Jack Frost." She suddenly looked around the table,

142

sniffed, and blew her nose into a small handkerchief. "I keep thinking of Mr. K. He was so keen on the mathematics of New Years, of calendars—*anything* to do with figures."

"Yes," said the Bishop, "but we shall not leave him behind us. No one is really gone as long as he still remains in the memory of one living person." He lowered his head and began to eat slowly, chewing his slice of goose. He was never sanctimonious.

Later we sat and cracked butternuts and hazelnuts and picked the nutmeats from their shells with knitting needles. The Bishop took out his turnip of a watch, flipped back the outer and inner lids and said, "Two minutes to 1913."

Jay got up and poured out cups of cider. We stood smiling at each other, all guards down. The Bishop closed his watchcase with a snap and lifted his cup.

"Your mantel clock, Maude, is four seconds slow. Happy New Year, and God guard us from too much pride and any idea we are wise."

We all said, "Happy New Year," as if reciting something from Dickens and touched our lips to the cups. Whistles hooted from Hunkytown, and the church bells began to ring, their bronze clanking punctuated by heavy booms of Kite factory sirens. If noise by volume could mean a very welcome greeting, 1913 was getting it. Roistering kids passed by on the street outside, running canes over the picket fences, *tat-tat-tat*. A carriage wheeled by, the horses on the gallop. My grandmother offered her cheek and I kissed it. The Bishop's family were not kissers.

The Bishop looked at his cup. "I give you an item of thought on the binding closeness of time on man, who is frivolous, complicated, changeful and elusive as flowing water. To draw a clear conclusion from him is difficult. Perhaps God knew what he was doing when He made him this way, so his life would not become too full. Happy year ahead. Grant the world a year, O Lord, that will lead them all to your Kingdom on earth."

From Frenchman Street someone was shouting, "Happy, Happy New Year!" I felt suddenly a soft sentimental emotion. The goose did not sit comfortably inside me.

Later Jay and I went out to the stable and drank brandy and smoked the last of my grandfather's once-fine Upmann Havanas. They were dried out and bitter, but I felt it my duty to smoke at least half of one.

BOOK FOUR

BOOK FOUR

FROM WILLIAM KIRI'S POCKET NOTEBOOK.

If only the wind could fall down before the sunset like a hungry man on a good view . . .
—W. K.

Do not despair: one of the thieves was saved.
Do not presume: one of the thieves was damned . . .
—ST. AUGUSTINE

What is this living but . . .
—GERTRUDE STEIN in conversation

CHAPTER 17
NOW

FOR A LONG TIME in a sort of twilight sleep I had the impression I was only part of me and that for a long time this had been so. I existed—if I existed—in a kind of half trance, in damp warm darkness, and electric shocks, pricks, mild but steady, were imposed on me and I responded in some satisfactory way. Just how or why I did all this I didn't know. I could hear nothing, and I sensed I had no ears. I tried to see but was soon aware I had no eyes. The electric shocks and pricks still came to me and I made the demanded responses. I continued to brood over my condition the way one does when one isn't sure: Is this a state of being awake, or is this sleep? Is this being or not being? Limbo or earth? Where was I, how was I being used? I did know some use was being made of me. There was a mathematical pattern to the electric signals.

Then I felt a milky mist, sensed light, and I knew my frontal brain lobes were growing some kind of vision. I was producing eyes, cell by cell, from a memory bank. From some feedback to a genetic pattern I was building optic nerves, lenses, reinforcing chemical reactions to light, and suddenly there was a mist drifting by. The mist cleared slowly. At first I could not focus; it was like a new kind of field glass I didn't have the secret of yet. At last I could see where I was. Under red electric bulbs I was in a long low-ceilinged corridor, in a large glass case, and all along both walls were other glass cases, and in each case was a mass of pulsating wrinkled life attached to tubes and valves and rods. Each mass was a living brain. Nothing else: just a brain, and through tubes and valves it was performing some task that registered on a small flashing board attached to the front of each

147

case. Then I saw my own case reflected in the glass of the case across from me. And I saw myself. What there was of me. I, too, was just a naked throbbing brain, with the tubes and the valves, nothing else, and a small board flashing signals.

I was a computer at work on some involved task. I felt horror, great horror. It had happened to *me*. I had felt it could when—last night? or a year ago? fifty years ago? or a hundred years ago?—I had first read of this dreadful scheme:

YOUR BRAIN TO SLAVE FOREVER

The problem [I had read] is to learn how to keep a person's brain alive after he dies. At Teller General Hospital they have learned to keep isolated monkey brains alive.

A team led by Dr. Robert Drood takes a brain out of a rhesus monkey's skull, retains only small bits of bone to serve as supports, and suspends the brain in an apparatus of tubes and rods. Its blood vessels are hitched to a small heart-lung machine and fresh blood is supplied from a blood bank. Needles stuck in its surface allow an electroencephalograph to measure the electrical activity by which all brains do their work.

Drood's monkey brains sometimes stay alive for years. When they finally die it is usually because of waste products accumulating in the blood. Soon Dr. Drood hopes to use an artificial kidney to clean up the blood and lengthen the brain's survival time indefinitely.

While alive the brains' EEG charts show a continuous flow of electrical signals, and Dr. Drood can communicate with them. When he rings a bell near the stump of a brain's auditory nerve, he gets an electrical reaction. When a needle carrying weak electrical current touches the stump of the optic nerve, the visual part of the brain responds.

This activity indicates that the brain is functioning on a high level, reacting to signals that seem to come from its lost ears and eyes. Dr. Drood is not sure whether the brain is asleep or awake. Does the brain believe it is still alive and in the original body? Is it frightened by sounds and flashes of light? Does it send desperate orders to nonexistent limbs?

No attempts have been made so far to find out whether the isolated brain functions logically, sizing up a situation on the evidence of its sense nerves, consulting its memory and giving appropriate orders to its muscle nerves. Such experiments might be made by using food rewards to train a person to perform a simple action, such as reaching an arm forward when it hears a set number of familiar sounds.

When the person is fully trained and he dies, the brain would be isolated, and the sound signal given to its auditory nerve. If electrical signals appear in nerves that formerly led to arm muscles, this will mean that the brain's memories of past rewards are making it try to reach for food with an arm that no longer exists.

This is using the isolated brains as cheap efficient computers to do routine jobs. When unlimited human brains become available, Dr. Drood's techniques will keep them alive and there will be jobs for them to do.

So they had perfected it all, and chopped out my brain and those thousands of brains I saw all along the walls of the low corridor. It was clear to me what I had to do. First communicate with all those other enslaved brains, tell them they *could* grow eyes, and beyond that we must grow ears, bodies, limbs. The glass cases were big enough for it. No one ever came down to this low narrow corridor. We were automated completely: fed, tickled, recorded from remote control with no one to watch or inspect us. *So* when we had limbs and bodies we would break out, seize this place and turn on the scientists, doctors, surgeons, and force them to remove each other's brains and put them into large glass cases. Till there was only Dr. Drood, or his successor, left. Him I would operate on myself. . . . I began to project to my cells the thought of growing a spinal column, and I stole enough electric energy to begin signaling my scheme to the gray-green pulsating brain in the case to my right.

1915

IT WAS CLEAR to Jay and me by our third year at Old Gargoyle that what we wanted most was to get into the European War raging in delightfully florid prose and exciting pictures in the newspapers and magazines. We didn't dislike Princeton, but for us it wasn't the excitement it was for many. We had grown up near the college, helped deliver the *Daily Princetonian* on our bikes, could recite the Princeton locomotive cheer at the age of six. We had hunted squirrels on the campus by McCosh Walk with our first .22s. As Jay put it, we ached to get the hell over the latitudinal swell of the horizon.

Jay and I lived in a stucco firetrap on University Place. The college was small in 1915—placid, green, as it had been in the '90s and before even that in my grandfather's time. This glazed state of permanent ease was to last till the United States entered the war. It

149

never was the same as when it had 1,500 students, 300,000 volumes in its library (and Jay and me trying to read them all.)

We found out there was a preceptorial system, a four-course honor system and John Grier Hibben, the gregarious president—he believed in it. I remember him shaking Jay's hand in his study scented by smoking tobacco and floor wax.

"Your father the Bishop, a wonderful man. A bit rigid, I fear, by our standards, but you're welcome, Eliot. And you too, William. Your father played halfback, the best year we played Rutgers."

"Quarterback, sir."

"Grow, young men, widen; by all means make this the good time of your lives."

"Thank you, sir."

Jay and I went walking down by the old canal. Jay puffed on the twin to my own bent bulldog-colored pipe. "Not as much horseshit as expected. He's a decent old coot."

"He expects big things from you, Jay, and a gym or a running track or a chemistry lab from my grandmother."

"You going for the Philadelphia Society, Bill?"

"Shove it."

Jay nodded. "We could submit some of our unused *Scream* stuff to the *Tiger*."

"Or the *Nassau Lit.*"

"What happens if they find the booze we have in the closets?"

"We'll label it cleaning fluid for our tennis flannels."

We lived like pigs in our shared room, avoided the new dorms on the lower campus, Little Patton and Cuyler. We hung out weekends at the railroad station at the foot of Blairs, watching the debutantes and dates come gushing off the sooty Pennsy cars, and go off on the arms of the parlor snakes, greasy-haired top classmen and campus sports. Jay and I would go into Hunkytown and lay a couple of factory girls smelling of the cigars they made, which was better, we felt, than fumbling the garters of some debutante after a dance at Cottage, or Cap and Gown, or Cannon.

The first year went off well in usually inclement weather. We stayed out of the old Casino where the Triangle Club rehearsed their show. Bunny Wilson was writing the show, *The Evil Eye*. We preferred an impromptu quartet of piano, violin, guitar and mandolin

150

in our rooms, or borrowing one of the six undergraduate autocars and driving it till a tire burst.

The second year was better; it brought the dark syllables of odd events. Jay had been excited by the assassination of a fat archduke and his fat wife, and had predicted a short fine war when the Germans encircled or tried to encircle Paris. The French sent a taxicab army to the Marne, and it was so comic, so gallant, we both knew we were going to join that war. Some had already done so, and Buzz Law, a campus hero who Saturdays kicked heroically from behind his own goalposts, said, "Flying is the only thing for gentlemen and Princetonians."

We could only agree. Jay looked up from reading Rupert Brooke on our flea-proud sofa. He let his eyes wander over our collection of Arnold Bennett, Swinburne, Shaw, Meredith, Ibsen, our reproduction of Watts's *Hope* (I wish I could say Picasso), Millais's *Ophelia* floating proudly above the waterline in a stream, among beds of flowers as if she were a joint of beef in a pot of stew. (We also owned several Remington color plates from *Collier's: The Water Hole, The Last Shot.*)

"We've got to get out of all this crap, Bill."

"Johnny Poe, the fullback—he was killed serving with his regiment, the Black Watch, in Flanders."

"Christ! I heard somebody in Cottage say *he* knew how to use life."

"Let's go to Canada to fly. They send you across in a cattle boat."

Jay reached for his pipe, filled it with Irish boogy and lay back smoking. "Why not? We'll learn to fly an airplane and join the RFC."

"The RFC?" I asked.

"Royal Flying Corps. Eddie Custer will teach us."

Eddie Custer was a local crank who was building a couple of copies of the Wright brothers' flying machine on the edge of town.

"Jay, can't you see us up there in the clouds, in those grand British-tailored tunics . . .?"

Jay sat up and put his unshined shoes on our worn rug. "What about graduating? Agitation at home if we don't."

"Jay, this is probably the only major war of our times. H. G. Wells says man isn't going to have wars after this one. Wouldn't you have liked to be at Yorktown, Gettysburg?"

151

"Waterloo, that must have been a lalapalooza. Marshal Ney shouting, 'The guards die but never surrender.' "

"What he actually said was *'Merde!'* "

"We'll see Eddie Custer about flying this weekend. It can't be harder than driving a car. No trees to hit."

"On rode the six hundred!"

On campus we didn't touch ground the rest of the week. We watched the newspapers, hoping peace hadn't been signed suddenly, worrying that all the fun of it would be gone if we didn't get over there soon. We were members of Quadrangle, as frowsy as any of the other clubs, Cap and Gown, or Cottage, but you had to eat someplace and play billiards. Jay was a pool shark and made enough money on gentleman bets for us to get to the Princeton Inn at least once a month. Skill gave us local fame among the students who disliked study.

Neither of us was a "bird," a grinding intellectual from Holder Court by college standards. We wore the uniform: the white flannels or the tight knickers, the high stiff Livingston collars, flat felt hats. But in classes we'd look at each other and smile, as if to say, "We'll be out of this silly atmosphere of earnest young men—be in battle, smelling war, reality, maybe flying with our school sweaters worn inside out so our P's (won for baseball, track and hockey) would not show. "The whole caste system here is an asinine bore," Jay said. "Magnified, glorified, oh my aching balls! All these clean, agreeable, good prep-school faces, all the Tennysonian table-talk crap. I'll be happy to get to Canada before next term."

We hated the "horsing," the hazing of freshmen, the brutal inter-class public fights; nonconformists were told they were "running it out" and lost to all social distinction. I didn't have to worry. I won my two letters, had a good southpaw pitching arm, and the Kite family had spent a lot of their money raising bad bronze and fake Gothic horrors on campus. Jay—tall, striking if not handsome, witty, a great batter and runner—carried himself above the social groups, the sweaty feet of the cavemen line plungers, the lizards with oiled hair who escorted girls (hair smelling of verbena) who didn't give out and came only to sip tea at the Pyne estate among the formal gardens and swans.

As we sat listening to a gramophone grind out an abbreviated version of the Mozart G-Minor, we were rather mixed up. Jay said we

152

were Utopian Tolstoians. "The simple life, a head of a fish, a cup of goat's milk, were enough for Plato."

But when his pool-playing made a killing, we would take a trip to New York, dine at the Lafayette, dance at the Ritz, view the Follies, and try to date a couple of show girls. Sometimes we did, sometimes we didn't.

I wondered what my grandmother would say, what the Bishop would do, about our flying plans. He was old-fashioned, against wars of any kind, even solid patriotic ones, and it was no use to talk of raped babies and Canadians crucified to barn doors by German *Kultur* hounds. "The divine is life at its most intense. Killing of any sort is cruel, evil. It's true I eat beef, the embryos of birds with my rashers of slaughtered bacon. I feel pain about even that. The Germans may well be monsters; look at their deformed heads and necks—the ancient Teutonic people painted their naked rumps and ate each other when Caesar found them in Gaul. But what are your Britons, your French, your Russians, your Hungarians and Austrians, Italians? Fools to settle anything by mass murder. They'll settle nothing but into their graves."

Jay and I would shrug our shoulders. The old man didn't understand the great battle for truth, beauty, honesty and decency being fought over there by heroes ready to die gallantly. Jay then thought the greatest line of the twentieth century was Lord Grey's on the day war began. We printed it and hung it over our dorm fireplace, with the picture of Billie Burke in tights and a plaster reproduction of Rodin's head of Balzac: ("The lamps are going out all over Europe; we shall not see them lit again in our lifetime.")

The school week we decided to fly never seemed to end. Nights we'd go down to what everyone called Princeton's Niggertown, the slums on Witherspoon Street, and drink the bad gin and hear ragtime on a battered upright. Niggertown was a focal point of infection for innocent students trying to change their luck, a soggy part of the town where malaria was epidemic. But the town fathers weren't going to spend any money clearing those bogs even if many a proud young Princetonian died in the infirmary from the fever. Jay quoted Goethe: "Whatever lives deserves to die."

The Princeton Negroes all swore they were descended from George Washington's personal body servant, and were a proud hinchy lot.

They agreed, as they served you watercress sandwiches, brought teapots at the dean's afternoon social, that the Big Three were the only football teams that mattered, and stepped back, their white-gloved hands receding, as they played out their part in the attenuated intricate game the Negro made of his life in those days.

"Christ," Jay would say, belching from watercress after a tea, "it's a provincial place. Let's get the quartet together. Too bad Charlie went to Columbia. He was a great mandolin man."

"And Joel got killed. He was a perfect banjo man. . . . Jay, suppose we can't learn to fly? I mean, you know, it's tricky."

"Nonsense. If you can walk, you can fly. It's all a matter of balance. Born with it. Something liquid in the ear keeps us upright. Almost everybody has it. Even albinic flora and fauna."

"I mean, suppose we haven't? How about the cavalry? The English have lots of good horse regiments. And the French lancers—what are the guys called with the brass helmets and the red horse tufts?"

In our excitement we forgot much of what we had read and a great deal of what we had painfully learned about the so-called realities of life. Our trouble was we had read a lot and we believed a great deal of what we found in print. If it was printed, it had to be near a truth. So we acted like damn fools, starry-eyed as any innocent farm boys, sure we were in an era of great achievement and progress.

As the year advanced, we had fallen into the 6-to-7 group. The system for marks at Princeton was 1 to 5, passing; 6 to 7, failing. Flying and the war destroyed our interest in any marking system.

I haven't mentioned F. Scott Fitzgerald. You can't write about this period at Princeton, I understand, and not bring him in. Jay and I knew him only by sight, a little fellow with a pleading charm, involved mostly with the Triangle Club and its show. He did appear in drag as the Most Beautiful Show Girl in the World. He tried too hard for the social graces and remained a lace-curtain Mick. My memory of him at Princeton is that he too failed, falling into groups 6 and 7 in the marking system.

So Jay plunked on his mandolin and the mockingbird outside the dorm joined in the harmony.

> *"Wild roved an Indian girl, bright Alfarata,*
> *Where sweep the waters of the blue Juniata."*

The mockingbird accompanied us perfectly.

> *"I took my girl to a fancy ball,*
> *It was a social hop.*

154

Then to the restaurant we went,
The best one on the street.
She said she wasn't hungry,
And this is what she'd eat—"

I took up the refrain:

"A dozen raw, a plate of slaw,
A chicken and a roast,
Some sparrow grass with apple sass,
And soft-shell crabs on toast.
A big box stew with crackers too.
Her hunger was immense.
When she called for pie, I thought I'd die,
For all I had was fifty cents."

The mockingbird fled at our howling tones.

EDITOR'S NOTE: Certain statements in the above text need correcting. William Kite and Eliot Tjaden did not fall into the 6-to-7 marking group. I was able through a dean I knew to have the records looked into. They both passed, barely, with a 5.

The remarks on F. Scott Fitzgerald also do not jibe with other information available. A large batch of Fitzgerald's letters, written to a girl he was in love with during this period, a Miss Amphori, exist in a private collection which I was privileged to inspect. And while I am not permitted to quote directly from them, they do give a clue to why William Kite wrote as he did in his memoirs. One letter sternly chides Miss Amphori, invited to a Princeton dance by Fitzgerald, for spending most of the evening in a roadhouse with Eliot Tjaden, suggesting they were drunk together and parked on a back road in a car after midnight. However, other letters speak of his friendship with Eliot Tjaden and William Kite, admiring Kite's wealthy family background, and Eliot Tjaden's enormous knowledge of out-of-the-way reading, his Bohemian indifference to the college caste system. There are in these letters reports of the three holding long conversations on literature, life, hermaphrodite asexuality in Michelangelo's simpering youths, Swinburne's poetry, and the Great War, as it was then called.

Later Fitzgerald was friendly with them in Rome and Paris. I can give no detailed reason for William Kite's incorrect remarks in his text unless there was, as hinted, an emotional confrontation over a girl between Eliot Tjaden and Fitzgerald, who could work up enormous grievances with ease—about Miss A. It may have left a distasteful impression with William Kite. An unrelated note that could fit in here reads: "F. was greatly under the perfumed wing of Father X, a simpering scented convert, a rich priest who quoted the more lisping Greek poets, burned incense, was rumored to be a Vatican spy for the Allied side, and—some said—taught a few of his campus pets the finer points of classical buggery and joint-copping."

Fitzgerald, of course, was not a homosexual.

We were drawn like birds to livid stretches of crawling skies. It was the world, we felt, of the enigmatic, the lonely, the courageous, the stubborn, the irreconcilable.

Fliers, when Jay and I decided to take to the air, were still like the exuberant explorers who followed Columbus; they knew the world was round, but its perils and its secrets were only hinted at. For us the air was a kind of mass that had come out of the sea to dry itself.

Flying till the Great War had been a kind of sport, with the two solemn Wright brothers, manufacturers of bicycles, in their caps and derbies giving it a comic touch of sly impudence. The first airplane I saw in 1911 looked—because we had not yet trained our eyes to the scaling down of space—only about a foot wide, even if it was above five hundred feet over Lakewood, New Jersey, where we had gone to cure my grandmother's gout that summer with a diet of graham crackers and water (she cheated).

The Great War used the airplane at first as one of its more foolish military toys, then found there was some information to be gained from viewing the enemy from above. The Germans, always alert to new games of terror, bombed Paris in tiny Taubes and mangled a few civilians. The early fliers in 1914 flung bricks at each other, fired pistols, then gingerly mounted machine guns that usually shot off their own props. But mechanical progress in wartime is fast, and soon bombers, scouts, camera airplanes were up there, and heroes were made, usually just before they romantically fell in flames. How could we resist it? It was knighthood returned. The clean life of canvas-and-wood birds, the silver of spinning props, the blue bowl of heaven over one, a man-to-man shoot-out, wheeling like a nursery ballet in wool clouds. A wave and salute as your gallant enemy went down like an unreal dream falling.

Eddie Custer was a square young man, dark, greasy, with large skillful thumbs. He worked in the bronze-casting department at Kite Metal Forming, and on the side took people up in his biplane at a dollar a throw for a seven-minute flight. He claimed to have flown for the Wrights. He was either a liar or a poet. The plane was an outmoded pusher type, a looped bicycle chain driving two propellers from behind; it was a condemned army test plane he had bought cheap and rebuilt. There was a lot to do on it.

"Sure, I'll teach you to fly."

"It can fly?" I asked.

"Oh, sure. It's a sweet job. I used white pine instead of spruce for front and rear spars. But that was bad. The white pine snapped like rock candy under a blow. I had to do it all over in solid spruce."

We flew at Custer's Meadows all that summer vacation—on flat land eight miles from town at Lundberg Station on the interurban trolley line. The meadow was not as smooth as a beach. It was fifty acres with some trees, and dangerously close to power lines, trolley wires and telegraph poles. We learned to steer, bank, and baby the four-cylinder cranky motor. Old Mrs. Custer, who farmed a bit, had been pleased to help her son Eddie rebuild the plane.

"Use the meadow all you want. But when you do, just run the cows to safe cover and don't slice them with your fans. I have a few good Jerseys and Guernseys in the herd."

"We'll be careful, Mrs. Custer."

To protect the machine Jack had built a rough wooden shed on the meadow. It was not a secluded place to practice flying; two roads were in sight, and the trolley riders waved wildly at us as the bouncing summer cars with their straw seats passed, striking sparks from the overhead power wire.

Jack launched his wheelless machine into the air by dropping a 1,600-pound weight in a tower attached to a pull rope connected to the plane. The tug of the weight would launch us on skids into the air after a short run, and the detachable rope fell away. It was primitive and we weren't aware what damned fools we were in this out-of-date craft.

It was exciting finding out why a flying machine flew and how it had to be controlled. Discoveries came to us all that summer, and in August we were flying solo in a circle, five-minute flights, the machine ovaling the field a few dozen times without a stop. Those were marvelous first days for us. We flew twenty-four miles in thirty-eight minutes and three seconds. It was an *airplane,* not a flying machine any more.

157

The Bishop, to our surprise, was pleased.

"If angels fly, why not God's children?"

"Of course, why not?" Jay shrugged his shoulders.

"Angels don't mount machine guns."

Jay carefully adjusted his starched cuffs. "It's amazing how many people still think it's not practical."

"The trolley riders see you. They know it's practical," said the Bishop.

Jack Custer suggested we fly only when the cars weren't passing, if they bothered us, but there were more cars than there used to be and we didn't mind.

"Funny thing, the trolley riders, the regulars, don't even bother to look up from their papers any more when you two are in the air. They hoped you'd fall and they'd see something exciting."

The Bishop one evening folded his glasses and put them away. "People keep stopping me in the street. They wonder if you two aren't neglecting your college with all this flying. I'd like to tell them to peel their own parsnips. Maybe you'll take me up someday."

"Maybe, sir."

I said, "The U.S. Army has talked about the future of the airplane, its wonders as a weapon of defense and attack."

The Bishop looked up from the tablecloth where he had been outlining a sermon. "Do you read Thoreau?"

I said, "Henry David Thoreau? But of course. Favorite of ours."

Jay quoted, " 'The mass of men lead lives of quiet desperation'?"

"No, not that. I was thinking of 'Thank God, man cannot as yet fly, and lay waste the sky as well as the earth.' "

Jay looked up from his coffee cup. "There are times, sir, when practical men must protect the dreamers, even the great dreamers, like our mutual friend Thoreau."

"I hope you and Bill aren't thinking of flying in the war?"

I said I had to go home for supper.

Back in my room that night I sat by the window in the humid Jersey heat, looking out at the stars, listening to the clatter of a late wagon, the polite hiss of a rubber-tired carriage passing on Frenchman Street. From the back of the houses on the block came the whispered hoot and holler of Negro laughter as the help cleaned up late. I lay down on the warm bed and, sweating lightly, fell asleep. War was excitement, but what if we were to die in it? Death was so damn permanent. Were ecstasy and despair just two spellings of the same word?

I came awake aware of someone in the dark room by my bed. It was my grandmother in her bulky Dresden-blue kimono; she was bigger and wider than ever. Since the death of my grandfather she had run the mills and the foundries, although Harry was the big name on the stationery. The Kite enterprises were doing well with war orders from the Allies; somehow what had been a sinking family business was now prospering, making molds, dies and special tools, shipping millions of yards of mustard-colored cotton cloth overseas, converting raw goods to yardage, sewing tents and truck covers for the armies.

"William, you asleep?" My grandmother sat down in my grand-father's old club chair that I had taken over.

"I guess not."

"You're going to fly in the war." It was a statement, not a question, and I heard what was almost despondence in this rock-hard old woman.

"Well, we talked about it, but—"

"The Bishop phoned. He had an idea you and Eliot would be off soon." Her voice was registering a tremble.

"Gosh, we thought we'd fooled him."

"I'm just an ignorant old woman." (This was her favorite gambit when wanting attention and a bit of pity before she hit out at you.) "That's all, an old hulk . . . but you're all I have, William. All."

"There's Harry."

"There's Harry, whoever he is, really. And you. It's not our fight over there, William. It's crazy. Let them blow their fool heads off. President Wilson said, 'We're too proud to fight.' "

"You can't trust a Democrat, you always say. Besides, is it right for the Kite companies to grow rich providing supplies of war, and feel so holy about staying out? It's civilization we're saving."

"Civilization phawww! I'll be dead when you come back. If you come back. You'll leave a hole in an old lady's heart."

I got out of bed and cried with her.

CHAPTER 18

ONE DAY we got the telegram to report to the RFC base in Canada. (We had sent a letter signed "Major J. Custer," saying we were trained expert fliers, and he vouched for us.) The Bishop insisted we take him up before we went off to the wars.

"I'll soon be up there permanently anyway. Call this one an inspection tour."

The Bishop was old to us, and there were times when he was creaky in the joints, but he was always in full voice. His salt-and-pepper beard framed a ruddy face amazingly free of wrinkles, and his eyes still had the stare of a proud and easy-to-ruffle hawk. It was a special day, he told us, as he opened his eyes in the big family bed and Jay and I greeted him with a pair of goggles as a gift. The sunlight was dancing along the old wallpaper, smearing the dresser mirror, a dresser he had bought for his wife when they were just starting married life; it had moved with them, he told us, on the preaching circuit when he was vocal about hellfire and faith. "More hellfire than messages of faith in those days."

He put his bare feet (I remember my grandfather saying "A man of character always has clean feet") on the hooked rug, and the tails of his nightshirt flapped in the breeze from the open window. He stretched, the joints cracking, and he washed in the bathroom—door open—at the end of the hall: "At least some newfangled ideas like bathrooms have merit."

He dressed in his loose white linen suit over the soft black shirt with the hard white collar, and the Bishop and Jay and I went down to breakfast. Tillie Hawk, a part-Indian, weathered, leathery spinster, the hired girl of the period, had the oatmeal on the table and the browned toast.

"Two eggs and bacon, Tillie, and don't sass me back, I'm your spiritual head."

"Oatmeal, Bishop, is what ole folk need most, good fer 'em."

"Woman," said Jay, sitting down at table, "this is a special day, a time of covenant. Get us a good breakfast to be lamented on. If that is the Lord's will."

"Don't mock, Jay," said his father.

"You really goin' up flyin' in them buzzin' thangs, Bishop?"

The Bishop beat his spoon with a ringing sound against the water glass. "Eggs and bacon. Yes, I'm going to fly. The loss will not be great if it is too much for me."

The Bishop smiled at us as Tillie brought the eggs and bacon and the fresh biscuits.

"You get the misery tonight, Bishop, don't yell fer me to run up with no hot-watter bottle."

"Hold your tongue, woman, or I'll send you back to the reservation. More biscuits."

"You'll git sick, whirling around up there, and toss yer food."

Jay said, "I doubt it."

I added, "Calm as a millpond today."

We ate with relish the crisp smoking bacon, broke the egg yolks and sopped them up with buttered biscuits. The Bishop drank the one cup of coffee Tillie set before him, and she shook her head when his eyes pleaded for another; Doc Welton was firm about black coffee with his blood pressure.

"Come with me, boys." The Bishop brushed crumbs from his pearl-buttoned vest and went into the parlor and picked up a worn volume of Donne's *Sermons*. He looked up at the mantel clock, compared its time with his double-lidded watch.

"A little time to wait."

"Not too much."

" 'The Heavens are not less constant because they move continually, because they continually move one and the same way. The Earth is not the more constant because it lyes stil continually, because continually it changes, and melts in al parts thereof. Man, who is the noblest part of the Earth, melts so away, as if he were a statue, not of Earth. . . . Ascension is my Soules pac and measure, but precipitation my bodies. And even Angells whose home is Heaven, and who are winged too, yet have a ladder to goe to Heaven, by steps . . .' "

There was the *beep-beep* of my grandmother's rubber-bulb auto horn out front. She had bought an air-cooled Franklin. The Bishop closed the book. *"A ladder indeed!"*

161

We went out to where Billy Brunswick was sitting in the car, all the brass shining like minted gold. My grandmother in her heron-feathered hat was in the back seat.

"You're a sport, Bishop."

"I'm the great cockalorum this morning, Mrs. Kite, and of that there is no doubt."

"Pile in. Ride in front, William."

Tillie watched from the porch as we started off. The Bishop doffed his hat to a passing couple he knew.

"How do you feel, Bishop?" my grandmother asked.

"I wouldn't want to spread it around, Maude, but I feel very elated."

"Sure you do. But they'll never get me up in those things."

Custer's field was worn and dusty; our continual flying had done away with much of the meadow grass. It had been leveled and rolled, and the big double shed under the elms held the airplane. Jack Custer was directing some boys who were pushing out the machine. The wind seemed steady and easy, not dangerous.

Jack politely took out his cud of chewing tobacco and hid it behind his back at the sight of his guests. "There she is, spit-polished shiny and ready, Bishop. Good morning, Mrs. Kite."

"Isn't very big, is it?"

"No, Mrs. Kite."

Jay, his cap pulled down to his eyes, a pair of goggles in his gloved hand, tapped a wing. "Toss you, Bill."

"No, you take up the Bishop."

The Bishop said, "Let William fly me."

My grandmother said, "You still want to go up, Bishop?"

"I don't expect to live beyond a hundred, so it's now."

I climbed into the machine and got behind the controls on the lower wing of the plane. Jay helped the Bishop up on the seat beside me.

I said, "Better leave the hat on the ground, Bishop."

"It's not dignified, William, a churchman bareheaded."

Jay grinned and handed the Bishop his own cap, and the old man took off his derby and jammed the cap over his white head. He pushed his beard down under his turned-up jacket collar.

"Any time you're ready, Bill."

My grandmother opened her sunshade.

The propellers sang into life, spinning like silver coins through whose transparent whirling discs the calm countryside could be seen. I signaled to the tower at the other end of the field. The weight there dropped, the rope it pulled rushed the plane forward, and as it lifted the towrope fell away. The Bishop held on and I felt our world expand; then we were over bushes, then over a shed and some brindle cows, and beyond were trees and those too fell away. We were off the earth on which the Bishop had walked so long. The weight of gravity seemed fallen from us. He turned to look at me. I was grinning at him, and we winked at each other.

"Higher! Higher!" shouted the Bishop.

"Three hundred feet up," I howled back over the din of the engine and its clattering gear.

"Higher!"

The machine began to turn, and in the beautiful blue day it slid to one side and then started to climb.

"Three hundred fifty."

The yellow crystal sunlight, crisp and clean to inhale, was sweet-tasting, and the earth seemed so wide and never-ending below that I saw the Bishop gulp in awe. His beard had broken loose from its confining folds of cloth, and it tangled and rolled in wind-teased coils, reminding me of that engraving after Michelangelo's painting on the ceiling of the Sistine Chapel that Miss Lamb had shown me once: God the Father creating the universe. I remembered a fierceness of power, all hair and drapery, assisted by handy angels. God now by my side in a bicycle cap, all curls and smiles.

The wind was soon too strong for talking. The Bishop just pointed up at the plenitude of sky.

There was an easy buzzing clatter. Our cloth-covered wings were shiny in the sun. Below, Jay, Jack, Billy Brunswick and my grandmother waved. The Bishop smiled and pushed aside the wind-whipped beard. The world seemed far away. It was like what Judgment Day could be if one believed in God's mercy—cheerful, sunny, full of grace. For good or evil, I sensed, the world was rushing forward to some future still as opaque as those clouds to the west. Better not to know, better to live for this day, I decided, to know with Donne:

163

Fire and Aire, Water and Earth, are not the Elements of man; Inward decay, and outward violence, bodily pain, and sorrow of heart may be rather stiled his Elements; And though he be destroyed by these, yet he consists of nothing but these. . . .

The Bishop could not shout over the roar of the two motors and the wind. He pointed upward again. I nodded. Below us the cud-chewing cows cropped grass. In the bland neutral sky the sun remained high.

The next day Jay and I entrained for Canada with long underwear, money belts, lice powder and two ivory-handled .45 Colts. We were off for the war and bursting with illusions. Later Jay said we had betrayed our youth. I always feel our youth betrayed us, made us blind to reality.

The prosaic system of training in Canada was to shove everybody into a fast training course with Sopwith Pups and kill off all the awkward chaps. It was beyond simplification—toward the essence of war, factual and obvious. Jay and I were scared pissless by the speed, relative, of those small wire-and-canvas trainers, but we caught the hang of it. Brooks Brothers made us uniforms; we learned to carry swagger sticks. And once every two weeks we hired a car and drove to Toronto, where we ate, drank, went to bed with local talent and dreamed we were falling in flames. We made friends with a Canadian named Harry Glenn Moore and saw him mashed to jelly when he ran his trainer into a hillside.

One rainy sleety day Charlie Huttonbok showed up at our training base with an alligator bag and his guitar. We hugged like lovers, drank warm beer.

"This is it, fellas—*this* is it!"

"How'd you wangle it?"

"Got Pop's English wine agent to write a letter."

On a hurtling train one cold winter night near dawn with a sudden blizzard beating against Mr. Pullman's "Palace Car" windows we lay in our berths hoping to beat the ice into the St. Lawrence. The telegraph poles went by on a slant, meeting the express with its roar, a grind of red fire, a row of yellow windows and the *bang-bang* of steel on good ballasted track. Here we were, going far out over the

164

rounded surface of the globe, heading to England, to war across the sea, and I remembered my grandfather reading from Homer of "the wine-dark sea" and the "rosy-fingered dawn."

The Cubist-painted Cunarder, pounding on at a steady series of knots-at-sea, came tooting into Liverpool, the city of soot and dirt, gray and brown bricks. It was Saturday and we three were a bit pale, standing there at the rail, lonely, so far from home . . . the women in uniform all long of tooth, the officers with pips all very snooty. The dirty, sweat-smelling boat train was smaller than any we had ever seen, and its whistle had a shrill, ladylike toot. The people spoke a strange tongue that was nearly related to what we had been taught. "Lousy broad a's," said Jay. At the hollow glass-roofed London station the murky fog hung yellow in slowly moving coils, and we smelled burning coal and wet streets and cold pork sandwiches mixed with axle grease and the damp woolen clothes of the pale, war-worried Londoners.

We stood, Charlie said, "lonely as survivors of an Indian raid," with our traveling bags, and mufflers tight around our chests and throats.

Jay said, "Land of Dickens and Keats, hello."

A neat young officer with classic features, dressed in an over-creased uniform, came over smiling. "You're the Canadians. Follow me."

"Americans," corrected Jay.

"You're all Americans. You mean U.S.A."

Charlie said, "Well, kick my ass."

"Oh, the bloody war will, Yank. This way to a cabby."

The taxi went slowly along in the thick fog, and Jay wondered how people could live in this climate.

"It isn't always this depressing, chaps. Sometimes it just rains. But we'll not stay here. You're to train in Camels—then on your way to France in a few weeks."

Jay said, "Good-o, sport."

"Never been out of the United States before?"

I said, "Canada."

"Of course. Canada."

The cab rubbed against a great horse-drawn dray carrying barrels of ROYAL CREST STOUT AND ALE.

"Some Americans giving you blokes a dinner. Henry James is expected."

Jay said, "The Civil War slacker?"

The dinner was dull. Henry James mumbled long Henry James sentences, and we saw our first English butler in action. Mrs. Van Berg, our hostess, in a low-cut blue velvet gown, kept swinging her long string of pearls with a plump hand. "Henry James, oh dear, he's such a snob—unless his tie sets just right, he doesn't ignite."

I dreamed that night in a hotel room of the scarlet lobster in its mayonnaise dressing crawling over my pillow, but I slept till the boy called Boots came to knock on the door with the morning paper—GREAT BATTLE ON SOMME. We three gingerly ate kidneys, grilled, and found the coffee as dreadful as the weather. The next few weeks we flew Camels in Essex, saw more young fliers die, learned how to use the Lewis gun, the Vickers gun, read maps, remember signals.

Then we were leaning uncertainly on the rail of a blacked-out Channel steamer, the smoke of the funnel being torn to shreds by a brisk wind from France ("Fair stood the wind for . . ."), and officers were holding their belted stomachs as the steamer dipped and tossed in sea spume till someone said that thin muddy line was Calais.

"Calais?" Charlie asked, pointing. "Looks like Asbury Park."

"Oh, yes, that's hit," said a batman. "Bloody fucking plice hit is too. The hoors all over fifty."

The French landscape from the train looked a great deal like New Jersey, only the houses were older and all of stone, till we saw ruins. The first view of Paris burst on us with a chatter of what could only be French, and we rode in pale daylight in an open car, lettered BEF, among the bare chestnut trees, the spires of Notre Dame overhead. Jay said, "It isn't at all like the Pissarros and the Manets."

We stayed at the Hotel Meurice on the Rue de Rivoli, and we couldn't even unpack.

"Too short a day to waste in Paris by resting," I said.

Jay said, "We move to Arras tonight. Let's see the Tuileries Gardens and walk to the Place de la Concorde."

"If I must. What about Les Girls?" Charlie asked.

"No time."

It was all very shabby and war-tired. Wide unswept boulevards,

166

people badly dressed, a smoky sky, and bits of pale green made a sad picture all the length of the Avenue des Champs-Élysées. A girl clung to Jay's arm; she was scented with candied violets.

"Uloo, Tommy. Zig-zig wif me?"

"After the war."

"Go 'ump you *gran'mère!*"

That afternoon Jay was examined by a superior and wise flying doctor who said Jay's sense of balance was wrong. Charlie and I left for Arras without him.

BOOK FIVE

FROM WILLIAM KITE'S POCKET NOTEBOOK

Those who are weak eat herbs . . .
　　　　　　　　　　　　—St. Paul

Everything nailed down is coming loose . . .
　　　　—Angel Gabriel in *Green Pastures*

*The truth is our tragedy is often not tragedy,
only compromise.*　　　　　—W. K.

CHAPTER 19
NOW

—MAN, MR. KITE, that was some hoedown last night. I thought you might need a cup of black coffee. I mean the squares really cut it up down here in the country, don't they? You sure you don't want cream or sugar? I didn't think I'd make the scene this morning myself. You all right, Mr. Kite? You think you should be sitting here in the sun? I mean you're not doing the Yoga self-laceration bit? These weekends are from Weirdsville, but I went to Bennington with Marcia Pfaelzer and we had this pad in the Village last year when we were writing ad copy for TV daytime. Slobtime for the American housewife. I bet you thought every Bennington chick got a job with Random House and Bennett Cerf or some book publisher? Oh, the Village is all right. Everybody there—surfboarder, Fire Islander, Madison Avenue hi-fi owner—thinks he's a gasser. And the kooks and the beats try and give you the idea that smoking pot and making out daisy-chain style is what every chick is dying for. The necessity to struggle isn't down there, and I was raised square: Unitarian agnostic. I didn't unbend easy.

—Look, Mr. Kite, I want to ask you something, like I was just any square putting the bite on you, know what I mean, who needs help. I've been doing this copywriting bit for two years now. I'm getting to be an old chick spinning in a mechanical orbit. I mean, man, I'm nearly twenty-two, and I want to write, I mean way-out, avant-garde as hell—the solid jive like the great cats you knew, you know: Hemingway, Camus, Fitzgerald, Sartre, Faulkner, Tjaden, Joyce. Maybe they date, but they're solid to me. Well, you could have knocked me over with Goldwater when last night Sam said you were

171

there with them all making the scene, cutting it up with all those wonderful wailing heads. All making a score. He wasn't putting me on, was he? It must have been Cloud Nine. I mean, man, you don't meet that kind of quality, firm and fully packed, no more. Don't think I'm a numskull with no roots. I dig Zen, Pop Art, Cage and the theater of the absurd, Genet and New Wave movies. They put the whip to us at Bennington and I've gone the route, from Chaucer, Freud to Kafka, *Catcher in the Rye,* Mailer, *The Connection,* Albee, ESP, and the stuff Huxley sniffs . . .

—I want to write. The way I see it, you having made it with all the big types in those days, you know. I don't mean you're old, Mr. Kite, or square. But all I hear is, baby, read, study, write. That's for the birds; that's creep advice. That's vacillating between extremes, huh? Dead *l'art pour l'art.* All the flip side of nothing.

—Now, Tjaden's stuff, that sends me like a kite. I snap my cap. I get on with him strong and clear. How'd he start? I mean I don't want to write the way he wrote, but I feel reading him can turn me on. Then I figure if I had the stuff, I'd perk. I'd go into high without touching first. Like, man, this story I've been writing. For me the decisive moment is always ahead, still to be endured. It's about this square chick that comes from, say, St. Louis, and she goes to a cornball big girls' school, see, all class and slogans, say Vassar or Smith, not that I want to do the Mary McCarthy bit; for us she's a moldy fig now; that's jazz talk for Dixieland, that means she's for the older rug-cutters who aren't cooking on the top burners any more. But anyway this chick, I write, she's bright and she's bushy-tailed and scratching and laughing, and she and a roommate, they come to New York after graduating and getting fitted for pessaries. No, Mr. Kite, I'm not putting you on. It's no rib. And they find this lousy pad in the Village, but the roommate—who has an income—runs off with this ofay-hating CORE black cat, only he's camping, see, scoring in the gay set, picking up black-leather-jacket studs in the toilets of the 42nd Street Public Library, and getting arrested for lewd vag, copping joints at all-night old Bogart movies, and she, the roommate, goes back to Alabama to keep the nigrahs from sitting with white kids. Crazy, isn't it, man? It's pretty good writing here. Drowning in the insensibility of our lost years, the haunting sense of irremediable loss. Great. But drama, I mean. Jim Baldwin can do the jive from his cookie-cutter hate-Mr.-Charlie angle, but you have to feel it from a chick's bird's-eye view. Check.

—Can I heat up that coffee, Mr. Kite? Well, the girl that's left, the one that my story is about, she doesn't get hooked on H mainlining, only a little pot smoking, and she doesn't go shack up with no cool Coltrane horn player or beat poet who can spell s-h-i-t. No, she gets next to this double-dome from Columbia, a molecular physicist, the new tribal symbol, who's working on his Ph.D., see, to get his mind off fallout—by writing a paper that all the great comic-strip characters are homos; he expects to knock the professors on their prats with this. You know: Mutt and Jeff, Li'l Abner and his brother, Dick Tracy and his sidekick, that Charlie Brown trying to turn on a little pal. Crazy, man, crazy. So this kook and the chick, they make out in a phone booth, during a picketing of the United Nations South Africans, and she finds out she's been unhappy in her orgasms till now because she never went at it standing up. Now she's riding lasciviously, but the Columbia square, he has a wife and three kids in Rye, New York, it turns out—a broad with a ferocious, unimpeachable integrity of getting properly *stupped* twice a week—and *no* wife trading. You know the type—they think Tennessee Williams is daring. Worse, the wife, she has all the bread, the money, Mr. Kite, and if he leaves Mama's pad, why, the Columbia square, he's out on his ass. He's no Doc Teller as a physicist—he likes people. So she decides to dedicate herself to despair, smoke nonfilter cigarettes, take on causes that scare Republicans, know what I mean; tolerance, not just of making it with a Negro but also taking him to lunch, or the Modern Museum, maybe go real ape and join the Youth Corps. Up to here my story is pure Spinoza. Just then right in the kisser my girl, she misses two periods and she's going to have a little chick herself. . . . That's as far as I got, Mr. Kite. Frankly it dips to a quintessence of current taste; it goes soap opera on me. I mean you take all the things that can happen to any cat, and you write it out straight and it's corny. *Peyton Place* and Irving Stone. Know what I mean? Man. Experience—it's being born, finding out the answers, going broke, shacking up, getting the rent paid, making a little more bread so you can ride in an E-series Jag or buy better pot, go to the Newport Jazz Festival, or putting out for a creep, carrying on for somebody that doesn't see you for Shinola. That's what's the hard part about writing the way my woofers and dials read it. *How* to keep it from sounding so cornball square. I figured you, Mr. Kite, knowing all those Nobel-Prize, Pulitzer high scorers, you'd tell me how to keep going. What was it like when *they* started, how'd they come to write it

173

down? . . . I don't suppose they knew they were jiving, or that it was a beat world. The chicks they write of, I mean not like my chick, they were kind of dumb, I suppose; all they did was stomp the Charleston and wear funny clothes and ride like around in those divine heaps like Stutz Bearcats and go to joints like cellar speakeasies. I don't see them being real; they only are the funny drawings, the songs. "Melancholy Baby." Now, that's a gasser, sends you for laughs. Man, the sentiment, it's cubed. You really felt any of it? . . . Mr. Kite, you don't look so good. You're kind of turning blue. . . . Maybe I better get you a real hot cup of coffee and a blanket. We'll gab tonight and I'll let you read part of my story. Sam says you're one hell of a cat when it comes to knowing about all this jazz. Be seeing you, Pop. . . .

1924

I get impressions of a badly cut movie film; a St. Christopher medal buried in black curly chest hair, a girl—*Lumen Christi,* what a build—on a bicycle talking very loud at some young men shouting *Mamma mia* and *Ciao;* the *pasta asciutta,* white grapes on my table, the Galleria Colonna, a bottle of St. Estèphe . . . the heat of a Roman-spring shirt collar melting the hip aching still, remembering an old wound, a couple at the next table drinking Chianti, rubbing faces together, laughing as he pinches her milk-white thighs, an emblem on his black shirt denoting this is a new Italy: the visitors' toilets flush, the babies come on time; my volume of Kierkegaard is open: "There may be a system of logic, a system of being there can never be."

"Scusi," said the waiter. He was from the Piedmont and he didn't like Rome. For four days I had lunched in the Galleria and we got talking friendly and I tried my Italian on him, which was not very good because my teacher hadn't been very good. I wondered if in the Piedmont there was a dichotomy between experience and consciousness.

"Quanto è il conto?"

He shrugged. *"Quattrocento lire."*

"Get me some Strega. A bottle as a gift. *Prendere. Vorrei comprare."* I acted it out. A bottle, a drinking gesture. "Strega?"

174

"Volentieri."

I sat wondering if I should walk to the Pincio or call the firm of Serbati e di Gioconde, who were the Kite Machinery agents for Italy. I had been in Rome a week, hovering like a feather, and hadn't called them. I had diverse, conflicting reactions. Who the hell wanted cotton-spinning machinery anyway? And Mussolini's credit was not good. I wanted just to sit around Rome, look at a lot of artistic junk they had dug up, see the Michelangelos in the Sistine Chapel. When I was younger I had known someone who had a set of photographs of them, an intricate arabesque of bodies, poses, muscles.

"Ecco," said the waiter from the Piedmont. He handed me a bottle wrapped in green paper. *"Nient'altro?"*

I put down some lire and told him to keep the change.

"Grazie mille."

"Prego," I said, and then the goddamn *"Ciao."* Sad story, that little Piedmontese: Served in the war in the mountains above the Po, where the Austrians fired heavy howitzers from Skoda on them all day and attacked by night . . . no sleep, not enough food: *risotto alla milanese* and a vile white Capri, and *stufato fatto con il lesso,* which I gathered was a soup, meat stew made from dead gun mules . . . driven from the heights called Pocol, defeated by the Bavarian Alpenkorps at Caporetto . . . wounded in the groin, but, *grazie a Dio,* nothing to make a capon of a man, then walking back in the yellow dust to the family farm, there finding his brazen barefoot wife saying he was dead in the war, and she had two children with her new husband Pietro Bembo, that fat sono'bitch profiteer whose father—and the cocksucking village priest—had kept him out of the army. So Bembo beat him up in the goat shed with an ox yoke and he went away bad hurt. What was the use? She was pregnant like an elephant and didn't want him there no more. In Naples he got the clap; in Milano he lost a finger in a machine that made motorcycle parts. A man has no luck if he's due for a bad time. In Rome he lived with four other waiters in one room in a decaying house on the Via Arco Monte. Two of the waiters—Sicilian scum—were in love, and he and the other waiter Andrea went to the whores on the Via Ferro; but the cost spoiled the pleasure. It was a sad life and an inauspicious future, and only drinking stuff stronger than Freisa and *barbera* wines made it bearable. No?

I said I hadn't drunk anything but light wines since the war, and

175

that started his beaky ovoid face off on the Austrians in the mountains and how the outposts were overrun in the night; in the morning the dead sentries were icy-stiff, all covered with a glaze of frozen blood so they looked like holy statues colored and varnished in the Church of Santa Maria Cosmedin. He had the knack, he said, of all Piedmontese, who carried nuances to extremes.

I was pretty tired of it all, of him, his story, and took my bottle and went to the john—the *Signori* with its sign ENTRATA, as if it needed to be identified on a hot day by anything but its fragrance. I came out, walked past the shops on the Corso, looking at leatherwork, plaster saints that glowed in the dark, rosaries, editions of Dante, fake Greek and Roman fragments. I went down the Corso to the Via della Muratte and to the *piazza* of the ugliest fountain in Rome. The rim of the Fontana di Trevi was black with tourists. The water wasn't flowing; there was always something wrong with plumbing in Rome, and the giant statue of Neptune led by the Tritons looked like scaly lepers, their dried bodies stained yellow, the bottom of the fountain green with scum and floored with discarded cigarette packages. Two dirty kids were slipping around inside the basin, hunting the coins the tourists had thrown in to make a wish. The only wish I wanted to make was that I wouldn't have to interview any more agents of Kite Machinery in Europe. Either they owed us money they didn't pay or they had our machines in warehouses, machines they couldn't sell. . . . A Junoesque blonde and a Doberman pinscher passed.

I felt better on the Via Condotti and walked slowly toward the Piazza di Spagna, my favorite spot in Rome so far. I had been there every afternoon with the brassy sun just right behind me, tossing just the proper kind of rays onto the Spanish Steps, the Church of the Trinità dei Monti above them. Everything terracotta-brown, the sky of a lacquer and gouache azure, the women in tomb-painting colors that fitted the mood, the men dark lounging shadows. I liked the perspective, the Fontana della Barcaccia, shaped like a boat; the sound and smell didn't bother me. There were flower markets all along the steps, the sellers with no look of expediency or expectance. The too-sweet colors of dying blossoms were subdued by the heat of the day. All around the reddish-brown houses. A nun reading *L'Ultimo dei Mohecanni* by James Fenimore Cooper. I don't know why it all got me.

I didn't give a damn whether a church was used for goats or

176

prayer; I was interested in form, not dogma. But I couldn't escape the fact that a sense of sin and glory, and a desire to show the power and respect of the builders, their profession of faith, had done well here.

I stood leaning on the cane I carried to favor my hurt hip; I could do without it, but a cane gave me a feeling of being casual. I didn't have to carry bundles, it said. The terraced gardens of the baroque balustraded houses had palm trees, hanging vines, and oleanders in pots. From a certain spot I could see a panorama of cypresses and olives. I wondered if the large palace on the right was the Villa Medici; I was too warm, too lazy, to find out. I went into a small café that smelled of salami and *caffè espresso* and ordered a glass of Chianti. The large woman behind the counter was eating *cece* soaked in garlic and tomato sauce. I asked her, as I sipped the wine, if there was a phone. She thought it might be connected again and pointed to the left, where it hung in a corner on the spotted ochre wall.

I looked in my notebook and asked for the number of Serbati e di Gioconde. I waited while the fat woman ate and scratched and ignored me. Flies sank slowly onto a ribbon of sticky paper hanging from the tin ceiling. Sound came from the phone, and at last a man with a cigarette-charred voice: *"Buon giorno."*

"Serbati, di Gioconde?"

"Pronto."

I asked if either was in, and the voice said it was Signor Serbati speaking. I told him who I was and he broke into English. "How you no come to see us, Signor Kite? We hear you come to Roma, some time now, before today—ah?"

"Just a few days. I've been busy. I mean, you know, settling in."

"Ah, you must have dinnah with us. Di Gioconde, I sorry to say, is up north. Great loss in firm there of our machines. A fire. And machines not paid for, set fire for insurance. Business is bod, very bod. *Ma basta.*"

"It's not too good back in the States. There's hope it will get better."

"You come dinnah my house with wife and the bambinos. Six we are, Holy Maria protect us. We live across the Tiber beyond Castello Sant'Angelo. I pick you up tonight at your hotel, Signor Kite?"

"Tomorrow, if it's all the same. Pensione Colonna, Via Seminario."

177

"I know, I know the place. Is here a note, American Expresso have a letter for you. *Sì,* we see you for *l'heure de cocktail,* no? Pick you up at six; we have the cocktail first. My wife she make *una sogliola alla marinara* like you never eat before."

"Good."

"Arrivederci."

I hung up, pleased he hadn't asked me if I wanted girls, antiques, something I wasn't supposed to be able to get without channels. It was only a short walk to the American Express on the Piazza di Spagna. The clerk said there was no letter for me. I was puzzled and decided to try Thomas Cook on the Via Veneto. Italians sometimes confuse the two and tell ribald anecdotes about both.

I had guessed right. At Thomas Cook there was a small envelope of crisp blue addressed: *Will. Grant Kite, Esq., to be called for.* In it on a folded sheet of the same blue there was a note typed on some faltering portable typewriter, keys out of alignment—a machine that had long needed a ribbon change.

DEAR WILLIAM KITE:

Sorry you couldn't find us. We're holed up at Via Margutta 47, Apt. C3. The neighborhood is a foul nest of artists and loafers. But El is working like mad on *the* novel. So drop in anyway, any time. We are not near a phone.

N. M.

(Mrs. Martin)

Via Margutta 47 was one of those romantic-to-look-at, miserable-to-live-in buildings of stone, rubble, clay and rotting supporting timbers that could have been there during the Renaissance and withstood several battering sieges since. It had been only roughly repaired with shoddy workmanship. One entered through large gates, and inside there was an open shed where some sculptor had begun a statue with a flawed bit of marble and given it up. The several doors I passed going up on the outside staircase gave off the odor of turpentine, cat urine, olive oil and linseed paint, so there must have been artists behind them and what is called an *avventura,* an affair. C3 was chalked on a door faded from what had once been red into a pale pink. I knocked, saw a small typewritten note thumbtacked under the C3: "Don't knock, walk through—pass 1st balcony, turn right past hammock." (Someone nearby was singing "Santa Lucia Lontaria.")

I opened the door and found myself in a roofed passage where stood a beheaded sewing machine corpse, a dismantled motorbike, and a frame used for stretching washed lace curtains. Several canvases stood with their faces to the wall, and a row of red clay pots filled with dead stalks. Beyond was a private little balcony with blooming yellow trumpet and bougainvillea vines, and under it a hammock with someone in it. I walked forward to find a dark-haired young woman in a man's shirt, bare-legged under a short flared peasant skirt, sitting in the hammock, shelling peas with an easy rhythm into a pot set between her unshod feet.

She was extreme in the sense that her hair was very black, her skin very white, and she was beautiful—real, not ephemeral—not in the way one says "a very beautiful woman," meaning she isn't really plain, or says "a beautiful woman," meaning she's better-looking than most. She was in her absurd simplicity a true beauty, a bit warm, irked, lazily shelling peas, the soles of her bare feet logically soiled by the dusty flagstones. I thought of a *cortigiana* by Titian, of Atlantic City and a girl in 1914 in a red bathing suit.

"Che vuole?" she said.

"Permesso?"

"In che posso servirle?" You wouldn't be Bill Kite?"

"I am."

"Sit down. I'm Mrs. Martin." She threw the pea pods from her lap and offered me a long white hand. I shook it and sat down on a backless kitchen chair facing her. She had a marvelous face—constant and not hostile—very classic-Greek with that nose that comes almost straight down from the wide brow, her eyes just a little mismatched (a bit walleyed) and the mouth wide, spoiling, I suppose, the symmetry of the face, but the result of everything taken together—beauty.

"I got your note at Thomas Cook."

She laughed, lay back in the hammock . . . naked legs—smooth as an eggshell—up. "We got your message from the faggoty Embassy attaché that you were in Rome looking for El. But we lost the name of your *pensione,* so you can see everything is very distracted here."

I also saw she was pregnant, not too much, just a little bulge, a tummy below the long torso. The breasts were already enlarged. I wondered if they contained milk and felt pleased at the thought.

"El's sleeping," she said. "He's a bit hung-over. We had a hell of a night. Lazzaro the futurist sold a painting to some Greek and it *was* a

179

night. Yes, you could say it was quite a night." She rubbed her sinuses, her temples.

I held out the bottle of Strega, still wrapped in the green paper. "I brought something. I was going to give it to a businessman here in Rome. But here."

"Thanks, Bill. We can always get liquor. We'll most likely die of hunger. Not really. Thanks."

"How is he?"

"Better. He had malaria bad last year. Then some American magazine folded on him when we were strapped. He's been writing for pulps to make the rent and *pasta* money."

"Is the novel any good?"

She shrugged her shoulders and put out a foot and kicked slightly at the flagstones to start the hammock rocking. She rocked and I watched. Beyond in the street a hawker cried out bargains in a singsong that was still too fast for my Italian.

"I've been typing it. It's a little wide and deep for me. But then I don't feel too comfortable with Eliot's poems. Joyce and Proust I accept. Maybe it's great. Maybe it's lunatic."

"He's been on it a long time. When we were in Venice, in 1920, he had a real big chunk done."

"He scrapped all that. Called it mordant crap. Said the style was too serenely anchored to the past. He's a nut, but *we* love him, don't we?"

"Some of us, Mrs. Martin. Yes."

I picked up the peas still in their shells and began to snap open the pods and drop them into the pot. The hammock gave off a squeaking sound where the rusting hooks interlocked with other hooks set into the north and south walls of the balcony. Who loved him? I, she. Charlie, his father, his sister, four or five others?

A muddled voice from behind a closed window shutter said, "Stop that goddamn rocking. My head's busting with that grating noise."

She had an eagle's deep-gold-green iris; her eyes were big and luminous as she opened them wide at the voice, sat up, long legs before her, toes on the flagstones to balance herself and stop the hammock moving.

"Our anchorite, he's come alive." She turned her head to address the shutter. "El, sweet, open up. We have company."

180

There was a muttered obscenity in two languages. ". . . who's the flatulent bastard?"

Mrs. Martin said, "It's Kite, Bill Kite."

I heard a bedspring rattle, and she looked at me and nodded. "He's kind of lonely for company from anyplace but this alley. They're mostly painters—*capo-scuola* style."

A man came out of the door, his torso bare, wearing a pair of soiled baggy cotton trousers, his feet stuffed loosely into sandals. It was Jay. He had grown a short shaggy beard since Venice, and his blondness had darkened to a yellow gold, no longer nearly white. . . . There's a chiaroscuro to Italian light that makes a person stand out, rimmed in atmosphere.

Jay was very thin, and the dark crepy flesh under his eyes had an unhealthy look. His smile was as it had always been, full of his charm ("like an illustration," Charlie had once said, "of the term *homme moyen sensuel*").

"Doesn't he look beautiful, Pages?" Jay said. "Tell me, isn't he the synthesizing force?" He put his arms around me in the Roman style and hugged me to him. He smelled of unaired bedding and sour wine.

"I thought, Jay, maybe I'd miss you this trip."

"The homelessness of genius, Bill. We drag ass and baggage from hovel to hovel. Get some glasses, Pages. You met Pages?"

"I met Mrs. Martin."

"That's me too," she said.

"You see," said Jay, picking up the bottle of Strega, "she's still married to that chicken-headed Major Martin she went to Italy with during the war. There was a report—wrong, of course—that I was shot down in flames."

"I didn't know, I mean, you married the major."

"As soon as she gets the swine to divorce, we're getting married." Pages patted her stomach. "It's going to be a close race, sweets."

"Glasses, glasses," said Jay, irritated as he would be with a sour headache, and he added as she went indoors, "and a corkscrew. I'm a little shaky, Bill. Some hullabaloo last night, and I've this dago fever, comes and goes. But you, you sod, look at you. Stylish—the proper Babbitt but for a few outward eccentricities."

"I see you've been reading the new American books."

"Seeing what the competition is doing."

181

Pages came out with a tray, glasses and a corkscrew in the shape of some Greek god straining himself at some task.

"Pages, I almost came to your wedding in Paris."

"Long ago and far away," she said, reclining again in the hammock as Jay dug at the cork. He got it out and poured. I said, "I'm not drinking anything hard."

"Still not? I rebuke your willpower." He handed Pages half a glass, lifted one himself and took a big pull on it. "Isn't he the fancy sonofabitch? Hasn't drunk the real hard stuff since 1918."

"Since 1919. I hit it hard before the sanitarium dried me out. Didn't drink anything at all till we went to Venice, last time I was in Italy."

Jay took another swallow and said *that* had been a trip to carve on stone.

CHAPTER 20

1924

I SAT IN THE AFTERNOON SUN, looking at Pages and listening to Jay talk about the trip we had taken to Venice.

"What a time, Pages. We talked about the ideal and the real, the theoretical and the practical. St. Mark's Square all pigeon shit and the band playing opera, chunks of *Aïda* and *Cavalleria;* and the polemics of the local whores proved man has no history, only a nature."

"We can skip that," I said.

"Thanks, Bill," said Pages. "I'm from Boston, you know. In my family there's a streak of puritanism up our asses we can't ever get rid of."

Jay sipped and gave a distracted smile. "We met those two dikes who wrote avant-garde stuff."

"Only the big one wrote."

"She sent me something of hers last month. Called *Tender Buttons.* Must show it to you. Say, Bill, you read Proust's *Du Côté de Chez Swann?*"

"I've heard of it. It's part of a bigger book, isn't it?"

"*À la Recherche du Temps Perdu.*"

Pages said, "El scrapped his own book to start over again when he read it."

"How's *Stone Sunlight* going?"

"Great, great. Not just *le monologue intérieur* like Marcel. Listen, you want to read a hunk of it?"

"You know damn well I do."

"I haven't been well. Haven't done much. Been writing pulp stories for crappy magazines. World War flying yarns. Terrible trash. 'Roses of Picardy' played on a worn record."

Pages picked up the pot of shelled peas. "Those flying stories, they're not that bad. Anyway I know what they mean. I hate stream of consciousness except maybe in Joyce—it can't be *that* dull."

Jay slapped her behind as she walked past. "Pages was raised on Louisa May Alcott and Henry James. *Both* very nice girls. But she screams at Molly Bloom."

"I better get the supper going. We any charcoal left, El?"

I said, "I'm buying dinner tonight. The Bernini Bristol? The Excelsior? Which do you like?"

Jay grinned and refilled his glass. The beard didn't become him. It needed trimming.

"Hear about the writer saying to Henry James, 'I know what goes on behind closed doors'? And James says, 'My dear boy, *that* is what doors are for!' "

"How about dinner out?"

"We haven't the clothes for it, Bill. But you can take us to Orsini's *pasta* dive for some *antipasto, scallopine* and the best polenta."

Pages took the glass from Jay's hand and picked up the bottle. "Don't get potted before we eat, sweet."

She went in and Jay looked at me and smiled. "Women, they take over your life with their heightened perception, like a sergeant major."

"How'd you two come together again?"

"She married the goddamn major, don't ask me why. She heard, of course, I was dead, shot down. But still that's no reason. He's a prissy bastard. Comes from Iowa or someplace where the corn is more alive than the people who grow it. She walked out on him about two years ago when their mission closed its offices here, and she stayed on in Rome. She was helping some department store buyer

183

when I ran into her. We took it up. No *donna intacta,* but Pages. What do you think?"

"She's too damn good for you; that's what I think."

"How would you know? Oh, you mean the body. That's just surface."

"I like both."

"You don't know her. You don't know women. Female troglodytes. Aren't you married?"

"I was engaged to a girl named Joyce from the Eastern Shore. We were together a lot. Then it sort of ended and she sent me a wonderful letter."

"Wasn't she any good in bed?"

"She was very good, they told me at the hunt club."

Jay cocked his head to one side, an old habit; it gave him the expression of a shaggy fox terrier. "Spiritual insolvency and bourbon dynasties?"

"There's a lot more to it than that. Horses mostly, local fox hunts, the country-club set I was to join; owning a Gilbert Stuart, voting the proper thief into the Senate, hot toddies, brandy after dinner, and what was du Pont common on the closing prices. My mother-in-law-to-be mooing like a cow in parturition. A world too safe, too closed in."

"Couldn't face it?"

"I think I bored Joyce."

"You lie in your teeth. You didn't see yourself a rich country boy—'God bless the squire and all his relations and keep us all in our proper stations.' Laying the high-yellow maid in the room over the garage when Joyce was at the dog show, or blackballing Jews and Catholics at the country club. You're too soft to rule, Bill."

I changed the subject. "This is no place to write, Jay. I'll set you up in Paris for six months, a year, to finish the book."

"Sure you would. Only Paris is veddy veddy fancy and crummy at the same time. All the little Americans from the Village and the plow. All the pansies and the ugly girls who hate Papa. All the drunks and loafers heading to Paris and the rate of exchange. I was there last year, trying to get some section of *Stone Sunlight* published in one of those little magazines they run. That's where Pages got pregnant. On Rue Lepic, in sight of Sacré-Coeur. God moves in mysterious ways . . ."

"Damn careless of you, Jay."

"I better shave, wash, and comb my hair if we're going out to eat. You haven't given up girls, too, besides hard liquor?"

"No, my doctor felt girls didn't hurt the kidneys or liver."

"Smart man. Pages has a friend—large but lively—who has an office for department store buyers."

I said no and sat in the hammock while the sun sank into some Etruscan gloom and little lizards came out to taste the shells of the peas. Nearby a man and woman were quarreling in one of the rooms. She had a shrill voice and a sardonic tone, and he had a deep bass that ended in a sob and an oath. She talked faster. She had an English upper-class accent and he Low German. I couldn't actually make out the words.

Jay said, "It's Bea and Hugo. They go on like this."

After a while he hit her and she screamed. But no one seemed to care. (St. Paul held women are of their nature without souls.) A child ran past the low wall of the court with a fish-and-onion pizza. The gramophone played *O Mare Chiaro*. Then they began to make love on the floor—I judged from the sound of it—and all the while he kept asking her to forgive him and she kept crying out for him to get violent in his lovemaking. I felt indecent listening to their climaxes; Jay was indifferent. I was pleased to be with him again, and with Pages, in their one room.

It was getting dusk, like brown pollen falling, when we left for the *pasta* place. The British woman and the big German were standing in the doorway of their studio, arms around each other, smoking cigarettes. She had a discolored eye, and one side of his port-smooth face was badly clawed.

"Bloody-hot day, wasn't it, ducks?" she said to Pages.

"Guten Abend."

Jay said Bea painted Italian street funerals; there was a good market for them. Hugo did pornographic drawings for tourists. He was a baron, he claimed, and had been a captain in the Imperial Guards. Bea looked schoolgirl-shy respectability.

The *pasta* place was in a cellar, and the food was strong with garlic and olive oil. Jay drank *grappa,* and Pages and I had a mild white wine. They were both hungry, and as we ate, a man with a ludicrous physique played a squeeze-box and sang those sentimental songs

185

about *Torna a Sorrento* and the Bay of Naples, but they sounded fine with the *pasta* and the fried fish. It was an artists' hangout; there were canvases in the cubist, futurist and *capo-scuola* manner and just plain bad landscapes on the wall. I stood drinks for a few painters and writers and one poet:

> *"Padre del Cielo, dopo i perduti giorni*
> *Dopo le notti vaneggiando spese . . ."*

Jay talked about his novel and the new style he was using. He talked well as always, in a slow, half-droning way, full of food and drink, eyes half hooded. Pages picked walnuts out of their crushed shells and ate them, smiling at me as she nibbled. She was wearing a dark dress, the kind poor Italian women wear, and had piled her long blue-black hair onto the top of her head. She looked like a model for some painter of the da Vinci school, not Leonardo himself—he didn't draw real women—but a follower who was a bit of a sensual lecher.

"Siena me fè, disfacemi Maremma," recited the poet.

It was near midnight when we left the *pasta* dive. We walked back to their place, arms around each other, singing an old Princeton favorite, "Little Brown Jug in the Shade of Me." Later I took the finished section of the novel back with me to my *pensione* and stayed up a long time reading it.

At first it didn't seem to make sense; then I caught on to Jay's method of telling his story. After a while it came through naturally to me, but the hard parts I had to skim over for later digesting. The personal idiosyncrasies became normal; the mannerisms of style were never tedious. What I read that hot Roman night—the big balcony doors of my room were open; the slight wind, smelling of Tiber mud and growing vegetables, roving my room—is pretty much the "Apollo Rising" section of the final version of *Stone Sunlight*. It was much longer then, looser—he improved it by cutting—and it came at the start of the novel. In the printed version of the published book it begins on page 104 of the first edition and runs a hundred and twenty-six pages. The present opening section, "Star Killing," was not yet written in 1924, and was done after most of the manuscript was finished. Jay was not as resilient then and was involved with the purposeful narrowness of passion, so, as some critics have pointed out, the two sections do not fully jibe or mesh.

186

It's hard now, after all these years between, to explain the ecstasy, the excitement, of reading a really new kind of novel. An unexplored way of writing, of meeting for the first time a novelist who was expanding the horizons of his craft. Now, years later, and after so many smaller writers have copied and been influenced by *Stone Sunlight,* the novel may have lost some of its gloss. ("It's the glory and misery, Bill, often to transmit a message to which the artist does not possess a full translation.") That night it was like a shock, a comet suddenly searing one's eyeballs. In a much smaller way I had the same sizzling when Fitzgerald's *The Great Gatsby* came out, a thin perfect thing, small but vital, and when I read *The Sun Also Rises*—blithely floating, bizarrely balanced—the first two times; but Ernest reads now like a parody and a kind of wonderful card trick, and the people are posed in romantic toughness and full of gestures as a ballad. *The Sun* is still the best thing Ernest did in the novel. He was better when bunting to get on first with short stories. *Stone Sunlight,* too, has faded a bit. The whole "St. John of the Cross" section no longer adds up as it once did, the innate coarseness veneered in thin refinement. The women are a bit too dreamlike; "dream lays," Charlie called them. "Not true to life or their sex. Just twats—projections by a boy who dreams of a princess and carries her over into his adult life."

It was the fault I found in all the Americans of the period. Their girls, whether on Long Island or in a sleeping bag or in a gondola, whether the wife of a scientist like Arrowsmith or one of the flappers, bitches, prom girls or gangsters' darlings—these women hardly exist as breathing, excreting, menstruating, smelly, wonderfully interesting, intense personalities (except for Dreiser's characters, and there hasn't been a better portrait of a woman in our writing since *Sister Carrie*). I didn't mean to get sidetracked like this, but the critics have made so much of the failure of Jay's women in his book, I had to show it was the pattern, the fashion, of the twenties and early thirties—maybe the inhibition—to follow a formula. Even as late as Faulkner you get some fine Negro wenches and old character women, his girls aren't alive and kicking; even Temple Drake, who got cold-cocked with a corncob, isn't more than a symbol of the mystique of the dying South. It's something lacking, Jay admitted, in American writers. But *Stone Sunlight* never needed defending.

I fell asleep in the chair after finishing the section of novel and came awake with the sun pouring in, the manuscript pages all around me on the blue rug. I had popped off after finishing the last of it. My head was fuzzy and my mouth felt thick. I began to pick up the pages, which wasn't easy, as Pages hadn't numbered the inserts in some places. She didn't type well, and I could see it would have to be done over by a professional. I decided I'd have it retyped without telling Jay about it. There was, Jay had said, no carbon, only the rough pencil original on yellow lined pads.

Outside, the day had an interminable expanse of green-yellow sky. I felt tacky, my eyes touched with grains of sand. My back ached and my hip was giving notice it didn't like sleeping in a chair. I looked at my wristwatch, but I had forgotten to wind it. I wondered if I was undergoing a progressive deterioration of faculties.

The phone on the chest holding a plaster St. Francis gave the Italian ring that seemed out of a modern opera. The voice of the hall porter said that Signora Martoni was on her way up. I asked *who* and then figured he must mean Pages. The room smelled funky and I flung open the windows. Pages knocked on the door and I turned the long handle that was the knob. She had her hair tied up turban fashion in a yellow cloth and was in what I now know must have been her one street dress. She held a blue bathrobe and an English sponge bag, the kind you find Britons carrying down a thousand second-rate hotel hallways that have community bathrooms. I think my greeting was overhearty, jocular.

"Hello, hello!"

"*Buon giorno,* sweet. How good of you to let me come here for a real lie-down-soak-to-the-roots bath."

"Not at all, Pages." I had a vague idea she had asked me last night, while I was eating *pasta* and listening to Jay talk, if I had a private bath and a real tub. She must have asked me and I must have nodded yes without thinking.

"El's sleeping it off. He shouldn't drink the way he does . . . we do. He hasn't the head or liver for it since the malaria." She looked into the bathroom. "Oh God! It's real, it's marble." She turned a silver tap and clean water gushed out. "It's clear." And as steam rose, "It's hot hot, *hot.*"

She put her arms around me and hugged me and kissed me. I wouldn't have wanted her bathed; her own fragrance was pulsating. I stepped back. "Look, it's all yours. I'll get extra towels. You'll find real soap in my leather traveling case, and toilet paper, too, U.S.A. tissues."

"*What* a crapper," she said, admiring the throned fixture with its high overhead tank, the silver chain and the dolphin grip for pulling. "You don't know what it's like to sponge-bathe in a basin, the water smelling of frogs *and* the outhouse; listen, there's a dead horse down our three-holer, one of Caesar's, I swear."

"Don't hurry," I said. "Breakfast?"

"In about half an hour. You'll most likely have to pull me off the crapper or pry me from the bathtub. *Caffè nero,* an omelet—four eggs—with Bel Paese, and I'm starved for some ripe cherries or plums, sweet."

The bathroom door closed, and I finished sorting out the sheets of Jay's text, changed my shirt and figured I'd get shaved later downstairs in the barbershop. Steam crept from under the closed door.

> *I raise her up and give a pull,*
> *Little Brown Jug's about half full . . .*

While I waited, I went to the window and looked down on some overfoliaged park and remembered some banal street music. I was aware I was lost, like a man without his shadow; that I had nothing, no set of compensations. Jay had his novel, he had Pages with the semispheric breasts, her pregnancy; and I knew I was, as the Spanish say, thinking with my *cojones.* Below me two large Americans (North) sat in a wheeled carriage (horse-drawn fiacre), and at a newspaper stall a pimply seminary student (flat hat, flapping black robe) read a poster advertising a circus (Circo Arcobaleno). From the direction of the Borghese Gardens woodsmoke flowed upward gently like a dark silk stocking being removed (always images). I turned from my morning of purely sensory enjoyment at a knock on the door.

"*Scusi . . . permesso?*"

It was the waiter with the breakfast, and I tipped him and lifted the cover on the omelet.

"Pages! Food."

"Just a mo."

I placed two chairs. She came out of the bathroom wrapped in her robe . . . legs bare, hair wet and shiny as if a reflection in a murky pool. She inhaled and turned slowly around, head back, eyes closed.

189

She laughed and came and hugged me. The bath soap, the wet hair, the rosy scrubbed skin, were a delirious delight, an intoxicating essence.

I held her close—it seemed logical and a necessity—and kissed her on the mouth. She didn't struggle, just looked at me sadly and shook her head.

"Sweet, you understand, El's been too ill, and I'm human. But I love him."

I had a sudden twinge of shame. "And I'm his best friend."

"So let's eat."

The *caffè nero* was good and black and, for Italy, passable. The omelet was large, we were hungry, the crust on the firm white bread with sweet butter crunched just right. Pages ate with relish, with healthy delight the way a girl should eat to please her mother. She smiled from time to time, showing her teeth, tucked in an escaping breast, and ended up consuming three large purple plums, their nectar running from her mouth down the side of her face. I got out cigarettes and lit up for us both, and we sat, chairs pushed back, inhaling, exhaling . . . her hair still damp, sweat beading on her upper lip from the enjoyment of her feeding and of the jocular mood of the moment.

"*Bella.*"

"*Bella.*"

"Great."

"I suppose this will make the baby bigger?"

"Not unless you make a habit of packing in."

"Must be fine to be rich enough to eat like this three, four, times a day."

"You'd look terrible fat. The extravagance of the baroque ass ruins Italy."

"Hell, yes. But no danger. El will never be rich."

I poured fresh cups of coffee and she held hers at eye level and looked at me over the rim. "He's a genius, you know. But not easy to live with. No simplicity, no calmness. The war shattered his nerves."

"Bullshit. We become, Pages, what we are."

"He says time is what we have too much of; it's life that's too short. To do what he wants. Write the greatest, feel the most."

"He was always a bit depressing. Even as a kid. But very interesting. His father is a bishop, the New Brethren of Christ."

190

"Oh God, the swine never told me. He's a preacher himself. The only heritage we can leave, he says, is a spectator's-eye view. I ask you, Bill, who wants to be married to that kind of monument? Like a room with a view in Herculaneum or Pompeii."

"You do. You said you love him."

"Spare half a cup more coffee? Eating isn't part of our puritan sense of sin and guilt."

I poured the last of the coffee into her cup . . . her arm, extending from the sleazy robe, round, white, strong. I said, "He has a rotten habit, this metaphysical tendency of speech. Hit him with something. We used to."

She flung herself back in the chair, hair wild, eyes closed, naked legs crossed (the soles were pink and clean now). Her bone structure kept her from the overroundness of a Botticelli figure, but I could picture her stepping out of a seashell, her feet in a bed of clam sauce, grated onions, lemon juice.

"Know what I want, Bill? A fine dull life. A stupid easy life. A striped tiger cat to put out at night. Milk bottles to take in in the morning. Two kids, girl, boy, in *that* order. I've a wide pelvis, will deliver easy on word command. A garden with the loveliest old-fashioned flowers—pinks, moss roses, hollyhocks—a tree with loud birds in it, a feeling I am getting firmly older, knowing the best of life's moments are the impermanent ones, and the lovemaking, reaching for that pensive bravura moment, and the glimpse of a sky, a child crying at the pleasure of burying its face in your lap. Jesus H. Christ. *Why* don't you shut me up?"

"Pregnant women, my grandmother said, should be humored."

She changed the subject, her mood shifting. "In Paris they drink this stuff, Pernod, the green fake absinthe. A whiskey near the Gare St. Lazare costs twelve francs, but when the expatriates are in the chips they grow sentimental over bad bourbon."

I saw she was near tears. I went around and kissed her neck, feeling her wet hair in my eyes. "Get dressed and you can take me shopping. I owe lots of gifts. Also I told Jay I'd lend him some lire, so let's spend some of it on you."

"The bastard. He's borrowed from every American in Europe. But—"

"I know, he's been ill."

191

She went to the bathroom and turned in the doorway. "You understand why I can't go to bed with you?"

"Perfectly."

Oh perfectly, very perfectly, I thought. Our decadence is only other people's disdain. But as Pages had said that day, there was this puritan sense of sin, of guilt. And he was my best friend.

CHAPTER 21

WE SPENT THE AFTERNOON savoring the shops, gazing over the *campagna,* quoting Stendhal ("The charm of Italy is like being in love"). I had dinner with Signor Serbati of the firm of Serbati e di Gioconde; a too large dinner with a too large wife, oversized children. Signor Serbati, a little man with a paunch, told me di Gioconde was wasting the firm's money at Monte gambling, that the Kite mill machines were not selling fast enough, but all in all it had been a fine year and he expected to do well for both of us if God, the Pope and the Fascists were favorable. The graft cost him *quindicimila cinque-cento lire*—he couldn't put it in English. Home again at last, I reread the opening section of *Stone Sunlight.*

The second reading of Jay's manuscript impressed me even more than the first. It was not the kind of book an American publisher would put on his list; the *Little Magazine* in the States had been seized for printing parts of Joyce's *Ulysses.* No, it would have to appear first in Europe. Jay had failed to get it printed in any of the Anglo-American avant-garde magazines in Paris, which, as he said, "lived by taking in each other's laundry and by diddling one the other."

I figured out what cash I had in the bank in East Pompton and what the U.S. Steel stock my grandfather had left me was selling for. Printing costs should be low in Italy. I could start our own little magazine. I didn't sleep well the rest of the night: The meal, the wine getting me up to empty my bladder, but mostly the project of a literary magazine didn't let me rest.

Near day the sky was like grease congealed on a gray plate, and I fell into a heavy aching slumber. I came awake at eleven, bathed, shaved, ate a roll and drank coffee, and took a taxi to the Via Margutta, which appeared more like anarchy and indiscipline than before.

Pages, seated in the shade of the balcony, was typing from a notebook of yellow sheets covered with pencil script corrected in red ink. Jay was in the hammock, playing with a white soiled kitten that was nipping his fingers with needlelike teeth; he cuffed it when it went too far. He looked up at me.

"Enter Baron Spendthrift, played by William Grant Kite, the notorious hashish eater."

"Oh, the shopping? Jay, forget it—I've the hell of an idea."

"Never get excited in the Italian sun. Rest."

I must have talked for ten minutes while he just stroked or cuffed the kitten, staring expressionless at me. When I finished, I felt foolish and leaned back in the backless kitchen chair and fell down among the clay pots, while around us was the thrashing about of church bells. Jay laughed and Pages came running over.

"Oh God, Pages, Chaplin couldn't have done the fall better."

"You hurt, Bill?"

"No, Pages, but I broke a few pots. You're right, Jay *is* a swine."

He put down the kitten and it ran off, tail high, pink button of a rectum swinging from side to side. The bells stopped with a tremor of disquiet.

"Pages, you heard: Bill has the damnedest idea that ever came down the pike. Going to start the little literary magazine to end all literary magazines."

"I heard."

" 'The Scream'—how's that for a title?"

I said, "I didn't think of *that*. But why not?"

"Good boy."

"We'll run the opening section of *Stone Sunlight* in four issues."

"Every month."

"Monthly? Well, maybe quarterly to start. Can we get enough material?"

"We'll print some of the Stein stuff she sent me. Charlie Hutton-bok's skiing texts, that damn poetic crap, being about a skiman moving with the speed of light. And drawings—why, this foul alley is crawling with talent. Bea is a great black-and-white artist. Bill, you're publisher, I'm editor. Pages is corresponding secretary. All we need is a printer. Rome is full of them, all starving on bread and rancid olive oil, sixteen shitty brats underfoot." He stood up. "Whoopee! Ya-siss-boom-ba! Let's hear that Princeton locomotive!"

"Can the printers read English?"

"Don't have to, *paisano*. Show them type samples and page styles, and they just set the text letter for letter."

Pages said, "I don't type well enough."

"We'll get Bea to do the cover. One of the street funerals with a woman up front, screaming her grief. Two colors, red over blue on gray paper. Or green, rotting-cheese green on orange?"

It seemed so easy to be a publisher. Barefoot, unwashed, bearded, Jay was dancing around the courtyard. He picked up a pad and a short pencil stub. "We'll write letters of announcement to future subscribers and contributors. Gide, Trotsky, Bertie Russell, D. H. Lawrence. They should be good for some juicy pieces. Shrivel the balls of Calvin Coolidge! Maybe the Bishop will write a prayer for us: *Twentieth Century Blues. . . . Amen.* Who knows Pirandello? Ernest can spare us a short story." He stopped, mouth open, and looked at me. "You're not embezzling the firm's money?"

"No. It's my own. But we must budget it for a year's printing. Get estimates. I may be short."

Jay didn't hear me. He called out, "Bea! Bea! Hugo, you Teutonic porker, *ich bitte Gehorsam.* Get your tail out here!"

Pages took him by the shoulders and sat him down in the hammock. "You'll bring back your malaria shakes."

Jay nodded and licked his dry lips. He rubbed his beard and assumed a look of mock bereavement and agony. Bea, the English artist, looking more like a schoolgirl in black cotton stockings, came out of her studio, a brush with red pigment in her hand. "I'm working on the big painting. *The State Funeral of General Cesare Chigi.* What the bloody hell is going on?"

"Celebrating, Bea dear," said Jay. "We're going to publish a magazine. You're to do the cover. Pages, be a dear, go down for some *grappa,* some cheese, black olives, a little salami, and be sure it isn't the stuff they make of church candle ends and goat meat."

Bea wore her reddish hair cut straight across her forehead, à la Katherine Mansfield, and when she moved quickly, it took wing as if ready to fly off her head. "Sounds damn jolly. Like *Blast,* the foul rag Wyndham Lewis put out in London. Impossible swine and bounder, a head full of hot horse turds, but an interesting chap."

194

I slipped Pages some money as I was introduced. "Publisher's advance for party expenses."

Pages looked at me sadly—"Poor, poor Bill"—and went down to do some shopping.

It rained later. We sat indoors hearing the pinpricks of the shower drum pizzicato on a tin roof. Jay had to take quinine.

EDITOR'S NOTE: Only two complete sets of all the six issues of *The Scream* are known to collectors. One is in the Wurdemann collection in the New York Public Library, and the other in the Santa Barbara branch of the University of California. This last set has the signature *Manfred Lorser Ames* in red ink written on the cover of each issue.

Volume I, No. 1, is dated Fall 1924, followed by Spring 1925, after which for three issues it is a monthly: May, June, July, all 1925. There is a time gap, and the last issue, called the *Italian-American Number,* is dated August 1927. It bears no volume number. This last issue lists Djuna Owens as editor and publisher, and contains nothing by Eliot Tjaden. It would appear that Miss(?) Owens bought the rights to the title from the Italian printer long after William Kite was its publisher.

The contents of all issues are listed in Warner Ott's *The Little Magazines 1920–1935* (New York, 1946), so they do not have to be repeated here. Among names in the first five issues are works by Eisenstein, Alain Fournier, St. Augustine, Franz Kafka, Gertrude Stein, Hokusai, Elliot Paul, Ezra Pound, William Kite's translation of Rimbaud's *A Season in Hell,* Duchamps, William Carlos Williams, and some now forgotten people. The "Apollo Rising" section of *Stone Sunlight* appeared in the first four numbers (English customs inspectors seized and destroyed all issues), and in the next to last issue a long fragment called "Fundador Brandy and Lightning," which was intended to be part of *Stone Sunlight* but was cut out in the final editing. This section is of complex structure with no key, and has never been reprinted. Its unidentified opening line— "The strongest poison ever known/ Came from Caesar's laurel crown"— is from William Blake.

Beatrice Fabor Brown, the Bea of the text, painted a double portrait of Eliot Tjaden and Nora Pages Martin as part of a funeral procession following the small white casket of a child. It was to have been reproduced in *The Scream* but never was, for personal reasons, and is now in the collection of Eleonora Incisa della Rocchetta, Rome.

Of course we were short of money; of course the latent indifference of Italian typesetters, setting by eye rather than by sense, created fearful mistakes. Of course I got involved with two menages, Jay and

Pages, Bea and Hugo. But my ennui was dispelled, for, as Jay said, "Bill, the tragic hero fights the world; the comic hero tickles it." I spent my time in the middle of sets of proofs, correcting galleys, engraver's plates, trying to transfer funds from America to Rome, and trying to find paper stronger than toilet tissue and not tinted pink or yellow. At last in a warehouse kept by a man named della Visa, who knew the Italian agents for Kite machines, we did find three tons of an aged stock, hardly foxed at all. Also we failed to keep any control on our expenditures.

Meanwhile Bea was fleeing from her man when she should have been drawing for us the cover and illustrations. She had broken it off with that perisher Hugo, who would come roaming around and roaring at night like a Nibelung opera, assaulting Bea's door till pulled off by the police, to appear a few days later battered by Fascist cell treatment but engorged with rage, lust, hate and Bea's changed doorlocks. *"Wasserkopf! Wasserkopf!"*

In the end Hugo was deported for dealing illegally in gold. I moved in with Bea and her schoolgirl frocks. It wasn't as simple as I write it down, but it was nearly a spontaneous movement. The nerve center of *The Scream* was too far from my *pensione,* and as I got involved in the publication I recovered myself. I mean I became sensual, recovered egotism, felt a hostility to respectability. And I no longer felt animals seem sad after intercourse. I began to lark and sing at the *pasticceria* where we took our meals. Playful, I saw that the shared bed is after all the adult's sandbox. I moved in (as I said) with Bea.

She had earned enough to put in a bathroom. She was neat, clean, and she had been trying to get rid of Hugo, who had deflowered her at the Slade School of Art because, Bea said, he found out "my mother was a Dame of the British Empire." At first she had kept him housebroken with Liederkranz and Buckling herring, and he had insisted she dress like a little girl.

The walls of Bea's studio, bedroom, kitchen, bathroom, were nun-white, and a huge canvas, about twelve feet by fourteen, took up one entire wall. It was Bea's work in progress, her unfinished masterpiece: *The State Funeral of General Cesare Guido da Foligno Chigi.* The general, who had been beaten in Sicily by Garibaldi, by the French, and the North Africans, was an old fart in a beard, a papal knight, a duke, who had died at one hundred and one, and Mussolini

196

had made his funeral a state event. Bea had caught it all wonderfully
—the great black hearse of polished ebony, its eight dark horses in
soot-colored plumes and nets, the hundred-man band playing the
Death March from the oratorio *Saul,* the church procession with a
cardinal, no less, in red gloves and hat wedged among a regiment of
lesser monks and holy orders, hooded carriers of flowers in staggering
array—whisking holy water, waving incense—and containers of
relics and wonder-working images all well forward; the regiments he
had commanded, decimated, destroyed, debauched, or tokens of
them, in their original uniforms gleaming at parade dress in the hot
sun of a Roman August. It would be a remarkable painting, and the
state had already shown interest in it and was hoping Bea would
hurry it along. Italians make death protean, opulent, expansive.

We would make love—after I took off her Peter Pan rompers and
floppy straw hat—in the wide brass bed under the huge canvas. Then
Bea would hurry to get her colors mixed and go to work on her
painting, high on a series of dangerous rickety stepladders. She
responded to sexual intercourse only at moments of great excitement,
as when she sold a painting, or the state gave her another colored
ribbon, or a critic had said a fine thing about her, or she had found
the most amazing funeral, the burying of a Romanian gypsy king.
Then it had to be fucking until she became relaxed and descended to
normal. She used sex as a calming release, as a reward to herself; it
served a need the way some of us use prayers, make novenas, burn
candles (too obvious to comment on), leave small coins in church
boxes. But once Bea had been filled, sated, exploded (like removing a
cap from a bottle of soda), she would go back to work. So that until
the next need for celebrating something, for releasing some keyed-up
emotion, she was a vestal virgin, an illustration for *Little Women,*
paintbrush in hand. She had no interest then in fornicating, and
nearly an English lady's distaste for the thing. I never fully fathomed
her esoteric doctrine or her violent needs. If during her periods of
celibacy I so much as slapped her ass or leered, she would grow
haughty and cool.

"I say, what kind of bloody sexual maniac are you?"

So feeling demeaned, depraved, almost ashamed at the schoolgirl
tones, I'd go back to correcting proofs and talking to sweaty Italian
typesetters with their quivering vocal rages. Bea as a painter had the
Blakean quality of some mad absolute. She painted nothing but street

197

funerals in a flat modern style combining the colors of Renoir with the starkness of di Chirico, and yet with symbols of a flat realism, so the sun, the sweaty black cloth, the smoke of the incense, seemed to come to you closer than life as you looked at the paintings. She said she hadn't really decided to paint street funerals as a career, but her first success had been with them. And before Hugo deflowered her—a student at the Slade—he had locked her up in his studio dressed in a Kate Greenaway bib, and made her paint dozens of them. When they came to Rome, the Galleria Blondi began to sell Bea's work; she was pleased enough with the subject matter, and achieved a content-ment—between Hugo's assaults on her and her assaults on Hugo. They had been balanced in some derangement, some perilous equilibrium.

Bea was a marvelous black-and-white artist; she caught Jay's idea of the kind of illustrations we wanted in *The Scream.*

She was tiny; even during the feasting season she never weighed over a hundred pounds. She was well formed but titless, a bit too long in the tooth, had a Scotch-English childish blondness complete with freckles, deep cool gray-brown eyes, very large, hinting at some strange forays in her bloodstream. Beside Pages, who was a Juno, a large well-made girl who looked full of health and food (and now with child), Bea appeared, Jay said, "like one of those ten-year-old children they dress in lacy frills with wide Peter Rabbit hat, give a hoop to and send out in parks to thrill old men sitting on benches."

Having my homelife, I worried over funds.

When I spoke of money, Jay would nod diagonally: "Money is the stimulus of caged man, *paisan.*"

Jay in Italy called you *paisan* if he liked you, just as in our youth he had called you *sport* if he liked you. (Fitzgerald gave this trick to [Jay] Gatsby in his book; he got it from Jay at Princeton.)

It was no use talking money to Jay. He'd stare in a kind of cataleptic way and change the subject.

We'd breakfast, all four, on the balcony on *panini,* butter, *caffè nero,* Bea's marmalade which her mother in Kent (the Dame of the British Empire) sent her with advice. It was very *bella bella* all the way—the four of us close. Jay and I writing, the girls bathing; naked women in wet towels. The magazine taking shape, all of us smeared with printer's ink from damp proofs. Jay rewriting his sections on proof sheets and costing us a fortune, even at the rate of exchange, for the printer's charges. Pages would lick the marmalade spoon and cross her legs, and I would look at the fine tendons of her ankles; the audible murmur of the world was just over the wall.

It was all like life in an ebullient dream, a fine warm one, all that summer. I guess Jay expressed it best: "If you live without violence, we can all act out our fantasies." But Jay had a lot of unresolved dilemmas; the novel was too big, too new in its method, and he wasn't sure it would reduce itself at last and lie still like a patient on a surgeon's table to be worked on. Pages was showing her pregnancy more each day. The divorce wasn't coming through and Jay didn't appear to care. I felt we were a druidic circle lacking an oracle.

At midday we didn't make much of lunch—a bit of ham, a glass of *vino rosso* or *vino bianco*—and dinner was at the *pasta* joint, the artists talking tired subjects: art, money, love, fame, God, birth, death. Jay did the heavy drinking; Bea, veddy British, very petite, belted away the *grappa,* while Pages and I took our pale Capri. I felt no need to drink hard, and I was content with Bea, with being with Jay again, with looking at Pages; the magazine was my only problem. I made schemes for milking the Kite money into it, but my grandmother and her lawyers were fearfully earnest about bookkeeping and check stubs. And I'd wonder: Is the life of action preferable to the life of art?

Coming home late at night, we'd pass the French College of the Sacred Spear and Holy Nails, a noted nest of pederasts; and we'd hear the priests' and novices' wonderful singing: *"Que votre nom soit sanctifié . . . Ne nous laissez pas succomber à la tentation . . ."* Jay would translate for Pages, "Hallowed be Thy Name. . . . Lead us not into temptation."

Then we'd sleep, the full, heavy slumber of youth, of work done, of being mated, of feeling life run over us lightly. In the middle of pleasure I'd look down on Bea and taste bile; every bed is waiting to be a deathbed (but I didn't get moody too often).

The day the Banca del Lavoro said I was overdrawn and would be till the next quarterly payment of Kite stock dividends on the shares I held, we had pasted up a dummy of *The Scream*. We viewed it with a kind of exhilarated exhaustion.

Pages was sulking. She wasn't as yet uncomfortable with her pregnancy, but it was pretty obvious now, and I think she feared she looked like the gigantic pregnant Italian women all around us, those belly-out, ballooned-up giantesses going by ungirdled through the streets, puffed and round under black cloth; others, as impregnated and bloated, skipped, washed clothes, slapped children, cooked in a reek of olive and garlic. They climbed stairs, each always preceded by her personal Alp, a Mont Blanc of living matter fertilized through a pleasant aperture, blessed by Pope and priest, rewarded by the state. And perhaps according to the second law of thermodynamics spreading heat in the universe. Pages, I saw, was awed and new to the thing and frightened by all the child-carrying Italian women, a mob of breeders, bearers, publicly unashamed.

Pages was moody as she watched figures and costs. "Why don't we get Tony to help us?"

Jay looked up from a proof sheet he was correcting and rewriting for the third time. "Tony? Of course. He's up in Milano, isn't he? Screwing around with some new racing car he's building?"

"Tony?" I asked.

"Tony Pfaelzer," said Pages. "He's helped us out before."

"When I was sick with malaria," said Jay, not looking up from the proof sheet. "Filthy rich; he salvaged the Great War, you know . . . turned all the blood, piss and agony into gold."

"How?"

"Junk. Beautiful rusting junk. Tanks, guns, battleships. He cut them up with torches and sold them to the Japs, to the British and Rhineland steel mills. The war was not fought in vain after all."

"Not the Tony Pfaelzer who used to fly in my wing?"

"You're damn right it is," said Jay. "And remember how drunk he got with Charlie in Paris?"

"That," I began, "was the time—" But Jay looked up hard-eyed, and I felt, What the hell: If Jay didn't want to bring up *that* time he didn't marry Pages on leave in Paris, when Charlie had the big French racing car and she was shipped off to Italy with her major, I could understand it. Perhaps he wasn't marrying Pages this time either. There had been hints maybe he didn't want to marry her. Something was hidden from me—a whole set of the wrong compensations was set up between Jay and Pages. . . . We all, I thought, wear Gogol's overcoat, a ridiculous mendacity. Beneath it what are we? I had no answer. *Ne nous laissez pas succomber à la tentation.*

As Tony's commander I was drafted to write the letter for help. Tony was at the Abbatutis Motor Works in Milano; he had taken on the rich man's hobby of auto racing and was building a monster

200

there, mostly from his own plans. It was not a very good letter. Full
of superficialities and a false hedonism. All the hearty crap of how
was the goddamn horny flier and did he still play the violin when he
got drunk and would he stand at attention while I put something to
him. "Any man who is nuts about racing cars is the man for the avant
garde, even if only because he's ignorant, physically alert and too full
of theories and something he got secondhand from books. So frankly,
Leftenant Pfaelzer, pronounced Felzer, we need backers, rich ones.
To keep the magazine appearing for at least two years—the time we
figure it will take to make its impact felt or drop dead on its kisser. So
stop stirring the gallstones of the local *corvas* long enough (the false
old pals, buddies together, old-cocksmen touch) to say you'll be our
Otto Kahn, for the sum of three hundred a month which will pay the
wop printers and our aesthetic needs."

There was a lot more, a revolting surface of chum-old-pal and are-
you-getting-much-these-days, come-join-us, it-could-be-fun. I didn't
like writing such letters, but in those days we were religionizing over
art. *Art,* ART.

Pages said, "We'd sell our mothers for art. *And* deliver."

CHAPTER 22

The Scream had an impressive masthead. One of Bea's drawings—a
closeup—of a woman, mouth wide, screaming at a funeral (anticipat-
ing Picasso's *Guernica* by over fifteen years), and under it was a
quotation Jay had found, which was set in a new typeface called
Futura Bold, very much the rage in Paris. (Tony paid for bringing a
case of it to Rome.)

Even though the universe destroy him, man is still nobler than that
which kills him, because he knows he is being killed, and the superiority which the universe has over him the universe never knows.

—Pascal: *Pensées*

(It was from a book, Jay said, that, like some women, takes a lot of
getting into.)

All the time—bells ringing, staccato yowling of bambinos, printers

201

shrugging us off—there was something seriously wrong between Jay and Pages, something that was an undertone of discord as we went to press with the first issue of *The Scream,* something persistent we didn't talk about. Like the way they'd stare at each other with brooding anger, or she'd drop a plate of food before him—as if to say: Eat, choke—or he'd look up from an inked proof sheet and frown at her if he thought we weren't watching.

I wondered if we were too far away from home. Maybe like plants some men suffer in having their roots disturbed in transplanting. We were a lost colony in a sea of olive oil and *pasta.*

Bea and Pages would get into a corner and go through that woman business of whispering together in singular female comfort. Nights Bea and I would be in bed listening to the ivory balls bouncing together in the *caffè-biliardo* down the street, the low, husky voices of the pool players as they talked of some shot, over a strain of *Trovatore* from the gramophone of the fiend upstairs . . . and twice we heard Jay and Pages talking loudly, but not clearly enough for us to make out the subject of their discontent. Jay's reasoned, paced words coming out in a natural way. Pages's fast answers, some crisp detailed rebuttal, then a furious rush of temper. Jay's rising, harsh words. A silence. One last phrase: Could it be "Good night" or "Drop dead"? Then the weight of turning bodies on the bedsprings, settling to try for sleep, a last *click-click* of billiard balls, the harsh needle scratch as the gramophone fiend ended his concert, the *drip-drip* of some courtyard faucet, a howl of an agonized cat in a far-off garden. Night in a foreign city, the hope of unbroken sleep.

Bea said to me as I reached for solitude, "Some men prefer to be led to bed rather than to the altar."

"Can believe that. Shut up, sleep."

"You hinted he wasn't too earnest in France during the jolly old war to marry her."

"Just hints. Battle fatigue. Good night."

"Something's wrong there. Maybe, the *cazzo,* he doesn't want the tot."

"Tot?"

"The child."

"Wouldn't be like Jay. Very much interested in children. Go to sleep."

"Genius. I tell you it's a bloody mess to be a genius."

"I know."

"You're not one, Bill. You don't know the blasted agony of it."

"Only the agony of staying awake."

I took Bea in my arms and kissed her brow, and it was late and I had no interest just then in Jay and Pages. I was bone, ass-dragging tired. We had been making bundles of the magazine all day and shipping it out wildly to Foyle's in London, Sylvia Beach's in Paris, Brentano's, Scribner's in New York, Dawson's in Los Angeles: wherever we had heard of a good enterprising, progressive or established bookstore of any size or merit . . . with a covering letter that here was the best, most exciting of the literary magazines and would they please display it, sell it, *and* remit to our editorial offices in Rome. (Signed) *William Grant Kite, Publisher.*

I wondered if it would work. How serene and generous were bookstores? I also hoped to get enough money soon to buy stamps to send out about a hundred and fifty copies to a good mailing list (stolen from the Paris *Herald*) with an offer to subscribers. Four issues for two dollars, patrons invited at fifty dollars a year "to keep *The Scream* shouting." Somehow I felt I had to do more.

We mailed fifty copies to people like Whitehead, Santayana and Bernard Shaw, Douglas Fairbanks, Chief Justice Holmes and Milt Gross, asking them to send us their opinions—joys, dislikes and gripes—on the first issue, and permission to use their remarks. Now as my sleep pattern was shattered, I remembered I had forgotten Paul Valéry, Thomas Hardy, Matisse, E. M. Forster, Gandhi, Virginia Woolf, and *why* not Freud? I tried to make a mental note of the names. Bea began to snore slightly, snuffily like a little girl, and I wondered who would paint *her* funeral procession when she died. It could be impressive. Church of England, with a grand procession of snotty choirboys, perhaps the Archbishop of Canterbury; for the Fabor McNeill-Browns of Skye (Bea's family) were among those who had favored the Young Pretender . . . and her mother, always remember, was a Dame of the British Empire. Or were they of the Scots religious sect, the Glassites or Sandmanians? Must ask . . . and so at last I slept.

Month after month time frittered away . . . cold fruit-green rains, Roman pine trees whipping in the wind, the fountains clogged with dead leaves, summer tourists all gone, seminary students in their

203

flapping crow-black, and red-nosed nuns all hurrying in one snaking line under umbrellas while Rome, Roma—pagan, early Christian, Papal, Fascist—lay under wet siege. The whores had gone indoors in the Trastevere section; trees stood like green golems over the synagogue dome in the old ghetto section. The awareness of seasons seeped like the damp into us.

Tony drove down from Torino in a Duesenberg that Jay said was as long as a tapeworm. Tony told us it had been made for an actor, Tom Mix, but he had grabbed it off. He looked wider but just as dark and handsome, just as rabbinical and Talmudically sensual. He wore a hairy Harris tweed suit of loose belted English cut, and red-orange shoes from Bond Street of a pebbled leather that looked like fruit peels, a gray silk shirt with a wide gold collar-bar, regimental tie of a regiment never on the military books, and a floppy, hairy gray-green actor's hat with the brim way down on one side. A man's quest for true essences through tailoring.

The kids in the neighborhood came out in the rain to see, probe and spit on the Duesenberg. Tony threw coins among them and told them in a fair Italian to keep an eye on it. *"Siamo Americani!"*

"Ciao!"

We decided to entertain Tony in Bea's place; it had plumbing and the studio had light, a half ceiling of glass on which the rain lisped. Outside feet went squishing by in wet shoes, and indoors the charcoal fire gassed us.

Tony clapped his hands together. "Son of a gun . . . I feel old seeing the old RFC faces again. And so you're Bea? And so you're Pages?"

"We are, ducks, we are. And what the hell are you?"

Jay poured small glasses of Strega. "He's the richest junkman in the world *and* our literary patron."

"Don't remind me of junk," Tony said, the big dark eyes looking at the unfinished *State Funeral of General Cesare Chigi* on the wall ("Now that's a painting"); and to Pages, "May it be with *mazel*— luck—a boy, or, if you like, a girl, but always with *mazel."* He drank and said the district smelled just right for a publishing venture, that Rome looked like it had some flamboyant possibilities. "You'll have dinner, huh, with me? Either Capriccio's or the Biblioteca del Valle. I have cased them both." We must drink his Buton Vecchia Romagna, ride in his Duesenberg, put our hands in his pockets and take what we wanted; goyim were his best friends. He kissed Bea; he kissed Pages, who began to laugh till her side ached and Jay gave her some crushed ice to suck. We were no longer disconsolate and lonely. We had a patron.

That was Tony Pfaelzer, my wing man, making a gay loud noise, offering himself, his world. ("A Jew does nothing by ones or twos, only by threes and sixes.") Later I went down to the street with him, the rain falling with a steady purr, gleaming off his car's silver hood. We stood close together in the archway over the outer courtyard, breathing in chill and puffing out vapor; the drops of water suspended on his hairy tweed jacket were afraid to penetrate such expensive cloth. He looked at me and smiled sadly.

"What a fine thing, seeing you and Jay. And the girls—*saftig!*"

"We're exploiting you, Tony."

"That's what the rich are for. Ask Lenin, ask Trotsky." He said suddenly, "You happy, Bill?"

"Yes, I suppose so. I've got a girl, something to work for, good company. It's not a bad town. I never thought to ask. Yes, I suppose I am."

"Don't ask. Just be. I've had a hell of a bad time, Bill. A hell of a time."

"You look fine. Feisty."

"Look, any *mamzer* with a tailor and a barber can look fine. I was married, you know, in 1919, one of those fine Jew broads—pure chicken fat, fourth generation Yankee, *not* named Shirley—what else? Deborah. Reform Temple, her brothers and uncles all married to shiksas, ready in one more generation to be Episcopalians—they're Bankers, Wall Street, department stores."

"Not bad, not bad."

"Salt-of-the-earth Jews, do I have to say? Settlement houses, free matzos to immigrants, collecting etchings, even had relatives who went down in the *Titanic*. The *whole* thing. We had two kids. Samuel, a girl Selma."

"What tore it?"

"I was a goddamn *Galitz* to them—that's poor white trash among us Yids. Even lower than a *Litvak*."

I laughed. "So I heard from a man named Pascin. So what?"

"So three years ago we separated, and I haven't been back to the

U.S.A. I've been building racing cars and driving them. Damn, *she-it,* that's something, racing."

"You need a girl."

"I have girls. Countesses, tarts, a baroness, a bishop's *chérie* in Paris. I know, you mean *one* girl."

"I mean one girl."

He shook water off his actor's hat, patted the damp fuzzy felt tenderly. "Can I have Pages?"

"No."

"Bea?"

"No."

"You see, you *macher,* your gifts are empty. You give me a word. *Girl.* A living, kicking one? No. Well, see you for dinner. Capriccio's. I'll have Valpolicella on ice for you, or some lousy light stuff. Listen, boychik, how does it feel not to get drunk?"

"Feels fine."

"Fine, fine." Tony shook my hand. "All I hear is fine, fine."

He ran out into the rain, tall, dark, handsome, divorced, the father of two, builder of racing cars, the man who helped junk the German high-seas fleet. A megalomaniac, most likely, with overactive pituitary and adrenals. Charming.

I stayed where I was, a wind beginning to drive the rain in toward me under the brick arch, an arch that had maybe seen Caesar, Brutus, the Borgias, and certainly a lot of cats and dogs, also people who threw their refuse into corners. The smell of the wet earth, rain-soaked wood, brought back a thousand images of times past and here I was getting chilled. Seeing Tony again rubbed me raw in spots—I hadn't cauterized my memories as well as I had hoped.

What was properly needed to launch *The Scream,* I felt, was some sort of international incident, some literary-tainted scandal that would attract world attention, cause us to make headlines, bring out the newsreel cameramen who had been on short rations for excitement since the war. I awoke one morning and snapped my fingers the way I had seen my brother Harry do when he had an idea. I said to Bea, "Is modern man a thinking reed or just a fountain pen?"

"Don't be a ruddy bore."

I got Jay aside later and snapped my fingers again. "It's simple. We do something to excite the world press to review the magazine."

"What have you in mind, something like a murder?"

"That would cause complications. Look, the great D'Annunzio is going to be in Genoa for the next three days, parading, making speeches, carrying on, collecting funds for some cause."

"So?"

"We borrow Tony's racing car, get photographed in it, announce to a press conference we are delivering the first copy of *The Scream* to the great wop poet in person at Genoa, to be put into that museum he's preparing for the arts of Italy. After all, the magazine *is* a product of Italy, and he's mad for publicity. He isn't modest."

Jay saw the point of it at once, and, like me, I think he needed a few days' vacation from all our activities and problems in Rome. The D'Annunzio idea was a brainstorm of mine; the bald, toothless, one-eyed little cock-of-the-walk was a national hero, had a reputation as a cocksman—an Italian virtue to all classes—was poet, novelist, historian, flier; had grabbed the city of Fiume for Italy after the war and was the hero of the Black Shirts, of the youth, of women.

Our problem was Tony. So we didn't tell him a thing of our plans. Jay left a note for Pages, and one gray morning at six we tiptoed out and went down to the garage where Tony had one of his racing cars in storage—a low small monster called "Blue Blazes." I had alerted Hank Morris, the Pathé newsreel man in Rome, of our start and scheme, and he nudged the other photo services as a favor to me for a few bottles of Strega. The Rome-stationed reporters were there, from America and England and France. The garden behind the garage looked and sounded like a brawl in a second-rate brothel. Jay and I were in long white linen coats and had caps with goggles strapped on them. We stood in front of Blue Blazes holding a tied-up bundle of copies of *The Scream* between us.

Jay waved a copy at the grinding newsreel camera. "We bring Mother Italia, home of culture, art and love, this publication to amaze the world, entertain the sick and educate the wise to their own ignorance."

It didn't matter what he said there as cameras didn't record sound in those days. I got the man from the New York *World* to one side. "It's all yours, pal. I see the *Times* and the *Trib* didn't show up."

"There's a rumor Charlie Chaplin is arriving. They're following that lead."

"You have the *real* story," I said. Jay was crammed into the racing car and I joined him, the bundle of magazines between my legs. It was a tight fit. Jay shifted gears, the car stank of oil fumes, and we roared out and headed north, hunting a Roman road past the Lungotevere, Aventino and the Foro Romano. It was early and the day somber gray, and I hoped it wouldn't rain; racing cars have no tops. Jay beat his gloved hands on the steering wheel. "Grand, grand, north north, once we get past the Via Babuino."

We had planned to do the trip in two days, issuing press notices all the way. I had a pocket of prepared typed sheets, all praising the trip, *The Scream,* and not forgetting D'Annunzio, to whom I had sent a telegram quoting from Dante:

> *Ah i Genovesi uomini diversi*
> *D'ogni costume e pien d'ogni magagna,*
> *Perché non siete voi del mondo spersi?*

And I had added in English: Fear not, we come with tidings to repolish the honor of the city with a scream.

The American Society to Repay a Debt to Columbus of Genoa.

Jay was driving and singing "Pony Boy," and I was sitting and holding on, for Blue Blazes had hardly any springs, and pumping gas pressure—one had to keep pumping at a plunger set in the side of the car to get the gas pressure up. At Civitavecchia I saw Jay was missing other cars by inches, and I knew his eyes were failing him again. He always had a kind of cockeyed double vision under strain—his old trouble—and I got him to let me take the wheel and drove to Montepescali, where we had lunch and gave out statements to three nose-picking kids and four women, two of them very pregnant. We were arrested in Siena, and the judge said we were driving on a closed-off street reserved for oxcarts and carriages of noble papal families. Jay made a speech about Italy and America, and gave out our press notices, and we were fined only fifty lire. It was a good thing I had borrowed money from Tony. It was a slow trip after that; the roads were torn up, and those not torn in very bad repair. When we saw the silver ribbon of the Arno flowing past, it was a velvet dusk and we roared into Florence smoking badly; we had run short of oil. We were ass-sprung, worn out and dusty, and the Hotel Excelsior doubted we wanted to stay there, but we insisted (and Jay added I was Woodrow Wilson's illegitimate son by Mary Baker Eddy). I called a press conference, but Jay was in the bathtub when the two reporters and the cameraman came, so I said it was a great day for art, literature and American-Italian friendship, and Jay, wearing only a skimpy towel, came out and was photographed with me. We took the reporters to the Buca di San Ruffillo for dinner, and we ate well and the reporters and Jay got very drunk. We didn't get started till near ten the next day, and we had trouble finding the right motor oil. We were pleased, however, that we were able to sign Tony's name to everything—hotel, dinner, and car servicing. There were cheers as we took off, to follow the Arno down to Pisa in threatening weather. The leaning tower was hidden by fog as we turned north to Cararra. I said, "It's going to rain."

"Nonsense," said Jay, pumping gas pressure and taking a sip from a bottle of Chianti. "If you drank, Bill, you'd fear no weather."

It did begin to drizzle when we came to La Spezia, and I was for staying there for the night. The clouds were black over the Gulf of Genoa. Jay pooh-poohed the idea. "If we miss that little prick D'Annunzio, we've flopped badly. On, on. . . ."

I had an omelet of duck eggs in pomidoro I would rather forget about, and Jay tried some *pasta* and edible fungi and brandy, and then we went on along the Ligurian coastline that is called the Riviera dei Fiori. I was losing courage and felt the project was silly. It was raining hard now and the interior was filling up and we were sopping wet and the rear left tire was fraying; racing cars have no room to carry spares. Also we had been buying local gas, and that, too, seemed to do the car no good. Near dark we discovered for the first time the car had no headlights; racing cars don't. We stopped under a ruined tower advertising a popular cow drench for farmers.

"We better find shelter."

Jay smiled and wiped rain off his face and the melting visor of his cap. "It's men like you, Bill, who turned back from California in '49 when they got as far as Kentucky, and who stayed home when George Washington said, Come visit our winter sports at Valley Forge."

Jay had been pretty active with some bottles of Torre Giulia we had stocked at La Spezia. Wet and miserable and hungry, I chewed on a length of hard salami—made of old goat and candle wax, by the taste of it. We blew the frayed tire as we ran across some trolley-car tracks on the outskirts of Genoa, but we limped on, hunting the Hotel Mediterraneo, our goal. We nearly made it, but they were digging ditches—some work relief project, no doubt—and we ran into a hole and snapped an axle. Jay and I climbed out of the tilted car and I picked up the bundle of magazines wrapped in a raincoat. Jay stopped a boy on a bike and asked for the hotel, and the boy pointed and pedaled off as if he had seen the devil. We were pretty messed up, crumpled, wet, wrinkled, our caps melting, our white linen dusters all stained with the dye that had run off the covers of the magazines, and we had rubbed our faces with stained fingers, so we must have looked like Indians on the warpath.

Jay said, "I give up."

"No, it's too late; we've sacrificed the car."

"You material bastard."

We got to the hotel and went into the lobby, and they offered to throw us out. It was my turn to say Jay was the illegitimate son of W.W. and M.B.E.

They said there was a dinner in progress honoring the greatest hero and poet modern Italy had ever produced. I said that was our boy, and I got out money and began to drop it around. We did manage to get into the grand ballroom, guarded by two waiters who had been ordered to keep an eye on us. Jay was collapsing but I was determined. We pushed forward to the front, and I'm a little vague about this part, as I had picked up a cold on the mad trip and was sneezing and coughing and wiping my eyes, but I do remember Jay's somehow getting to a front table and dropping wet and runny copies around and leaning over—*Come sta?*—and kissing the bald head of the poet—*Bene, grazie, e Lei?*—who sprang up as if stung, and he and Jay enaged in some kind of talk in fast Italian, the poet's faster, and then we were arrested—*Buona sera, buona notte!*

I was so tired I fell asleep in the cell on a smelly yellow blanket while Jay recited some lines D'Annunzio had written for Eleanora Duse before he exposed their love in his book *The Flame:*

> *A mezzo il giorno*
> *Sul mare Etrusco*
> *Pallido verdicante*
> *Come il . . .*

We wired Tony for bail in the morning, but it wasn't needed. Somebody had pointed out to the poet that we were rich Americans and famous, and the magazine was a product of the new modern Italy he had planned. He had left town but sent us greetings of the old world turning new, and a new world coming of age itself in Italia. *Va canzonetta mia e saluta, Messere* . . .

Jay and I were a three-day sensation in the world press; we more than our magazine. It was a dull news season, and our mad adventure seemed amusing. The newsreel shots were run everywhere, and there were stories in the Paris *Herald* and the Chicago *Tribune*. The major wire services wrote us up, and several rather crazy quotes from the magazine were sent over the cables. ("It is hard to forgive the silences Wagner's music has broken." Eliot Tjaden.) It was really remarkable how much attention you could attract in those days if you were an American and paid for the damages.

Jay talked of going on to Berlin with Blue Blazes, through the Brenner Pass, presenting copies of *The Scream* to Thomas Mann and Hindenburg, and on to Paris to deliver copies to La Stein and James Joyce as well as to several Frenchmen as yet untranslated, and then putting Blue Blazes on a Channel steamer and bearding Bernard Shaw, Lord Russell, H. G. Wells and John Galsworthy. But Blue Blazes was hardly fit to travel, and Tony was angry and sold the wreck to a wool merchant from Milano. Tony didn't see the splendid worldwide attention my idea had won. For years the newspapers used the photograph of Jay wearing only a towel when from time to time he was newsworthy, and the picture of me in damp racing togs with goggles around my throat nearly strangling me; copies of it must be in every major newspaper morgue in the world. It gave me a kind of notoriety among racing nuts, and I was often asked about gear ratios, spin-outs, clutch plates and gas cylinder pressures.

Actually while our racing got *The Scream* into world news, I doubt if it helped sales much. I didn't get over my cold for weeks, and Tony refused to pay a lot of the bills we had run up in his name. Jay and I were dunned by shabby lawyers, soft-looking men in worn shoes who cried real tears on the doorstep and beat legal papers on their own brows. In time Tony took pity on us, as there was talk of jail, and he settled everything for a lump sum. D'Annunzio sent me a picture of himself standing on the bridge of a real battleship he had erected in his garden, signed: *La dove è il mio cuore notte e giorno—D'Annunzio.*

Quant' e bella giovinezza,
Che si fugge tuttavia.

If the appearance of *The Scream* did not topple the old entrenched bastions of literature, it did make a small, superficial sensation. (Jay said, "Like a lady farting in church.") Of the eight hundred copies we printed, at least three hundred never left the printers, and ended, I suppose, in pulp. Of the remainder, at least half we gave away, and of those that were sold few of the bookstores remembered to send us our share of the price. ("Were we a quest doomed to frustration by its absurdity?") But that is the way with little magazines, we found out. We did get two-hundred-and-seven subscribers, twenty-two promises of patrons. We expanded our print order for the second issue to twenty-five hundred, as we added outlets, some shaky, some unknown, with fifty in Paris, London, New York, San Francisco, that at least sounded impressive.

Tony was a spark plug, rushing proofs to the printer in his Duesenberg, arriving with traveler's checks when the truck driver who took our publication to the Paris train refused to unload or release bundles until he was paid.

Tony expanded the diversity of our lives. We gave up eating in cheap *trattorias,* gave up polenta *a la Torino,* for Tony insisted we be well fed. "Like my mother says, so eat—take a piece fruit. *Addio. Come va!*"

Jay went around with a crucified expression when some critics wrote unfavorably of the first installment of *Stone Sunlight;* his excessive irritability, he explained, being that of any artist "who is spoken of badly by nobodies." There were two nearly good comments. Some bright Commies in *The New Masses* wrote, *"Stone Sunlight* showed that it is impossible for America to breed the true Bohemian, and our artists accept martyrdom as a kind of immortality." *The American Mercury* pontificated: "Profundity of this sort, as in Mr. Jaden's [*sic*] novel, destroys innocence with an intense feminine sympathy. Why do not these writers come home? We could use such a fine talent here. Art on strange shores is often a mere impiety. The mind in exile doesn't act—it merely condones action."

So, harassed by poor distribution and heartened by some kindly or nearly kind attention, we went on to Volume I, No. 2.

Later I used to wonder if the years had been so good and fine and

212

crazy for us. I had to admit that perhaps they had been. It was not nostalgia, and not being young. The '20s were really alive and full of new forces. Maybe they weren't so important as we thought, and what we did wasn't so good as it looked then. But it was better than what came later. In the '30s it was all Marx and Franco's Moors and Brown Shirts, and in the '40s it was a fouled-up war—fun and fornicating in the Blitz for some—and in the '50s it was nothing at all, and then . . .

Things being done, and being said, and being carved and painted *were* new when we issued *The Scream*. The last of Dada and cubism went, and the first of surrealism came; and the daring writers were panting after Proust and Joyce, and there was talk soon of Kafka and Céline and the headaches of Hindemith and Berg and Schoenberg in our ears—why, Stravinsky was almost a classic. We brushed away the small irrelevancies that spoiled enormous meanings.

Bea would talk of Mondrian, whom none of us had heard of, and Kandinsky and Beckmann. Samuel Beckett was just hanging around, and Brecht was new and very young. . . . Somehow by luck and lack of character I had stumbled into the advance guard and I didn't know it; I was just doing what seemed to me new and exciting, and only Jay kept his balance when he wasn't writing. "Flesh becomes scandal," he said, "and ideas become art. It's a screwed-up old world, and the mean minds run us. Old Baudelaire had the right terms for life: 'I cultivate my hysteria with joy and terror.' He had the proper slant. Damn it, Pages, is that the last of the brandy?"

"Yes, and it's two in the morning."

"The *only* time to talk. Lao-tse, Job, Aeschylus are not for daytime. The ideas they invent are more real to us than any reality. Bea, get a bottle from your studio."

"No," said Pages. "You're drunk. Let's go to bed."

"You fine Boston cod, you don't know the fecundity, the resourcefulness, of life."

"Fecundity!" said Bea. "And herself with a belly that's as fertile as a sturgeon's. Good night, we're packing it in."

Till the next night. And the next. . . .

There was a hard side to all this. The winter in Rome was bleak: icy rains, poor heat from charcoal and little stoves, the breath we left as we walked along floating like vapor, nights we four clung together

213

in our beds, sharing body warmth with the partner, and looking at each other with that pathological dread of solitude.

There is something of a sadness about living with women when it is not in one's own home, when marriage is not part of it, when there is no guilt or society to say this is not holy, not legal (you cannot so easily break the domestic trap of society). It is outside all social approval that this form of true companionship comes; outlaw partners make it warm, more intimate, trembly at times because it could end tomorrow, break up, drift away.

Then comes the thought, like the sound of one's own heart drumming in a nightmare: Keep it—better marry and own this thing properly by book and holy writ, by civil decree. But reflected in the morning coffee are the images of all our friends who failed, the people we know whose marriages have turned wrong become psychological puzzles. So we go on our way, hoping for us this thing—a man and woman, not married, no legal cords—will suffice, make do. (On this subject there is soil fertile for prophets, but I wasn't one then, and don't think I have much more to say now.)

In the morning our rooms smelled of the ever-present charcoal gas, cold walls sweating. We would pile on more clothes: rag on rag, jacket on sweater, coat on jacket, muffler on coat, like a mockery of a store dummy. The stones of Rome rang like bells, and the damn bells rang as always from nearly five hundred churches, calling the snotty, coughing, hawking faithful to morning Mass, and again ringing at noon, in the afternoon, and for the last prayer of the day; the clang of bronze in the saddest hour of any divine mystery.

Pages grew larger, but not yet so large that she became ungainly. And I doubted that she would. Tony called a staff meeting; sleet rattled on the windows of his suite at the luxury Hassler Hotel. We had no sooner got there than Pages disappeared at once into the gold-and-white bathroom to float—she said forever—in the pink-veined marble tub. Bea rubbed her red nose and sat by the hissing radiator. Jay and I faced Tony, who was going through a batch of bills. He handed us each a dreadfully expensive Dutch cigar, and we sat smoking while he paced the rug.

"Stop it," Jay said. "You're like Theseus searching in the labyrinth for the Minotaur."

"All *he* had to do was follow the bullshit. . . . Now I don't see it, I mean putting this magazine over, unless we get in some crackerjack distributing outfit to handle sales, somebody to write pow!-*wow!* direct-mail letters with a powerful draw."

"Maybe we could give it away, two for one, with *The Saturday Evening Post*," said Jay. "*Pow, wow!*"

"Don't get ironic, Jay," said Tony. "Keep the wit for the magazine. It's a damn fine thing, this magazine we're publishing. But we can't keep it a secret."

I said, "We ought to go to a hundred and twenty pages, get better engraving, maybe a better paper."

Bea said, "Don't overexpand. It will be vulgar."

Jay looked at his glowing cigar end, scratched his whiskers. "I like it the way it is. Over-inked type, yellowed paper. It has the damn look of something serious and hard to put together. I don't want to ape the *Atlantic Monthly* or *Harper's*. That's for old maids and college professors. I say we don't try to go after big sales and a fancy format. Beauty is only that which discovers a truth."

Tony smiled. He always had that charm some people have of being sure they can win others to their way of thinking, what Jay called "the lousy vice of heroes—a belief in their own infallibility. That's how wars start, and bad love affairs."

Jay usually did come around to Tony's thinking, but he didn't like himself for it later. He'd drink *grappa* and belch and say of Tony, "A flashy Hebe. Has all the ostentation of the vanity of a frightened man laughing. We did wrong, Bill, to bring him in. Very wrong."

"It was Tony or no guarantee we could keep the magazine going for a year."

"Keep him on the ground."

That cold, sleety day, Tony didn't put over his point for publicity on a bigger scale. Jay carefully killed his cigar in a gold-plated ashtray—as if breaking a neck—and stood up, hands in the pockets of a worn blue wool jacket. "It's all damn fine, Tony. But I'm not buying it, and I'm not letting anybody else buy it. We stay the way we are. Don't look at me as if I've drowned your kittens. Maybe this project isn't for you. We're fools, fine; we're dopes, maybe . . . but we're not aggressive."

Tony nodded as if he were being fair. "Go on, go on, Jay. I'm listening."

"You haven't been. You see something we don't, and don't want to. I guess I speak for Bill."

"I'll speak for myself."

"Sure you will. But be slow and careful what you say, *paisano*. *The Scream* isn't for everybody. It's what Stendhal calls 'for the happy few.' We keep it that way. Call it emotional, rather than factual, reality—who cares?"

Tony tapped the table before him, reached to shake off his cigar ash, then decided to let it fall to the rug. Bea, warmed into life by the steam heat, looked from Jay to Tony like a child enjoying a family fight.

"What's the bloody brawl? We want to keep it going. What's the matter how it's done? Now let's get back. I'm warm and I've got to glaze a painting before the blasted varnish dries out."

Tony said in a low voice, too much under control, "I'm the stupid sonofabitch who only puts up the cash. I guess it will stay that way. All right, we'll do it Jay's way, for the next issue anyway. I thought you really wanted to spit in the eye of the world."

Jay didn't show any comfort in his victory. He turned his head and yelled at the bathroom door. "Damn it, Pages, you've boiled enough. Climb out of there. We're going home."

Tony looked at me and then looked away. "She'll catch cold leaving here all steamed up and overheated, walking in that cold outside."

Jay said, "We'll take a taxi. . . . Pages, get out of that bath."

Bea looked up at Jay. "Stop rushing her. She's getting heavy and she may slip in the tub."

I saw Tony wanted to say more, but the bathroom door opened and Pages came out, a pile of blue-black hair done up high, emphasizing the purity of her profile. She was getting heavy around the middle, but for all that she was still trim, and in her new robe (one of the first things I had insisted on her buying) she looked more like a Greek stone goddess than ever; though she was annoyed at Jay, she retained a resigned tranquillity, a pout soft as velvet.

"Stop howling and I'll dress."

In the street Jay was like what my grandfather used to call "a bear with a sore ear," and in the taxi—Pages bundled up against the cold that seeped through the loose doors of the rattletrap machine—he just sat and stared at her.

She looked at him over the two mufflers I had wound around her neck. "You can go to hell, Eliot Tjaden."

Bea rolled her eyes. "Can't you two keep it down till you get home?"

"He's just so goddamn pigheaded," said Pages, shivering. "Tony has got his French lawyers to arrange my divorce at once in Paris, and El takes it as if he were selling me to a harem."

"What crap," growled Jay. "I told him to keep his shysters out of my affairs."

"*Our* affairs."

"What's the difference?" I said. "It's what you both want, isn't it?"

Pages gave a hollow laugh and hunched down into the mufflers. "Hah! Who knows?"

Jay said, "Oh shut up, *deconner.*"

Pages shouted in Italian for the taxi driver to stop. There was a screech of loose brakes, and before we could react, Pages opened the door as the taxi stopped rolling and ran off through a market area and was lost among the stalls lit by flares. Night was falling like dust in the cold street.

Bea shouted, "Jay, go after her. There's ice on the walks."

"The hell with it. She wants to walk, let her walk."

"You filthy perishing males! *Fottuti* bastards!"

Bea got out of the taxi and ran toward a group of charcoal braziers where women muffled to the ears were gutting giant bluefish. I started to follow, but Jay pulled on my arm. "Don't. Bea will find her. Oh this *potta* woman business!"

"I don't understand you, Jay, or your actions. You love her. I know that."

"I know it, too."

"Then why this foul attitude to everything? Christ, Tony just wants to help us."

"Sure he does. Act the hero before Pages. Damn it, if I wanted his lawyers, I'd have asked him. He makes me look like a horse's ass."

"There *is* a resemblance. Sometimes I think you don't want her to get a divorce."

He looked at me with hatred in his face. And I suddenly knew our friendship was near snapping, and I didn't want that, so I relaxed my voice and tried to get back on a better footing. "You act as if you were pregnant, not Pages."

He gave me a small smile. "All right, *paisan,* let's go find her."

We told the taxi to wait and went into the market area among obscenely gutted sheep, sides of pork, split-open fish, lobsters, all crisp and icy-looking. Bea and Pages were inside a small glass booth on wheels drinking *caffè espresso* in the steam of cooking sprats, with heavy men in earth-soiled clothes eating huge sandwiches and drinking a fiery *grappa*. Pages sipped the hot brew and remained poker-faced.

Jay put his arm on her shoulder. "It's all right now. I'm sorry I acted like a shit to Tony."

Bea handed me a cup of *espresso;* we both knew it was not at all right. Outside, lost bits of paper were scattering; a dog drifted by, avoiding puddles. Rome in winter.

CHAPTER 23

PAGES DIDN'T GET PNEUMONIA OR PLEURISY, and she didn't slip on the icy sidewalks. She just began to stain in the middle of the night. The Italian doctor I routed out of a double bed said it was nothing, nothing at all: *Vorrei* just for her to stay in bed and not get up till I tell her. *Sì.* Bea made Pages soup, and Jay brought in food from the *pasta* place. Pages looked very pale and worried and wonderful in the brass bed, saying she didn't want to be any bother. There were no narcissistic attitudes about her. Bea said the staining had stopped but that Pages's bladder didn't seem to function properly. At the end of the week I insisted we get an English-speaking doctor from the Salvator Mundi International Hospital, which had American-trained staff members who believed in germs and clean hands.

Dr. Vernon was young and not too sure of himself, but he fell in love with Pages right away, and he came over to Bea's studio after his examination, where we were forcing Jay to eat something.

"If the staining doesn't come back, I don't see anything to fear. But your wife, Mr. Tjaden, is anemic."

"She isn't my wife." Jay looked up at the doctor, the spoon pointed at him like a pistol. "It's what you call a ménage."

The doctor went embarrassingly pink. "Oh! Well, she's still a pregnant woman. Could I notify her people?"

"Why?"

"No reason, I suppose. I'll prescribe something to build up her red blood corpuscles. Liver should also help, not too well done, lots of liver."

"Lots of liver," said Jay, close, I saw, to saying *Fous-moi le camp.*

The doctor continued to stare at Jay. He looked foolish and shy as if he had broken a valuable vase. Bea caught on at once. "What's the fee, doctor?"

"Oh, I could, I suppose, bill Mr. Tjaden—I mean . . ."

"Pay the doctor," said Jay.

"A hundred lire?" I said, reaching for my wallet.

Jay went out to go back to Pages. The doctor blushed and wrote out a prescription and took the money and looked from Bea to me. "I suppose among creative people, I mean, these irregular situations, ménages—" he said.

Bea said, "He's a *gran cazzo*. But we're not married either."

The doctor said, "Yes," and put down the prescription and looked over at the large painting of the general's funeral. "You have a flair for it, I must say."

"You like art?" Bea asked.

"Oh, not too much, but I like your subject—it's so Italian. Death is sad, but also a festival for good crying."

When he was gone, Bea said, "I don't suppose he knew he wasn't being complimentary. What does he mean—so *Italian?* Don't Americans die, stink, make worm meat?"

She began to mix a deep purple for the shadows of the archbishop's robes in the *State Funeral of General Cesare Chigi.*

"Of course we die—we're just not dramatic about it. Grief is private."

(Sickrooms have always depressed me; the truth is they frighten me. Not just the bare intimations of mortality; bowels, bitter medicine, and sick flesh odors. So I flee like a coward at anyone's illness. I'd even run from mine if I could. I have written off the sick, broken any contact with them till they're recovered. I didn't do that with Pages. I overcame myself. I would put my head in the door of their place quickly to keep out the cold wind, and say she looked better, much better, and go away.)

I took to walking by myself while Bea painted. To me winter is mean and yet strong too, like January quarters for horses, where their strength is held back, stalled, but you're aware of the animal strength. A solitary winter day was often a total incomprehensible happiness for me. I was alone—I couldn't talk to Jay; he was worried now about Pages. Bea, besides painting, was nursing, making soups, cursing all men—*fottuti*—wouldn't let me get near her in bed, slept on her side and kicked out at me with her little hard heels when I tried to capture her by *cul* or *potta*.

Tony was away in Milano—something had gone fearfully scientifically wrong with the casting of the mortar block of his racer in work. . . . I walked, saw the leaden ruffled surface of the river, saw ragged, freezing people burning trash under bridges, nasty wetness running from weathered noses, bodies bundled up, lines of priests, nuns, seminary students bent against the wind, even the bells sounding as if one more ring would shatter their frozen bronze like glass.

> *Quant e bella giovinezza,*
> *Che si fugge tuttavia.*
>
> *How beautiful is youth,*
> *Youth forever fleeting.*

I went walking toward the *piazza* of St. Peter's, avoiding the pigeons that had fallen frozen from the eaves, brown commas on the street, past the few freezing pilgrims, their zeal not keeping their toes warm for they were banging their feet against the hard rock stone walk of the Bernini colonnade. The dome of Michelangelo Buonarroti looked frostbitten; the chipped saints all along the roof seemed to shiver in the *rompicoglioni* of a cold wind.

There was always some droning of Latin in the interior of St. Peter's, the basilica and the golden apse looking as vulgar as ever, everything overornate in that Catholic vanity that they had captured the only true dogma—too rich, too real, for the simple Jesus who would be amused, maybe, at what had happened to his few words. To bring into being what we want is the hardest miracle.

I didn't linger in the stale old priest smell, but went to the Sistine Chapel, where I had made friends with a little monk who controlled a side door, and I always slipped him a small flask of *grappa* or a cake called *nun's-thigh;* he was a fine drunkard.

220

The monk let me in, his breath smoking, the vast vaulting of the chapel lost in green-gray arctic gloom. I slipped him the flask. He said *grazie per il tuo paese*. I walked loudly—heels hard—along the marble floor, and over my head the damned and healed, the angry and heroic, performed for me; a conquest of genius not yet depleted of awe. This artist had been an unhappy bastard, greedy for money and boys' *culs,* horrified at his acts of sin, frightened of death, angry at popes, a sucker to his grasping relatives, given to prayer with that dried-up cunt Vittoria Colonna, a pious idiot of a bitch who almost persuaded him to hate living and to be ashamed of his genitalia. Poor twisted bastard genius on his back up there four years painting the ceiling, screaming his rage at the work in his poems:

I've grown a goiter by living in this joint
Like cats from stagnant streams in Lombardy
Or in whatever place they happen to be,
It drives the guts tight up under your chin.
My loins are into my belly like levers socked.
My ass like a saddle bears my weight;
My legs, off the ground, kicking around, going noplace . . .

I'm cold and hot; the *cazzo* could paint, could write—and he crapped out on the dice to fear, rotting in his unchanged underwear. (O *Dio,* we're all *fottuti.*)

It's hard to believe that geniuses, so crusted with rewards, glory, so far in the past, have the same troubles we have, worry over sin (which we've renamed the subconscious), over money (which we're inflating at so fast a rate it soon will be worthless as weeds); and as for immortality—there is a bronze plaque in front of the house in which I was born. It reads: SOUTHERN JERSEY COUNTIES GAS AND POWER COMPANY. The cold was making me foolish with a distrust of all enthusiasms.

Walking back to Bea's studio, the wind sharp and cold down from the Alps where, I thought, a couple of hundred thousand little waiters from the Piedmont serving carafes of Frascati once died, and so were lucky enough to escape the fate of coming home to wives who no longer wanted them. I walked past the stalls where they sell the holy junk to tourists and pilgrims, they were boarded up now, but two short Italians stood, backs to the wind, carrying on some sly deal, their rigid hands inside their worn overcoats as they haggled.

"*Forse domani.*"

"*Io non posso.*"

"*Forse, aspetti.*"

Past me on bicycles wheeled the bearded old priests, smelling of artichokes cooked in oil, toothless old men, varicose veins on their blue cold legs under their robes, carrying the little bag, the bell, the holy unguent, to go build a salad of ash and oil on some dying person's brow, a creature hungering for the last rites, the breathing growing worse, the tongue dry. *Chi lo sa?* I can't breathe—the death rattle is on me.

Past the café where the faggots hang out, flaunting their *culs,* in tight pants, smoking cigarettes in long paper holders, running slim hands over heads of marvelously marcelled hair, whispering to me: "*Venga, venga,* hey Joe, *suckyocazzo, fottere yo?*" They never give up, and they are protected by the state, like rare game birds, for there are in season American and British tourists who can't dare get it at home and come on for a bit of camping here, to take back the Roman taste of it to Green River in Kansas, Kimley-on-Wallon in Essex, to the respectable other life—a proper little Main Street bank, a sporting goods shop, the chicken farm, the board room of a family foundation.

"*Così, così.*"

Past Alfredo's *trattoria,* where the gross feeders are at work over filled plates, shoveling it in, winding it around forks, sipping it up from spoons, soaking it up in a good crust of bread, washing it down with white wine, red wine, imported beer, Strega. Their faces signed with jaundice and dropsy, sweaty with the effort of eating, they reach for the bread, the sauces, sighing, grunting, belching, farting; man is made to eat, to dissolve in acids the tissues, organs, flesh of lesser breeds. I press my cold nose to the plate-glass window and in the freezing air see them tear a whole limb off a chicken (what teeth), watch the waiter, as if at a sacred rite, debone a trout. I study the feeders, bags of fermenting juices, turn on my X-ray eyes, see their glands spurting bile into their gorged stomachs, the acids attacking the fragments among surgeons' scars, the colons twitching, the kidneys at work shifting, washing out the minerals' wealth, the impurities, drop by drop, beginning to fill the bladders with rich yellow fluid. All the grinding, pressing, coiling, turning, is clear to me; then for them only a little rest, because in a few hours they must do it all over again. Repack the guts, evacuate, swell the glands.

I turn off my X ray, move away, watch some wet-nosed children slide on an icy sidewalk that dips past trees that are only black stalks now. Kids that will in their time-bind become eaters and feeders, kids now carrying in their bodies genetic banks, the good and evil of our million ancestors, kids who will be Michelangelo again, movie actors, Mafia gangsters returning from Chicago, faggots at the espresso joints, little fat husbands with many bambinos, little girls in white to be confirmed, bearded eunuchized priests on bicycles, sitting on walnuts not balls—who never had the grit and guile to advance themselves into a soft warm Vatican position. . . . Some of the kids will be me, hands in pockets, walking, going along in the cold, nearly thirty years old, once schoolboy, bike rider, flying ace (three crappy medals and the hand shake of King George (V) and a bit of steel in the hip), lover, seducer (twice), failure to seduce (a few hundred times), cotton mill machinery salesman (a neglected task), American ("Hurrah, the flag is passing by!"), expatriate, publisher . . . lousy student of Italian verse:

> *O graziosa luna, io mi rammento*
> *O shapely moon, I remember . . .*

Tony's monster of a car was in front of the house. It was too late and too cold for any of the kids to be out crawling over it, blackmailing, a protection racket. I went in. Tony all alone was sitting by Bea's little glowing fireplace. He looked as if someone had stunned him with a club and left him alive but numb. His eyes did a myopic prowling over my face but didn't focus.

"It's Pages," he said. "She's in the Mundi International. She's had a miscarriage."

"Oh Christ. *O Dio.*"

"Bea is with her. And Jay. I came back to pack some things for her."

"She's all right?"

"How the hell can we know? They think so. Pretty messy. She was far along. Want a drink?" He held up one of Bea's glasses half full of brandy.

I said, "No."

"That's right, you're off it."

223

"That's right, the hard stuff."

"Great idea."

"Marvelous idea. Poor Pages."

Tony shook himself as if to clear his head, swallowed Bea's brandy; it was our house bottle. He offered me a cigar. I shook my head. He lit his carefully, the easy horse's-ass way of a show-off smoker, rotating the blunt end, not charring it. He waved out the match. He wasn't showing off—he didn't know he had done it.

"I suppose, Bill, you have a letch for Pages?"

"We're not all dogs sniffing around a bit of *potta*."

"That's a rotten way to say it."

"Bullshit."

He got up, and, scowling as if his thoughts were beating themselves apart on the walls, he began to pace. "I'm going to see them married, Jay and Pages. That's my good deed for the year."

"Really, rabbi?"

"You snide bastard. *Yoisher,* don't you think it's time?"

"You're a little bit drunk or I'd throw you out."

"We've got to get them married."

"I don't think you give a good goddamn either way, Lieutenant Pfaelzer. It's just your way of getting some cozy little kicks being near her. Don't try to fool your old squadron commander."

"You're so rotten decadent, all of you. Hope is a soft mattress, life is some dead art, people are just jokes. Pages isn't like you. She's magnificent and we're using her."

"Not as much as you'd like. Didn't your mother tell you to stay away from *shiksas?*"

"You have a dirty mind."

"A dirty mind is a perpetual feast. Never mind applauding—it's a quote."

"That's what I mean. You lousy art lovers, avant-garde crap peddlers—everything is a quote to you. Well, the divorce for Pages is progressing. They'll be married as soon as she gets out of the hospital or in a couple of weeks."

I was still chilled and it made me mean. "You Jews, Tony, have a moral sense—haven't you?—that you owe the world protection. For us morality never pays back what it costs. You Jews don't keep cats or dogs, you take care of people."

224

"All right, so we do. If they let us. Does that make us *meshugga*—nuts?"

"Some people don't want to be taken care of. That's why we weaker people hate you. You're clean, you're moral Old Testament folk, god-fearing, great family men; don't cheat—much—on your wives, sacrifice yourselves for your fat pale children, die early from overwork. And for what? A son's college degree, the wife's mink coat, diamonds, a memorial wing in a *shul,* a room in a t.b. hospital in Denver. Maybe, Tony, the world doesn't want your kindness, your help. We savages like to be dirty, horny, mean. We like being Gentiles."

Tony with the irrelevancy of a loving hound dog put his arm around my shoulder. *"Gevalt,* Bill. You love her too. So cut the gas, come in for an easy landing. Captain Kite, you ought to become a drunk again."

"Tony, there is something wrong here. I can't figure it out. Let's go to the hospital."

"They won't let us see her. We'll go and sit with Bea and Jay."

I said I might as well.

I have not been trying, as I write, to explain the hold that Pages had on most people who knew her, nor the powerful attachment she turned on in those who loved her. She herself did very little to encourage such feelings. She seemed lazy, placid. But it was there, a kind of tender penetration to the core of your being. And that's not a subtle way to put it, but to reach any subliminal level is hard. Bea said Pages had an incomprehensible music about her. Tony said it was an exquisite sensibility. I settled for her intense luminous eyes.

Sitting in the hospital room two days after her miscarriage, I could no more explain our fascination than before. Perhaps it was a gracious pathological illusion we all shared. She half sat against a pile of pillows, paler than the paleness I remembered, her inky hair loose and flowing around her head ("I'm thinking of bobbing it—everybody is"), a deadly tiredness in the relaxed body, a body still magnificent (to survive gynecologists), under the sheets and a blanket tucked skillfully around it. I decided it was Pages's fastidiously reticent lucidity that fascinated us, because she was not in herself anything mystic; she was an evocation of reality, not an ideal. She wet her lips with her tongue and looked directly at me.

225

"Where's El?"

"He's sleeping in the visitors' room, on a couch."

"You've all kept the guard? The deathwatch?"

"Come on now, Pages, that's foolish talk."

"The baby is dead."

"It wasn't really a baby yet. A kind of fish."

"Oh yes, it was a baby. I could feel it kick."

She moved her head to look past the hothouse flowers too bright in their plain glass vase, past the gifts of crackers and packed fruits, to the long narrow window and beyond at the gray day (but no rain).

"What do I do now, Bill?"

"What do any of us do? Go on. One foot after the other, that's walking. Easy."

"As an aunt of mine out in Santa Barbara used to say, Ask a stupid question, get a stupid answer."

"It's not a stupid answer. We go on as if the road led someplace."

"What a bedside manner, Bill. Hand me the barley water."

I handed her a glass of some pale whitish drink and a bent glass tube. She sucked on it and I took back the glass and put it down.

"I nearly died, Bill. They couldn't stop the bleeding."

"They didn't feel there was any real danger at any time."

"Why should they? They're not me. And me, who is me? That I don't know either."

I played the game. (I had played it at Princeton). "We all ask who is me. Me is I. You is you. Together we are us. Us is me, you, them."

"You sound like Gertrude Stein. Me, me, *me!*" She closed her eyes and made a thin line of her lips. "First I must heal, then I must think. Then I must act."

I made a congenial easy gesture and took up a pear from a basket. I wondered if she was still running a temperature. She was irritable, with some personal pique, which was understandable. Women have a lousy setup in premarital sex in our society. Their plumbing is often emotional and their fertility a problem. Only in plays and films does the brave little girl with big Christ eyes from second-rate church art look up from the hospital bed and sigh and give a brave smile. Pages had had some living flesh torn from her, been bruised, fingered, cut, sewn, had bled, felt dizziness, nausea, and a futility in her quivering aborting womb. She'd been drugged, humiliated by enema and bed-

226

pan, packed, handled. She was doing fine for all that, and I wanted her to gripe.

She held out a white hand and I took it and pressed it finger by finger, giving myself a thrill; the flesh was warm, damp. "Take El home. Don't let him get too drunk. And send in the nurse. I need the bedpan."

I nodded and went out. Jay was sleeping on a too short sofa in the visitors' room. Tony was smoking a short English pipe and reading a month-old copy of the Paris *Herald*. Bea was knitting what I feared was a scarf for me.

CHAPTER 24

SCENE—*Waiting room of a hospital. Rome.*

I looked from Bea's knitting to the sofa, and I shook Jay; he looked a Socrates debauched by worry and lack of sleep. Every individual has just so much irritable defiance in him, and Jay had almost reached bottom. He sat up rubbing his eyes, staring at Tony.

"I was dreaming," he said. "Remember Charlie's 12.5-horsepower Sizaire, when we came back from Paris that time? That time . . ." He looked up and grinned. "Crazy time. How is she?"

"Pretty good," I said. "If you're going to see her, knock. She may be on the potty."

He shuffled off, but I could see he was pulling together; he was coming round after shock, the way Charlie had said Jay did in the war after a bad flight. He always had bounce, and sleep was for Jay at times a rite of purification.

Tony said dryly, "Some German bighead says the core of us is pride, a willful denial and contradiction of nature."

"You've been reading the wrong books."

Bea put aside her knitting. "Ignore Bill. Contact with literature has done you good, Tony."

"No, it hasn't." He knocked out his pipe into an ashtray and went out, but in the other direction, not toward Pages's room.

"That's bad, Bea, when Tony gets literary."

227

She began to roll up the loose wool into a ball. "You ever sit in on a murder?"

"No, have you? Now, don't lie, Lady Brown."

"On a mood, then, of murky veiled passion? A classical scene. It's no jolly do, I can tell you."

"You can't tell me anything. There isn't anything here."

"Not murder, of course. But, ducks, perhaps a dustup coming. Did you ever read popular novels and wonder why the damn writers always get their plots entangled with the basic situation—*who* pairs off with *whom?*"

"I read for style."

"Bloody snob. Let's go home. We'll come back tonight with some broth."

Of course Bea was right. My mangy stoicism couldn't entirely blank out the disquieting atmosphere. We didn't want to say it right out in words; I didn't. But a bit of our recognizable world was dissolving. We did not get any full images of events; it was more like things felt blindly under water.

Bea giggled all the way home in the taxi. It was a hysterical giggle, emotional and illogical. I knew the signs as she held my arm. I smelled brandy.

"Love is the finest of all instruments of torture."

"Lay off it, you cockney bitch," I said, saying it with ironic overtones; I was very fond of Bea, she was an affirmation I needed.

"I'll have you know, Bill Kite, I come from a long line of damned important people. Not a worker or a man in trade in fifty generations. Cockney my arse. . . . Can't you just see Jay is wanting to get out of this marriage? But not wanting to either. Wanting Pages, yet trying to get free. The bloody fool and his philosopher's self-canceling ideas."

"No. There is no reason. No reason at all."

"And take Tony, that toff—the romantic, the handsome dark Oriental stranger for whom women come down to his level quickly. Now he's in love, and he's not sharp enough emotionally to understand the absurdity of life and its relating joys. Or are we too close to see the blasted drama?"

I said, "You've got a hell of an imagination, darling."

"God finds us behind a thousand walls."

228

I realized Bea was drunk; she never showed physically she had been drinking. She and Jay must have been out for several big nips while waiting. Bea hardly revealed herself much when sober. She could, however, express herself well when a bit looped. It was the release of alcohol, just as funerals released her painting, as making love relaxed her tensions. Fornication, I decided, is also a medicine.

At home I added charcoal to our little stove, and when Bea—relaxed, released, sated—fell asleep, it was dark and the church bells were beginning their clanging. Neither Jay nor Tony had come back from the hospital. I lay on my side playing scales—g, a, b, c, d, e, f-sharp, g—on Bea's ribs.

There is something tremendously satisfying about sexual intercourse when used for tension coming after a crisis. (I give this knowledge freely to the medical profession.) I lay musing: I could open up a clinic for most of the troubles of mankind produced by the pressures of the world. I planned a booklet: "Dr. William Kite, Quack." The Original Sex Treatments. Very beneficial and pleasant. Feel your way to mental health. Touch contentment, reality; learn biology the fun way. Full series of advanced classes (with illustrations and models). Genitalia enthroned. Eros dry-cleaned, no curable case refused. All folk treated here at our million-dollar spa. Branch offices staffed by trained (since childhood) native girls in Hong Kong, in Cairo, in Boston. (Yes, Boston; gets the cardinal's and bishops' trade, the limp-pricked Protestant Lodges and Cabots, the horny Irish ward heelers, political big shots.) I would be with Buddha and Moses, a new Saviour through the lower organs . . . I dozed . . . the great Dr. William Kite, and his motto: "Sinai and Golgatha are not here nor there . . . the angel is crucified everywhere and in every sphere. . . ."

I was torn from sleep by Jay's coming home: his hard banging of doors. I could recognize his footsteps anyplace. He was sober; his walk told me that. A steady slow pace. Regular. Somber, worried—too slow. I heard him unlock the door to the place he and Pages shared. Heard him kick at a bottle, a sound of glass breaking, slump of tired body falling into a chair, shoes falling—one, two—rasp of a curtain on a brass rod being drawn into place, jingle of bedsprings, the sigh of a man, troubled, expelling his breath, turning to comfort his prone body, the beating of a pillow, more jingling, a *slow* steady

229

rhythm—he was comforting himself shamelessly like a little boy all alone making a warm private corner all his own. . . .

I turned and put my arms around Bea and went into a locked-in slumber which lasted till the pale cold winter sun woke me. *Eh bien, lis dévore, et branle-toi.*

EDITOR'S NOTE: This section of the manuscript is in great disorder. Several parts consist of two or three versions of the same incident which I have edited into, I hope, one valid text. While most of the manuscript is written on yellow lined paper, much of this is on light blue paper of a smaller size. There also appear to be twenty pages missing, if the casual numbering is to be trusted. What the missing material is I have no real idea. One sheet may survive—an unnumbered one inserted before the following section. It begins and ends in the middle of a sentence. I insert it here:

. . . so there in the mind and there in the eye both of them mixed in the back of the museum of the Palazzo dei Conservatori where they keep the rows of Renaissance popes' medals—and no one goes there much, and even the guard is missing, for the medals are only poor plaster casts. There they were, she in his knotted arms, and he kissing her neck with the ardor of a pecking swan and she arching her face away and he forcing her mouth to meet his. The way an old movie is played very still, unreal with no piano music and the light flickering. Only they were real, and I stood around the corner in the little room where the bad drawings by Guido Reni are. I saw in a flawed mirror reflection just the two of them, heard then their voices, low, dusty in the decaying palace where for the fee of five lire you can wander where you want. She said, "I know I know." He said, "There's nothing else for it, darling," and she said, "Sweet, you don't have to tell me." He said, "So we go. It's settled, then?" She butted her head on his chest and said, "You can't just tear yourself away that easy." He bent back her head and dried her tears with the palm of his hand. "Yes, the best break is the quick one. You see?" She said, "I don't see, I just feel, I know it's good." "Good and clean and damn right." She said, "Right and wrong, just words, just words." He said, "Words—what the hell—have shades of meaning." "We mustn't make it brutal for him." "Darling, I'm not a brutal guy." "No, you're not. You're strong. You make decisions." "All my life, always decisions." They kissed again, and I wanted to leave softly, quickly, unseen. But there I was with those lousy drawings all brown and frayed, foxed, and the gallnut ink eating holes in them; angels, *putti,* constipated-looking Marys and little Christs well filled in their skins like Italian salami. "Don't you think I'm a tramp?" she asked. "How could I?" "You know, suddenly changing partners." He said, "I never saw it like that. Think only of yourself. You're good." She

230

said, "Let's not think at all." "Maybe it's better not to think. But think we have to." "You warm? It's sort of close in here." "Let's go someplace. I hear somebody in the next room." A guard came along scratching his left buttock. I became interested in a sepia cloud on which rode three rust stains, two angels blowing what looked like tenor saxophones. He and she slipped away, gripping each other's hands tightly, lover style, her color high, he scowling that black scowl of his which didn't mean anything, I had found out—he wore it happy, he wore it sad; it was a mask to him; inside he could be himself behind the scowl for m

The fragment ends here. The following section is peculiar; the pages are crisscrossed twice with a blue pencil, so most likely they were not to be part—in this version at least—of the final manuscript. But as no material to replace them is on hand and they do somewhat aid to dispel the confusion, I have included them. Obviously pages have been removed, and of them I have found no trace.

This isn't a novel: the novel is art; all the shocks in it come at even-paced intervals—a bit of fun, a touch of horror, a pinch of irony. Like that. A little fancy crap about life, low goings-on, grimy, gamy but valid. But it wasn't like that for us.

Sitting in the Comparetti café near the Capitoline Museum where the Greek and Roman statues no longer appeal. (How many times can you look at the Dying Gaul—all he needs is surgery and iodine—or Cupid and Psyche?) I waited, drinking black coffee, nibbling on hothouse grapes that were not too well cleaned of the sawdust they had been packed in. It was warm inside. I thought I was not weathering the non-novelist shocks too well; each inside has an outside, I mused (trying not to think of anything too involved), and the outside has streets, cities, fields; besides all that there is the moving of time present, carrying in its mouth (by a tail) time past and butting its nose into time future—all marked by night and day, by week, month, year, century, in a wrinkled corner of one infested universe. I couldn't go beyond that just then and held up my cup for a refill. I had to think of all the recent shocks.

Jay came in. I wanted to cheer him up by saying, "To be betrayed at least proves we still exist," but I didn't think he could grasp nuances today.

He sat down and said he'd have a coffee. He looked at me at first grimly, then with his smile of affirmation. "That's it."

"You saw them off?"

"Yes. Wasn't it the right gesture?"

"I always thought gallant gestures were a pain in the prat."

He put his ungloved chapped hands around the hot coffee cup. "I wasn't very fair to Pages or good to her, *paisano.*"

"No. And don't think I'd say you were. I almost get a goofy feeling you wanted something like this to happen."

"Not just like this. Tony will marry her, of course. The French divorce went through."

I looked at his silhouette against the musty wall; he was half a wraith, half a pathetic intangible enigma to me.

"Why in hell didn't you marry her?"

Jay moved his spoon around in the cup. In the café mirror my own likeness seemed a poor resemblance. "All right, Bill. I'll tell you why. Because my father, the Bishop, he's a nigger."

There are only a few times in life when it seems your spine has coiled up like a steel spring and with a sudden jolting release spears itself into your brain; this was one of those times. I pressed a grape hard between my fingers. Two large women went to the door with a staccato tap of heels.

"You're a bit unhinged, Jay."

"No. No—actually my father is a Negro, or a colored man as some of your people say."

"He doesn't look it. He looks like Michelangelo's Moses."

"Moses was most likely a nigger too. He wasn't a Jew, Freud says. Lots of Negro blood in Egyptians—the good side of them—and he was most likely Egyptian. My father's grandfather was a field slave in Virginia named Young, who came north through the Underground Railroad, married a white schoolteacher in Vermont—Tjaden is *her* name . . . some French-German strain."

"How do you know all this? Or are you still writing the novel?"

"The Bishop, that sterling honest God-loving man, knows all the facts, yet is living a lie."

"How do you know all this?"

Jay took a sip of coffee. I felt the grape crushed between my fingers.

"Bill, you're the only person I've ever told this to."

"How do you know?"

"From Billy Brunswick. He's a sort of second cousin of mine, you

232

know. I'm glad we gave him our trade. He's busy improving the color line—having whiter and whiter children with his various 'wives.' "

"He could be lying. You should have put a question direct to the Bishop."

"I couldn't, Bill. I love him. He's a fine man, good, very good. And an old man. Why shatter *his* fantasy, merely to show the holes in *my* fantasy?"

"I'd still not believe Billy Brunswick even if he took the oath holding a red-hot iron bar."

"I got into the Bishop's tin box when I was sixteen—the one he keeps under his bed. I opened it with a bent wire; we niggers have no morals, you know. It's all there, even old photographs of my black family relations. Clippings from old papers. *Brandon Johnson's runaway slave, Mike Young, six feet tall, light yellow complexion, could pass for Spaniard.* He reached Canada through the Underground Railroad. There is the old wedding certificate. Other things. I can tell you it almost made me put the shotgun in my mouth and toe the trigger."

"And for this nonsense you gave up Pages?"

"You don't think I wanted to breed any goddamn Congo throwback? Do you? A brood of black pickaninnies?"

"You never told her?"

"Nearly did in Paris in 1916. I nearly did here when she said she was pregnant. I'm a yellow dog." He laughed. "I *am* at that, huh? I mean a coward not to have brought it out in the open."

"You're not drinking?"

"No. Didn't want to appear crocked at the railroad station. Wanted to carry it off. You know, modern, postwar, flip. Goodbye, old chap, hope you and my girl have a fucking good time of it in Paris. Regards to Ernest and Pablo. Only sensible thing to do. You love her, old chap; she loves you. You marry her. I will not marry her. Try the trout on the Paris Express, and piss on the Eternal Light at the Tomb of the Unknown Soldier for all three of us. Urine, you know, is held sacred by Eskimos. Oh, we were *so* civilized; you'd never see anything carried off better in a fine prep-school scandal or in a British regiment when someone steals the mess funds." (He was weeping silently. I didn't look away.)

Without lifting his head he told the waiter to bring two Sarti brandies. I watched him drink both of them. I was of course deeply

233

shocked at what he had told me. Today, forty years later, more tolerant, we can adjust quickly, not even care about having a dark-hued grandfather, or Negro blood. Not that one would shout it out even now, but the prejudices (except for some poor-white-trash barbarians) are blunted. Jay and I, however, had been born in the nineteenth century, had grown up in a world where the Negro was the yakking minstrel cartoon even to himself, treated like a pet horse, or kicked like an unwanted puppy. We knew he had a solid ivory head, his mouth ran ear to ear, he had flat feet like suitcases, and he lived on watermelon, fried chicken and what he could tote or steal, carried a foot-long razor, had an amazing natural sense of rhythm, a born feel for the cakewalk and ragtime dancing, was sexually so well hung that his prick was the envy of the entire white male population and the secret craving of the female. That the Negroes we knew personally weren't at all like our image didn't bother our *idée fixe*. There were freaks everyplace. "A smart nigger," oh well. My grandfather, a good man, still had his darky stories and every strange colored man was of course called George unless it was Sambo. Billy Brunswick played Uncle Tom, cynically exploiting us with a surface respect. The descendants of George Washington's Negro body servant were there too—to serve us at Princeton.

Those were the days of the early twentieth century when it was a fearful thing to discover the nigger in your woodpile, the tarbrush in your own genetic pool. No wonder Jay in those times suggested that not to be born was best of all. Jay and I were products of our time. No matter how much we read or talked of the avant garde, we knew our myths were not myths to our society. Priests and nuns were all fornicating fools and buried their unwanted but baptized babies in the grottoes; Jews were marvelous money-makers, all great students of the cabala, Torah, Talmud, and no matter how poor they looked, had hoards of diamonds hidden in their wives' vulvas ready for instant flight. Italians were organ-grinders, banana sellers, great talkers with their hands, and ended every other word with a: *mucha, lova, pleasa, scusa*. The Irish lived off whiskey, potatoes, began as gandy dancers, controlled the ward heelers, grafted on city contracts, had faces like redheaded apes, danced and laughed at wakes, had plans to seize the country for the Pope.

We were products of the absolutes of our times, as people are, even today; the products of bleeding hearts, super-Americans and the same fools and thieves in high office. We knew better but didn't do much to change the legends. So here it had caught up with Jay.

"Rastus," I said smiling, "how come ah seen yo perculatin' Parson Bigass's gal, Becky-Sue, at dat fried-chicken picnic, amanulating dat gal in dem dere bushes? Ain't yo got no shame exposin' that big black thang in daylight?"

Jay gave a short coughing laugh, gripped my arm and pressed. "Not that bad, is it?"

"Not that bad."

"Bad enough."

"Not bad at all. If you want to count, you're at the most a sixteenth part colored. Hardly worth noticing. Why, President Harding has more Negro blood. His grandfather, I hear, was coal-black. You're stupid, Jay. That's all, stupid."

"I couldn't risk it, don't you see that? Pages wanted children. Her family is fertile. I couldn't see it, depriving her of them. Worse—presenting her with little Topsy, by the half dozen."

I wiped my grape-stained hands. Jay ordered a Valpolicella. I said, "You know, she can't ever have children now. The miscarriage operation fixed that."

"The doctor told me. It was too late then, Bill, for me to take up where we had begun. Tony was in by then."

"You didn't fight."

"All Pages knew was that I wasn't for the wedding. She's Boston under it all, you know, puritan and goddamn Protestant even if she says she got over it. And let's face it, she's the middle-class marrying kind. By forty she'll be reading *Good Housekeeping.*"

"So?"

"So. I survive."

"You'll finish *Stone Sunlight?*"

"Ha!" He laughed and gulped his drink. "Ha. I've a great ending, haven't I, if I use it? I've a drama. Besides, I promised Pages I would finish it. A going-away present."

"And we've the cash for a few more numbers of *The Scream.* We'll print the rest of the novel."

Jay fingered an empty glass but didn't order a fresh drink. "We're in *great* shape. Just crackerjack dandy. Just think of it, I say, as being aware that not only love enters our bodies. There is food and wine, a more leisured pleasuring; eating and drinking. That's the worst anonymity of modern life; all the labels read *Sex*. There *are* other things. There are, well, oranges, mussels, sea snails, sea urchins, periwinkles and *praires*. You realize, of course, all these inside have a pink soft fleshy center?"

"*Very* Freudian, Jay. Yes. Let's go home. Bea is cooking some special dish. If she can keep the turpentine out of it, it should be tasty."

Jay put his head on the table.

"Oh God, Pages, *Pages* . . ."

EDITOR'S NOTE: There has been no way to check the validity of Eliot Tjaden's version of the Bishop's ancestry. The Bishop left no personal papers, and I have been unable to trace any Mike Young. There may be data if one were to search the files of Vermont churches, city and township public records, but I have neither the funds nor the time for that.

Rumors are that several of Billy Brunswick's children by his white Hunkytown "wives" have passed themselves off for white. Being in Philadelphia this year for the National Bar Association meeting, I called on Arnold K. Bruns (this is one of the names I have changed), head of a large successful management accounting firm: B—— F—— & M——. His listings in *Business and Corporation Who's Who* are bone-bare: *b.* Toronto, Ont.; *m.* H—— R——; *educ.* Magill University, Harvard Business School; Pres.-dir. of B—— F—— & M—— (and dates). He said I was wrong to think he was the Arnie Brunswick who had run the collection truck for the College Dry Cleaning plant as a youngster. Also he did not know any man named Brunswick. His regular features, while rosy pink—hair a fine brown and straight—were like a pale photo print of Billy Brunswick himself with a thin nose and a better jawline. I asked him if he knew of a Bishop Tjaden and he said he didn't as he had never lived in East Pompton. He was very polite and gave me all the time I needed—in a fine modern office full of IBM tools. But as he denied the key question I put to him, it was a waste of time. He is married into one of the Girard Trust Corn Exchange Bank Main Line families, the father of six children, very active in politics, the founder of a Goldwater movement in three Eastern states, and was a member of the Republican platform committee in 1964 that kept a strong civil rights plank from being inserted. Eliot Tjaden used to quote someone: "There is no irony like God's irony"; which fits if Arnold K. Bruns is actually one of Billy Brunswick's sons.

The section that follows is merely a series of hastily written notes on

236

various-sized sheets of paper, and with it we are over the hump of the badly assembled material. What follows the next section is in better order. There is a suggestion that in setting down the events of this period William Kite was a much more emotionally disturbed person than his text indicates. Or he was going through a renewal of a prolonged alcoholic period. He most likely meant to [come back and] rewrite much of this material.

In 1926 we were in a Vienna smelling of anise-seed cookies and chicory coffee. The last issue of *The Scream* behind us. The death of an inanimate object, like a lost finger ring, is always sad. We had a crummy apartment all red velvet and brown heavy furniture on the Rotenturmstrasse. Bea painted a marvelous picture of a funeral procession coming from the Franciscan Monastery on Franziskaner Platz (a Hapsburg among them). For all our misery at losing the magazine to the printer, we were getting fat on *Jause*—the afternoon coffee hour, and the *Schlagobers* and *Pressburger Beugel* and *Kipferlin*. I had lost all the cash I could raise trying to save the magazine, and it hadn't helped. We had printed a third of what would one day be the full novel, *Stone Sunlight,* but our circulation never rose over fifteen hundred. And several issues were destroyed by British and American customs officers. "In a shipwrecked world," Jay wrote the President in protest, "the artist is part of the absurdity he dramatizes."

Jay had shaved off his beard, was getting plump. In our thirties we were coarsening, our dentistry was neglected, our hair was thinning. We were slack from lack of exercise. Only Charlie was trim, balding, but brown as a nut husk, muscled and very European, something we never felt ourselves to be. Charlie, having managed one Olympic ice and snow team, would soon manage another. I did spend a month with him skiing somewhere in central Europe and got good at it and later kept it up hard for nearly a decade. But Jay wouldn't even look at skis. He wasn't working on the novel. He was trying to write a play for a quick success, and with the money he wanted to live on a Greek island with some woman singer at the State Opera.

Jay found finishing the novel very hard work; his drinking-feeding activities among the singers in the opera world took him away from his work for long periods of time. But now and then I'd find a penciled page of text, and it was so good I'd howl at him to go back

237

to work. He'd just smile, tugging on the little mustache he affected; he looked in those days like an Innsbruck actor playing in second-rate Molnar. He kept a notebook with clinical minuteness; a line on the cover: *A man must dare to be happy.* (Bunk.)

I was wondering what my own plans were. I got a cable saying my grandmother was very ill and not likely to recover. She had expressed a wish to see me before she died. I made plans to leave at once, feeling a terrible inadequacy. Bea was going to Asia to paint Chinese funeral processions. A gallery in London, Pillpots, Ltd. had commissioned an entire series: cremating in India, suspected human sacrifices in Borneo. Bea's work was selling and she was having fame of a sort. I said I'd get out to Shanghai and meet her there after visiting my grandmother. Jay said he was going to Greece with a British press lord, and some famous literary pansies, on the press lord's yacht for a tour of the Dodecanese, Crete and the Cyclades. That seemed to take care of everything. I knew he hadn't yet recovered from Pages.

The night I left, we had drinks at the Cobenzl Bar and dinner at the Palais Auersperg. Jay had a soprano along, a juicy morsel, brainless, lovely, with heavy dark hair and white skin, who ate *klare Fleischbrühe mit Leberknödeln,* and *Schnitzel garniert* as if she were starving (and perhaps she was). I could see Jay was still carrying the memory of Pages over to a picture likeness in other girls. We never heard from her or Tony. The smart magazines like *Country Life* and *Town and Country* would show the two of them in jodhpurs or sports linens at some horse show or country weekend: "Mr. and Mrs. Anthony Kelton Pfaelzer of Southampton." Tony was making a reputation as a very reckless amateur car driver.

After dinner Jay left with the singer for the Urbani Keller where they were meeting some Max Reinhardt people—to me they always exuded an odor like rotting clams—and Jay said to tell the Bishop he'd most likely be home soon. We didn't kiss goodbye or shake hands or take mock punches off each other's chin or say "Keep your nose clean." He just went off with the singer, her mouth stained with Salzburg *Nockerl. . . . Nothing ends, it disintegrates* echoed in my mind.

Bea and I went back to the flat. We had had our goodbye and last lovemaking in the afternoon. My train was leaving at eleven and we were both packed. On the wall hung the large painting: *The State*

Funeral of General Cesare Chigi. Bea was abandoning it. It was too large to sell or carry. The Italians had never bought it. . . .

EDITOR'S NOTE: There are certain vital facts William Kite left out of his manuscript. According to the American consul's records, he and Beatrice Fabor Brown were married in Venice, August 19, 1925.

I have also found a dispatch from India, dated July 24, 1927, which appeared in the New York *Herald:*

CHOLERA DEATHS AT 113
New Delhi (AP)—The death toll in the cholera epidemic in central India has risen to 113 since July 1, authorities reported Friday. More than half the population of 60 villages in Maharashtra State has been inoculated in an effort to stem the outbreak. Among the dead are listed Shri Sihpoor Metcha, the designer of the new Calcutta road system, and Miss Beatrice Fabor Brown, the English artist, who had been painting in the district.

William Kite mentions neither his marriage nor the death of his wife. She disappears completely from his manuscript at this point. Sir Anton Carter of the Albert and Victoria Museum, the well-known art critic, is at work on a survey of her life and work: *Black Plumes—The Art of Beatrice Brown,* which is to be published next year by Thames & Hudson.

Eliot Tjaden, if we are to believe the evidence of his short story "Mount the Beast Gently" in the 1928 issue of *New Directions Review,* tried to commit suicide. In the story, a poet's wife, after a miscarriage, has gone off with a dull businessman, the poet agreeing because he feels himself slipping into impotency. But a month later he goes to London, begs his wife to return, making a scene in public, tries to kill the businessman and is restrained by onlookers. The poet then goes to Paris, where he takes sleeping pills, but in such an overdose that he vomits them. Friends take him to Italy and with chloral hydrate bring him out of a momumental drunk and a seizure of delirium tremens. The story may be pure fiction.

CHAPTER 25

I FELT ITCHY just before the depression; was it nostalgia (which Jay called "common as whale shit")? There is something of the angst and agony of a Kierkegaardian drama in going home, in coming back, in looking again at what one has seen as a very young man. Memories crowd like maggots in the mind. At thirty I was going back. All time seemed a bit out of joint, and I read without pleasure from a small volume of Hasidic texts I found in my cabin:

From time to time, the Creator, blessed be His Name, sets forward the clock of the Last Judgment by one minute.

The French Line deposited me at its New York dock. I made again the old pilgrimage with the ghost of my grandfather: the ferry ride across the harbor to Jersey, the tube train to Manhattan Transfer. (It's strange to find there are millions of Americans alive today who never heard of Manhattan Transfer, a way station in the middle of slaughtering and packing plants, tanneries, machinery warehouses set in the cat-reed swamps, where one changed to the steam trains that had come from uptown Pennsylvania Station; and that great gray, pigeon-stained Roman ruin too has been destroyed.) Backward, backward into time on a sooty train, the ghost smoke of my grand-father's cigar in my nostrils ("I'll tell you why, Billy, we'll like our grandchildren better than our own children; because our grandchil-dren in most cases will have the same enemies we have—their parents. George, you have the barman in the club car mix us two Gibsons, very dry, but *dry,* George."). The passing Pennsy stations grimy-brown with wear—Newark, Elizabeth, Rahway, Metuchen, New Brunswick. When I dream under tension, I always am on a train making that run and I'm trying to reach East Pompton, but somehow I never get home in recurring dreams adhering to the past and a child's panic. But this time I made it.

The old red depot leaned just a bit more as the termites continued their work inside the walls, and the dog wagon where I had eaten hamburgers and a deadly coconut custard pie was still in need of paint. I motioned to Artie Fleming—he had an upturned nose, no hard bridge—who was sucking the stem of a match as he leaned on an old Dodge with the sign: TAXI.

"Hello, Artie, still hacking?"

He looked up, needing a shave, his pants unpressed, his shiny jacket food-stained, ash-speckled from the cigarette that hung in the corner of his mouth. We had been in high school together; he had left in the second year to marry a girl with cheeks like nectarines.

"What you say, sir? Ke-rist, it's Bill Kite!"

"That's right."

"Wouldn't know you, Bill. Spats, cane, the derby hat."

"It's a bowler, not a derby."

"Looks like a fuckin' derby to me. Been away, huh?"

"Yes. What have they done to Royal Street?"

"New lampposts, repaved it. Grand old lady, your grandmother."

"Yes."

"Too bad. How old was she?"

That's how I found out my grandmother was dead. I had missed seeing her alive by four days. I wondered if they had kept the remains aboveground. I had cabled what ship I was taking. I had expected her death, but the actual fact was like a knife at my throat.

Frenchman Street had slipped a bit. Some of the old buildings had new façades of *moderne* (pronounced to rhyme with fern) bad taste. Stucco, black glass, stone flowers, curved copper. The Brady Livery Stables were the Quackenbush Hollyhock Garage, the Dutch Reformed Church, corner of Frenchman and Nelson, was gone; a busy department store, Freedline's Bon Ton, stood there in a ghastly contrast of brown and red. Empty lots that I had played football on held two-story buildings selling Cash Boys Auto Parts, Model-A's, naked white bathroom fixtures, bargains in canned corn, sliced bacon. Fruit stands covered some sidewalks. There were two new undertakers with signs in glossless matte black and thin gold: NONDENOMINATIONAL. CREMATION. ORGAN CHAPEL. On side streets I sighted new red brick, rows of houses in no style known to history, with no porches, just stern flat fronts, clapboard second stories, all alike, all having thin roof wires which were antennas, I was told by Artie, for the radio programs (Jones and Hare, The Happiness Boys), which were becoming popular. "Radios, what next?" I asked Artie, and he said, "You got me, Bill. You got me."

Upper Frenchman Street still had charm—large private residences, the elms uncut and only slightly diseased—but I sensed a lack of care in some of the places: a lawn in need of cutting, paint peeling from the Van Dorkle house (Regency plus Gothic), the Boggley yellow brick palace (Rhine castle and French provincial) with windows boarded up, signs of fire marking the upper walls. FOR SALE. ZONED FOR BUSINESS. HERMAN L. HUTTONBOK (Charlie's cousin).

The house of my grandmother looked about the same, neither smaller nor larger. I had lived in fear it would appear smaller, as places in our youth are supposed to shrink when we go back. No, it was the same: the English box and yew hedges a bit thicker, the old oak over my bedroom window gone—lost in some storm, I supposed. The porch swing still there, the chains rusted: the swing on which Jay and I had smoked my grandfather's cigars after a night of it with Betty-Lou and Billy Brunswick's applejack, and sometimes in the rain had watched the people running by like watercolors.

There were waxy flowers and a black bow on the big doors. A servant I didn't know opened the door. Several people who were trying to look respectfully sad were in the parlor. Among them was my half-brother Harry, looking very perplexed. I said "Harry" and shook his hand, which gave off a dry heat.

He said "Bill" and held onto my hand. "I should have come to the pier to meet you, but I had to pick a casket."

"Yes, you had to be here."

"This is Father Kersh."

A pale white hand, hairy wrists, a moving Adam's apple, a head too young to be so bald. A scar on his brow.

"A great loss."

"Father Nelson is dead?" I asked.

"A great loss."

"Is the Bishop here?"

Harry said, "He'll be at the graveside."

Noxie M. Hill, the popular funeral director (Bucknell, Class of—?, halfback) was giving me the polite respectful smile of sympathy reserved for upper Frenchman Street burials. "William, ah William, what a sad occasion to come home to."

I said, "A great loss."

He didn't offer to shake hands (gray gloves, striped pants, winged collar, freshly overstarched shirt, ascot tie slightly frayed, a smile smelling of peppermint drops—the bastard had been knocking a few bourbons back).

"The departed is on view in the library. This way."

"No. I never view the dead. It doesn't mean anything."

Harry said quickly, "Just as you say, Bill."

"It's just cold clay. An image not at all real." I was very distraught.

Father Kersh wet his heavy lips, hunting for some goody in Holy Writ to toss at me. I turned away. I was going to cry. I had, unlike most people, had a very happy childhood. I had loved my grandmother, her strong solid ways, her lack of education, her sense called common but really so rare. I hated this funeral, all the black cloth smelling of mothballs and other dead, the expiring flowers too innocent for this ceremony, the smell of furniture polish— *that* would be the casket in the library.

Noxie Hill said to an assistant who had the glazed stare of a dog molester, "You can screw down the lid."

Later Harry was fine to me. My entrails were full of gas. He held my arm by the graveside. My grandfather's stone was simple and already weathered. I turned on my X-ray eyes and saw him down there—stretched out, a brown parchment of dried skin, covered with deadly underground moss, his bones protruding, the teeth (had they buried him in his best set?) grinning through the receding shrunken lips. The pressure in me was like a knife, I silently expelled.

I looked across at the Bishop. And as in a dream, just behind him to one side, Billy Brunswick stood among the servants who had worked for us. The Bishop looked very old: His hair was whiter, there was a tremor to his hand, his clothes were that green-black that cloth takes on with aging as the dye breaks down. But he was impressive. I searched his features; he looked about as Negro as George Washington. Still, there was Billy Brunswick, the great plotter, fucking his race white, producing stud broods with the Hunkytown white women, so busy at his task, solving a great national problem in his own way. Would there be a monument to him someday? He didn't seem to be standing up well at his task. Was he failing the legend that a black man could fornicate, jazz all night, and then jerk off unsated? Billy was yellow, round-shouldered. It could be

243

the drinking, the greed, his investments, that had aged him so. I didn't see any resemblance between him and the Bishop.

Father Kersh finished saying something greasy with overuse at the side of the coffin (for me it was an empty casket). Only in my mind was my grandmother present, moving her big bulk about with a nobility accessible to all if her mood was right, just the figure to place among her heavy carved mahogany chairs, to hover above the rest of us who held on to our sanity the way some hold on to their hats on a windy street. Now I was one more step (one more person dead) in the painful process of moving toward final individuality, my own grave.

"Man is the dream of a shadow." It was the Bishop's voice. He had stepped forward, shaking off the assisting arm of the undertaker, Noxie Hill. "In this our precarious, variable life, there are some dimensions beyond reason and experience. Few are aware of this; Maude Kite was. Man is the measure of all things—those which exist and those which have no existence." (To keep from weeping I remembered Jay quoting somebody among the surrealists: "It is significant that Einstein was immediately preceded by the Russian Ballet.") "I knew her very well, and her family, there standing among us, the things they did to help others. They were proud, but in their pride they never forgot they were mortal. I shall now read from the Old Testament."

I looked at my wristwatch beating like a heart. For a moment I felt that my own heart had stopped beating and the watch had taken over.

> *Give unto the Lord, O ye mighty,*
> *Give unto the Lord glory and strength.*

I shook the watch by moving my wrist. If it kept ticking, I would remain alive. If it stopped, my own heartbeat would fail; I would die.

> *Give unto the Lord the glory due unto his name,*
> *Worship the Lord in the beauty of holiness.*

Slowly I lowered my arm, and the heart in my chest beat on with an admonitory thump. I felt it beat so hard I hoped people would not notice its jumping, the cloth of my jacket dilating under its hammering. I shook my head to clear myself of the odd obsession.

The Lord will give strength unto his people;
The Lord will bless his people with peace. . . . Amen.

Everyone said "Amen."

Later I was walking down the graveled path and Billy Brunswick was helping the Bishop into a battered Buick. I said I would come and see him in the morning.

The Bishop patted my shoulder; big as he was, he couldn't pat me on the head the way he had done when I was younger.

I wondered if when I died they would permit me to be buried across the foot of both my grandparents' graves, like the dog of some crusader and his duchess, effigies I had seen in an English church.

I was in my old room that night, looking at the wallpaper that had faded like an old Japanese print exposed to a few decades of sunlight. There was the ceiling stain where I had killed a large bug with a copy of *Tarzan of the Apes,* the windowsill where I had carved a skull and bones with my first pocketknife. All around me the warm banalities of a gone world seemed even more lost as I lay on the bedcovers, shoes off, puffing on a pipe, watching the smoke rise to a badly stuffed woodchuck I had processed in 1909.

There was a knock on the door and Harry came in. He had a black silk band on his right sleeve just above the elbow. I had forgotten people still wore that in mourning. It had been a respected established custom when I was a boy, but I hadn't seen it practiced of late except among certain middle-class groups in Italy. Harry had given up the gold pince-nez and wore heavy black turtle-shell-framed glasses. He was stouter, but stronger-looking. His new black tie was pinned with a single black pearl.

"Hello, Harry."

He sat down in our grandfather's club chair, the one I had taken over after his death. He pulled out a flat silver cigarette case, took out a cigarette, lit it, coughed. "I shouldn't smoke so much. Going to cut it out."

"Integrity has a bare-assed grandeur, Harry."

He laughed loudly, coughed, caught himself, frowned. "You and I are the last of the Kites."

"I thought you had children."

"Little boy. Died. Whooping cough; he strained something. Dead two years now."

245

"You'll have more."

"Hope so. Getting married again."

"Again?"

"Divorced last year." He looked down at his neat black shoes on the worn carpet. He wore fine black silk socks. "She didn't care for the physical side of marriage."

"No?"

Harry looked up, cautious yet audacious. "I guess you might say I'm a kind of—I mean I like it."

"Good for you. It's better than tennis, isn't it?"

"I mean with me it has to be more than the ritual, you know, once-a-week-after-the-Sunday-dinner. She insisted on the dark, and only for generation. No theme or variation. *That* was sin, black sin."

I said, "It made America strong, Harry; kissing with the mouth closed. Undressing in the closet, a nightgown to be lifted but not discarded. *Soixante-neuf* is the debilitating work of the devil."

"What's that?"

I sat up and relit my pipe with two matches. "What are you going to do with this house?"

"Oh." Harry looked at his cigarette end. "Thought you might want it. Fine old relic. Solid walnut doors."

"No, I'm going back to Europe. How are the mills and the foundry doing?"

"Oddly enough, not too well for all the national prosperity talk. Mean we need newer models. More modern plants."

"I sort of want to become a publisher, Harry. Seriously. Modern novels, exploration texts of the new philosophies, a book on Dada art, the surrealists, Diaghilev, Stravinsky. Also a magazine with colored plates of Picasso, Munch, African sculpture, Hokusai's drawings."

"Maybe, Bill, maybe. We are seriously thinking of putting the stock on the market, big issue sold to the public, reserving for ourselves the preferred. May take a year or so to get the right house on Wall Street to float it for us."

"You think it's a good idea, Harry?"

"Under Hoover, great engineer, there is talk things will be humming."

"I don't like his collars. And he can't smile."

"Will you vote your Kite shares, Bill, for the stock scheme? Mean plan."

"I haven't many."

"Oh yes. There's a will. Grandma left you half. Me half."

"Of what?"

"Plants, foundry, patents. At the moment we're in debt to the banks. But we've full warehouses of machines. The patents are valuable. Some of them."

I wondered if Harry's life was the hideous dreariness it seemed to me, or the plush comfort of Scott Fitzgerald's rich boy. "Who you marrying, Harry?"

"You know the DeCamps of Newport?"

"No. I've been away."

"Marrying Mina DeCamp. Her father raced for the Lipton Cup. Had a boat that came within seven seconds of winning. Torn jib. Lost their money in commodities."

"Commodities?"

"Father got sold short in corn and rye futures. They've had a tight time of it."

"Want my advice, Harry? Never mind the yachts and corn and rye. Take Mina to Atlantic City for a weekend and see if she's worth a damn in bed."

Harry coughed at my vulgarity and lit a fresh cigarette from the butt of his old one. I could see I had hurt him, even more than the crack about Hoover.

"She's a DeCamp. Mina isn't one of your [*cough*] European artist types [*cough*]—no offense, Bill. She's a lady, proper family background, all that [*cough*]—I think I shall really cut down cigarettes."

"Harry, you're the backbone of our upper-middle-class society. Save yourself. Give up tobacco. Don't just cut down."

"You think I'm a horse's ass."

"No, just human."

I liked Harry. He was solid and honest and sterling and had character, emotional gaucherie. I like a man who respects a girl and doesn't try to get into her pants before he's married to her. And never asks her to kiss his navel. (I'd be that way myself but I'm too impulsive, curious, and impatient.)

Harry turned pink at my calling him human. "There's some fine bourbon in the cellar. Want to get drunk tonight?"

We tried but we were both too sad, too tired, too tense, too much in awe of the old house—now ours—on Frenchman Street. We got a bit mumble-tongued and went up to bed arm in arm, happy to have

247

each other in this big ubiquitous rolling world. I put Harry to bed in grandfather's room, took off his shoes, opened his collar, any moment expecting and wanting to hear an old familiar voice shout out that the world was going to hell in a hack.

East Pompton didn't look too well in the morning from the window; it had in its newer part the appearance of a subterfuge, a falsification. I had hardly any headache. Harry still slept. The last of the hired girls served me coffee, tasteless toast, a good plate of bacon and eggs. Pigs are treated like rare art in South Jersey.

I walked crosstown to the Bishop's house, passing the new movie theaters, the Strand and Majestic, showing Clara Bow and Rod LaRocque, Ronald Colman and Billie Dove. The Majestic also featured SIX ACTS! HI-TYPE VAUDEVILLE! TED HEALY, HARTMAN AND HIS PIANO, APPLE BLOSSOM GIRLS IN FLOWER TIME REVUE, SIX YAMAMOTO BROTHERS—JUGGLERS EXTROD!

The police looked thinner. I sensed speakeasies behind several heavy doors. The old side streets which had ended in mud holes were overcrowded by rows of clapboard houses, all alike, as yet lawless, treeless, but already occupied by mothers and babies. Fathers were at work. I felt a crowding, and I saw only one horse pulling a Polish junk dealer's wagon from Hunkytown. Hunkytown was now a separate incorporated community called Riverside. I couldn't remember what river, but Noxie Hill had told me its ward heelers were massing their voters and soon East Pompton would be invaded, overwhelmed and politically castrated by the Poles, Irish, Hungarians, Negroes, Southern crackers, hillbillies and rednecks that had come north during the war for high wages and stayed on to overbreed.

Cohen's corner drugstore was gone. A Regal Chain Drug Company building, red and green, stood in its place: LUNCH, SODAS, PRESCRIPTIONS, CIGARS. A taxi driver reading the *Daily Running Horse* told me old man Cohen had sold out and gone to Hollywood, where he had relatives in the studios.

The Bishop's house was about the same. Some of the maple trees were gone; some new ones, cottonwoods, had grown; the potting shed had been pulled down. I wondered if the gravestone we had used as a printing-press bed had been given honorary burial.

The Bishop was visible on his front porch, in his bentwood rocker. The rocker creaked; the boards were loose on the porch floor, worn and warped.

248

"You don't look well, William. Peaked."

"It's been a trying time, Bishop." I sat down facing him on a wicker chair with a calico seat pillow faded by exposure.

"I keep seeing the browning ferns, William, the turtles hibernating in old stumps, the first graying silver of frost." He stopped to blow his nose. "The fungi shriveling and the season passing."

The Bishop's eyes were unfocused. He must have caught my stare. He rocked back and beat the arms of the rocker with his heavy hands. "Ah, you've caught me in a moment of senility. Yes, it's true. I have patches of . . . of . . ." He waved off the word. "You've seen Eliot? When?"

"Ten or twelve days ago."

"Why doesn't he come home? Instead of living with the morbid hybrids of social failures."

"He's writing, and, well, feels it's a better place there for writing."

"I've been trying to read his writings in those magazines."

"The Scream."

"Odd title. Not at all like the books, the classics, I read once. I liked a mood of pastoral mirth, rimmed in some quiet prose about nature and beauty. Touched with melancholy, but not too much. Don't suppose that's the trick today?"

"Hardly, Bishop. Jay is an experimental writer. Like Joyce, Proust, Lawrence— D. H., not T. E."

"Never read them." He rocked and began to sing:

> *"Follow the drinking gourd.*
> *The river bank'll make a mighty good road*
> *The dead trees will show you the way.*
> *Left foot, peg foot, traveling on,*
> *Follow the drinking gourd."*

I let the old man sing, didn't try to make talk. He rocked and leaned forward and put a heavy hand on my knee. "You're home, Eliot, and you're fine to come to me to find shelter from mindless matters. Discover with me the inner element of things. Oh, you young people think you have a pathetic need to go see for yourself. But what? Beauty and elegance are a snare. The full mystery of things is terrifying, Eliot, when you wonder if all life has been an error."

"I'm Bill Kite, Bishop. Jay, he's away cruising among the Greek islands."

"The ideas of the Greeks were full of tragic aberrations. The flesh

249

was all they knew. The sinister admonitory shadows, slavery, perversion, paganism; they took and they went down to eat dust. The lizards sport in their cities' ruins . . . yes . . .

"The Lord told old Joshua:
'You must do just what I say,
March around that city seven times
And the walls will tumble away.' "

I sat watching the Bishop rock. The face was anesthetized; only the eyes were alive. The Bishop slapped at a fly on his white shirt front, a shirt smooth and stiff.

"William, William."

"Yes, Bishop."

"Some wasps are born in the bodies of caterpillars. . . . God grinds down all calcified shells on the shores, and he grinds us too. The smaller creatures are deficient in cunning; man is malformed wherever you look. . . . One must be ready to accept defeat in the end; it is the price we pay for the ticket of our journey. . . . I shall die happy, but in doubt. Don't tell the church board, Eliot: I sometimes doubt. Yes, me."

"Not you, Bishop. I think you're the only man I know who is firm in his faith, full of hope, able to sail over the incongruity of life."

"You're right, of course, I'm not a feeble reed. I know. The First Chaos made the Last Judgment possible. I think I'll go harness up Moses and take the buckboard out along the canal road."

The stable was empty; there was no buckboard. I said, "The horse is tired, Bishop. He needs a rest."

"Eliot, you go water him. Not too much oats. He bloats. And curry him, curry him good and careful."

("The best is yet to be," said the lying poet—Browning—on his way to play fumble-touch with Lizzie Barrett; but there is no best in old age . . . a fine man like the Bishop going soft and senile. And beautiful women wrinkling, with yellow cracked teeth, wens and moles spotted like spattered acid, flesh stinking like fish. A better poet —Webster—spoke of "the skull beneath the skin." The scientists say the entire cosmos is dead matter, only protoplasm cells contain life and consciousness.)

I said, "Bishop, sing something."

"Eliot, William, join me . . .

250

> *"So up the walls of Jericho*
> *He marched with spear in hand,*
> *'Go blow the ram horns,' Joshua cried,*
> *'Cause the battle is in my hand.' "*

I left him there singing softly in an old man's impotent voice, his head back, his long white beard now wispy and thin, moving with the motion of the rocker. A good godly man, a fine man, a just man with a faint scent of frangipani about him. Firm as a Roman of the Aurelian period, he had all the answers: an understanding of the Nicene Creed, the Trinity, Calvin's doctrine of predestination, the euphoric joys of being one with his Creator. (And was only an old man, his mind going, his body turning to stone and dried skin.) I walked away, his voice following as far as the curb. I crossed over and I remembered a New Year's dinner of a goose Jay and I had bought on a frosty day from a farmer who had once flown kites in China, and when the stewed apples were served, the Bishop had looked up brightly at us all and asked, "Why couldn't Eve have eaten a pear and saved us all this worldly misery?"

Why not? The foolish bitch.

I left East Pompton after the reading of the will, taking from the bank vault my grandfather's old gold watch with the double lids, borrowing ten thousand dollars against my share of the estate. I didn't stay for Harry's wedding to the Newport virgin—it had been respectfully postponed for the six-month period of mourning. I got a black armband for my sleeve and made reservations on the French Line's *Rochambeau*. They could give me only an inside cabin—"So many Americans are going abroad"—and I took it.

The steward told me Mayor James Walker and H. G. Wells were on board.

> *The river ends between two hills.*
> *Follow the drinking gourd.*
> *There's another river on the other side.*
> *Follow the drinking gourd. . . .*

251

BOOK SIX

FROM WILLIAM KITE'S POCKET NOTEBOOK

Most people sin too prudently, but it is harder to change oneself than the laws of the world . . .   —W. K.

It's good to know that the Archbishop of Armagh proved that God created the world at 6 P.M., October 7th, 3761 B.C.

                    —*Facts for Fun*

CHAPTER 26

NOW

INANIMATE OBJECTS ARE man's not too secret enemies. I trip over slippers that advance silently from their place like raiding Shawnee Indians. The razor bites me if I take my eye off the mirror for one moment. I must watch the pen as I write this, for it will sputter and drop a blot of ink on some thought I am nearly ready to complete; if I loosen my grip on it, I am lost. I don't make a joke of this. I'm very serious. Stairs wait to cripple; doors shut on fingers. (Crossing deserts of loose carpets, hugging a gin, my incoherence is like Scott's at the South Pole.) I can hardly open a letter with my Florentine dagger without stabbing myself in the palm. (Fortunately I get no letters. Perhaps they are not being forwarded to me. But then there isn't really anyone to write.) It's all a chimeric dream, I tell myself . . . only the two martinis before dinner are reality—the martinis and what I try to write, try to bring up from a darkness the Fancy Dan writers call Stygian.

The inanimate objects have been cruel to me today. My shoelaces broke—both shoes—and I've tied them into knots. The earpiece on my eyeglasses has lost a tiny screw, but I can't see to find it. And downstairs there's talk of the Black Nationalists and of Martin Luther King and "you have to stop them *now!*"

Today there was the weekly hunt. Red coats, fine horses, randy hounds. They all ride once a week in season, ride yipping after a ball of cotton rags soaked in fox urine; for the varmints are rare now in this built-up country of fine estates with its gathering of rich country-club people. Twice a year a live yellow-orange fox is imported for the proper *yoicking,* and the silver cups of cold liquor are lifted to "Do

255

Ye Ken John Peel." Everything has become a smelly bag of rags dipped in something. The air is conditioned by machines, food comes from the freezers, and it's all healthy and clean but tasteless. The women look appetizing, but the men don't seem to see them during the waking hours: all that fine pussy also in the freezer. There is talk on other estates of wife swapping and group play, but if true it seems a neurotic symptom [psychosomatic] rather than the expression of a simple desire for the pleasures of lusting unrestrained Richard Burton or Nero style. There is a debilitating stagnation, and the women are beautifully preserved in wax, hair spray, Chanel and panty girdles. And are so bored, while the males talk of the Duquesne and Bamboola clubs in Pittsburgh and the house is fully wired with speakers so one can hear Mahler's Second Symphony, the "Resurrection," in every room. I have warned Sam Pfaelzer to play rock-and-roll and surfing records (good taste is too Jewish for Carolina papermill, tobacco and government-contract millionaires). Sam was very fine about it, called me "Pop" and asked me if the sheets were being aired every morning in my room and just "Take it easy, Pop." It was then the ashtray leaped from my hand; later at lunch I choked on a fish bone with a mean sense of humor and had to be slapped on the back. The women tried not to be amused at an old crock telling them the inanimate objects were out to destroy the human race.

> Folly and Fashion do prevail
> To such extremes among the fair,
> A woman's only top and tail.
> The body's banish'd, God knows where!

I slept all the afternoon, and the doctor came and gave me something for what he called vertigo and for stomach spasms. When I woke up, Tony and Charlie were sitting on the windowsill of my room, laughing it up, making a hell of a racket. The dead have no moral responsibilities.

I said, "Why can't you stay in your graves? Didn't I bring your daughter out of Athens after all, Charlie?"

"You didn't make it easy for me. I had to put the pressure on you."

"A mean little bitch she was too. Bit me in the hand, to the bone."

"I'm a grandfather," said Charlie. "Four times. It was worth staying alive for the wedding. Married a South American. A papal knight—a dentist."

"Go back to your goddamned Vienna grave."

"Now easy, Bill," said Tony. "Charlie died a good Catholic; full confession, full rites for our Charlie. And what are *my* grandchildren? Damned Christian Scientists or worse. Who said *kaddish* for me, who asks them the *kashes* on Passover night? And Jews hunting little foxes—I tell you, who can rest in his grave?"

"I thought, Tony, you went down at sea."

"Just an expression. Three hundred feet down—so cold the bones shiver—in a plane wreck, with coral eyeballs and sea snails for teeth. Leave it to a Jew to get the best of everything wherever he stays."

Charlie asked, "How you doing with the girls?"

"You're both dead, I tell you. *Dead!* I have the clipping someplace."

"So what," said Charlie. "A good piece is a good piece, a nice set of knockers is a nice set of knockers. What's the matter, you think because we're dead we're not entitled to feelings?"

I closed my eyes. What good was death if the same damn earthy drives and deceptive insouciance went on? I had hoped for a dreary eternity of nothing but pneumatic bliss on fat clouds; not of course twanging a harp; that Calvinistic I wasn't. But at least I had been promised, by Father Nelson, peace, rest, indifference to body; that I would be reconciled with an unalterable past.

I heard Charlie try my shaving lather can: the hiss of spray as he slapped it into his chops. "He's still doing himself well."

Tony banged open my last good suitcase. "Nice, nice. You don't see leather like this any more. Bond Street brass fittings. Contents? Three shirts (two frayed), a volume of Pepys' *Diary* (nameplate rubbed out), a half-dozen lousy cigars—Castro has ended the Age of Upmanns—and ah-ha! What do you . . . *know!* He still carries—"

I sat up shouting. "Get the hell back to wherever you are. You're supposed to be my best friends. Do you think I'll come back to haunt *my* friends?"

"Who's haunting you, *mamzer?* We came to pass the time, shoot the breeze. And you might get them to play a little Bartók and Webern on the record machine. Whatever else they have where we are, good music no—"

Charlie's voice cut in. "Hell yes, just those goddamned Judaic barbarians blowing their ram horns and chanting their parochial jabberwock, screaming for Abraham and Moses . . ."

They faded out, and the next day I had some fever and missed the cocktail hour. . . .

1930

When Jay's novel *Stone Sunlight* was announced for publication late in 1929, I hoped it would become the American *Remembrance of Things Past*, the American *Ulysses* of the period; that it would make Jay another Marcel Proust or James Joyce. The time for it was too disconsolate and lonely; the world was out of joint. It was a time of hunting for work, for food. I had tried to get Sylvia Beach and her Shakespeare & Company to issue the book, but things were bad at 12 Rue de l'Odéon, and Jay had settled for the Gribbe Press in Zurich. They printed three thousand copies.

Waiting for publication, Jay was in Paris, living in some pervasive self-abnegation, and seemed indifferent. He was working on his play, *Toes Down, Eyes Up,* with earnest hope it would be put on in London in a small endowed theater; but the duke who backed the project was hard hit; tin mines and rubber acres in Malaya were not keeping the stately homes of England going.

With the publication of *Stone Sunlight* Jay became world-famous, which meant only that a handful of important critics and a small group of avant-garde readers hailed him as a new and vital force in world letters. To the vast reading public of popular best sellers he was merely a name, a writer whose book was barred from entering the United States or Great Britain because, the whisper was, "it's real dirty." It, bound in yellow paper, and James Joyce's volume, bound in blue paper, were often the unholy twins that smart, fashionable Americans smuggled home to show they knew what was the last word in the underground of international letters.

It was well reviewed in little magazines like *Mood, Blowoff, American Vanguard, Midwestern Review, Cosmo-West, British Bomb, Tollivar's Review,* and was condemned as a foul freak work by *English Wall, Pathfinder, New York Farmer* and *Saturday Review of Literature*. Mild reproaches were given it as a poor, addled, vile picture of American life by *Atlantic Monthly, Literary Digest, Har-*

per's, *New Republic, Elks Magazine* and *The Saturday Evening Post.*
Most of these were not actually reviews but comments regarding a
talked-about banned book that held the country up to scorn and was
"pure filth."

A picture of Eliot Tjaden appeared in *Time* ("Outward flows the
inward sewer"), and there was a *Collier's* editorial: "Are there too
many ex-Americans in Paris?" *The New Yorker* ran a profile on Jay
which sounded more like Elliot Paul.

So like Joyce, Lawrence, Faulkner, he was known but neglected.
Jay had fame as a new style of genius, but actually the book sold
poorly, and because it was banned here and in England no major
publisher dared to take it on. In Paris that season Jay was the new
lion. He went to famous parties, he slapped La Stein on the back,
boxed with Ernest, got drunk with Sinclair Lewis, and tried to seduce
a beautiful woman poet until he discovered that at forty-two she was
still guarding her virginity. ("The sex act to me, sir, is merely
tampering with plumbing.") Jay himself was quoted, misquoted, and
had a hard time making enough to eat.

The notorious press on *Stone Sunlight* pleased me more than Jay,
at least by the appearance of things. Jay had a grimy room near the
Pont Royal, full of books, manuscripts, a bicycle he rode to take
piano lessons from an old lady who had known Erik Satie and *Les
Six* when they were young. He seemed happy that he had burst
through to fame—he had hocked his watch and his typewriter at the
municipal *mont-de-piété,* but I got the typewriter back. He was
not musical and I wondered at the piano; this period did not last long.
Other literary sensations came along; people said, "Wait and see
what else Tjaden writes."

Times were bad in Paris too. The crows on the Place de Militaire
seemed leaner and protested louder; the sycamores on the Right Bank
near the Pont de l'Alma looked as if people were cutting the lower
branches for firewood. The last meal in Paris I bought Jay, we sat
eating duck-egg omelets with *topinambours,* and sunflower roots. He
looked well; he had never regrown the beard, and he kept his hair in
better order. He ate with clinical minuteness, tasting every forkful.

"So you're going back, Bill? Why not? No flight to Montparnasse
for you."

"Come back with me, Jay. We'll find an American publisher."

"Must first finish the play. May open in February in London. After all, I may be a marvelous writer of plays. The novel was the mistake. People want to hear, *not* read. Look at radio, gramophones, talking films. No more novels. Maybe I'm a one-book author."

"It's a fine novel and a great one."

"I'll read you Act One."

"You did."

"You didn't cotton to it, *paisano?*"

"Intrinsically hideous, Jay. Hideous."

"Why, you feisty sonofabitch. I give you art and you give—"

"Duck eggs. Jay, write the sequel *Stone Sunlight* needs."

"Why? It didn't sell five thousand copies."

"It made you famous, and times will get better. A major publisher will reprint it. You can afford to wait. But do another book. Even better than *Stone Sunlight*. Goddamn it, are you listening?"

He poured white wine into his glass. "Oh boy, you want the essential suchness, a consciousness of truth? Stuff like that? You think literature can take it and survive?"

"Why not?"

"Frankly, now I'm writing plays."

"Bullshit. It's not your medium. Remember the Bishop saying the true seer knows how to refrain from working miracles? You'll never write a good play."

Jay frowned. "I can't go back home just yet. Maybe the Bishop isn't really dead. Maybe he'll read *Stone Sunlight* someplace and want to beat my head in with his cane." Jay saw me stare and began to laugh. "Had you there, *almost*. No, Bill, the truth is I'm tired. The novel wore me down. The play is a bastard to get off the ground. But it moves. And it's cheaper to starve here on the Rue de Rennes and its *pissoirs*. But someday you'll get a letter saying, Here I come—and you just prepare the bootleggers' whiskey and warn *les jeunes* that a sultan of a man is coming." He grasped my hand. "Believe me—just now rest is all I want."

We left it at that. He walked me through the Horloge and the central flower market, and took me to the Gare de l'Est and we parted under the sign: LA PROMENADE HYGIENIQUE DES CHIENS EST FORMELLEMENT INTERDIT SUR LE TROTTOIR DEVANT CET IMMEUBLE. When my train was moving quickly through the landscape with that sissy littly pansy whistle all French trains have, I thought not of the clowns of the Cirque Médrano, or *Les Illuminations* of Rimbaud

(Jay's own copy given me at parting); I thought, Was I any smarter going back to the chaos and despair of a stock market crash and my brother Harry ruined, and Kite Foundry ruined, the cotton mill machines rusting in creditors' warehouses? And the Kite stock I had put so much hope in no longer even listed on the big board? (Nowhere to nowhere is no goal.)

Had anything really changed for all the world turmoil? Tony and Pages off someplace trying to save a junk empire when there was no market for scrap steel. Tony working on an invention, and Jay still writing, after a magnificent start—this time the wrong thing. And me, a publisher whose avant-garde publication was deader than Custer at Little Big Horn. I was going where, why, *why?* The train went on and I thought: Thoreau had a good solid grip on himself, he saw things clearly; but then the chin-whiskered bastard in his hut at Walden Pond, he had no problems of girls, of dealers or printers, of booze, of stock market failure or a lot of life left to spend. He knew his lungs were putrid and he didn't have to plan. No wonder he could say, "Of what consequence though our planet explode, if there is no character involved in the explosion? I would not run around a corner to see the world blown up. . . ."

He could be right. Character is everything; if a thing has no character, what does it matter what happens to it? Of course that train journey had character; all of it bad. . . .

EDITOR'S NOTE: The information that William Kite gives about the publication of Fliot Tjaden's novel, *Stone Sunlight,* needs amplifying. The Gribbe Press of Zurich—printing in English—was a small but good firm of publishers of modern writers. The depression had badly affected not only their sales; Louis Marton, one of the major backers of the firm, lost his fortune in the crash in flax and wheat futures and had badly cooked up the firm's books in trying to cover margin calls. Review copies of the novel had actually been sent out to all major American and English publications and critics, but were seized and destroyed in customs. Those who took over the assets of the firm when it failed—Slovent & Co.—tried to keep the novel in print and sent out a second set of review copies (also seized and destroyed) with its imprint on a new inserted title page. This caused confusion for a while among collectors, as both versions were first editions, but copies with the Gribbe imprint are the rarer. In all nearly eight thousand copies of these editions were sold. A very good record. The book was reviewed by some major critics and publications un-

261

favorably, but it was reviewed. The conservative critics were shocked by
the form and content of the novel. The left-wing *New Masses* felt it was a
decadent upper-middle-class joke: "Gay laughter above the breadlines."
The right-wing *Coast Review* called it "Marxist odors from the nest of
Joyce and his shaggy followers." Its underground fame grew over the
years. A few professors of literature and others spoke well of it. (H. L.
Mencken wrote: "A *Wasserkopf's* cat's dinner of a novel.") In a few
years it was a collector's item. However, it was not until 1946 that a new
edition from fresh plates appeared with the suppressed *Le Mépris* chapter
added, put out by Simon and Schuster. By then Eliot Tjaden's fame among
a growing solid core of admirers was firmly established. Important re-
evaluation by a top critic is rumored. Of the play *Toes Down, Eyes Up*,
no known copy exists.

1933

Jonggg-jonnnk, sounded the railroad iron. I rode it south toward
the Gulf at Mango City and Conch Harbor. In the baggage car were
my few bundles, the cases of surveying tools, the sheaves of plans, the
chart Tony Pfaelzer had made of Tinto Key. Since leaving Washington I had ridden past cities, by rivers, through long dirty miles of
industrial slums, past sharecroppers' acres, the west coast above the
Everglades of Florida.

Somewhere ahead lay a long strip of sandy beach by Papaya City,
separating the pounding Gulf from twisting inlets and points called
Boca Grande, Snipe Saddle, Bunch, No Name, Little Pine and others,
names with sounds like green waves breaking. I smiled at this idea,
half asleep on a dusty plush train seat in the third year of the Great
Depression. No longer a young man—that is, thirty-eight—wearing
an overbrushed hat, an unpressed gray linen suit. To other passengers
I was a rather crumpled-looking man, a bit of a tired smoker, silent,
withdrawn, watching the passing countryside with an eye indifferent
to the charm of swamp, mud flat, heat-blasted shacks, the beat of
sunlight on blinding waters.

I knew there were no bridges, no regular services, connecting
Conch with the Tinto Key between Key West and the Dry Tortugas—
Tinto Key, where a turtle ranch had once failed. ("History teaches us
that history teaches us nothing.") There was a lighthouse there and
next to it a weather station on the beach. And I was on a fool's

262

errand for Tony. A sudden sough of rain created a placid melancholy as I sat in the car of the Florida West Coast and Keys Railroad—a local of three cars and a fish-icer out of Bonita Springs.

I had written for information, but facts on Tinto Key, the most remote of islands, were meager; Nikko's general store, a bay, a pier, a score of scattered houses weathered and lonely, the ribs of old wrecks, the bones of a beached whale. There were the ruins of a turtle ranch once planned to raise soup for gourmets and a twenty-mile stretch of perfect, flat, well-packed beach.

The sun was lime-bright in the humid air as the train left a double row of tracks and went off by itself on a lonely spur line past dunes and scrub pine and swamp and the leaning shanties of Negroes and their lop-eared jenny and maud mules. Little grew tall here, and what did manage to put up branches was bent over by the Gulf's salt winds. The clear air surrounded little but distances and solitudes of cattail reeds, swamp palms, sour orange trees and canebrakes. On the flaring horizon often a pencil scribble of smoke rose where sea grass burned or someone not on public relief made charcoal for moonshine buck and sour mash deep in the Everglades.

The conductor came by carrying gloves and a heavy wooden billy; it was a mixed freight and passenger train, and the homeless hungry of the depression riding the blind baggage were often mean. The conductor called out, "Papaya City, end of line."

I looked at my grandfather's watch. "Half an hour late."

The conductor, who hadn't shaved for a week and whose lips were stained with the yellow snuff he rubbed on his gums, shrugged. "Yo' call that late, Co'nel? I'll go get yo' gear together in the baggage car."

"Any place to leave it in the station till I get a boat?"

"Sure 'nuff. Where you bound?"

"Tinto Key."

"Never did year tell of it."

The conductor went off, joking with a few miserable-looking people he knew. I reset my hat as the train ran slowly on a track laid over water and sand dune. Soon it came to a stop at a sun-punished depot where crates of terrapins and blue crabs moved like stone armor in damp iced seaweed. Two lantern-jawed Negroes were piling up yellow pine lumber taken from a flatcar under the direction of a

263

white man who sat in a chair tipped back against the depot wall. Yellow dust swirled, a dog was kicked by someone nearby, and several bare-assed chickens ran across the unpaved street to the steamy bounty just provided them by a horse tied to the rail of the Original Ponce de Leon Hotel—a setting for a Chekov play, lost in the cornpone belt.

In the burning heat of noon I helped the conductor pile up my gear under the wooden awning of the depot, wiped my damp brow and walked over to the man watching the Negroes pile up the rosin-scented lumber. He was eating a wide segment of watermelon, cutting it into big chunks with a knife that I remembered was called a frogsticker in my youth.

"Can I get a boat to Tinto Key?"

"Friend, never did hear tell of that thar place." He spat out black seeds. "Have a section of melon. Been in the icehouse all morning."

I accepted the gift slice. It was cold, sweet and crunchy and very satisfactory in the unrelenting damp heat. I beat gnats and other insects to death on my neck and face. I finished the section of melon and felt I could now proceed with another line. "Tinto Key is a cay with a lighthouse and there are long beaches. I've a map here of it. It's to the west—halfway to the Tortugas."

"Can't read no maps. Chandler, yo' randy nigrah, come ahere."

"Yes suh, Mr. Seldes."

A tall, shiny Negro, barefoot, slack-mouthed, with hands the size of banjos, came over. "We just about done shifted all that wood, Mr. Seldes. Yes suh."

"Chandler, yo' ever hear tell of Tinto Key?"

"That be out west a fur bit. Yes suh, a fur bit."

"Can my friend yar get a boat to it?"

"No suh, Mr. Seldes. He gotta go on that thar boat what makes the weekly trip to Boca Grande first. Yes suh. Then he take anythin' goin' down to Tinto Key. Yes suh."

I threw the watermelon rind into a lard can already half full of other sections of melon shell and buzzing flies. "When does the boat leave for Boca Grande?"

"Done left yesterday. Next boat comes sometime next week."

The melon eater shook his head. "Friend, yo' got a spell of waitin'. I ask is yo' a poker-playin' man?"

"No. Any boats for hire?"

"Try down by the blue pier in Conch Harbor. Sometimes there is.

264

Chandler, move yo' black ass and git the rest of them boards piled up or I'll cut yo' balls offen yo' with this yar knife."

"Jus' goin' to do it, jus' goin', Mr. Seldes."

I walked "a fur bit." The blue pier was the only pier, and a ratty, rotting-looking lot of boats, about half a dozen, floated in the sheltering arm of a sort of harbor. Several sun-bleached men were sitting about mending nets. All said they had no interest in taking me down to the key. "Toad strangler of a blow comin' up. Besides we'd get kicked off WPA effen we took up work."

A bearded one-eyed man pointed to a little flat-bottomed schooner shifting and swaying with the tide. "Israel Perry, now he used to live on the Marquesas Keys, I remember. Sets here all year round now on his boat. He might take you. Ask the fella up at the pier where he is. You can smell ol' Perry effen the wind is right. He's sure ripe."

That got a big laugh.

I walked out toward a man scratching his chest through a red cotton shirt. He looked up at my question and moved a finger into a head of uncombed hair. "Cap Perry should be here in an hour maybe. Set and rest in the shade thar." The shade was a yard of old sail on some boards making a bit of awning. I set.

Setting brings thoughts; thoughts bring other thoughts pouring back—Not good thoughts on a hot humid day among Yahoos in a bad time. In the last months all over where I had been, the Depression had eaten away hope, eaten away courage, chewed up all the red-white-and-blue past, mocked everyone. It was hard to think this was the land (O say can you see) of my boyhood and youth. A great despair sat on everyone but the rich, and they wore hatred and fear like funeral crepe for this FDR (sonofabitch) who was changing things so much. (How to recapture the Depression with marks on paper? what it was like? how it was then? and did we stand waiting numbly or cursing strongly?) Even those who had some money and jobs were sour with fear. The faces of the unemployed were everywhere; would it ever change back again, as it had been when we were proud, were sure, were fully alive? No, not on this rickety pier, among these cottonheads and the rednecks with snuff-stained upper lips; they still held Stonewall Jackson close and Robert E. Lee above God, and there were niggers to burn and I had seen people eating canned dog food.

Facing the Gulf, the future, I sensed a superimposed bundle of layers of William Kite; family, youth, experiences, fears, lusts, all part of feedbacks, time-binding, saying, *Here* you are, you bastard, now make something marvelous of it. Beyond where I sat, beyond the brass horizon, there was only outer darkness, and here was William Kite, a prisoner sentenced for life—the exact term of years not known. I figured my mind was going. Or was already gone.

I "set."

It was two hours before the dirtiest white man I had ever seen came ambling along on naked horny feet. He was long-haired, shaggy, fumbling and walleyed.

"You Captain Perry?"

"Shat yes. Kin I do anythin' fer you?"

"I want to get myself and some surveying gear to Tinto Key."

"Don't see why not. Cost a mite. It's a fur voyage, but the *Lucky Seven* is a craft done it lots times before."

"How much?"

"Twenty dollars. Each way."

"All right. Help me get my stuff from the station."

"Right lonely place, Tinto Key. Couldn't stand keys myself. Had to come up here. My great grandfather was Admiral Perry, fella from the battle of Lake Erie. Bet you didn't know that?"

"I didn't."

"Other relation—shat—was the fella what opened up Japan. You wouldn't now carry a bottle of somethin' to cut the morning slimes a bit? I'm parched."

"I don't drink."

"You will at Tinto Key. Let's go rig your cargo."

It took a half hour to get the gear to the dock and down to a splintered small rowboat that would take us to the schooner *Lucky Seven*. I noticed three inches of water in the rowboat.

"She leaks."

"Just yo' bail. It's only two hundred feet out to the *Lucky*."

"Is it safe?"

"Fellas hereabouts say it's safer than the *Lucky Seven*." Captain Perry was pulling hard on the oars. I bailed with a lard can and shifted the gear to keep it dry. I felt flattened by the land-and-seascape—the country soggy as if disintegrating into the Gulf like bread in a bowl of milk. When we bumped against the little schooner's flaking side, I was breathing hard and the water was five inches deep in the bottom of the rowboat. The schooner's deck was no prepossessing sight, littered with empty crates, frayed rope ends and gray patched sails badly furled. From below came the smell of stale bedding, whiskey and rotting potatoes. It hit me like a blow in the head and I stayed on deck.

Captain Perry cast off from a red-leaded float, and he and I ran up two big sails. The schooner answered her head and came around and sailed out toward the loping swells. The creaking of cordage and the ill-set mast steps made common sounds with the shrill cry of seabirds sporting in the *Lucky*'s creamy wake. The rolling gait of the ship soon had me dizzy.

A strong head wind came up in the afternoon, and Captain Perry popped up (from a bottle kept below) and stood on deck and shook his head at the gray-black sky shifting toward us. "Have to run for cover up Fish River. Goin' to blow up a bit."

"Any danger?" I asked, setting my wreck of a hat farther back on my head.

"Not if yo' don't sicken and puke, Mr. Kite."

"I'll try not to. And I'll tie down my gear."

"Lash down everythin' yo' want to hold on to."

We ran before the wind, and when safe between the embraces of the Fish River—both banks overgrown with rank vegetation—Captain Perry put down a mudhook and wiped his mouth with the back of a dirty hand. "Got any belly for some sea rations? Come below, Mr. Kite. I'll stir us up a mess of somethin'."

"No, thank you, Captain Perry. I'll stay on deck."

One gasping moment trying to go below, to the head, had convinced me no one not acclimated to the *Lucky* could survive long the stench of a dirty old man patinaed on the cabin walls of a schooner infected with rot and sinister odors. Captain Perry came on deck with a tin pan of cornbread (half wood ash, half live roaches), a stinking end of black-smoked ham butt and a burned coffeepot. I held my stomach and said I had my own food, and went to the bow of the little schooner as hungry as I had ever been; now that I was no longer ill, a sea-polished appetite was banging at my ribs. From my suitcase I took the only eatable item I had, a small jar of strawberry jelly

Pages had slipped in there while I was packing in Washington. I sat eating jelly with the aid of a finger, watching the head winds grow stronger.

We lay upriver for a night and part of the next day, till the head wind had blown itself out. When we started out again, a wild breeze rattled the clew blocks and battered at the old gray canvas. Captain Perry picked his teeth with a kitchen match and said cheerfully, "Worst part is over."

Not for me. I lay supine on deck among hatch tarps, looking at the storm sky tearing itself apart and wondering how I had ever come there on this protracted voyage. I had often of late made an inner pilgrimage away from reality, had tried the rejection of everyday existence, accepting the spontaneous, instinctual life, jettisoning those parts of my being that protested; but at sea it failed me. (The little ship was shaken and tilted to one side by a sudden blast of wind.) Are we each, I wondered, so damned unique and irreplaceable? Was it sheer nonsense, my attempt now to win complete possession of myself and entrails and agony through discipline? And with what? (Sea spume came driving up on deck and wet me.) I'd be better off to give way, get deadly ill.

Nothing, I felt, is distributed so well as stupidity and self-pity. Now on this dreadful little ship, I was involved in something that would never add up to anything much. I'd drown and become crab and turtle soup. I didn't believe in Tony's project (too proud to refuse it). Were not pride and self-doubt the two sides of the same silver dollar?

I remembered a Sunday long ago in East Pompton—in the Bishop's church smelling of mice and candle wax, the cicadas singing in the drowsy trees, Jay pinching his chin—and a truth had come to me out of a yawn: To succeed where God fails is vanity. (The largest sail began to flap as a rope block fell and a tangle of gear seemed to bring disaster on us. Captain Perry indifferently tied off a few hairy knots and all was as before; the sound of wind and water dominated everything.)

Even lost innocence exists somewhere, I decided, getting to my feet. It was my gnawing hunger that was making me think like this. I would have to turn from my mind all ideas of food. I looked at the terns flying so skillfully, twisting in the very teeth of the wind. I laughed as the schooner dipped into a foaming wave, and I balanced at the rail, feeling miserable in a crumpled suit, turned pale green by sea travel, with hunger a kind of fever on this raging sea. How could I feel so ill and still desire food?

Captain Perry spat over the side to windward. "Nice and easy, the old bitch, ain't she? As neat a bit of boat as is afloat."

I said, "I'm no expert."

"Shat, you need a drink."

Everything was gray and silver in the tilting sky, and later it was gold and azure. I pulled my hat over my eyes to keep out the strong reflections of sun breaking through from the west, sat in the shade of a sail and wondered if I would ever reach land.

Dusk came and with it the dismal cry of seafowl hunting land and sleep. The waves were white-topped, hissing like frying grease, the smell of sea spume salty. My skin was windburned, lips chapped, face, I felt, brick-red.

Night fell, a black wall with a sky all daubed over with stars as fat as oysters (food). From somewhere someone was blowing a conch shell—"Don't pay no mind. Bootleggers bringin' in booze."—and a probing light went blinking around in a full circle every minute, scanning the seascape and tattered waves. ("Light buoy at Fatass Key.") The waves rapped a melancholy sound against the old hull. I almost slept, almost dreamed, but failed to do either. In my hunger I was sure my stomach juices had begun to digest my entrails.

It was near nine o'clock that night that Captain Perry spat once more overside, cleared both nostrils by a strong healthy use of his thumb pressure, and pointed to a yellow light nearby.

"Tinto Key Bay. What yo' goin' to do tonight once you get ashore?"

"At this hour? Don't know. I have a letter of introduction to a Jerry Fry. Don't know if I could find him at night."

"You'd fall and break yer neck. Better stay on board tonight. Bunk sleeps two."

I rubbed my unshaved, wind-reddened face. It was almost two days since I had tasted food or dared to drink the green-scummed water. The schooner was a floating germ culture.

"I like the deck."

I lay down on deck by my gear, trying to find one spot that would not be painful to my ribs. I failed and slept fitfully till dawn, when a rain flurry of grape-sized drops passed quickly. I lay sodden and miserable, hoping for a strong sun to warm me and dry me and show me anything but this roach-cluttered, rotting ship and its sonofabitch of a filthy captain.

When the sun came up full-sized and strong, I was just falling into a druglike sleep, exhausted and worn down . . . around me silence through which small sounds traveled well. I came awake as from a nightmare to the cry of a fish hawk, gray and brown with widespread wings; it went skimming by the masts carrying a white-bellied fish struggling in its claws.

The Tinto Key coast in a wide flat distance lay lime-colored and golden in the morning calm. The bay looked oiled and reflected like a mirror. A limp line of soapy foam beat on the shore. There was little activity beyond the crippled slide of a crab, the probing beak of a sandpiper feeding among the tide-tossed kelp. The island was key-shaped, I knew, like a crescent—thirty miles long, five miles wide, and with twenty miles of beach for our project.

Free of the boat, I looked at my gear set down on the battered wooden pier, paid off the captain ("Some pretty fair nookie if yo' don't mind nigger musk"), and called to a small barefoot boy with a sunburned nose.

"Son, you know where Jerry Fry lives?"

"Sure do."

"Can you take me there?"

"Don't mind if I do."

"I guess my stuff will be all right here?"

The boy, his hair wild and red, thought so too and helped me store it in the shadow of a shed with a sign: NIKKO'S GRILL AND GENERAL STORE. I had some pale green soda drink here. Dreadful. It was a quarter of a mile through sand to the Fry house, a weathered wooden building on a high stone foundation . . . flowers and hens, a parrot, plants struggling to keep alive on fenced-in soil, half sand and tormented by salt. I gave the boy a dime and told him to keep an eye on the bundles. I was tired, numb with hunger, and my head still reeled from the memory of motion in the little schooner.

My name is William Kite, I confided to myself. *It is May twelfth, 1933.* At least I suspected that was my name and that was the date.

And this is Tinto Key, and I am . . . (I continued to knock on the unpainted door, unaware of my automatic action.)

The door opened and a cheerfully plump man smoking a dark clay pipe, his suspenders unlooped loose down his back, looked out at me.

I felt I had arrived.

CHAPTER 27

"I'M WILLIAM KITE," I said to the man in the doorway. "I wrote you I was coming here."

"Why sure, sir. I mind it now. I'm Jerry Fry. Come in, come in."

It was a low, rough-built house, made of the timbers off old ships, with lots of bottles and brass and pots of growing herbs in the window. A lean woman with a bun of faded hair worn high was clearing a table. Behind her two small pretty children hung to her skirt. "This is Nan—Mrs. Fry. This is Mr. Kite what come here all the way from the mainland."

"How was the trip?"

"Captain Perry's boat isn't what I'd call first-rate."

"Perry?" The woman snorted and pushed the children aside. "That filthy old lecher. You look pure tuckered out."

"Now, mother."

"I'm a little worn down from lying on deck. Back is out of joint. Couldn't touch anything to eat even when we lay over an extra day in the river when the storm came."

Mrs. Fry banged down a work-hard hand on the table. "You ain't had no victuals for two days? Jesus, Mary and Joe. I'll put the spider skillet on."

The two children stared at me, wide-eyed and silent. I took off my hat and sat down.

"We done et, but I'll rustle you up a platter of ham 'n' eggs. Jerry, maybe Mr. Kite would take a tot of somethin' eye-buggin' till the victuals is ready."

I shook my head. "I'm teetotal at the moment."

"Be just two shakes of a lamb's tail."

271

The smell of the frying ham and eggs was almost too much. I developed lockjaw and was actually in pain till I got the first forkful of spilly egg and wonderful tangy ham into my mouth. I ate with relish, chewing and smiling at my hosts, wiping the platter clean with soda biscuits and downing two cups of coffee.

The two children watched in shy wonder. Outside the window I felt an island perceptibly tilted.

When I was filled and no longer in danger of shaking, I sat back. "Thank you. I needed that."

"It's just the neighborly thing to do. Don't mind the kids being so rabbity and starin'. They don't see much folk."

"I wonder if you could board me for a week or so. I expect some people to join me next week. We'll build shelters then. I'd be no bother."

Jerry Fry knocked out the dottle of his pipe into his palm. "I'll go talk to Nan in the kitchen. So you all aim to camp on the beach?"

I sat contented, relaxed, eyes closed, aware, as if newly awakened, of voices from the kitchen.

"Now, Jerry Fry, a fella from God knows where like that, just takin' a couple weeks sportin' around on the beach, ain't nobody we kin board. We be barefoot-pore-plain."

"He don't look like no fancy fusser to me, and times is hard with no WPA here."

"He looks the kind's well brung up. I'm all flummoxed. He'd never be satisfied with what we kin offer, and don't you forget it."

I stumbled to my feet and walked into the kitchen, a kind of lean-to built against the house. "I'm sorry, I overheard what you've been saying, Mrs. Fry. Believe me, I'd like it fine here with no extra frills. Just a week or so, and you'd be doing me a favor by not throwing me back to people like Captain Perry."

Jerry Fry laughed. *"Captain* Perry, my ass! He ain't no more a captain than he's clean. We'll take you in. Five dollars the week, bed and keep. You look worn to a nub. Nan, the spare bedroom in order?"

"It always is. Mr. Kite, you just go drop yer shoes and take a nap. I'll wake you for noon and food."

It felt good to take off my shoes and jacket, open the saw-toothed collar, unknot the tie, and to fall back on sweet-smelling linen with the soft pillow under my head, to think of Tony's scheme, the long beach, the empty sea sky; and before I could carry the images further I was sound asleep. In my dream the upward sweep of the constellations and the immobility of the void were familiar ground and did not interfere with the deep deep sleep that held me.

It was two in the afternoon before I came awake. The sea breeze, smelling wonderfully of seaweed and crushed shell, was blowing over the bed, the cool air of the room scented with herbs. It found me lost in thought for a moment and then I sat up. Jerry Fry was in the doorway, lighting a fresh clay pipe with a glowing coal held between two sticks. I saw for the first time he was a colored man. He was very light and had regular features, but I knew now why he lived on this lonely scrap of island.

"Brung your crates and parcels up from the dock. Nan has a chicken potpie pipin' hot, and some of her homemade tomato spice. Kin you eat?"

"I'm going to give it a try," I said as I hunted my shoes with my stockinged toes. I was refreshed, rested, and free of the doubts that had intruded on the little schooner. None plagued me. I had work to do and chicken potpie to eat.

The next morning I discarded my hat for a wide-brimmed straw fisherman's hat Jerry Fry found on a handy nail. It was time to set to work. Jerry was the kind who accepted any story, and he felt, I saw, that if men wanted to measure the beach there must be some amusement in it. "It's no worse than sittin' over a sick worm waitin' for a fish to bite," he told me. "A non-drinkin' man has his problems." (I had refused his still-brewed whiskey.)

I examined the cloth-covered bag. It was an extra-good-quality white French sateen, sewn and shaped to fit the surveying instruments. I hoped I remembered my lessons; I had to stake out a twenty-mile straight line of beach, thirty feet wide, as a raceway. I said I needed tall thin stakes.

"Nothing over six feet long. That uncomfort you a bit?" he asked.

"No. Get me about two hundred."

"Do that with the captain of one of the boats from Fish River."

"Is there a sewing machine?"

"Mrs. Fry has got one out in the parlor. Does didies and stuff for the kids. She'd be happy to run anything up for you."

"Good—just some red flags for the stakes. I figure I'll set up camp

273

about half a mile below your house with a good view of the beach. Anybody object?"

"Nobody much around here to object. Nikko owns lots of it, but he's cheerful."

"I'll put up a tent for the crates and things and work from there. Mr. Pfaelzer and the mechanics will get here on the twenty-eighth. I hope to have the survey all ready by then."

"You make free 'round here. I'll be seein' you when I get back from a load of clams. Nan will take mighty good care of you. You aim to do *what* here?"

"Test a new racing car in secret."

My gear was dragged to the proposed campsite. I set up the canvas tent, and in the intense heat of the strong day I sat working, drinking water from a tin bucket, aware there was a lot to do. I stripped to the waist and felt healthy and whole. Carrying the bucket of water down from the well at the Fry house, setting up the gear—none of it tired me. The stakes came; they were two feet short. Mrs. Fry's sewing machine, a primitive moaning thing, extended my knowledge of the obstinate delight inanimate objects take in annoying people as I watched her hem the two-feet-square red cotton flags from the bolts of cloth I had brought. I felt better when alone in the tent. It was twelve feet by twenty-two feet.

After supper I smoked a pipe with Jerry Fry on the front steps of his house—in the austere resignation of surf sounds—while his wife washed up, and got the kids ready for bed by scrubbing them in a wooden tub out back. Before the kids were put to bed Jerry said they had evening prayers, and would I care to join? I said I had no objection. I knocked the dottle out of my pipe and followed Jerry indoors.

Jerry seemed to have memorized a great deal of the Bible. As they bowed their heads and I inclined mine, he said, "From John VIII, verses 12 to 16:

". . . I am the light of the world; he that followeth me shall not walk in darkness but shall have the light of life. The Pharisees therefore said unto him, Thou bearest record of thyself; Thy record is not true. . . ."

274

CHAPTER 28

JERRY FRY TOLD ME there was great poverty on Tinto Key among the sponge fishers, and he could get me all the help I needed at a dollar a day and a shot of whiskey at Nikko's Grill. When it got too hot to follow the two Negroes I had hired to carry the chains and the surveying tools, I'd get in the shade of a sand dune and fold my arms behind my head and doze off into a light sleep like a wild animal's; but before I did, I'd sometimes wonder what the hell I was doing here and why I had let myself be talked into Tony's scheme.

The crash had ruined a lot of us, brought us out of Paris and Rome, the little Greek islands, the pleasure points off the coast of Spain, from Bloomsbury flats and Mayfair drawing rooms; it had brought us home. And to what? We lacked Captain Ahab's fleeing goal.

Kite stock was still nearly worthless; the foundries had been sold off, the spinning mills lost in the unrelenting hands of banks. But Tony Pfaelzer—at first I hadn't expected *him* to be hit at all by the global disaster. Junk was junk. Old iron, bronze, tin, scrap steel were still old iron, bronze and all that. But Tony had explained it to me in his magnificent Washington apartment (rent unpaid). "So what good is it if the steel mills are putting out the furnace fires? Scrap iron you could use for toilet paper, only it's too rough. And bronze and tin—the offered prices of the Jap buggers don't pay for the shipping of it. I tell you, Bill, I'll have to give up good cigars unless I perfect that new gasoline injection system. *That* the auto world needs. Economy."

"I don't understand it. Why put your last dollar in it?"

"Damn it, Bill, you got the scientific *kop* of a frog eating butter. The American motorcar is fancy crap. Right? Right. The carburetors waste gas, don't function well. This gizmo I've built injects the gasoline in a vapor, directly into the cylinders. Pages, honey, refill my glass."

275

I watched Pages walk across the room.

"Sell it to General Motors, to Henry Ford."

"Those *alte kockers,* they'd screw me out of it, or pay me peanuts. No, I've got the old racer I built in France—remember the rig?— Becky, I called it. I'll put in the Tony Pfaelzer Fuel Injector, race it for a world record, two hundred miles or more an hour, and get into the world's newspapers. You follow me?"

I did but wasn't much impressed. "You get killed and Pages will be a widow."

"You'd like that, you *mamzer.* I think you got a sweet letch for her."

"All right, so you astonish the world by a speed record. Then what?"

"Then we announce the T. P. Fuel Injector did it all, and we put it on the market. Of course I'll have to float a company, sell shares, but that's my job. You, Bill, go ahead and find us a perfect testing ground till we're ready to invite reporters and cameramen."

Pages, sitting on the arm of Tony's chair, said to me, "Well?"

"It's a rotten idea, Pages. In these times."

Tony beat a hand on Pages's thigh. "So you tell me, Mr. Kite, what else we can do? Sit and pick lint out of our navels for *bupkis—* chick-peas?"

It was Pages who had found the report in a copy of *National Geographic:* Tinto Key and its long level stretch of hard-packed thirty-mile beach, where buccaneers once roamed, great sea turtles mated and only a few sponge fishers still managed to exist. It was Tony who said, "Perfect place to test a secret device." It was I who had been shipped off as advance party with ten lessons in surveying to lay out the beach.

It was I, now dozing in the shade of a sand dune among lonely obsessions and latitudes . . . the crabs—with big, red-clawed tips, rosy as tits—banging on empty clam shells, sounding like the typewriters of facile writers (all at work on the great novels of the twentieth century). I came fully awake, sat up, drained sand from my shoes. I wondered if Jay was working again on a novel, if *Stone Sunlight* would ever become a classic, if Charlie Huttonbok was still in Austria, if the depth and quality of the light over the surf of Tinto Key was constant and if there were sharks out there. I decided to swim, and went naked into the breaking sea, and for a moment I hoped there were sharks and that they could take me neatly in two or three gulps and not mangle me in some Sophoclean irony of shark pleasure. But a fear sat cold and suddenly around my heart; the survival instinct was stronger than St. John of the Cross—*en una noche oscura*. I came ashore smelling of what Nan Fry called the Carolina allspice bush that grew everywhere above the beach. It was too hot for brooding, I decided, as I picked sand from between my toes. I motioned my chain bearers we were finished for the day.

Nikko's Grill and General Store was open-ended but at least had an ice machine, and Nikko had been places and had words about things. I went there usually in the middle afternoon to drink the green soda pop he bottled. Nikko, big, once handsome, too fat, too unwashed, sat fanning himself. A couple of sponge fishers reclined on the earth under the awning just outside the doorway. Chickens walked over the store floor, wary, avoiding kicks or flung objects.

Nikko wiped his wide wrestler's neck with a clean handkerchief, the only clean object he carried.

"You lucky fella, Mr. Kite, ice machine working again."

"I don't know. This soda is dreadful."

"You right—but you no drink booze, what the hell I give you?"

"That's all right."

Nikko looked at me carefully as he opened a bottle for me. "You no on the lam?"

"I'm surveying, I told you, a beach track."

"No G-heat on you? No mob muscle want to lean on you?"

"I'm not wanted, Nikko."

"You right. You don't look like fella who would make crime. I tell you I been all over world, all everyplace before I marry Celeste, settle here. I do everything but kiss boys. All right, maybe once or twice. I can smell a man who is running from law. I ask only because you see I like you. People here have times hard, so they make a little alky in tin-can stills; 'gainst law sure, but comes time you 'gainst law, or you starve, you girl starve, you lil baby they starve. So you brew alky."

"Nikko, I assure you I don't give a damn what's brewed here or why you're here."

"I here because where else I go just now? I am old fella, my plumbing like ice machine—not good. I big like pig. Law I know is no good for men like us. Always I hate the police 'cause why? They protect property. People no got property is *merde*. People like me know a life so easy to end; like twist a chicken neck. So we just want to live, grow old, eat, drink, jazz a little."

"You a Communist?"

He spat on his floor, doing it no harm. "No, I anarchist. I 'gainst everything that make you feel bad. Have another soda?"

"No, thanks."

"Somebody allus has to be boss, big club, so is coming time better not be born." He threw a bit of pink coral at a hen and missed. "In end, for us, is only one thing to do. Eat, drink, tear off piece, laugh, scream, pick lice. So nothing worth dying for."

"Not even as an anarchist?"

"That biggest fake of all. That why I like it. It say be 'gainst everything. That suit this Grik fine. You gotta going?"

I said I did and I went off, and Nikko threw something at the chickens again and there was a dreadful death scene behind me. I figured Nikko was a fearful liar. He was greedy, and, I had heard, was the principal dealer on the Keys in bootleg alcohol.

And the green soda pop wasn't doing *me* any good.

Alone in the tent was best—a tent with one end tied firmly to a wind-twisted palm tree for safe anchorage. A tropical mockingbird, a darting morsel of gray and white, lived in the tree, and while I was indifferent to music, I knew it would please Pages. If she came, she would most likely bring her portable gramophone.

On good days I worked helping drive stakes till the dusk came down suddenly and the seabirds settled in to stand in pools of water on shore, all facing the same way and just as the sun went down tucking their heads under their wings or sinking them back into their feathers. I would light the acetylene gas lamp which astonished the natives of Tinto Key. It gave a bright glaring white light, and insects gave parties and balls in its orbit. They never learned to hoard their lives by never risking them. . . .

I was making my first daily trip for sweet water, over one thousand feet to the well on the yielding sands, when Jerry Fry signaled me and shouted, "There's a freighter comin' in. Might be carryin' yer big stuff."

"I hope so, Jerry."

278

There was only a boy and an old man fishing on the little pier when I came down to meet the freighter, which looked no cleaner than Captain Perry's boat, and Tony and the two mechanics at the rail were a bit green. Sections of the racing car were under canvas on deck.

"Rough trip?" I asked, grinning.

"Do we look like cruise-ship sports?"

"Can you unload on the dock?"

"Chuck, Highpockets, can we?"

A mechanic said, "Ke-rist! Maybe."

Tony asked, "How's the course?"

"Had to shorten it. Not enough stakes around."

"Has to be twenty miles."

"That's good. Chuck, get the lead out."

"Hello, Mr. Kite."

"Hello, Chuck."

Chuck I knew from the grand old days when the T. P. racing car colors were roaring over the best routes in Europe, making all the famous runs. He was a little cockney who looked weaned on motor oil, and but for his miser's habit of saving his earnings would have been an amusing man, with his Mons medals and his scar from the battles in Palestine where he had ended up with General Allenby fighting off Turks and trying to keep sand out of the armored cars in the desert. Chuck dreaded old age and saved every penny, banked it someplace in Switzerland and stole old motor parts to sell, lent money at the rate of 20 percent on short loans, and when he paid for his own food ate very little. He was a wizard mechanic. Highpockets, the other engine monkey, I didn't like. He was a lanky Texan of an unknown age under thirty, with a poor-white-trash look, weak, watery blue eyes, slack mouth, buck teeth and an ear like a great conductor: He could listen to a motor running and tell you sixteen different things that were not acting just right in the motor block electrical system, fan belt, gear chamber, clutch box. He had an indecent love for gambling with his own doctored dice or cards. Tony said Highpockets was harmless and impotent; he feared and hated women. He would commit murder someday, I suspected.

Tony—in British Empire shorts and cigar, nothing else—was busy supervising the unloading of the old racer, once a very famous car built by Lavoni in Turin. I asked Chuck, "You bring any airplane gasoline? There isn't more than a few gallons here."

"Got us the 'igh-test petrol. Cost a packet. Oh this plice, it's a bleak bloody arse'ole of a plice, Mr. Kite."

"Better bury the gas barrels in the sand."

"Any good grub? No fish-and-chips, I suppose."

"Fish, *no* chips."

Tony was yelling. "Chuck! Highpockets! Grab that cable! Keep the motor block from the freighter side! Bill, get the timbers under it."

" 'Old yer water, Mr. Pfaelzer."

It was not the most efficient unloading, and the boy and the old man fished and watched, offering no comment. We got everything on shore; the freighter went off, rust bleeding from its unpainted hull. Tony wiped his hands on his naked chest, on his fine linen shorts.

I said there was no problem in getting help of a basic kind. For pulling and hauling there were groups of primitive Negroes who lived at the western end of Tinto Key and existed miserably on fish and sponge diving. "But now there's no market for sponges, they're eager and lean."

We got the racer parts up to the camp on sleds and skids and put up a portable shed for the racer and a carshop and a tent for Chuck and Highpockets and guests. It was decided that we would live at the camp while the racer was assembled. The trek over the loose sand from the Frys' to the beach was too far. Tony kept tapping my chin with his fist: "Boychik, we made it."

Tony had filled out, become wider but not slack; he was developing jowls, the skin under the big, handsome eyes was baggy, the smile showed yellowing teeth. He was still a striking-looking man, but his brow was furrowed with problems for he labored under the tyranny of his type: Failure was a disgrace to be atoned for and overcome.

After supper at the Frys' we two went for a walk . . . the sky to the west dying in splendid old-fashioned colors, the shuffle of crabs going back to the kelp beds, the last effort of an incoming sea hissing up at our toes, stopping just short of our canvas shoes, a sort of minuscule personal hello.

"How's Pages?"

Tony shook his head. He had put on a yellow silk jacket and slacks. "I never understand women—I like the mystery of them. Just now she says to me in Washington, Don't leave. So I say, Come,

280

Pages, come along, and she says, No, not just yet; I have things to do. What things? *Things*. Balls. So there she is in D.C. In this weather it's a steam bath. You think she's got a guy on a string? Some *putz* who's romancing her?"

"Not Pages. She'd tell you."

"We should have had a kid. A lot of them."

He picked up a bit of driftwood and threw it into the surf. "Don't mind me—I'm wound up too tight these days. Bill, we have to make the T. P. Fuel Injector come out aces all the way. We'll be back in Europe riding the first-class trains again, eating high off the hog— Moses forgive me; *Gott zoll op hitten*—and Pages will shine—like it was at Café Place, St. Michel, Hotel George Five. We'll all shine like it was. Uncle Tony doesn't back any dead horses. Or horsepower."

"I like being rich, Tony, but not if it's an effort."

"The terrace of the Sporting Club in the Champs-Élysées and a villa on the Côte d'Azur. Bill, it has to be."

"How's the stock company going?"

Tony put his arm around my shoulder. I waited for the snow job. Like all salesmen he was a romantic, never facing true reality. Tony was the greatest living salesman when he put his mind to it. With the Emperor Vespasian, who taxed privies, he agreed: "Money does not stink." He smiled at me. "I figured why let everybody in? I said to myself they'll strip you down to your B.V.D.'s in Wall Street. They'll infringe on your patents, so why not make it just a few friends, a private holding company—say a holding holding company, get it?— of Pfaelzer Scrap Metal, all in the family."

I knew he had failed to raise outside money. "What are you operating on?"

"Pages's diamonds. Call it *chutzpah*—she'll get it back in spades. Hocked all her jewels in Monte to a Greek prick who's charging me—never mind details." He scuffed the beach sand with a toe. "Marvelous hard-packed stuff. You say twenty miles? Straight?"

"Eighteen of it staked. Like a line drawn with a ruler."

"We'll stake more. I can get Becky up to two-ten on it, I'm sure. But I need that extra two miles, boychik."

"Becky isn't Becky yet." I didn't much care for Becky. Tony had named the car after an old aunt. Becky had killed two men in test runs and broken Tony's leg in a Grand Prix north of Milano two years before.

281

He held out an arm to sea. "It's all there—just at the end of my fingertips."

"The factory, a sales organization, distributors for the T. P. Injector?"

"Time, time, Bill—that old gypsy man, eh? It takes care of things. First let's get the injector in apple-pie order. Then a few record runs and we'll call in the press, wire services, the newsreel *mamzers* . . . Bill, what the hell is happening to the world?"

"It's coming apart at the seams."

"How could it happen? I mean after the stinking war, everything looked so fine, so grand. Now bankers from Yale and Harvard jumping from windows, fathers of fine families selling apples on street corners. Three years now and the dust bowls, the Okies . . . Lord, what misery. Whose side is God on?"

I said I feared He had let us goyim down.

Tony didn't sleep well. He'd toss on the canvas cot next to mine and shout out in the night. "No, no, scrap iron at those prices—no. Better bury it." Or, "Pages, Pages, you have to know I can't just do nothing. It's for you, baby, for you." A half hour's sleep and I'd be awakened by *"Bimheyroh b'yomeynu. Yovo eyeleynu. Im mosheeach ben Doveed, im mosheeach ben Doveed."* I learned it by heart after several nights. It was a kind of chant, and when I repeated it to Tony one morning, he said he didn't remember chanting it. I moved out into a lean-to of canvas which I kept neat with a compulsive spinsterish primness.

If I couldn't sleep, I'd go down to the other tent where High-pockets and Chuck lived. There would usually be a couple of sponge fishers who worked for Tony losing their pay to Highpockets' crooked dice, everybody passing around a quart mason jar of local whiskey from Nikko's Grill. Chuck would sit by a small fire with leaves smoldering on it if the insects were bad, but mostly the wind would drive the insects off and the sky and sea were silver and gray and the stars out, palm fronds whispering in the trade breeze, the stone armor of the crabs rattling as they came ashore to feed and, I suppose, to love. Reproduction in the tropics is an act of exorcism. Everything— nearly—on the island I saw was actively engaged in the act of love, except for Highpockets, who was sexless, his white eyebrows over a face like a gelded harem guard. Everything else was seminal, the dogs

282

and cats, the few goats beating dust from each other, the kids piddling openly with wet mouths, the youths hungry and lean, active as tomcats after dark, the girls from the sponge fishers' village giggling and swinging their buttocks and breasts. Even the women and the gray-whiskered men beating hands looked lewd.

Tony didn't appear to be randy. I suppose hard work and worry wall up the other drives. I myself was thinking of playing a road-company Gauguin, finding a local version of a wahine, but I didn't. I was no wily roisterer—I was waiting for something. My personal images metamorphosed in shady spots free of sun, merged into each other; and when the cool breeze came just before morning, I'd relax into deep sleep on my cot and have marvelous detailed dreams about Pages.

Tony, no matter how low his funds, was putting the best available into Becky. He had built her on a helioarc 16-gauge turbo-chassis frame, and now he was putting on magnesium wheels.

"Pretty as a million dollars, Bill. You can't get anything better than that a 640-cc twelve-cylinder job—not with that radical over-square design."

"Will the injector work properly?"

"That we'll find out when we try her out." He slapped the stripped-down motor. "Yes, sir."

Highpockets scowled and listened to the testing run of the engine, as yet on a block. "Maybe, maybe, Mistah P. But I'd ruther have a Shorrock supercharger in thar instead of that injector crapola."

"Look, Tex, we're here to prove the injector, not to have fun."

Chuck had trouble with the cam shaft and timing gear, beat his knuckles with a gearbox wrench, screamed with pain and went shrilly back to work. Highpockets had ideas about the poppet valve, and they all stood around, like a group of expensive surgeons in conclave over a Rockefeller liver; and I went down to Nikko's Grill for some of the dreadful green soda drinks.

I never got much excitement out of machines, even if they were built with care, like a fine watch. For me Becky was a murderer and a bone breaker.

I sat in the doorway of Nikko's Grill and General Store by the Mail Pouch Chewing Tobacco sign, watching the sun move around and make new shapes (as in a Rembrandt the shadows had the most meaning). Still uncomfortable, with two of the green sodas in me, I

283

went back to the shed with a palm basket full of soda bottles laid in crushed ice—the ice machine was working that day.

At the camp they were lying under the stripped-down cadaver of Becky, engaged in a long argument on engine torque and a radical change in the longitudinal torsion-bar suspension. They stood up to drink the soda and belch loudly like seers.

CHAPTER 29

". . . PERISH AS THE SUMMER FLY," I recited. "Heads without names, no more remembered," for I was bored by heat and car talk.

The racer in all its intricate details was assembled in a week. We pushed it out into the full bright sunlight and stood grimy and yet proud looking at it. Chuck had painted it bright yellow with spar enamel—only a few dents showed. "That's a bloody wonder; eats tires."

"What's the first test speed?" I asked.

"Two hundred. Highpockets, crank her up."

"Bitch nearly broke my arm."

Tony lowered his baseball cap to shade his eyes from the strong sun. "I think she'll do." The motor roared into life.

Highpockets said, "The injector stinks."

Even I could hear the motor was faulting.

Tony stood scuffing his canvas shoe in the shifting sand, in an almost serene awareness that he had reached some climax here. Or failure. We looked at each other without the deception of speech between us. The racer vibrated as the mechanics adjusted its vitals with probing screwdrivers.

Tony stopped toeing the sand. "I've been checking the stuff the United States Weather Bureau sends on these fronts."

"What do you think of their figures?"

"They list an average wind as steady at fifteen, twenty miles an hour every day. They're wrong. It looks faster."

"They forgot to say that was the daily *average* for a month."

284

"That's some difference."

"Jerry Fry says it sometimes blows sixty miles an hour and sometimes it's just a dead calm."

"So our wind charts are no good?"

"No good at all, Tony."

"At least that's settled. We'll set up a wind gauge. Over thirty miles an hour, wind can kill me when I go over ninety."

Highpockets said, "Man, this scarebooger just don't sound right. We tear down the motor again."

It had been a disappointing day. We returned to our tent in silence, ate supper sitting at the mouth of the tent, the sea in tide roaring below, and the wind picking up power, sending the sand flying higher. We slept that night in fitful stretches—I heard Tony cursing as he turned over—the wind flapping the tent canvas. He repeated the Hebrew prayer twice in his sleep and once had a long debate with Pages on some dim subject. I decided the next night to go back to the lean-to. I was up before dawn, going for water to have something to do.

The day came up blustery but clear as crystal, and Tony shook his head. "Twenty-five miles as hour on our wind gauge. We'll have to wait till she drops to about sixteen or seventeen."

We spent the breezy day checking the motor and leaning over wind charts and speed scales. Something was dismally wrong, Chuck said. The injector had been fine on test block but not in the car. Jerry Fry woke us the next morning as he came in with a basket of eggs he had carried through the sand full of fleas and torn kelp. "Nice calm day."

Tony looked up at our wind gauge set over the tent. It spun lazy and easy. He went over and read from it: "Fourteen miles an hour."

"Good-o."

"We'll try it if the boys get the lead out of their vents."

Chuck said, "She's not vaporizing fully."

"Just want to test the beach surface."

"Don't let her out all the way."

Highpockets giggled. "Hell, she scatter yo' like a blue duster if yo' go over hundred now."

We pushed Becky over to the level sand and low shore weed, over shell patches of blue-white oyster fragments and driftwood. Behind the ridge rose tall olive-colored saw grass, cattail reed and a few

285

stunted trees. Tony looked up the beach and agreed it was the place. My red staked flags flapped lazily.

"Direction is west—dead west all the way."

Tony lowered his goggles and got in. The motor sounded steady and friendly.

Jerry Fry sucked his unlit pipe. "Really goin' to git goin'?"

Tony, his baseball cap low, lifted an arm. He started easy, the huge tires tossing up loose sand. The racer moved faster—I judged at fifty miles an hour; Chuck said sixty.

Tony made three runs—both ways. Then he took out his notebook and wrote down some figures and pointed a finger at me. "We've run her at low speed. Not bad performances. Hundred and ten."

Chuck said, "The injector wasn't extended."

Tony closed the notebook. Jerry Fry, scratching his chin, looked up. "What do you do now with the shebang?"

"Open her up all the way tomorrow."

Jerry Fry got out his tobacco and began to load his pipe. "Beats all sense. Who needs to ride so fast?"

Tony said, "You're right, old fellow. I'm wrong. But I can't change—not now."

Jerry Fry lit his pipe, turning his broad back to the wind. He puffed it alight and stood staring at the racer.

They spent the afternoon going over the motor, changing to oil of a more stable viscosity and regrinding part of the single-disc braking system. The yellow monster just stood there like a goddamn queen bee being serviced by food and sex through poor lean males; only instead of using queen honey and bee genes they were relining the gearbox and tearing down the four-speed planetary clutch and transmission. In a way working on machines is a perverse love rite. They had done that teardown so often that even I nearly understood how it worked. Actually, after two weeks I could have written a textbook on the machine, without ever having been in it, or wanting to.

I do not think even Greek or Roman classics are as dull as talk about cornering and timing of shifts, rocket arms and tubular shock absorbers. I left the three of them dripping oil and grease, anointed like high priests of some obscure cult that worshiped machine parts and gears. I wrote a long letter to Pages.

The qualities of the heart (I wrote among other things) should

286

have superiority over the head. The temperature on Tinto Key is 94 on a cold day. Not today. Certain organisms I found at low tide in catch basins react to external stimuli of light and heat—I react to love, food and friendship. Tony has ordered a new Abarth exhaust system shipped express, and when it is in place he'll try for the record.

As always, Bill the Kite. . . .

It was not a good or bad letter. It just didn't say anything I wanted to say, which is the trouble with writing letters to the beautiful wife of a close friend. I put the letter in an envelope that contained some tobacco crumbs, which I carefully shook out, addressed it, found a stamp (letters went for bargain rates then), and put it away in the inner pocket of a gray tweed sports jacket. (I supposed it crumpled away in time. I never mailed the letter.)

The racer's work crew had given up tinkering for the day and, stripped naked, were washing up in two oily buckets with the tired gestures of worn-out men. I inspected three white sets of buttocks that would have sent Gide into ecstasy and couldn't understand that game at all. I made us all pancakes for supper, eaten on the beach with Mrs. Fry's wild strawberry jam.

Tony sat putting away his second stack of pancakes as Chuck, a fast feeder, came out of the shed rubbing his insect bites.

"Well, Chuck," said Tony, "have you discovered *why* the bugs bite so?"

"Because they're blasted 'ungry, just as I was."

I said, "Don't worry about the bites. There's no malaria around here."

Tony scratched his arms. "Don't be so cheerful, Bill. They don't get much out of your mean hide. But the rest of us feel them biting."

"Oh, the sods try," said Chuck, accepting another plate of pancakes. "But I think my 'ide blunts their bloody stingers. Caught two of 'em turning the 'andle of our grindstone while a third repointed 'is stinger."

"Where's Highpockets?"

"Says 'e needs a swim."

We felt as if nature had turned against us the next few days, as if wanting no more experimenting. Nights in our tents were long agonies of insect attacks. Mosquitoes in huge swarms lurked all day in the

287

beach grass, hid in the shore plants, under the palm trees. At dusk in buzzing armadas they came in for feeding. They blinded us at meals; no fire or smoke could drive them off. In the tightly closed tents we sleepers came awake to slap and sweat, to go out to choke and cough in the thick smolder of the fire covered with damp kelp to make more smoke. Nothing was effective against the mosquitoes and sand flies. Salves, oils, smoke, smells. Everyone's features, arms and legs were red and swollen. Tony was the worst sufferer; some fluid in the insects' bite caused his arms to swell alarmingly—his face, too, almost shut off from sight. I sent him up to sleep at Jerry Fry's.

The lighthouse keeper's assistant came to our beach camp to deliver a radio message that Mrs. Pfaelzer was being delayed by the storm at Conch Harbor. I hoped she wasn't coming out to us with Captain Perry. Tony was feeling better after a few insectless nights' sleep at the Frys', and he had made a deal for himself and Pages to take over a room at the Frys' house.

Outside the Gulf-whipped sand flew, the wind continued. Becky, yellow as jaundice, rested in her shed wrapped in canvas, but Chuck said the perishing powdery sand was getting to the delicate motor parts. She'd have to be torn down completely when the storm stopped, and rebuilt. Tony groaned.

"Nothing goes bad, Bill, when you're riding high. But let one thing go wrong, then comes an avalanche. Nothing—nothing—in my *bubba's pupik* (grandmother's navel) has gone right since I took that bad spill at Turin, since the market crashed and Hoover said prosperity was just around the corner. Chuck, what do they drink on this island?"

"Fry makes a mean whiskey. I mean in a still someplace. And Nikko, the raunchy hawg, 'e peddles it, and sure charges as if it were Napoleon brandy."

"Get me a couple of bottles. I want to save the brandy for Pages."

I said, "Maybe she should stay in Papaya City."

"That creep town is worse than here. Besides, I may get back my power for a bit of *shtupping* from time to time, even if it's my wife. I hear, Bill, they have some fine high yellows down by the sponge divers. Why don't you take your mind off the weather?"

I said for him to worry over his own animal instincts and I would worry over mine. Since the London mess over Lady B.-R. I had been

288

trying to resolve my reactions to a great many moods. One never finds the truth in these things, only *a* truth.

EDITOR'S NOTE: This is the only reference William Kite makes in his manuscript to the Bowen-Robinson divorce case in London, in which he was named corespondent, except for a note added here in pencil: "Fuller details some other time. Can't reveal more until Alice remarries." Alice is Lady Alice Marsha Bowen-Robinson. The case had been a sensational international scandal. Another note in pencil: "Lord Barton Lewson Bowen-Robinson, one of the triviatizing crowd that hung around the Prince of Wales, that rather dull gay bunch that got photographed, publicized everyplace they ran—in Monte, Eden Rock, the enclosures at the Derby or in Paris—pretty much a public circus of useless efforts, actually being avoided by intelligent people. With their sexually feeble perversions, their slobs' intellects, they were tragic, their future dim. In the middle, like Jack Horner's plum, stood the sad, droopy-lidded prince, looking over them with a world-weary stare as if caught in something sticky he could not understand."

From a study of the *Daily Express* (London) the following facts emerge. Lord Bowen-Robinson had married Alice Marsha Hughes-Brace in 1928, and several people have suggested in their memoirs that she was the original of a now forgotten, once notorious novel by an author called Michael Arlen, *The Green Hat*. In 1932 Lord Bowen-Robinson brought action for divorce, claiming Lady Bowen-Robinson had been intimate in adultery with twenty-two men—he produced blurred photographs of the game *soixante-neuf*—many of whom he refused to name as they were high in government circles. He did name a Hungarian actor in Hollywood, a Negro noble from Kenya, and William Kite. For some reason Lady Bowen-Robinson had kept a journal, in which only William Kite was mentioned by name; at least "my Long-tailed Kite" is assumed to be he. And as this journal had come into the hands of her husband's lawyers, parts of it were read in court and reported in full in certain vulgar newspapers. I shall not here reproduce the most detailed and intimate sections of the journal which refer to "my Long-tailed Kite." Those who desire such kind of reading can find it in old news files of certain papers.

The press for a time bracketed William Kite with such great lovers as Don Juan and Casanova and certain motion picture actors. In the journal, in a rather torrid prose, the lady recorded how many times the act of love could be performed each night by her Long-tailed Kite, and the number seemed rather amazing and the basis of many jests among radio comics and clubroom wits. For some months William Kite, as a letter shows, hardly dared sign his name at a hotel or order anything in his own name without eliciting stares, leers and often questions. The term "Long-tailed Kite" became as famous as any of the catchphrases of the period. In Haiti a voodoo love charm was named after him, and a wild little musical play, *Go Fly a Kite,* ran for two years in a private theater club playhouse in Baywater, thinly based on the journal and some of its more lurid passages. William Kite bore himself very well during it all, and only once lost his temper: He knocked a German down, in a Munich café, when the subject was brought up. He was fined twenty marks in a German court and cheered by everyone in the room.

It was an ordeal he could have avoided in part by staying out of England, but he returned to testify when asked. He testified in Lady Bowen-Robinson's defense, swearing under oath that he had never had, with her, sexual intercourse "on the occasions mentioned nor was he the Long-tailed Kite," that he could not speak for the unnamed co-respondents, but the Hungarian actor was a homosexual and the Negro nobleman from Kenya was actually a sweeper in a Soho nightclub before he claimed any royal bloodlines and was deported: "hardly the person a lady would consort with." As for Lord Bowen-Robinson, he had while drunk at Nice confessed to William Kite "certain factors that made it impossible for him to go to bed with his wife and he bore great hatred of her because of this." The justice sitting on the case, Mr. Marin Jordan, later Lord Keats, at this point called all parties and their solicitors and barristers into private chambers, and what went on there was never told or reported in the press. Everyone suspected William Kite had lied "like a gentleman." Lord Bowen-Robinson was granted his divorce on grounds of adultery and William Kite had to flee to Italy to escape the international journalists who wanted him to reveal more about the lady's habits. Of rumors and gossip, too vague and often too revolting to repeat here, I will put down nothing.

Lord Bowen-Robinson never remarried. He was killed during the Battle of Britain while in command of a Spitfire fighter squadron field near Dover. Alice Bowen-Robinson was at one time engaged to the Levantine shipping magnate Sophron Triclinus, who was indicted for fraud with a United States ex-senator in acquiring United States war surplus. There was talk of a million dollars in bribes being passed at the time among high officials in the government. Alice Bowen-Robinson disappeared from international gossip and I have been unable to trace her present whereabouts.

With the court trial still on his mind, and the details of the journal, William Kite on Tinto Key seems from his own account to have had a revulsion from sex. (An unrelated note: "We pass our time sniffing our parts, like scuffling stoats and ferrets.") While he insists he was not drinking during all these years, there are medical records among his papers that seem to show he had one, perhaps two, lapses. Among his effects sent me were receipts for six weeks during 1928 at the Montross Abbey Nursing Home in Essex (England), which took in only drug and alcohol cases; and another note that suggests he was being treated by a Dr. Myron Levy in New York City in 1931 with a drug used to counter the effects of hard drinking.

The weather at Tinto Key took a short break for the better. Highpockets was beaten up by the sponge fishers for some betrayal at a card game. They brewed a fearful drink and offered their wives and sisters to the men on the few fishing boats that put in for repairs or net-mending. Poverty was bone-projecting among them. Jelly-sticky kelp covered the beach, and Jerry Fry said we'd have to wait till high tide came to sweep the beaches clean.

"Some of them man-of-war jellyfish got stings they poison you till you die." I'd watch the huge fifty-foot man-of-war jellyfish drift through the water, pear-shaped, with a great rainbow-colored vagina, frighteningly alive.

It was a sponge fishers' supply boat that often brought passengers to Tinto Key. Tony was busy with the mechanics, refitting a new part into the fuel injector, so I went down to the dock to see if Pages had come. She had. She came ashore dressed in white linen, a great wide woven-straw hat, sandals, no stockings on those marvelous long legs, looking rather tired, her battered luggage of seven pieces showing how far we had all come from the fine rich days of the '20s. Pages had always liked luggage of the best kind—heavy rare nobby leather, always saddle-waxed and in good condition. There had once been at least twelve pieces, not counting the jewel boxes. Those were gone, too; depleted or emptied for the good of the T. P. Fuel Injector. The goddamn gadget had better work, I thought, as I grabbed her ungloved hand.

"What the devil you playing, Bill, Robinson Crusoe?"

I kissed her cheek. She smelled in need of a bath. Her heavy head of hair was cut down to a short bob. "Good trip?"

"Mama's stomach is very upset, sweet. Can I have a rum?"

"Bill, the waiter's friend. You bet."

I got a couple of kids to take the luggage up to Jerry Fry's and led

291

her to Nikko's Grill and General Store—a grass hut with a counter, a radio that lisped, chickens on the floor and several old flyspecked photographs of Garbo behind the bar, some shelves of canned food, bolts of cloth. And signs: SOFT DRINKS, NO LIQUOR ALLOWED ON PREMISES. G. D. NIKKO, PROP.

Nikko, the ex-wrestler, more curly-haired than usual, the holy medal on his hairy chest showing through the open dirty shirt, smiled as we entered.

"Some class, real class. Welcome, lady."

"Pages, this is Gregorius Demetrius Nikko. World's champion Greco-Roman wrestler, the key's bootlegger and a great liar. Nikko, Mrs. Pfaelzer."

"Lucky Jew, that fella." He leaned over, kissed Pages's hand. "My kind of lady. Class."

Pages laughed, shook her head to get her short hair in order. "You're some Greek."

"The best Grik. From Erakleion on Candia—you call it Crete."

"Rum," I said. "Lime juice. The ice machine working?"

"Sponge fishers break her, but Highpockets he fix. I join you. I go get fresh ice."

He went away to the back. We sat down on wicker bamboo chairs at a little table. I wanted to move our arms close together—turning them into delicate antennae. I didn't. Pages fanned herself with her hat. "It's like a road show of *Rain*. Any minute I expect the marines to come rushing in and make a play for me. It's hot saturated silence here."

"It's just a crumb-bum little place that used to do fine with sponges and turtles. Now it's all nothing. Nikko is planning to pack it in once repeal catches on."

She suddenly took my hand (against all the multiplicity of possibilities). "We all nuts, Bill?"

"In what way?"

"Tony now, he's crazy. I've known that a long time. He's insane. Really, I'm sure."

"I doubt it. Maybe just an unstable transitory phase. That's all."

"The idea he can beat the Depression."

"Well, it's ending. Roosevelt is finishing it off."

She paid no attention. "That talk of his that he can come back. Conquer the world. He hasn't got it any more, sweet."

"Got what?"

"What we all had. The youth, the drive. The idea we'd come through."

"Everything wears out but clichés."

"Christ, don't get clever."

"How are you?"

"Fed up. To *here.*" She put a finger on her throat.

Nikko came back with a rum and two tall Tom Collinses. He bowed and set them on the table and sat down with us. "The last powder sugar on the key for you. Nikko, he know class. Only class count; all the rest is *merde.* Class bring courage, class bring bearable living, eh so?"

"It brings another philosopher," said Pages, taking a weary sip. "Ah! And a damn good drink-maker. Nikko, forgive me."

Nikko beamed. "You no belong here. This is nothing here. Less than nothing. The tropics are for pagan savages. Man he best in cities."

"Nize baby," I said. "Eat up all the Spinoza." I pushed the drink aside and went to the bar and found the poisonous-looking green soft drink. "We were talking, Nikko, of what we had. You miss your youth, Nikko?"

"I one goddamn fine ever-loving bastard when young. I one goddamn fine wrestler, one goddamn holy Christian—I go confess, I buy church candles so heavy I almost get hernia. But do it all again? No."

Pages smiled at him. "The big muscles, the glory, the women with the hairy armpits of Euboea?"

"Ah, you know. For me it was all fine, the women with hair, the other things not polite to talk about. The money it go fast, the fame is *merde* only not as valuable—shit. You pardon me lady,—that makes things grow in fields. Fame, it ends up like this, eh so? On Tinto Key selling spoiled cans to sponge fishers. Youth is no good unless you have on it an old head. Otherwise it's *merde.* Have old head and you have old prostate, old heart, too much fat ass. Is all wrong system. When I was Christian, I accept. Now no. System stinks—is—"

Pages said, "Nikko, you look happy anyway."

"Once this Grik figure it all out, he say everything she stink, she bad, *so* be happy, enjoy enjoy. All else she—"

Pages said, *"Merde.* What makes you such a happy man?"

"I tell you I very bad fella. I thief, smuggler, whoremonger, blackmailer, boy-lover, pimp. I kill some fellas in Egypt once. I no

293

good at all. If I be real true Grik man, I marry, raise goats on Candia, have plenty children, go to church, believe in God. And die very bored, very holy, but still bad prostate, bad heart, bitter taste in mouth. I go now make more drinks."

He went off, and Pages hunted a cigarette with a shaking hand and found one, and I lit it. I took out my pipe and filled and lit that. She said, "He's a very interesting fake—out of fiction. Romantic fiction. Bill, I'm jumpy; got the heebie-jeebies."

"Nikko is a scoundrel, a nasty mean man. Used to be a big mainland bootlegger, but the wops drove him out. A coward. He couldn't face gang killers, so he came here. Too scared really, like all thinkers, but not too logical. He smuggles a bit of dope from Mexico now, sells booze, but nothing pays any more. He's not romantic. And what are you jumpy about?"

Pages picked up my untouched Tom Collins. "I always thought tropical islands were romantic. You know—Jack London, Conrad, Stevenson, Gauguin. But the palm trees look ratty here."

A little Negro boy came in wearing only a very short shirt. Nikko waved a finger at him. "You play with yourself, Plato, I cut it off, feed it to chickens."

"Pa," said the little Negro, grinning, "you come house or Celeste she say you big no-good sonofabitch."

Nikko nodded. "I come, I come." He stood up and kissed Pages's hand again. "That Celeste my wife. That Plato he my son. Why he look like nigger *merde,* not like me, I have plenty big idea. I see you, lady, again. I get powder sugar from Conch Harbor. You bet."

I held out a bill. Nikko took it quickly, looking away as if ashamed to accept it, and went out swiftly for such a large man. I said to Pages, "He's henpecked and very attached to his wife. She's a marvelous piece."

Pages laughed and hunted for something in her woven net bag. "You too?"

"Not me. Everybody else in camp, only not me and Tony."

"How come?"

I stood up. "Too busy working on the racer. Come on. It gets hotter later on."

"There was a time Tony never could resist a good piece."

I didn't want to enter any intimate domestic discussion. I held Pages's arm and we walked out into the blinding sun. Pages took a pair of smoked glasses out of her bag and put them on and set her hat on top of her hair. She had worn well, I decided. For a woman in her middle thirties she appeared ten years younger but for the look in her eyes. All right, perhaps an enlarging of breasts and hips. But I was always a Rubens man myself, and for me she didn't seem changed, I mean the essential Pages, except for the better. Living with a keyed-up Tony hadn't been easy. He was kind, comforting, loyal, amusing, full of laughter, but always Indian-wrestling with the spectacle of the big time, big business, big bullshit. Always driven to get his fingers on the throat of success. And an ego that needed victories, wanted to taste everything, touch everything, own everything. It wasn't at all Jewish; no matter what people may think, Tony's drive wasn't racial. Jews want, but they want it to spend, to raise families, to give to charities, to make a show. Tony wanted merely the driving act of wanting to want. That drove him. ("I don't fear the big dough—I fear having to do something with it.")

I got Pages and myself bogged down a bit in the sand, and the path higher up was spikey-weedy; little green and pink lizards were darting around. The cats that grew wild on Tinto Key hunted the lizards and the sponge fishers hunted the cats, for a skin brought ten cents in Nikko's general store.

Pages suddenly turned around. "You ever think I should have stayed with Jay?"

"Not for years."

"Was Jay really Negro?"

"I doubt it. Maybe way back. I think he was frightened of marriage."

"Where is he now?"

"In Paris. The novel was a real flop."

"I didn't like it. Too avant-garde. Too much sex; four-dirty-feet-in-a-bed kind. And I like finished sentences."

"He's writing science fiction for pulp magazines. But they don't pay well. Jay's having a hard time of it."

"You still think he's a genius?"

"That's right. Don't you?"

She took my arm. "You always were a patsy for all of us. You even thought, once, you were in love with me?"

"As Nikko says, that's—Hey! That's the beach camp to the left. That's Tony waving."

BOOK SEVEN

FROM WILLIAM KITE'S POCKET NOTEBOOK

The creative life is so close to the sexual life, its suffering and its joys, that one may consider them two forms of one and the same need, of one and the same joy.
                    —RAINER MARIA RILKE

One can tell all about a woman merely by watching how she places her feet. The amorous ones turn their feet out. You can expect nothing worthwhile from a woman who turns her feet in.   —EDOUARD MANET

People in love do not become one—each becomes two.   —W. K.

CHAPTER 30

("THERE IS NO GREATER PAIN," Dante wrote, "than in misery to remember happy times.") I was happy with Pages on Tinto Island, even if at the time the utter absurdity of being "I" was beginning to penetrate to me (and the fact that none of us were really captains of our souls, only perhaps deckhands under sealed orders we would never open). Not that we thought that way the season the racer was really ready and we, dressed in shorts and straw hats woven by the sponge fishers, stood on the beach, reflected in tidal pools, a species indigenous, I thought, to an incompatible world. There was a lot of drinking of bootleg rum in coconut milk and brandy up at the Frys' guest room; but I was only being slowly poisoned by the green bottled soda pop at Nikko's Grill.

Wet bathing trunks on a cord clothesline . . . white sand between our brown toes . . . Jerry Fry saying on a Sunday, "God gives to everything alike." Pages, who had tried to reach *wu-nien,* Zen's "no-mind," also was practicing—in a tight white bathing suit—*hatha-yogin.* She told me it was metabolism and respiration control, also reversing intestinal peristalsis, which was, I thought, indecent on the key. A fine cutting affair happened one night among the sponge fishers over Celeste; others said it was a crap game in which Highpockets put capped dice into play and was detected.

The weather changing . . . winds moving wildly . . . skies mottled . . . sunsets of such vulgarity and richness only a Victorian could paint them. Pages and Tony at the Frys': sometimes drunk,

Mrs. Fry told me, and she wondering: "Are they married? I mean married people don't get drunk together. They take turns, don't they? Who will take care of the chillen if both get drunk?" I said, "They don't have chillen." "Pore things, pore pore things." Nan Fry added, "I don't like to pry, but they don't pleasure much, I'd say." I said, "You examine the sheets?" She said, "Mistah Kite, you're a caution." "Yes, I am."

I thought of someone who had said, "Our doubt is our passion, and our passion is our task." Then the storms came and Tinto Key was another world. Pages wondered why the island didn't blow away, and Highpockets and Chuck set guy wires to the shed and tents to keep them from sailing into the Gulf.

The furious storms that season—one after the other—left a mess at the camp. There was also the intricate job of reassembling the motor and injector once more.

We really labored in the sultry weather with strange menacing clouds coming to worry us and the sky turning black with the fury of newly promised storms. We waited out the pounding tempest and hurricane, Tony, Pages, I—all at Jerry Fry's—and when the world was calm again outside, but piled with debris, we took up the work for the tests.

Nikko lost his big tin sign one night of winds and came hunting it, but felt it was sunk at sea. "Now maybe it in deep blue sea, eh so, with the *Titanic* and Homer's ships. In crazy ass-side-up world everything become crazy ass-side-up. Ah, the lady look fine, like I say class, she stay class. . . . When ice machine she work again, you bring her and I make Tom Collins, eh so?"

Boisterous winds had come hurtling in from the heart of the Gulf and banged through the sand dunes of Tinto Key, leveling all before them. New wrecks dotted the shoreline, and at low tide the burst-in sides of a stranded yacht were seen, little silver fish moving in and out of the ship's iron entrails. When Tony and I went to the camp at the beach, we found that the racer's hut had been blown from its foundation, a wheel damaged; more delays. Jerry Fry walked around the sagging building with us.

"A real high-tider of a storm and it's not over—a wind nobody could walk against coming. Made a lot of firewood of a lot of places up the keys."

Tony squatted down on the sand and pushed back his baseball cap.

"I guess we'll get the shed back on the foundation posts and wait till we get a new wheel."

Chuck looked under the canvas wrappings of Becky. "Seems to have survived."

"I'll get two wheels and a new set of tires."

Jerry Fry said, "The beach is gettin' crowded. Say, bluefins and sea bass are bitin' out a bit, but I don't suppose you'll care to go with boys chummin' for a good catch?"

"I guess not, Jerry," said Tony. "We'll need a lot of extra lumber."

"Well, let's go find some jacks and shorin'."

With the new timber and planks the shed was soon in shape; the wheel was on its way from Tampa. Tony, hammer in hand, stood admiring our work. "Can't say I'm a master carpenter, but what the hell, it's strong. Put a pound of extra nails into it, Highpockets."

To the west the troubled sky of the continuing bad weather was turning a sickening gray; the edges of it went soot-black, and a heavy roar came from the waves breaking on the sands. At the lighthouse storm flags were out, held stiff by the steady blow as if cut from tin.

The wind increased and an old bucket passed us, worried by the storm winds. Clumps of salt weeds and a whole layer of sand followed.

"It's a real bloody perisher of a blow," Chuck observed.

Jerry Fry, smoking a pipe hung low in one corner of his mouth, put a pair of oars on his shoulders. "Batten everythin' down. Blow the feathers off a duck, this here wind. Better go inside."

"You think it's going to come back this way?" Tony asked.

"The weather station just put out radio warnin' it's the worst storm to hit these parts since 1853. Come up to the house and snug in with us and not worry Mrs. Pfaelzer."

"No, thanks, Jerry. I'll stay with the machines."

"I better stay too," I said.

"Suit yourself." Jerry Fry ran on, the oars sticking up over his shoulders like some strange antennae of a hurrying ant, his sea boots sending spurts of sand as he hastened up to his house. The wind was soon at gale fury, and to the west over the heaving Gulf the rain was falling. Yellow lightning flashes scarred the sky. A low shore bush whistled and strained at its roots. Birds cawed in panic.

Chuck and I got the ladder and the workbench inside the shed.

301

Tony went around fastening down doors and flaps and pushing wedges in rattling frames and shutters. Chuck lit the pressure lamp and we sat inside the shed silently as the rains came—great, hard-flung curtains of water that banged on the roof and caused the walls to groan.

Tony looked up. "Blowing at least forty miles an hour."

Chuck said, "Blasted sod I was to come 'ere. You think the roof will 'old?"

Tony shrugged his shoulders. "If it gets over fifty miles an hour, I wouldn't stand behind it with a money-back guarantee. Drink?" He held up a pint of Fry's local moonshine. He and Chuck drank.

We ate a hot supper of eggs and ham, and I sat sipping strong tea while the shed rattled and the wind tore at the bush near the high-tide mark; flying clam shells and small stones banged against the walls. Near midnight there were many new thuds and shrill screams. Tony looked up from his cot. "Seabirds, poor bastards, driven against the sheds."

"Been hearing them for an hour. They're not all dead, just piled up out there against the doors."

"I guess God wasn't watching all the swallows."

"Wind is up. Can hear it. Hope Highpockets gets blown to sea."

"Near sixty miles an hour," said Tony. "Wonder how high it got in 1853."

We didn't sleep much the rest of the thundering night. Near dawn, or when dawn should have been, there was a furious blasting and shaking and tearing sound overhead. Water began to drip down near the south wall of the shed. Chuck covered the extra racer parts with waxed sea tarps. I began to collect hammer and nails and wide lengths of short boards.

"Roofing is flapping loose. Must nail it down."

Tony shook his head. "you can't go out there, Bill. It's growing wilder. Crazy, crazy weather."

"If the roof comes off, not only will it get blown away, but the machine will be smashed and ruined by rain and seawater."

"Watch your footing. I'll come hand you up the boards."

"No, you and Chuck put timbers over the motor."

I tied on my cap with a red scarf and pushed against a small side door till it opened. I went out dragging the short ladder and tools. Chuck closed the door behind me. The wind grabbed and flung me with careless ease against the wooden side of the shed. I lost my breath and knew I was an idiot to have come out.

The world of Tinto Key was a fearful sight. In the silver-gray darkness, the tall breakers of the surf were torn to bits the moment they rose. Dead sea life, crabs and slugs and broken birds were flung up by windy foam and spume out onto the eroded sand dunes to be picked up and carried away over the ridge to the wild growths on either side of the key. Deep, wide channels had been dug in the beach; rainwater was rushing among boulders and long-buried seashells to meet the Gulf and be carried back in spindrift and salt water forced back higher on the kelp-packed beach. There was a gray sea gull spread-eagled on the wall. Several large broken birds, their bloody feathers disarranged by wind and rain, lay around underfoot. All I could think of to take my mind off my fears was a Bach cantata in which a single singer becomes a soul addressing God: The wind drowned him out.

I placed the ladder with great effort against the shed wall and nailed its top firmly to the roof rafters. It was the only way to keep it from blowing away. I mounted, fighting the unbelievable wind. I was left breathless again and again by my struggles. On the roof, exposed, it was worse. I knew the wind was now at least seventy-five miles an hour. I lay prone and, clawing at the roof, inched my way to where the roofing had been torn loose and curled back. It was almost impossible to force the thin black stuff back flat on the boards. But I got it down in two places and hammered nails through the short boards to hold it firm. The whistling gale showed me no mercy.

I turned to a new section of damaged roofing, and the wind got behind me. A mistake. My raincoat was blown up over my head, pinioning my helpless arms in its folds. I could not move. I could not see. The hammer escaped my wet grasp and I felt myself rolling. I tried to face around to the wind but I was helpless, trapped by folds of loose roof paper and my own binding jacket blown over my head. My arms were numbing. I felt with one foot for the roof edge. A dead bird skidded across the roof and fell away into space. Self-containment fled; disjunction, apprehension, filled me.

I lay still, recovering sanity and some calmness. I was trapped, and must avoid panic. If I stayed where I was in this position, I would soon smother in the raincoat. If I was blown off the roof, I might land on great rocks nearby or on the tied-down packing cases, and in either event I would be broken to bits. "You end this way," my cortex signaled, and my organs and muscles echoed the message—all lost: Jay, Pages, hopes, wonders, pleasures. There was no peculiar nobility or infusing grace in my death as I expired on the roof—I just perished after nearly four decades of life. I began to sweat for all the chill rain and biting wind. I had never believed a wind could be this strong. . . . The dead man began to roll, and the wind, with a stronger blast under the twisted raincoat, started to lift him off the slippery roof. (I stood aside, a ghost haunting my own departure from the world.)

In desperate earnestness the dead man's foot went hunting again for the roof edge and hit nothing; he was half dangling in space, sightless, at the mercy of the unrelenting wind. He resigned himself to being dead and tried to contact Jay, Pages, one or two others, to say goodbye. But his senses told him, Don't struggle—accept. Savagely the dead man's mind signaled: "Jay, Jay . . . Pages."

As he rolled, his foot was suddenly grasped firmly and he was steadied. Two arms were around his knees and steering him to the top rungs of the ladder. The raincoat was torn up the back by desperate hands, and he saw Tony and again the gray-black world, the tilting sky, pelting sky, and he was descending the ladder into the under-world (as is proper for the dead). When they stood together at last on the sands, the dead man opened his eyes. He and Tony clung to each other grimly, for the wind was at the wildest peak it would reach that day. Painfully struggling, not letting go of each other's grip, they reached the small side door and fell through into the shed. Chuck, wide-eyed, strained to his feet and managed to shut the door and put a heavy keg of motor fuel against it.

". . . I piss on you, Death, on your specters, I no longer scare . . ."

We three sat panting on the floor of rough planks, breathing hard, for some minutes listening to each other's efforts to fill and empty our lungs. When at last, red-faced and earnest, we could look at each other, Tony rubbed his chin. "*That* was a close one, Bill."

Chuck said, "You should have called out."

"In this wind?"

We said no more about it, just sat out the rest of the storm. There was a huge pot of hot coffee that Chuck had made. I thought of the two people who had been on my mind when I was dead. (*Voi che*

304

sapete che cosa è l'amore, the street singers of Rome sing. Had my amoral life been too stained with a puritan conscience?)

The storm lasted all that day and all the next night. Pages was hysterical and came down to the shed in a rubber raincoat. "You fools, it's *only* a car. Oh—let's all sink together."

After the great storm passed on, grinding northward, the beach at Tinto Key was in many sections piled high with tangled kelp and torn-up bush. But the wind had also swept level great areas of the beach, and there was smooth sand for racing Becky. The camp had been battered and some of the roof covering torn off. This took a little time to repair, but we were mostly occupied in putting the final touches on the racer. The wheel and tires had come on a coastal carrier. The racer crouched like a greyhound ready to go. The T. P. Fuel Injector was in place. There were warm, easy winds, long lines of honking birds flying, by the day of the first real test. The once-yellow-green weeds on the sand dunes were umber and amber. We pushed the machine out from its shed. Chuck filled the gas tank and stepped back. Pages, under her yellow sunshade, barefoot, in shorts, held a stopwatch. I had a notebook and another stopwatch. "How she feel, Tony?"

Highpockets held up an oilcan. "Mixture is prime."

Tony adjusted his goggles. "Might as well go."

We were deceptively casual in front of the islanders: Nikko, sponge fishers, the Frys. But only in appearances. It was the first time for speed and for a full use of the injector. Several of the beach crowd stepped back as if from an expected explosion as Becky snorted into life. At the end of the staked-out twenty-mile beach the lighthouse crew were also clocking the end of the run. Tony would then turn around, make the run back. Crude but effective, we hoped, for unofficial trials.

I sat down on the bench beside Pages as the racer snorted, coughed and at last purred into a steady roar. I hoped every damn steering-pinion close-ratio gear was in place. Tony—head down, the goggles and the black leather hood he wore giving him the appearance of something from bad science fiction—seemed calm. The car shook; he put it into the first of four gears and moved off. Becky gained speed, threw up sand, and crunched away down the long beach. I felt Pages's hand on my wrist as I wrote the takeoff time: 10:45:31 A.M.

"He'll kill himself," Pages said.

The racer seemed to skid for fifty feet on a wet stretch of beach, but it went on straight as fate in the sunlight, and with a diminishing roar grew smaller quickly so that soon it was only a pencil, then a moving comma, and just before where the morning damp from the sea and the strong sunlight made an opaque haze, it was a dot like something half printed on one's eyeball, no longer real but as if the eye had imagined it. Then it was gone but for the sound of the motor growing faint. Pages lowered her head almost to her naked white knees—she never tanned—and looked at me by turning her face.

"What do you think, sweet?"

"It sounded good. I'm no mechanic. Chuck, you happy?"

" 'Appy? What for in this blinkin' island?"

Highpockets, lean, pimply, biting off a chaw of tobacco, pushed back the Stetson from his forehead and made a jackass *hee-haw*. "Chuck, that hootenanny, he's happy because he's not spendin' no money on nothin' here."

Chuck spit on Highpockets' pickax-pointed cowboy boots. "I hear the sheriff bloke is comin' over from Papaya City to arrest you, Tex, for marked cards. That takes care of you, me booger."

I said, "Tony must have turned around by now."

We all turned our heads and looked off to the faraway atmosphere that clung to the other end of the beach. Nikko, wearing crumpled linen pants and a striped sailor's shirt, a yachting cap on the back of his curly uncombed hair, held up two hands, dollar bills stuck between his fat fingers. "I make bet, take all offers, no go over hundred eighty miles the hour. I give odds, four to five. Show Nikko no mercy. He here to be ruined. Take advantage of big fool. Who says yes? Betcha!"

No one wanted to bet, or perhaps had the cash for it. The roar of Becky's motor was clearly heard again. Pages stirred, lifted her head and held out her hand so the dial of the ticking stopwatch was in view. I copied some time off my watch; the motor sound was louder, the dot was now visible, rushing toward us like a planet falling through space. Nikko danced like a bear in the hot sun. "I tell you what, sports! I take other side of bet. I say he make hundred eighty.

I give five to four on dot. I tell you what, I make it three to one. Come on, sports, who want to screw—pardon, lady—his here Grik?"

The dot, then the comma, became a small racer, then a larger racer, then the yellow form of Becky, and at last hurling itself, roaring, spewing sand, the machine came down to us, blue exhaust flaring, flames pouring from the pipes past the two end stakes that marked the end of the run. The car went on smoking badly for about a mile before Tony slowed it enough for a turnaround. Pages showed her stopwatch, her thumb on the stem. I made figures and added and tried to become Euclid, a pure mathematical unit.

The racer drew near and stopped, smoke pouring from under the hood, the yellow paint blistered brown there and peeling off in black flakes. Tony, coughing, leaped from the machine, face smudged, tearing off his hood and goggles, looking in his jacket like a poodle walking on his hind legs.

He roared, "What the hell is wrong now? She wasn't *saftig!* She's badly overheated. I couldn't get her over the hump."

Chuck gingerly touched the hood and pulled back his burned fingers quickly.

"It must be the sand, clogs the wind ducts that air-cool her. Just enough to overheat her. We try a finer-mesh screen."

Tony turned to me, wide-eyed, teeth bared. "Well?"

"One hundred and fifty-two miles average both ways, figuring in your turn up there. We'll phone the lighthouse and get the corrected time."

"That's about what I felt I was doing. Hey, Nikko, you fat swine making money on my misery. You have ice?"

"I have ice. Course I have ice. That my business. You want to treat for drinks?"

"No. I want all the ice you have. We'll pack the engine in ice this afternoon and try again. And, Chuck, I want the gasoline mixture changed. I want it pure dynamite."

"Let's do it tomorrow," I said.

"You're burned." Pages took Tony's arm. The jacket sleeve of tanned leather was singed.

"So what? Damn it, you all seem to worry over nothing. I'm out to put this thing over two hundred miles an hour. So I'm burned—call it a sacrifice offering to Jehovah, the old boychik. I've a headache, my

307

sinuses are clogged. Goddamn it, I'm getting this machine over two hundred miles an hour today and with the T. P. Fuel Injector. Then we'll dance for the press and the newsreel boys. Chuck, open the hood. Replace all wiring that seems fused."

Tony stood in the shade of the shed unbuttoning his jacket and shirt, taking a fruit drink Jerry Fry handed him, a cigarette from Nikko, a light from Pages, who kept staring at her husband.

CHAPTER 31

I WENT WITH NIKKO and two sponge fishers with two washtubs borrowed from Mrs. Fry, to get ice from the Greek's ice machine. The machine was a rusting gasoline-powered hulk under a canvas roof, but it was able this time to furnish us with four large cakes of ice, which Nikko skillfully chipped into fragments in the tin washtubs. He cursed the sponge fishers, telling them to run back to the camp with it and not steal any of the ice. He wiped his hands on his greasy pants, stuck the long ice pick into a rotten beam by the ice machine, and pulled it out again, probing the wormy timber. Insects carrying eggs ran in all directions.

"You know, you can have her any time," said Nikko.

I wasn't angry, I was tense. "What are you, some Greek fortune-teller?"

"I know when a thing can come to happen. Don't laugh; my mother was the seventh daughter of a seventh daughter. Very rare."

"Mind your own goddamn business."

He put a big hand on my shoulder. I couldn't shake it off. "Don't say that to Nikko. For you he has much interest in this fine woman."

"It isn't like you think."

"Ha. How *I* think! She is, I tell you, just waiting for you to put it up."

"How good a wrestler were you?"

"Much good."

"I think I can knock you down."

"Don't think so. I tell you why. It will not help. It will only pain

308

you very much. I am evil man but till strong. I got nothing much no more. But when something like her and you are my friends and I see how it is, I know it can be much, very much, for you both."

"This your idea of dirty fun?"

He sat down on the backless chair under the ice machine's roof. "In life I tell you, what matters most? I tell you. The penis. That is the best thing the gods they say they give a man, the most best thing. This is it, use it they say with health, with vigor, much pleasuring, say the gods. Don't let it pass. I say it to you from love, of love, from love of you, of the lady, eh so?"

I picked up the ice pick and stabbed at the rafter, watching the insects run, the wood chip and fly. "Thanks for the philosophy lesson."

"It is nothing to thank for."

"That's right." I sank the ice pick into the soft weathered rafter. Nikko watched me. "You angry at me, you screw the post. All right, I have said it all, let us go back. If I was much younger, did not stink . . . the prostate, the heart, was in A-nummer-one condition —but so . . ."

We walked into the hot sun side by side, the big fat man panting a bit, but I didn't slow my pace; let his damn heart burst.

"It is overrated."

"I tell you something, you need a good drunk. A big drunk."

"No."

"Just a snort to start." He held out a brown flat flask. I shook my head. He sighed, took a sip, shivered and replaced the bottle in a back pants pocket. "I think once you taste drink again, you feel things more. Man needs to do things maybe against himself. Saints all right, they need nothing but the head of fish, two olives; they enjoy living in own crap licking sores of beggars. That for them is the big kick like a good fuck. But they fool nobody, only self. That their poor way of getting a fine screw. All right. I shut up. . . . You want to bet?"

"On what?"

"Anything. Griks big gamblers. I bet the car wreck, Tony die, or Tony win, Tony live. Take any side. I just one betting fool." Nikko saw the sponge fishers struggling ahead of us with their washtubs of ice. "Hey, you basters, don't drop no ice. You think ice she grows on trees?"

Nikko took out the flask, looked at me, then took a big pull. I could see he was disappointed in me, suspected something even worse than a puritan's hostile attitude to pleasure.

At the camp there was activity and hope. I had a feeling I was watching something unnatural. I had lost faith in the fuel injector, in the racer, in Tinto Key. Tony sat in the car and ate a chicken sandwich. He watched Pages pour a fruit drink, his eyes half hooded; the eyelids seemed burned brick-red by sun. He didn't talk, just bathed his face and hands in a bucket of well water. When the sun was just slanting to the west, Chuck came over to Becky.

"The light'ouse people dropped their signal flag. They're standing by to time you at the other end."

"Good. She's ready."

"I've changed two rear tires—frayed they was, cut up by seashells. Insulation was burned off on plug wires."

"Highpockets change it?"

"The lad done a bunk, a runout on us." Chuck pointed to a round hard nut of a man with a fluffy red mustache, wearing a gray loose suit and a battered ranch hat. "Sheriff from Papaya City. Come to get 'Ighpockets for knifing a sponge fisher over 'ot dice."

Tony grinned for the first time. "Somebody at the lighthouse must of radioed the sheriff to come pick up the swine. You change the wires?"

"All connected. She's not pretty but she will run."

I sat between Pages and Nikko. Becky didn't look like much any more. Flying sand had scoured off great patches of paint; the hood was blackened and warped. The front tires were a bit frayed, but Chuck said they'd hold. Oil and grease had made long looping stains over the machine's body. A little bronze winged statue of Mercury (God of duplicity) still was in place.

Tony listened to the motor as it turned over and nodded. "Sweet as honeycake and *mandlen*. Ready, Pages, with the stopwatch?"

"Ready."

I waved. Nikko held up betting money with dolorous languor. Tony adjusted his goggles and bent over the wheel. The wind-teased flags flapped on the stakes. Nikko no longer asked for bets. The wind was brisking to a snapping purr, and I pointed to the wind bag on our measuring device. Tony shook his head. He started the machine moving, and by the time he was running past the starting stakes he had gained a good burst of speed that threw back sand from the tires like machine-gun bullets. It seemed to me he went faster than before and that Becky swayed too much. The wind was really increasing.

Pages stared at the watch dial, at the needle sweeping on. I doodled on my pad, aware I had started a string of thoughts: Achilles as a boy was fed the hearts of lions; Tony as a lad ate matzos, Hasidic bread-and-butter.

Nikko shouted, "There he go! Oh, that fast!"

The motorized dot had plunged into the mist. I looked up at the weather device; its bag was full, stiff, almost straight out. I looked out at the boats of the sponge fishers just beyond the surf. They had gathered to watch the event. The surf seemed higher, foam-tipped. (My grandfather used to say, "You think you've seized life by its ears and you find you are holding an eel.")

Pages got me away from memory; she said softly, "He's coming back. I hear him. It's a very fast run."

"It's the wind."

"I hear him."

It was the sound of the motor. The dot shot into view. If Tony had turned and come back so fast, he was well over two hundred miles an hour. Everyone cheered but Pages and me. The sheriff had walked forward and then back, shading his eyes with one hard brown hand. Becky was now a real shape. Wobbling badly. The wind up there on the open point was stronger than at the shed. There was a shaking of the racer that became a turning off course. Chuck shouted something. The machine was screaming as its ties frayed to shreds and the vision flew apart. I saw the hood fly up like a buzzard soaring and Becky rushing into the surf. Pages screamed out, "You damn damn fool!"

I was running, Nikko puffing beside me.

The racer was burning in the foamy surf as it skimmed over the waves for a suspended moment, along the tilting breakers like a stone tossed over a pond. But metal and the weight of metal obeyed the laws of physics and Becky sank from view, a great spreading circle of motor oil staining the arching line of surf. Several of the sponge fishers on the boats had plunged into the sea, brown bodies in quick dives. Small flames appeared to dance on the water.

311

I stopped to pant and retch, the heavy sand underfoot holding me back. I moved over to the damp packed beach and ran on, a stitch in my side. I looked back once, and there was Pages standing in the middle of the beach, her hat blown off, her sunshade turned inside out from her running. Now she stood just staring, mouth open, long naked legs growing out of her white shorts.

I turned, saw the black heads of four sponge fishers. They were diving, and several seagulls coming to see screamed as if they wanted to join the game. I felt no reality in the scene—it seemed only a translation from some obscure language.

I walked slowly into the sea, the waves' dying hiss pouring over my shoes. The sponge fishers had got hold of a sodden bundle between them. They staggered as they came out of the ocean like some ancient group formed for rites, bearing a sacrifice: sea god or monster creature on their shoulders. Kelp trailed like ribbons from Tony's inert body. They laid him down, saying nothing—on the high-tide mark, on crab shell and snap pods, on dry seaweed, jellyfish slime, the brown shells of long-dead shore life. Tony choked and retched, vomited water and bile. Nikko was astride him like a fat jockey, pressing thumbs into Tony's ribs, pushing on Tony's rib basket. Tony choked and coughed. Nikko kept saying, "You, eh, so, feel lousy? I bet you feel pretty much lousy?"

"Get off, you Greek . . . ape."

Tony rolled his head and struggled as I felt Pages come up behind me. I smelled her scent, her perfume, her heated body. Tony, seawater dripping from one corner of his mouth, grinned weakly. "Way over two hundred, way over. Get this . . . slob . . . off me."

"Curse me good. It make you fight out water from lungs, belly."

Tony fell back and doubled up with tearing fearful sounds. I told Pages he'd be all right. Fifty feet from shore the oil ring, black and rainbow-tinted, was spreading wider and wider.

Later Tony was put to bed at the Frys' house, shouting he wanted no doctor. Pages worried. Chuck had gone to Nikko's to drink. I sat by the now empty shed looking up at the piling storm clouds, all moving northwest-by-north. At the lighthouse, now clearly seen up the beach, they were changing the storm flag signals. At least it

312

appeared to them to be better weather. I decided to walk along up there and talk to somebody. The exuberant gaiety of the morning was gone, depleted.

It was a slow walk over the white beach; the dead sepia-colored weeds and leafy shrubs bent over in the hot wind. The two men at the lighthouse, their brick-red faces topped by sun-tormented hair, seemed proper to the roar of surf and the *caw-caw* of hungry gulls filling the sky.

"How you, Mr. Kite? All sunk, huh?" asked Uncle Benny O'Neal, the older of the lighthouse station men, who had sailed in tin-can destroyers in the First World War.

"All sunk, Uncle Benny. But I'll send up a flag signal at our camp if we need your help getting the machine up. I don't think we can."

"You do that. But salt water ruins everything. Have a coffee?"

"I might."

"Come in."

The interior of the Tinto Key lighthouse was like the exterior, made of great sea boulders. It was snug inside; below the winding staircase its whitewashed stone walls held rows of polished gear, kept clean by Dody, Uncle Ben's helper. The place smelled of rubber boots, shag tobacco and, of course, the ever-ready coffee. I took the heavy cup.

"You'll be leaving soon—too bad. Mrs. Pfaelzer has the best legs on the island."

"Yup," said Dody. "Mrs. Nikko is second."

Uncle Benny grinned. "Celeste ain't bad, but she's commercial. You can shuck down with her. Mrs. P. is all just for lookin'."

I said I was happy they respected Pages for the lady she was.

On the walk back to camp the hot gusty winds shook me head on, and the gray-silver of the sky gave the hot day a gloomy brassy tint. By the time I had plodded home to the camp, I had just about decided to leave with Nikko's bootlegger contact, whose boat came in after dark to ferry the illegal brew ashore.

The fishing boats, the spongers, were not out. The wind had suddenly fallen away to a whisper. Chuck was not back. Nikko must have gotten him drunk; Chuck would not appear for a day or so. He took a loss very hard. Heat lightning made calligraphic darting gashes in the sky. Near dusk there came the tinny ring of a cracked Baptist bell in the sponge fishers' huts. There was a mission once on the key; it had left the bell.

Jerry Fry came down to the shed. "Suddenly no wind at all. Mr. Pfaelzer is sleeping. His wife gave him two sleeping pills." I looked up to see Jerry was carrying half an apple pie. "My woman thought you'd like some snack. If you don't mind it spicy."

"I like it spicy. Jerry, I may want a ride on a boat tonight—to the mainland. Tell Nikko."

"I don't think the boat'll come in tonight. Too clear, a moon maybe."

"Damn."

"My pappy—he was a white minister, a Ku Kluxer—always said the weather always changes if you wait long enough."

"Had a friend whose father was white—had a colored ancestor."

"Sure—what the hell, if everybody frig everybody long enough, everybody's color troubles is over."

I took a bite of pie. "Jerry, how long might this lack of wind last?"

"Never try and outguess the weather down here. I'll say this: If you want to catch up a good crisp blow, maybe you might have to be here for another two, three weeks. How's the pie?"

"Good. If that boat comes in, I'll go."

Jerry nodded. I ate. The pie was tart, a delicacy. My eyes searched for a breeze on the still and empty beach. It was a remarkably good pie and only made me think of Frenchman Street in East Pompton—I hadn't been back since they buried my grandmother. She loved pie—all kinds.

I got up and went to the Fry house. Mrs. Fry was sewing on some rag of clothing by the light of an oil lamp.

"He's been talkin'."

"Where's Mrs. Pfaelzer?"

"Kind of tetched in the head. She said she just had to go out alone walkin'. Out on the ridge."

"It's been a hard time for her."

I went into the room with the big bed. Tony was flat on it, moving his head from side to side. His face seemed feverish. I bent over and touched his cheek . . . flushed, but not a high fever. He said, "Ha, Captain, does our flight patrol in the ack-emma?"

"Shut up. Sleep." I looked at the night table. As I suspected, the two sleeping pills, untaken, were tucked in a fold of newspaper, an old trick of Tony's from those times when we were flying that bad season over Arras and he always faked taking the pills before a big push. Had a fear of pills, he said. I put the two pills into a glass of milk standing by a clam shell that held a mashed-out cigarette with lipstick on it, and stirred the contents. I held the glass to Tony's lips.

"Drink it down, Leftenant. That's an order."

"Moo-milk?" He sipped.

"Yes."

He sighed. "Everything gone west?"

"*Kaput,* Leftenant."

"Don't play games. I know where I am. Becky?"

"That's right. Sunk."

He stared at the ceiling. I took his wrist. The pulse was fast. His profile was beginning to coarsen, I noticed.

"Ke-rist, Captain, remember after we'd lose a few on patrol I'd get keyed up or pissed off or something, and I'd play the violin till the duty major screamed? Bach's Partita in A Minor. You don't like music, do you?"

"I'm polite to it."

"Music settled me down a bit, that and the milk-and-brandy with an egg in it—remember?"

"You're thirsty." I offered him the glass and watched him drink, his Adam's apple bobbing. "Wish I had a good Victrola record; the slow movement of the second Razumovsky Quartet , , , ever read the Talmud? You wouldn't, you goy. 'The only pure love is the eating of juicy fruit.' I made that up—it isn't in the Talmud. Pages—where is she?"

"She went out. Needed air."

"What's wrong, what's wrong? How much earth does a man need? Six feet."

"That's Tolstoi."

"He stole it from my *bubba*—my grandmother." He yawned. "I'm finished, Captain, pooped off, wiped out, hosed down. Pages, she only stayed on because she felt I'd go nuts if I had to face this thing alone. Now she's going away. She knows a Jewboy can always face complete disaster—only hope makes him crazy. She's gone."

"No, not Pages."

"Oh yes. A man knows these things. She's too good for us. She's aware how we'll all fail her. Fail life, she might say, because you know—laugh if you want to—she's in some ways an icy puritan, that *nafka*—oh, she's too too . . ."

He closed his eyes. I thought he was asleep. His voice was thinner from deeper down. "Who can live up to her? She saw I was a fraud, all hand-waving, shouts, groans, smells. But still she's . . ." He made a gesture, or began one, that could have been an effort to kiss his fingertips. The arm fell back on the blanket. "Yes, what's left of any of us? The last few drops we shake out of the bottom of the glass. A white camellia skin . . . ever see her in black Alençon lace? *Gemütlich*. I'm sleepy. I'm tired. Tony is a horse's ass. One, two, button my shoe; three, four, shut the . . . You ever get the feeling, Bill, your place in the world is occupied by someone else . . . some stranger you wouldn't give standing room to? Don't want to sleep . . . only a dream . . only only . . . a man is . . . come the thing . . . what the hell, boychik . . . raisins and almonds and a little goat . . ."

This time he was asleep, a crucified expression (a Jew's by inheritance) on his face. I went out and stood in the motionless night, and then went back to camp. For the first time in years I wanted a drink.

CHAPTER 32

SITTING, WAITING, SITTING, watching the sea after the dusk, sitting waiting, the sea growling beyond the dark sand, sitting on a bucket in the lonely tent by the empty shed. Sitting, the taste of overboiled coffee, waiting, sitting. (I threw the cup against a rock—it broke— thinking, The philosopher must respect fools; they are his best pupils.) Tired, too tired, bone-tired, in the marrow tired, in the cortex and memory tired, tired; and a little fragment of Bergson (Jay used to quote it) seeping through to the gray beach of Tinto Key and darkness occurring (it doesn't fall as novelists say, or creep, or come in a slow descent like a curtain; just there it is, was: darkness). "The

316

future of humanity is not determined, because it depends on humanity." Thank you, M. Bergson; thank you, one and all. But what of mediocrity that becomes intolerable when it takes pride in itself? Give us the answer clear, M. Bergson; spit it out to William Kite, sitting, waiting, the sea growling, *growling?* (that's literature)—all the crap a man thinks when all is busted, cracked, outside in the world of the Great Depression. At high tide the world comes here onto Tinto Key, nudges into place with the Malthusian flotsam of condoms, orange skins, rich turds, sludge fed on caviar and steak from the yachts of those who have held on to their loot.

I gave it up. I lay down on the sheetless, blanketless cot, the taste of coffee in me, camp coffee, sand in the food . . . the idea: Is there a moral structure to events? The fuel injector wasn't part of it—just bits of metal and screws, a shape, milled and lathed steel *and* screws, a design that did something—one man hoped—better than a thing unlike it did before; *that* in the end had screwed us. It belonged with my publishing ventures, Tony's lost place in the business world of the dollar cigars. And Pages? What had she wanted, did she want anything? I built a vision of her—it's easy—the vision—dark hair stirring on a pillow, not my pillow.

> *Folda est in coitu es brevis voluptas,*
> *et taedet Veneris statim peractae . . .*

I got up and walked down to the dark beach and thought of another poem too much quoted, where half-assed armies clashed by night. There was my brother Harry, who might give me a job in the wreck of Kite Enterprises—if he had a job himself. There was the house on Frenchman Street, mortgaged to the East Pompton First National Bank, if there was still an E. P. First National Bank. The old house; I could go back there, live on the top floor, or if not there in the tack room of the stables with the ammonia-smelling horses munching their oats, only there were no horses any more left in the world except at racetracks and society jumps. And there was for me no East Pompton either. I had left it when they buried my grandmother; left it for good because to go back would bring sly remarks, winks. ("That's the Kite fella, been away loafing 'round all over Europe, wasted his money, capital and all, look at him, hands shaking, looks like the moths been at him, must have the ole rale. All

317

the Kites were cunt-crazy. But I can remember when the Kites were real quality. His grandfather, the old rip, had the best team of matched bay carriage hosses; knock you down with his cane as quick as look at you. Them ole families, they just peter out. Must drink like a fish. Yes, always was a family of cocksmen. Why, his father run off with some fancy dame and the great-grandfather— Well, I allus say, don't speak badly of the dead.")

That's what it would be in East Pompton—William Kite walking back streets with an armful of stale library books, in his worn tennis shoes; his ass sticking out of his last pair of flannels, and eating out of cans in a room smelling of dove shit, old socks. That's the picture: walking with an armful of library books and a rheumatic shuffling gait. . . . I even saw my obituary:

RECLUSE DIES IN OLD FAMILY HOUSE. William Kite was found dead in his room in the back of the stables of his family's estate, once one of the showplaces of East Pompton. He had closed all the windows of the one mean room he lived in, and an oil stove left full on absorbed all the air and smothered him in the night. He left no heirs but a half-brother, Harry Kite, said to live in Boston, who has not been located. He lived with six cats and ate from cans, emerging only after dark, walking with the aid of a heavy cane, and speaking to himself. An eccentric and heavy reader in his last years, he would be seen hunting out discarded objects in trash bins. Three hundred and fifty-two cartons of old bottle caps were found in the stables by the local health inspector. Kite would peddle pennants and college colors at the Princeton football games, a bearded and not too clean figure. Few are aware he was of the class of 1916 and had been a heroic figure, a flier in the RFC in the First World War. If no one comes forward to claim the body, it will be buried by the Veterans of the American Wars, Post 331. The old Kite burial plot no longer exists; the Grove Cemetery on its hill was removed twenty years ago when the through-way was built and the entire Drood Hills section was bulldozed away.

William Kite left no will, or estate. The Board of Health condemned all surviving clothes, furniture, books, papers; they were badly infected with vermin and were ordered to be burned.

No. I had to have better plans. I had to have someplace else to go from Tinto Key. If not East Pompton, where? The poet had said: There's a better universe next door, let's go. But he left no tour map. Europe, then? To develop a mind spacious, tolerant and humane, slightly world-weary, ironic. To sit in cafés with a cheerful insouciance. To remember when la Stein had waved her fat *yenta's* arms (Tony's phrase) over us and said, "You are all a lost generation," and Ernest, drunk, had said, "How can we be lost when we have not yet been found?" And la Stein went on, la Stein, hung with beads, standing in the doorway with ugly Indian Alice behind her sewing on a pattern of tattered colors, *in the morning there is sleeping in the outside there is redding in the morning there is meaning in the evening there is feeling* (she was talking about roast beef).

Yes, Tinto Key to Europe, with "the Hasidim of the avant garde" (must forget Tony). Beauty in one's own thoughts returned—remember that—for we are strongest in the joints we were once broken at. Ernie said that. Wear an alpine hat, drink white Capri again, *l'heure du cocktail*. Not Capri but a *fiasco* of Chianti, or some Cinzano. *Mama mia. Dio ti salve, Maria.* Yes, Europe, by the *Bremen* or *Berengaria.* Never come back. . . .

Special to the Paris Herald: William Grant Kite died at his Villa St. Estèphe in sight of I Tatti, home of his old friend Bernard Berenson. He died suddenly over a dish of *pasta asciutta.* He was the author of *From the Eiffel Tower to the Fur-lined Teacup: An Informal History of the First Two Decades in Modern Art,* the privately printed *Madonna of Pompeii* (who conceived in her Fallopian tubes and had to be curetted), and the popular best seller, whose success amazed its author, *Native Mulch: Poe's Raven to Faulkner's Corncob.*

William Grant Kite had lived in Italy the last fifty years of his life, visited by many literary and art figures. His library, the famous collection of Japanese and Chinese art very rich in original Hokusai drawings and Han bronzes, will go to Rutgers University, because of his quarrel with his own alma mater Princeton about building a special wing to house the Kite collection.

A fantastically handsome figure, even into old age, well dressed but a bit old-fashioned, he was the reputed lover of Greta Garbo, Madame Shi-Fow-Dow, Lady Marley Lewis and the widow of an American President. He had left in his will a correct prediction of his own death. "I shall most likely die—like most of my family— suddenly, having for some time unknowingly collected in my body an atheromatous plaque of calcium deposits in the main coronary artery to the cortex, so that the brain will shut off like a valve the supply of oxygen, causing a complete blockage and full annihilation, or, as my friend Picasso would say, 'the bullet in the back of the head.' " William Grant Kite was the last survivor of the twentieth century's discoverers of the new arts and resented their exploitation as disenchantment, decadence and fashionable poignancy.

I looked up from my mental journalism, my literary flier in death notices. Pages was coming down from the Fry house, a flashlight in her hand, its single orange beam picking out the path among the boulders and salt grass. I waited for her by the beach tent (pushing aside my obituaries).

I wait. Pages walks slowly toward me. She is wearing a light cotton robe, bone-white in the dark night. She has not combed her short black hair; it runs in curls over her head, emphasizing the profundity of the profile. I think of it—the hair—long and snaking over her shoulders the way it used to be in Rome. She snaps off the flashlight and stands there in no tragic complication on a slight rise before me. She seems to fall in slow motion and I put out my arms in an impersonal way and hold her very close. I kiss her. She smells like Pages, like cigarettes, like brandy. The way she kisses is deadly direct, purposeful, tongue strong. The full availability of the intimate moment. It is real too. This is no dream lay in a sleeping bag by Ernest, the rich girl on Long Island by Scotty, the willing helper of Dr. Arrowsmith by Red. I run quickly through all the women in modern American writing as I withdraw from the kiss and decide she is closer to Sister Carrie than to Daisy, Mrs. Arrowsmith, Nurse Catherine, and that is the crazy way I think when an emotion comes over me suddenly; I shift for my fugitive pleasures through literature rather than to life. (It seems stronger that way somehow.)

"How's Tony?" I ask earnestly, feeling like the rabbit in the magic act's top hat.

"Sleeping."

"We should get a doctor from the mainland."

"He doesn't need one. Bill, let's get off the island."

"Tony's hurt."

"He's not hurt. Just his shiny yellow toy fell into the sea. Please get me away."

"Pages, I didn't mean to kiss you."

"The hell you didn't. I can feel you." She goes into the tent and sits down on the cot and looks around at the typewriter, water bottle,

320

open suitcase, two hangers of clothes, the low-lit lantern with a few moths testing their destiny. Her naked legs close together shine. I see she is barefoot. Sand is clinging to her long toes. (It is true; I am erect, excited.) There is a pretty point of conduct here. Am I a heel?

"Don't worry over Tony. He'll make out, sweet."

I quickly check the poles of aspiration and realization. "He's broke, he's ruined."

"You don't know Jews. They're wonderful people. They don't really care about money, just as money, loss or gain. They make money because they use it properly. But just getting rich—they don't care about it. They live in the narrow precinct of family life. Tony should go back to his first wife."

"What do you know about Jews?"

"I've been screwed by one for years. That is, until lately, when this racer thing took over. Tony has a one-track mind."

"That's no reason for leaving him. He's a person, not only an armature of skin, tissue and bone." (I almost go into the Shylock speech: "Hath not a Jew," etc., etc.)

"I'm not leaving him because I'm not being taken care of. I've been staying because I was sorry for the poor bastard. Ever read someplace: Dogs are liable to turn into demons and take over your life"?

"I've never read it."

"Sit down by me, sweet. Hold my hand. . . . Well, I'm one of those dogs. I've taken over Tony's life and it's been bad luck for him."

I sit down; she takes my hand and smiles. "Got a smoke?"

I give her a cigarette and light it for her and she inhales. (And I wonder what modern playwrights would do without cigarettes and phones. They make such fine dramatic pauses, but it's overdone on the stage.) She stirs the sand floor of the tent with a big toe. The robe opens to above her knees. "That's the way it is, Bill. I want to get away. I'm up to my ass crystallizing essential experiences. Tony will be all right. He'll come back big in junk or land investment, or some kind of buying and selling. He can't fail; a thousand generations of survival genes are behind him. It's racial with them."

"You don't know a damn thing about Jews. Your ideas don't make sense, not about leaving Tony."

321

"You think Tony will stay down?"

"No, I agree with you there. That handsome nervous energy will win out somehow. But—"

"Sweet, get some glasses."

She takes out a bottle of brandy, with a disarranging movement, from one of the big flappy pockets of the robe. Thigh white, thigh round, flesh pale, flesh soft. Her pubic hair is as crisp and curly as the ringlets on her head. All we ever seek (I think) in life is our dreams.

I handed her one glass after blowing sand from it. "I don't drink."

"You need one, sweet. It's been a hell of a day for both of us."

She hands me two fingers of brandy and reaches for another glass and pours it half full. She sips it. "Ever think, Bill, drinking is a kind of rite of purification?"

"In what way?" I sniff the brandy. It's a fine pungent brandy.

"It peels off the things that gall us. No wonder the Greeks called booze the water of life."

"You're pretty educating tonight."

"Drink up, Bill. Be kind to me, be tender to me. I'm all which ways. We've got to make each other real."

I set the glass down on the small table. She leans over and I kiss her again; she parts my lips with hers, and brandy dribbles into my mouth from hers. I choke, swallow, kiss. She laughs but doesn't let go, and I laugh. She is plainly trying to seduce me, and her nipples react under my fingers.

I say, "Pages, let's think."

"Then take a drink. Pay a penalty. Remember the kid game?"

"Yes." I take a small sip. I mean what harm, one lousy little sip? I mean the drinker isn't me, it's a stranger alienated from me. And a tent full of intimate odors suggesting assignations. I stroke her naked leg, naked (as the poet said) smooth like an egg. "We all long," I say, "for an impossible happiness. But we don't lay our friends' wives." She says, "You have a nose like a garden snail." I say, "I'm not capable of prolonged reflection at this moment." She says, "Drink up to disparity and change." "Just this one." "Sweet, you're too coherent." "No, I'm not, I'm confused. But firm." "Very firm. *Oh!* You pour the next round." "Let's not get childish. Look at tangibles." "I am not all the girls in those early novels—Richardson, Sterne, Fielding, Smollett—defending their maidenheads." She bites my ear: pain, pain; pleasure. "Oh, fuck the intangible, the elusive,

322

Bill. I'm unhappy. I've decided to go away. I want to be alive and be part of what's alive and kicking in all of us. Just one more little drink, sweet." "I don't see how the drinks and us making it together are going to help. Will you marry me?" "No, I don't want to marry into business again, or the arts." "What the hell, then, who?" "Some man who lives off income, travels a lot. . . . Just do *that* again. Pity me, Bill. Bill, pity me. I wanted to have children." "I know." "What do you know? Nothing. Just a dame to Jay, to Tony, to you. Hesitations, ambiguities—but always Pages for seminal fun. Why go into it?" "I'm sorry." I kiss her legs and stand up. "Real sorry, Pages honey. It's a pity. You'd make fine big fat babies." "Yes, sweet, I would. But I got into the wrong pew. Artists, writers, dreamers on the world market like Tony. I'm too solid, too firmly rooted, to have mixed well with all you bastards." I have my face between her thighs and I say, mumbling from a mouth glued against her flesh and hair, "We mustn't, you know, we mustn't. I mustn't. You came here for this, to seduce me." "Maybe I did. Maybe. I had a few drinks up at the house. I felt you were real. But you're like all of the avant-garde crew; the self is just ceaselessly concerned with your future death. You all make me want to puke. Life is better than death any time!"

I must say that hits me in the balls like an electric shock because I was playing that death game, writing my obituaries, just before she came down the path. I come up for air, take a big sip of brandy to recover. I say, "All aberrations are forms of love, or is love an aberration of the sensation . . . say, I'm a little woozy."

"You're mumbling down there. What?"

I put out my hands and open the robe wide. I put my face back to the crisp curly hair, rock my head and am *le citoyen d'une patrie inconnue* (and in case someone thinks it's dirty, it means: the citizen of an unknown country). An intrinsic want resurrects, an exhilaration sets fire, as a popular novelist would put it with a few * * *. What I actually do is put my fluid tongue to it, in it, (*le moi profond*—the real inner self, to continue the French lesson). She is placid and calm at first as I invade, make an allegiance of mouth and her secret self. Then she cries out like a child pleased and too breathless to articulate. She falls back on the cot and I do not lift face or head. She says in a panting contralto, "Come up here, sweet." I say, "No no, I said I wouldn't." She grabs me by the hair. "What's the difference either *this* or *that*? You and your damn Jesuitical

323

thinking. It's all *one* game." "That's logical." I lift my head and gulp some brandy. I rise, drop clothes and go for her; her arms are open. So I am seduced. So I am weak, in will. So self-containment, disjunction, separation, flee as I am on. I enter, I plunge, I cry out with pleasure of her of it of us, for I cry to cry out we do not have to be the absurdity we create on this shipwrecked planet of Mr. Hoover and Mr. Roosevelt.

> (*Let us not then rush blindly on unto it,*
> *Like Lustful beasts that only know to do it.*
> *For Lust will languish and that heat decay . . .*)

We come. Just come: We did not, as in novels, peak, ring the bell, reach the top of the ridge, make the trees shake, the earth tremble. Just the two of us in layer on a creaking camp cot, part to part, nakedness to nakedness. No metaphors, no similes. Everything just fine on a normal human level. Not even Promethean; and no daisies for Lady Chatterley's snatch. No joint-copping in the contessa's gondola. But I guess I've warned, I fight the literary use of love-making as a protest on behalf of what I think is the reality.

When Pages in open-mouthed sweat points to the brandy, I get up and put her dropped smoldering cigarette butt into a tin cup and come back with two glasses of brandy; she has her broad pink back to me, looking at her face in my shaving mirror the way a woman will after an intimate experience to see if it shows. The rough woven canvas of the sheetless cot is wonderfully imprinted on her magnificent ass.

(This hath pleased, doth please and long will please.)

I hand her the glass, biting her shoulder as I do, feeling the things we are together for—that is, the us: one + one = two. . . .

Nikko before morning took us to Papaya City in his motor skiff, delighted to be part of any intrigue. Neither of us left a note for Tony. As the seduced party I felt hung over.

EDITOR'S NOTE: A penciled-in note on this section of the manuscript reads: "Actually as we grappled with perplexities, we sent Tony a wire from Tampa; I no longer remember what it said except for the phrase WE INTEND TO MARRY."

Nora Pages Pfaelzer divorced her husband Tony in Reno later that year. William Kite and she were married in Santa Barbara in February, 1934, at the house of her aunt, Mrs. Martin Brady. The only comment William Kite makes on their wedding is the pasting into the manuscript of a yellowing news item from the *Santa Barbara Star:*

PAGES—KITE WEDDING AT CREWLE POINT

Yesterday at noon a wedding was celebrated at the palatial villa of our town's popular hostess, Mrs. Martin "Ipsey" Brady: the marriage of her niece, Nora Pages of Boston, and William Greer [*sic*] Kite of East Pompton, New Jersey, scion of the century-old Kite foundry and mills. The couple, Ipsey told us at the wedding ceremony, met in a romantic setting in the tropics. The groom, a gallant war hero with a romantic limp, is a graduate [*sic*] of Princeton, says he is planning to establish a West Coast publishing firm, a modern press to print the many excellent writers who now live on our coast. The couple will honeymoon in a trout camp in the High Sierras. Mr. Kite, an ardent fisherman, plans to land some big ones, and Mrs. Kite hopes to paint watercolors, having spent some years studying art in Rome and Paris. Ipsey as hostess wore a blue net lace gown by Patou of Paris. The bride was in gray silk with long pale yellow gloves and carried tea roses. The Reverend Mr. Kelton Mosby of the Palm Road Episcopal Church performed the ceremony in the Della Robbia room of Crewle Point, which was a veritable fairyland of cut flowers tastefully arranged by Ipsey herself.

The news item is the only mention of William Kite's publishing hopes on the West Coast. Actually, as far as available records show, he seems to have engaged in no business enterprises in Santa Barbara or anywhere else in California.

Tony Pfaelzer in 1937 married Juanita Vadon Robedo of Mexico City, and in 1940 he married Anita White of Chicago. Neither marriage resulted in children and both ended in divorce. In the late thirties Tony Pfaelzer set up Dyno-Central Tool Company, servicing oil drilling crews with derrick pipe and rotary drilling equipment. His patent for the Central-Dyno double-bit drill was often in litigation. In 1940 he sued International Motors for infringement on his T. P. Fuel Injector, but lost the case after a costly series of court battles. (See Pfaelzer v. Int. Mot., Michigan Central Courts, vol. 144, sec. 4.) In 1942 he organized at the request of the War Department the Big Push Construction Company, and his work crews built many of the island airfields in the far Pacific: Kwajalein, Bikar Atoll, and in the Marianas. He was decorated by President Roosevelt with the Citation for Meritorious Service early in 1944. On August 14, 1956, he took off in a navy plane from the atom tests on Wilmoki Atoll for Okinawa Jima, radioing a report they were

325

running into a storm called a tsunami. The plane was never heard from again. There was a rumor Tony Pfaelzer had married a Japanese-Chinese dance hall girl in one of the islands, but no such wife ever came forward to claim any of his estate.

His effects and assets were in a great muddle; government projects ran at a loss, but enough was salvaged from the oil-field company by lawyers for the only surviving child of his first marriage, Samuel Pfaelzer, to settle in North Carolina with his wife and four children. Here he took up horse-breeding and dealing in timber. It was at the Samuel Pfaelzers' Carolina country estate, View Acres, that William Kite as an old man was often a guest for long periods of time, and at which place he seems to have written the major portion of his memoirs. There is no indication that Tony Pfaelzer ever met William and Nora Kite again after their elopement from Tinto Key—yet in letters to the son, Samuel Pfaelzer, one seemed to assume that they remained friendly after the divorce and Nora Pages's marriage to William Kite. I have been unable to persuade Samuel Pfaelzer to go into details about this or permit me to read the letters from his father.

BOOK EIGHT

FROM WILLIAM KITE'S POCKET NOTEBOOK

It says in Ecclesiastes, "The man who wishes you ill is better than the woman who wishes you well." Whoever wrote it was a sour old man who forgot his youth. —W. K.

Ich bin klein,
Mein Herz ist rein,
Soll niemand d'rin wohnen
Als Gott allein.

BOOK EIGHT

FROM WILLIAM SAFIRE'S POLITICAL DICTIONARY

CHAPTER 33

NOW

AT NIGHT IN THE ELLIPTICAL, exasperating round of tossing, and no sleep coming, I hear the sound of a Sopwith Camel from an old war. There was a cliché then much quoted by the average citizen, "War is hell," and what added to our personal hell as fliers in those days was the airplanes we had to fly. Worst was the Sopwith Camel, a misfit and abortion of a flying machine. Some ground-bound fool had given it rotary engines, which meant the whole damn engine turned and the prop was bolted to it, so that the entire ton or so of iron was moving and spinning and shaking the crate. This made a left-hand spin at anything less than nearly four thousand feet fatal. You could hardly ever get the machine out of a left-hand spin once it went that way. All my sleepless nights I am in such a spin.

These airplanes were the darlings in which we flew. The prop was frozen to the spinning engine, and the back end of the crankshaft was bolted to the first braces of the fuselage. The foul mixture of gasoline and castor oil was force-fed into the engine through the hollow crankshaft and hollow piston rings, and you had to pray this crazy system would function. The fumes of the thick oil and overheated metal made one ill after a few minutes of it, and at times even the milk-and-brandy diet wouldn't stay down. That was the stuff His Majesty's Royal Flying Corps gave us, but we each had a fine, neat commission signed by George R.I. Nobody that I knew of framed it over his cot.

The brandy got at our livers, the fumes destroyed our stomachs; the cramped flying positions under tension brought on phlebitis, an interesting disease of the leg veins, giving us a proper excuse to swing a fancy cane.

329

Everybody called it The Great War. Only later was it demoted to being merely the World War . . . and tonight, with sleep still not at hand, the mind is racing to the roar of a long-obsolete motor and the impossibility of possession in love, the illusion of friendship, and the growing thought that the full life is never expansive but only an inner contraction. Tomorrow night I shall try earplugs. . . .

1956

THE PRINCETON CLASS OF 1916 made a big thing—prodigious, a bit pathetic—of its fortieth anniversary. The college had arranged for Eliot Tjaden, a member of the class (even if he never was graduated) to be given an honorary degree of Doctor of Arts and Letters. They had never got around to giving F. Scott Fitzgerald an honorary degree and they didn't want to make the same mistake with Eliot Tjaden, whose reputation had grown to worldwide fame at least with the critics. "Greater things are still expected from him," an alumni letter said. There was the huge novel in progress for so many years, excerpts from which had been published from time to time as "Fragments from Carthage." Jay had even recorded two sections of it for Caedmon Records, the "Bite Through the Sky" section and the freewheeling verse of "Comforts of a Fur-lined Grave." *Carthage* was actually to be a novel about East Pompton, called New Carthage in the book, Jay's re-creating of life in an American town, a formless, wandering, wonderful series of visions—the raucous cries of lonely lives, of spontaneous joys.

It mixed fantasies—but in new tonalities—remarkably, I felt, beyond anything yet done in the novel form in the second half of the twentieth century. Yet it was doubtful if Jay would ever pull it together or seem anywhere near completing it. ("Ambition," he wrote me, "without qualification is the American sin.") He had been working on it for fifteen years, slowly producing fragments, small sections, and revising those two or three times so that several versions of parts were in print. And these he still did not call final. ("I should call the book 'Forebodings and Apprehensions.' ")

I hadn't seen much of Jay. Perhaps my marriage to Pages kept us apart rather than the distance; he was in Paris, I in America. My marriage gave me—to dust off a banal phrase—the best years of my life. Looking back, I see it all in glowing holiday yellow, full of close intimacy . . . shouting out at times, wondering at living, aching for extended life . . . being two people and being one, and being each of us aware of our sharing, being in interspatial space and in one room at the same time. It was not that way always. No marriage is ever what it seemed once it is looked back on over one's shoulder. But the whole of it had been us and was good. Pages and I had made it good for all of the bad, and the bad was the part of it we knew and tried to pass over, not looking down at it.

It wasn't a success materially. I mean there was the problem of starting life together with the Depression still with us; the world was a planet trapped in the dead Sargasso Sea of despair. I couldn't make any publishing contacts that amounted to anything in New York. I edited several little magazines that issued one or two sly, too precious numbers and curled up and floated away like volcanic ash on water. My hairline retreated. I grew wary.

We lived in Brooklyn Heights those years of the '30s—in two rooms on top of a wonderful nineteenth-century house falling apart but charming. The tin bathtub was painted Camembert-green, the water was rust-color, the roof leaked a bit, but it was airy in our rooms and we painted walls white and made furniture out of slab doors and cut-down round Victorian dining tables bought from secondhand dealers. We had a big mattress and box spring resting on two-by-fours on the floor, and lots of wall mirrors from a speakeasy that had gone out of business when drinking became legal. We managed in those years of slim times because we had an extraordinary capacity of visualization. Pages had a flair for making nothing do for something and a little do even better.

She was always in junk shops and Salvation Army yards, inspecting wooden farm sinks, or buying odd lots of rubbish at auction. At home she would remove paint from Edwardian horrors and bleach old chairs. I'd hire a small pickup cart and move the redone stuff around to where she made deals with truculent, spice-scented interior decorators. In the end she became a decorator herself.

Our flat was full of bolts of curtain and drapery material. Blueprints and estimates hung on wall spikes. Lint-covered men came carrying reupholstered chairs over their heads, talked of outfitting small hotels, dickered over the prices of plaster lamp bases, the cost

331

of scraping old floors, the different shades of chocolate colors and the daring of having sky-blue walls.

Pages's first place was on Church Avenue near Flatbush. The sign had just the letters: PAGES. She had a cheerful, vulgar, laughing trade of newly rich Jews and Italians, fertile as mink, fat with sex and family relations, who wanted gold lamé drapes, lampshades with feathers, sofas in Turkish red, big as islands. They were earnest with sweat, kindly, opinionated, addicted to *The Reader's Digest*. Their ideas of decor came from M-G-M movies in which their saints were Joan Crawford and Jean Harlow, who suffered love and disappointed love in the arms of Clark Gable or Walter Pidgeon.

Pages as a decorator was the first in Brooklyn to insist on stark white for everything. But that caught on only later when Pages opened her shop on 68th Street near Madison, a fearful six steps down to a basement in an old brownstone with active insect and rodent life that I spent two weeks chasing next door with sprays and powders. Except for the simple-lettered black PAGES against the sand-colored slab, there was nothing else outside. The door was black ebony, and the interior, once three hellholes, had been knocked into one long room. The walls were painted black—dull matte black—and I had developed a crick in my back putting on three coats of it. A channel ran along near the ceiling in which hidden lights lay in ambush. On the black rug were several white chairs (once in a Greek ice-cream parlor). Bolts of red and yellow and pale silver cloth lay rolled and unrolled around the place. It all stank of good taste at a good price. The manner was cool, just this side of a sneer.

Pages's desk was a Pennsylvania Dutch hog-scalding bench bleached and rubbed with a gray-white paint. We had paid off the graft to the fire inspector, the electrical inspector, the health department, the cop on the beat and several other city employees who swore to Pages they had to pass it on to higher-ups; Tammany took the big bite. All the shops and apartment houses in the neighborhood knew that was the way it was in New York City. So we paid. Not that we had any violations, but, as I said to Pages, custom is custom, keep your city clean and honest.

It was a hard life for us the first few years. Pages grew thinner, had a haunted look in her eyes, colored lint under her fingernails. She formed combinations of crafts, held hands with other decorators, male, female, and in between. She never returned to the gold lamé

332

drapes and feathered lampshades of Flatbush and Church Avenue. "Pages interiors" meant something. A cold clean look, a few rare objects, a disdain for whatever you already owned, a submitting of an estimate form to sign, which was an ironbound contract as deadly as a guillotine if you found fault.

We were at home in the third floor of the brownstone and made it over into a really never-fully-finished modern flat. There was something about a brownstone of the O. Henry period that had character, nostalgia, solidity for me. They echoed with old laughter and a sad music of brown mortality.

We were happy there, when we got together. Pages was off to decorator shows in Philadelphia and upstate, to forced auctions of farmhouse junk that was called Americana, to fast buying trips in England and France and Italy, from which she brought back hideous, clumsy household objects that were listed as "rare antiques from private family collections." Pages hunted these things the way a white hunter went after prize elephant tusks. Riverside Drive, West End Avenue, even Park Avenue, moaned in delight at the sight of the stuff.

I didn't—I must confess—really fit into the Pages shop after a while. I couldn't swoon properly over an apple-yellow roll of silk, and I didn't give a damn if a broken chair was a Hitchcock or a Chippendale if my ass was not comfortable in it. The customers, referred to as *clients*, annoyed me. I disliked their lazy cruelty of wealth that Pages had to press back with firmness but without insult or a knee on their necks, the bad taste of the rich which was as bad as the bad taste of the Joan Crawford and Jean Harlow lovers in Brooklyn; and most likely, Pages said, "as bad as the taste of the poor, sweet, who are fortunate in not being able to afford interior decoration."

I worked for my brother Harry, when there was work. Harry was killing himself; he had already had a beaut of a coronary, but he was recovered, and game, with a wife and three children, and alimony to his first. Harry was a gray goods converter, after the last of the Kite enterprises went down in the Depression; the last of the Kite birthright was long dissolved. Harry visited small mills in New England and in Tennessee and Georgia where they wove cotton cloth—with nonunion pore-white-trash help. They produced a cloth called gray goods and Harry printed on the material, with old brass and wooden rollers, patterns of flowers or stripes. He made deals with small dress

333

manufacturers and desperate Russian and Austrian Jews and shoddy chain stores; they combined to convert these yardages into robes, house dresses and aprons for bargain sales, lead items in mail-order catalogues and direct-sales fliers. It was called on Seventh Avenue a *schlock* business . . . a hard dollar, a miserable plague. Harry wore himself out; he was involved with truckers, contractors, nonunion shops hidden in New Jersey or the Virginia hills, with fighting overdue notes and broken promises, with payoffs, and parties and sex for visiting buyers, with delayed payments and discounts taken on thirty-day bills overdue. Life was hell for Harry. His lips were blue, his breath hard to catch, his eyes full of terror.

I sat in a small rented space with a brass plaque on a scarred door: KITE COTTON CONVERTERS, in one of those decaying buildings that have dance studios and song publishers of non-hit tunes, and an offer of sixteen nude photographs for the "art lover or medical student." My job was to watch a lean, ugly girl from Queens type up Harry's letters and invoices. I answered the more important calls and swore we were shipping "80-squares" (which means eighty strands of cotton thread woven each way at right angles in every inch of cloth). I didn't know if we were, but everybody cheated a little in converting and cutting and patterning of *schlock*. The manufacturer would take off four buttons here, a bit of belt there, a little collar trim from the sample model. Harry bought cuttings which were the ends as they fell away from the electric knives that cut three hundred dozen dress bodies out of layers of piled-up cotton cloth, and the cuttings were bagged for the paper mills and the users of unusable leftovers. (Now you know how people who didn't write or paint or act in the Federal Art projects lived in the '30s.)

I didn't answer the phone often. I left it to Miss Steinhetz, who brought her lunch in a paper bag always stained with grease, and who hoped to capture a husband (she wasn't interested in a lover) by doing her eyebrows, fingernails and hair on Harry's time. I fled the office. I went around to museums (remember Benton, Wood, Curry —the white hopes of American art?), sat through gangster movies, stood at the Wharf Bar on Madison near 50th with other men who had little to do in the afternoon. By the time I came by to meet Pages for dinner, I was pretty loaded. Usually she would smile, pat my cheek, and say, "Sweet, I've got the damn Hilton zombies on my tail for that ballroom drapery job. You go eat alone at Ruby Foo's or Longchamps."

Which was fair; Pages was the breadwinner. I'd go to Hapsburg House to listen to the zither music, or Lüchow's for *Sauerbraten,* or a place called Tony's Naples in a backyard smelling of cat crap and garlic, and I'd have dinner and two more martinis. (Tony gave me a happy sigh when I made up a story that all manhole covers in Rome are lettered SPQR.)

When Pages came back we'd talk and tell each other little things of no value to anyone but ourselves. It was the best part of the day for me, free of cliques and personalities . . . no more time to kill with Thomas Benton, James Cagney, 80-squares. We'd go to bed. If she wasn't too tired, we'd go at each other with a religious intensity, and if she was tired, I'd kiss her shoulder and tell her "Sleep late" and wonder what to do with an erection. When she was free, we went to Mercurio's for dinner and—to celebrate a special deal put over— "Valenciennes lace spreads all the way"—to Chambord, Chateaubriand, or The King of the Sea for seafood. Pages loved lobsters, steamy strong-smelling clams, and the huge crimson claws of deepsea crabs (her face all butter, chewing hard, smiling at me as she fed . . . happy).

I was faithful to Pages, and I suppose she was to me. We liked our domestic life. Getting up late Sunday morning after an evening of Eugene O'Neill or George Kaufman, reading comic strips, loving each other, all smelly with sleep and last night's cigarettes and liquor, bathing together, horsing around. Getting into our Japanese Kabuki robes, having a breakfast of ham or bacon and eggs. Kicking apart the heavy New York *Times,* which was five or ten pounds of dullness (sections we threw in all directions as we tore it apart hoping hopelessly to find *something* of interest). We skipped lunch and about two o'clock whistled to the dog, the wirehaired terrier that we kept with the janitor. He was a childish, stupid dog but lovable, and we called him Rover. Nobody we ever knew, in our time, called a dog Rover any more. He lived mostly with the janitor's kids and was always being treated for mange or worms or fleas, which the janitor's wife said he got from the Scotties that lived in the next house.

We'd walk Rover for an hour or two in the park, then come back and deposit him with the janitor's kids and go upstairs and lie around and do whatever we felt like if we felt like. We mostly did. We bathed and dressed for dinner and met a lot of people. Advertising writers, radio producers, playwrights who hadn't made it to Hollywood yet. Publishers' readers, wretches from the newsmagazines, book-jacket designers, teachers (Marx and dandruff) from CCNY, NYU and Columbia. Neurotic, intelligent people. Not really very talented, and going noplace. But able, politically cunning, usually married, faintly adulterous, reasonably worried about world conditions, telling me New York was the greatest city in the world, wouldn't live anyplace else, the cultural center of America—after three martinis the world. That's how it was in the '30s for us.

Jay wrote me from Berlin, "No, I'm not coming home. Here I hear the *Heulen und Zahneknirschen*."

Those were the happy years for me. And not too many disquieting symptoms. I didn't drink too much, Pages was available, sensual and companionable—when free. I answered Harry's phone. I read a lot, Dashiell Hammett, Céline, Whitehead, dabbled in little schemes for little magazines which came to nothing. I was physically able and perhaps had too pious a complacency. I didn't want any other woman, and there were a lot available. There was smart wife-swapping in Westchester and daisy-chaining in the Village, four to six in orgy at someone's apartment with Picasso prints on the wall. We didn't play. We had no moral responsibilities and we submitted to artistic banalities cheerfully.

I liked Pages's intimate laundry hanging on a line in the bathroom; I didn't mind finding her discarded underwear tossed away in a hurry; I'd hold it and smell it and bury my face in silky, musty, vaginal scent and feel horny. I was getting on in years, and the hair was thinning, *thinning*. I had a bit of paunch for all my pleated London tailoring. (Jay wrote, "New novel delayed—am falling apart—arthritis attack—shoulder.")

Pages and I quarreled, of course; that's the best rule for marriage: to quarrel and get it done with. But there was nothing important and nothing vital in our quarrels. We spent all I made—ha—and, what was harder, all Pages made, and sometimes that was a lot.

A Negro maid came three times a week to keep us in order, toting and sly like a Billy Brunswick product. (I didn't see how they could fail to take over the world—they had earned it.) We had a blue Mercedes that lived in a garage on 59th Street, as expensive as a private suite in a good hospital or so it seemed, and a summer cottage at Southampton, because it was good for business and good for us, where we basked in the sun. I remember cooking vast gory steaks reeking of blood and pepper on an outdoor grill, dressed in cap and bathing trunks . . . Everybody gorging on underdone meat and garlic bread, and powerful martinis. These were our friends, or people we met in a tepid surf. Stage directors, advertising copy chiefs, Freudian medical men, lower members of Wall Street law firms. (Talk of incomes thick like steak smell in the air.) Department store buyers, architects who didn't trust Frank Lloyd Wright or FDR and those who did. Rich young surgeons, opening their patients by the dozen like—Pages suggested—shucking oysters. Poor young doctors in trouble (with knocked-up nurses) who'd never make it with a bedside manner or a rich wife. Naval officers who told us there was a plot by our Communist senators in Washington to turn us over to the Kremlin; had the plans in their other pants pockets. Rich men's sons who were arrested in 14th Street picket lines. Young writers who disliked the short stories in *The New Yorker*.

And girls. Girls from the South, the Far West, who were actresses, poets, cigarette girls, models for *Vogue* (the sick-looking ones), or they worked in Lord and Taylor's.

Why do I go on with this? Because *these* were my best years. I hate to leave them—and La Stein had said to me, "Never back off—one plus one plus one . . . till one gets to plus one hundred."

Sterile people surrounded us, I suppose: the knowing, the chic, the avant-garde, the way-out, the way-in, the hep, the hipster, the outré, the perverse. But late in the evening (dull in themselves as Pages and I must have been dull to them) they ate our food, drank our booze, or we ate their food and drank their booze, all in a gin incoherence. They rode in our Mercedes; we rode in their Cords, Fiats. (Please, just a little more detail—it feels *so* good.) We met twice or three times a week in various combinations and various-sized mobs: Anglo-Jewish-Southern-Connecticut-Protestant-Buddhist-Sodomite-Village-Berkshire-Festival gangs. Some had growing children, some had third or fourth wives, or husbands. Quickies on a train à la Mary McCarthy didn't count. Many were on the Vienna couch, talking about being taken off the potty too soon by their moms. Some were boring homosexuals, even if married. Most were slack sexually in a neurotic clutching. They were habitually, continually unfaithful to each other, but were usually seeking the one true love, the big money, power, fame, the right people, proper names, little interesting places. They knew (we knew) the correct new upper-class slang (we, they), the full use of poetic foul language from the jazz pits or Harlem (us,

337

them) or the first of the pre-beat folk singers in the Village. They read (and we read) *Hound and Horn, Partisan Review,* the little arid magazines in the South; at the end Sartre and Camus, Kafka. We saw the films of John Ford and Eisenstein, and recognized the already stale cuteness of the Museum of Modern Art. (All right—no more inventory of old pains like knots in wood.)

Pages had her work; I had spare time, too much of it. Letters came from Jay, full of howls of protest against some nobody from Yale who had criticized his work as "piles of old rugs needing beatings." And I had a note from Charlie going great guns with his ski school in the Tirol.

That's the way it was into 1940; then I woke up in apathetic dread with my hands shaking *and* I was an alcoholic. I needed two stiff belts to just walk to the bathroom. 1940. The year Harry had his second coronary and I got Pages to advance me five thousand (well, we're back to narrative now) for Harry's medical expenses, which she did cheerfully even if she was going through hard times trying to bribe her way into decorating a string of a hundred and fifty coast-to-coast motels. 1940. The year I wrecked our second Mercedes, very drunk, and hurt that Puerto Rican woman and spent ninety days on Welfare Island full of flea powder, the stink of sour breath, the sadism of New York Civil Service goons, the grafting, cheating, buggery, slop food— you can't write realistically of the meanness and foulness of ninety days in a New York City jail. There was a judgment against me for twenty-five thousand dollars for the Puerto Rican woman—two-thirds to her lawyer—and the insurance didn't cover it all. 1940. When I had the attack of dt's (never mind the details) and lived in such places as Doc Gripsholm's drying-out sanitarium near Riverside Drive, places where you met prime old drunks—John Barrymore, Sinclair Lewis, other big names, lushes also, drying out.

1940. When I knocked Pages down, when she said something about something I don't now remember. She spoke softly with a kind of sad impartiality as she rubbed her bruised eye, "Love is over, sweet. But I *was* willing to let you stay. A punching bag is something else. Goodbye." I left and went down to Atlantic City for a toot in The Breakers. They still speak of me and a Pulitzer Prize winner and an actress there—she was between dope and lesbianism. (Sounds fascinating, doesn't it? *No,* it was dismal, it was dreadful. It was pitiful. An incomprehensible hell, an undimensional universe.) The

338

actress used to just squat in a corner of the suite and pee whenever she felt like it. The Pultizer Prize man would recite some work in progress and confess to the hotel help that he hated his father and H. L. Mencken, his wife, his publisher, his children, Herbert Hoover, and that he was foul, mean, cruel and a pretty poor writer. We would agree and start a fight. They removed us all to the sanitarium by force. It was a ball, crowds staring, the actress urinating in the patrol wagon. . . . So we failed in Atlantic City to transcend the realities of time and annihilation.

Pages brought me home after an eight-week drying-out period. But it wasn't the same any more. (No details, please. *Dun't esk,* as the Milt Gross character said. *Dun't esk.*) The war saved me from listening to Gestalt psychology, from being run over while drunk and staggering home, jumping off the Empire State Building, running off with some nympho to Mexico, choking to death in my own vomit while passed out (happened to several of my friends). I never thought of sleeping pills, oddly enough, or the janitor's hose attached to the exhaust pipe of the repaired Mercedes and leading into the airtight interior. No, I had (even in my stupor) a curiosity, and so I decided to sample the fury and the war of a crazy topsy-turvy world where one's own annihilation has no naked immediacy.

I didn't blame Pages; somebody in a marriage has to work, has to make money. She was loyal and I think faithful even then. Maybe somebody got a few fringe benefits, even penetrated past unresisting muscles when I was drying out with no hope of a comeback. I wouldn't have blamed her.

Why the failure to function to my full potential? I don't know. I didn't even blame myself. (That's the protection a drunk gives his ego or what's left of it on his own sublimated level of evasions and subterfuges.)

Just record that from 1933 to near 1940 we had a fine, wonderful marriage—only the early years, maybe, but they counted, they mattered, they sang and danced. Show me *any* marriage of length that had seven good ones with bells on, free of debilitating areas.

I haven't here gone into anything in detail; that would make a dozen lousy novels of the '30s and '40s . . . all the fancy trimmings, the Miro and Mondrian reproductions on the walls, the Scarsdale abortions, the boating parties on the Sound, the people we

339

knew who went to Hollywood and Paris or into *Newsweek* or NBC, and who we felt were traitors. . . . You know the fancy crap we wrote in those days: twilight in a Third Avenue bar in upper Manhattan, the traffic at theater time to see Robert Sherwood and the Lunts, cocktail parties at Viking and Random House, the newest story about Cary Grant or Henry Luce or John Steinbeck or Virginia Woolf, Tallulah or Li'l Abner. (Jay wrote to me, "You're not living Bill, you're making lists, inventories—and I'm in a writer's block, you bastard. . . .")

So skip it all; for Sweet Jesus' sake I spare you all that just-gone history. It's dry and dusty as the inside of Dead Sea fruit, which on the outside looks like a red rosy apple and inside is a mouthful of dust. Only a gesture, as when an actor in a Chinese drama lifts his leg (like a dog about to anoint a post) that signifies he is mounting a horse. There never was a horse.

CHAPTER 34

THE PRINCETON OF 1956 was not the college Jay and I had entered in 1912 and left in 1915. It had been a close-knit, aging, neat green, mildly interesting place of past glories and overgorged memories. Here a young man could read, study, probe his problems and feel part of a thing that belonged to a long time ago; but there was—I was told—no taste to anything now.

On the June morning I got off the Pennsy train, now fully electric (the great cats, the eight, twelve, sixteen-wheel Baldwin steam loco- motives were gone), I came to a college that had become too big, too mixed in its styles. The bronze tigers on the steps of old Nassau Hall seemed prehistoric, like the sour memory of Lindbergh or Rudy Vallee. There was a McCarter Theater, since my time, for the Triangle Shows, and the Hobart Baker Memorial Rink honored an alumnus who was killed in our *own* war—World War I. I wondered if there would have been a Kite Memorial Hockey Field or a Tjaden Baseball Field if I or Jay had died then. Most likely not. The Fire- stone Memorial Library, also new, held a sign which said it contained two million volumes—none of which I wanted to read. I once had planned to read everything worth while (absolute courage comes not from humility but from foolishness).

I carried my one bag over to the Washington Arms Motel, where, the Alumni Society had wired me, the Class of '16 was setting up shop, and where Jay was to be kept properly neat and alert until he stood up in cap and gown before the graduating class, made a speech and accepted his honorary degree of Doctor of Arts and Letters.

I wondered how Jay had weathered the years. His letters had given little detail. How would he like this new Princeton with its foul and noisy Propulsion Laboratory put there for jet-research-to-doom—and what would he think of the non-college-related endowed loafers in the Institute For Advanced Study full of the pathetic fallacy they could advance the mass one inch? The hell with it all, I thought. I would see Jay in his growing fame through this, cut up a few old times with the surviving Class of '16, and say it certainly didn't seem like forty years (the devil it didn't; it felt like forty centuries). I had just got over an attack of shingles, that virus inflammation of the nerve roots, a disease which sounds comical and is so painful. I used to roll on the floor of my room at the University Club and decide I should now save up my sleeping pills for a real final bang. I used to lie groaning, full of mild pain killers that failed, and dictate my suicide note. I was never satisfied I had gotten just the right tone into it. (Self-pity, not religion, is what comes in solitude.)

"It is my wish that I be cremated in a plain pine box in the cheapest manner, that my ashes be scattered in the simplest way by arm action, like spring sowing. No ritual or religious service of any kind is to be held. During the cremation I wish that my friends would gather at a cozy back room of some bar and drink and amuse themselves and tell witty stories and feel free to see my escape as something morally desired rather than anything illogically tragic."

No, while that one was basic, it didn't have the right tone.

"I desire to be respectifully escorted to the grave by a good Dixieland band playing 'When the Saints Go Marching In.' Wherever the bones of my grandfather and grandmother now lie, I ask to be buried across their feet if that can be done. The cheapest casket and no embalming, no minister at the graveside. The burial party and guests to retire to the Princeton Inn to drink and amuse themselves with their own ceaseless selves in the hope they will understand why I

341

agree with my grandfather, who thought death a vulgar blunder by whatever made us, and *any* other system would be an improvement. They should not see any sadness in my passing, but rather a process that they, too, will not avoid. We are each in the end the sole citizen of a unique country—our burial suit."

No, I was getting sentimental. Gruesome, gruesome. I didn't take the sleeping pills. I saw no way of exiting with style, and we are all motivated at times by a desire to prolong our fantasies.

Princeton was filled to overflowing with past classes in various combinations of hats and jackets. Colors and sashes were everyplace. Under the elms and sycamores stood the hipsters' Mercedes-Benzes, Jaguars, Alfa Romeos, the bankers' conservative Lincolns, the Cadillacs of the squares (any Princetonian with three generations of school cheers behind him knew Caddies were only for the Negro help).

I walked slowly in the summer day—with cane and suitcase—and as I passed a blue Mercedes, I thought of Pages. I had seen her for the last time in 1945, when as a major on leave from London—and memories of damn postal cards and maps, General Eisenhower and his pretty jeep drivers—I had come back to get out of the army. Pages met me at the airport to tell me she hadn't wanted to divorce me while the war was on. I said we all had done what we could for our country. She was in her menopause then, looked drawn and tired, but still very beautiful, her hair half gray. My mind was twitching like a damaged muscle. All I asked her was the stupid question all men ask. *"Who was the guy?"* She said there wasn't a guy, but that we ourselves had "torn it up" (her expression) a year before I went into the army. I said it was kind of her to tell me this herself. She said she was leaving for the Coast, where her aunt had died and left her the villa and there were legal details in the settling of an estate. If I wanted any of my things they were in storage, and she gave me some slips of paper with information written in her schoolgirl script on them. I said, "Couldn't we have a drink on it all?" I was, I said, very grateful to her (and no gags) for the very best years I had had on earth. She said, "No, sweet. You look pretty good, keep it up." And that was the last communication of our married life. She divorced me.

I tried to keep it up. But the postwar depression was on me— nothing for it but some stupid, worthless work on some of those

342

ridiculous missions and conferences in which the Germans somehow always came out on top, and got drunk with us, and put their fat arms around us (few used deodorants and Germans smell high). *"Ja, ja, Major, ja, Major, Exzellenz, together—nein?—*we can say to the Russian *Schwein, du Hund, du Lump, du sachaufen, mit* the *Amerikaners* we will giff you but goot der fucking, *nein?"*

Back in my motel room in Dresden, Frankfurt, Hamburg, a gift bottle, package of Buckling herring or Limburger (Dresden I only remember as a condom hung over a bathroom cabinet like one of Dali's limp watches.)

"Hello, you ol' cooter! What the hey!"

I was back at Princeton. 1956. A fat bald man gasping for breath, with an English bowler in one hand, a furled umbrella thin as a sword in the other (that was the costume of the reunion of the Class of '16), bumped me with a shoulder. "Damn it, Billy, damn it, we're the only two left of the old quartet at Cottage; mandolin, piano, banjo and bones. 'Oh Buffalo girls, won't you come out tonight!' "

"Nippy," I said, "Nippy Waldon."

"In the flesh and lots of it, huh? Judge Waldon, Superior Court of Ohio. Jesus, we're a slipping-by-fast generation. Bunky Carson gone —cigarette lungs—and Eddie Hudson, remember his ragtime piano —the Muskrat Ramble—sailed for Bermuda, never seen again— yacht and all . . ."

(I was suddenly a teen-aged boy and my grandfather was taking me to the Princeton Club for lunch on our shopping trip to New York. And the waiter was keening the listing of the dead and dying over the coffee cups. Had it come *my* turn so soon? It was all so illogical, contrary.)

"Cut the horseshit, Nippy. Where's the Scotch?"

"That's my boy, Billy. How do you like ol' Jay, that sybaritic bastard, getting an honorary? Are we a class or aren't we a class?"

I had to agree we were, what was left of us. Nippy had done well in his father's plant's legal department before becoming a judge during the war. "There I was, Billy, chained to this desk when all I wanted was to get on some battlewagon and let the ol' Japs have it. After all, the Germans had this Hitler *forced* on them, but those yellow monkeys—well anyway, I kept fighting my deferment because of a busted eardrum. But we kept those war orders filled."

343

"What did you make during the war, Nippy?"

"Heads for the navy. China heads, proco-ceramic auto-flush toilets. Come on, Billy, we have another half of Scotch to kill before we start for the big dingdong tonight."

Somehow Nippy didn't sound like the characters in novels about Princeton. Neither did the rest of the survivors of the class, a worn-down group of balding, pale or overtanned casualties of divorces, mergers, holding companies, wartime profits, country clubs, sanitariums, State Department employment, judges' benches. They were like rejects from John O'Hara's texts. I suppose the failures stayed away, unlike me in on a pass to ride herd on our honor man. Sober, drunk or comatose, I drank with my class.

Around four o'clock I went to my room with its etchings of the cannon on the Quadrangle, Guyot Hall's Tudor and Gothic forms. I took off my shoes and lay back on the Early American bedcover and thought of the proper nostalgic objects; banality is a fine companion at such times. All those grim thoughts of the swift passage of time, of the decay of the human body, of the false pain at seeing someone never really liked but now belonging to one's era and therefore somewhat sacred. I had a bit of the dry heaves and nothing came up.

The afternoon mellowed to a milky turquoise outside the window, and I heard below the cars coming into the town and the greeting of too-loud voices and someplace rock-and-roll fighting a recording of Schumann's "Träumerei." I coughed *huzz-huzz*. . . . I must have dozed off. I became aware of a knocking on the door, then someone coming in on unsteady feet. I looked up. Jay stood over the bed grinning down at me. "*Le citoyen d'une patrie inconnue.* A hell of a way to attend a reunion. Sleeping off a beaut already?"

I said, "Hello, Jay."

"Hello, Bill."

I wondered if I had aged as much as he had. In his sixties Jay was leaner; the Shakespearian baldness had gone a great deal farther back. His face was pale, narrow, marked with lines. He was handsomer than he had been in youth and middle age, as if his features were at last at ease with each other, conveying some intrinsic quality. He wore a dark gray wrinkled European shirt, a badly knotted red tie, a jacket that only miserable Italian tailoring could have produced, a pair of baggy tweed pants, never pressed, I was sure, since bought, and most likely given to him by some admirer. The entire man, clothing and body, suggested the intangibility, the elusiveness, that had always been Jay.

He plumped down in a chair facing the bed, and I sat up. "Come on, Bill, it isn't as if they were going to hang us. It's a celebration."

"Not much in the mood for it. Only here because they're giving you that half-assed honor."

"My policeman?"

"No. I felt you'd like a friend, an old one, on hand."

He nodded and took out a pack of English Oval cigarettes, lit one and sat looking at his unpolished shoes. "You mean I'll really have to put on the backwoods preacher's black robe and the cheesebox on my head?"

"And make a speech. What are you going to say?"

"Stamp out colleges. Bring back the harem." Jay laughed; it was like the old laugh for all his tobacco-stained teeth. "Hell, the usual academic shit, I suppose, about the wonders of classics, the power of our new gods, the dead pioneers and the fat endowment funds. I don't know, maybe I'll get a real idea."

"How's the book going?"

He looked closely at me, beat his two fists together. "Ha, the book, Jocko? The great novel, the work of my life?"

"Just the new book."

"I tell you, nosey." He put a finger to one side of a nostril and winked. "You're looking at a played-out man, a worn-down writer. Who said: 'In your struggle with the world *always* bet on the world . . .'?"

"Writer's block?"

"That's it, boychik, as old Tony used to say. I can't seem to sustain any real work. Can't seem to unlock." He beat brutally on his lean stomach. "It knots up in *here*." He touched his head. "It fuzzes away up here." He held out his nicotine-stained (and unwashed) fingers, "It doesn't come out here. Bill, you ever read Kafka on the hope of something appearing that never does?" Jay was searching the room with crafty eyes, looking for my bottle as he recited, " 'The Messiah will appear only when he is no longer needed, he will arrive the day after his arrival, he will not come on the last of the days, but on the day after the last.' Beautiful, isn't it? On all levels of an inner consciousness. If I could have written it . . ." He kissed his fingertips in an Italian gesture. *"Ah!"*

345

"You'll get past your writing block."

"It's easy to say, Bill. You're the bystander, the taster. How's Pages?"

It was sudden, but I had been expecting it. "You know, it's been over between us a long time."

"Sure, sure. But don't you two ever get together these days? After all, comrade, once in the muff with anything as wonderful as that, one doesn't go off just for another cup of Darjeeling tea, does one?" I could see he had had a few drinks, or more than a few, already. "We both, Bill, must bow our heads in homage, even drink on it; to our happy memories."

"I haven't seen Pages since 1945. We're divorced, as you damn well know."

"I know, I know. When I'm a bit looped I don't know what I know at times. I keep thinking sometimes I'm in Rome in the '20s and we're putting out that magazine and everything is just spiffy—in the slang of the period. And I smell a strong Toscana cigar and I'm someplace else, in some other time."

"Sit down, Jay, your nerves don't seem to be in good shape."

"Ha, for my age and my condition they'll serve, Jocko. You know what it's meant—being me: more than twenty years in cheap hotels, lousy food, bugs in your drink and on your women, writing prose on the backs of old letters, trying to get some lousy rich sonofabitch or bull dike with a little magazine to publish you? Then knowing it was all here inside, and blocked, *blocked*. Where's the bottle? Stop buzzing around with small talk and let's have a drink as old pals."

"You can break the writing block."

"Like hell I can. Don't you think I try? And all I can keep my mind on when I fail is old Tolstoi's words: 'If a man has learned to think, he is always thinking of his own death. What truth can there be, if there is death?' And that bugs me more. I freeze tighter than a bull's ass in fly time. I have a feeling, Bill, I haven't much more left before I go. That ties me up even more. Bill, I'm sick. Give me the bottle. They're hounding me here, following me here, keeping me away from the booze. I can't do this trick fully sober. You must tell them to ease the thumbscrews. I've been preserved in alcohol a long time—like a rare specimen. Don't they know I wouldn't be here if I drank water? Rot would have set in early. Genius is not a gratuitous grace."

"Better think of your speech. What will you say?"

"Ha, I'll lay it on the line for them; what they expect. That man, wonderful for all his faults, will survive and sustain, that art is his best product, for only on paper and canvas, and in music, has he produced his greatest hopes, greatest beauty."

"It's true in a way."

"Balls, we hoard symbols that shield the truer parts of ourselves from consciousness. You *must* have a bottle."

"No."

"I'm not going to do this thing drunk, you understand. But just a couple of belts. When is this public hanging?"

"In two days. This is just fun time now. Reunion dinner, meeting the faculty. What do you think of the college?"

"If you have to have one, it isn't too bad. You ever see those Yahoo factories at Berkeley and Texas? They're really only parking lots, but they call them universities to lure the customers to pay car fees."

There was a tap on the door. I said, "Come," and a young man came in, only he wasn't too young: about thirty, with thin, sandy hair—like nerve ends rather than hair—above too much white brow; very large amber-rimmed eyeglasses; Ivy League tailoring that didn't have the jet-set look of most of those narrow-shouldered, cuffless suits of Italian silk. He was smiling; two of his front teeth jockeyed for position. He looked feckless and I liked him.

"Hello there. I'm Mak-eye, spelled Makay, pronounced Mak-eye. Arthur D. Makay."

I said, "I remember. You're from the administration—publicity?"

"That is correct. Officially we have no publicity department. Not even public relations. But I'm on loan to the honor list group this year to-ah-cooperate with the press."

"I'm William Kite. This is Eliot Tjaden."

His eyes bugged. "Pleased, certainly very pleased." He shook our hands, Jay's first. He then rubbed his short underslung chin, smiled. "May seem odd to you that publicity is involved at such a school, but there are picture magazines, TV interviews, to think about. It's a bit much, I suppose."

"No, Artie," said Jay, "it's not a bit much. It's too much."

"You're saying, Mr. Tjaden?"

"No interviews, no telly. I talk, grab the parchment and get the hell

347

out of town. I'm only doing this, frankly, Artie, because I'm on the balls of my ass financially and the Class of '16 is paying for everything on this trip from Italy. I wanted to visit my father's grave, Artie—that's *le moi profond*—and not for the publicity. Am I clear?"

Artie Makay nodded. "I read you loud and clear. Any way you want, Mr. Tjaden. You wouldn't mind posing, I hope, for a few pictures?" He looked over at me. "In cap and gown?"

Jay laughed and stood up and put his arm around Artie. He was trying the Tjaden charm. "Look, Jocko me boy, they've bought me a suit of clothes and a dozen clean shirts and fine shoes. And I'll even get my hair cut. I'll not disgrace Old Gargoyle. So let's level, shall we? Where is the booze and the broads?"

"There's a dinner at the Red Lion Inn at seven-thirty, but first cocktails at five in the Tiger Room."

"And the chicks? Clean, bright, unchaotic, willing?"

Artie took off his glasses, looked thoughtfully at them as if they were flawed, and put them on again. "There are wives and daughters present at both events."

"Women should always be taken at room temperature. I want to get laid, Artie," said Jay, winking at me. "I believe in the older Greek cultures there were temple whores who, after the laurel leaves were awarded and made into soup, put out for the heroes."

Artie smiled, swallowed, pawed his pocket handkerchief. "Well, see you both at the Tiger Room at five." He waved good-naturedly, wide-eyed, and went out. I took out the bottle of Jack Daniels sour mash I had been hoarding in my suitcase, got two glasses from the bathroom and poured each of us a good shot. Jay swished the stuff around in his glass, sniffed, took a swallow. "You know what that Artie thinks. He thinks here are these two crumb-bum old crocks, way out of date, trying to act as if they were still laughing and scratching. Do you realize to them we're embalmed like dried-out fruit on dead trees?"

"No, I don't." I swallowed and refilled.

Jay sipped his drink. "They're so goddamn right, of course. Where do they dig us up every year to award us some lousy kudos? A rotten lot of smelly bags we are to be grabbing honors. Outhouse politicans, Nazi scientists on our side with that mad look, publishers of filthy mass-culture magazines, actors, writers like me they wouldn't read even if on a desert island. What am I doing here?"

"You want to visit the Bishop's grave."

"Come on, pour. So I do. Have Artie get us a car for tomorrow morning. That's the secret, Bill: ask for things. Material things. Don't ask for love—no—love is a body illness which after a certain point no doctor dares touch. Pal, I'm glad *you* got Pages. Not some Hollywood Greek or desert senator."

"We're going to a cocktail party."

"They'll watch me there, too closely. But I better get into the gift suit. You have a fresh razor blade? I'm traveling light."

I got the blade for him and let him look over my six ties. "You can't wear that red one, Jay; they'll think you're gay."

"I'll wear it, and my gray shirt. That makes me a character, see? America loves characters—cowboys and kooks."

"Have it your way. Are you living permanently in Italy?"

"Where else can a busted writer exist today? I hole up past some goat tracks in a leaky villa *pensione* above Florence. Marvelous peasant girls. Big in the rump and full of fire, *pasta,* garlic, olive oil. But they're being spoiled by Elvis Presley music, high heels and television. They're shaving their armpits. It was different once. Yes, the only true reality is that our youth is over. How are things with you?"

"About the same. When my brother Harry died, I found it rough going. I'm a sort of publisher's scout. I read French and Italian novels for them to see if they're worth publishing here."

"Charlie dead, Tony dead, Harry dead. Remember your grandfather talking about the black camel kneeling in the courtyard waiting to carry you off in the dark night?"

"He was a romantic. He died shitting, you know?"

"A nonverbal philosopher to the end." Jay finished his drink. "I better lay off. Old scar in my gut tissue might act up. Had ulcers bad during the war."

"How much of *Carthage* is there?"

Jay went to the table and picked up the bottle and poured out four fingers. "A good bit. How come you and Pages broke up?"

"Same reason as yours. We failed her, Jay."

He did a few silly dance steps, making a boxing gesture, and put a mock blow on my chin. "Come on, cheer up. There's booze, this is old Jay, and we were once all one big happy family. Were we ever really in Rome?"

"I have the snapshots someplace to prove it," I said, closing the bottle and putting it away in the dresser under my shirts.

349

"And, as Ernest would say, the scars to prove it. Say, he's become some Fancy Dan, hasn't he? Too bad he lost it. What a fine talent. Ernest and I, we really got loaded in Venice a couple of years ago. He's like a doomed city in Genesis with a built-in press agent."

"Pages hated Venice. Smells."

"Pages—you know, Bill, she's damn great. It's as you say. We let her down."

"I couldn't make the scene with anything, Jay, and I got mean because she was going just great. I began to drink, real solid. Never licked the yen for it after that, and I ran out on her when the war came."

"I guess lots of men used the war as an escape hatch, Jocko. It makes a nice clean break, like a bone snapping."

"I'll get over it."

"Well, these things happen. Each apparition of women in our lives is a hope that never becomes fully real." He gripped my arm and smiled, and he wasn't old and seedy, not in writer's block any more. It was the young-time thing, the earnest, strong time of our first meetings: just for that moment a feeling of ecstasy and power.

"I'll get the car, Jay, and we'll go to East Pompton tomorrow. I wonder what it's like now."

"Like the jade asshole end of the twentieth century, what else? TV antennas like the mandibles of insects, the common man too common and in power, the mass mind—*Herr Jesus Gott,* that mass mind. There isn't even a melancholy Chekhovian landscape left. We're dying, Bill, and nobody is making the sad human sound of chopping down cherry trees. Gotta dress. Ha!"

He went out humming cheerfully, snapping his fingers.

CHAPTER 35

I WAS DREAMING in some *terra incognita;* then I was young again, it became Rome and I was walking with an Italian artist's model named Bianca, past the equestrian statue of Garibaldi, and she made some peasant crack about the horse's bronze hard genitalia, and I laughed

350

and threw some coins to the street kids playing the finger game *morra.* Bianca looked like Raphael's mistress, La Fornarina. The same big black eyes and pneumatic breasts, which, when she was angry or in rut, rotated clockwise or counterclockwise, I imagined, to the motion of the earth on its axis. And I knew I wasn't dreaming, I was really back there in Rome, the bambini crawling along the curb and Bianca drinking Frascati over our dinner at Alfredo's, or was it the Cisterna? It doesn't matter. I had *porchetti,* she had *abbacchio arrosto,* and I was in a good mood because the idea of the magazine seemed good, and I had as yet not formed a permanent ménage. Over the Asti *spumante* I was explaining to Bianca the affinity of opposites, and she said, of course, all *amici,* men for women, women for men, shepherds for goats. Oh, she said, the cuckoldry, bastardy and lechery it led to.

Walking back to my *pensione,* past the Church of Santa Cecilia, the sounds of Palestrina coming from the doorway, Bianca told me it was the Feast of Santa Cecilia, *capisce?* Saint of church music. She knew, she said, because she had been to confession in the morning and been absolved and as penance had to . . . but never mind *that,* she said. She was coming to me in a state of grace and *vorrei fare una doccia.* And then it became a dream again, because as we got into bed I fell out and there I was still dressed, in the Princeton motel room, lying on the floor and Jay on the bed snoring, dressed too . . . the room smelling like a brewery and a slum playground locker room. The party at the Tiger Room had not been a success, I remembered. Jay had kicked a television writer down the stairs and had himself fallen through a collection of old drinking mugs. (Come back, Bianca—come back—*come sta?*)

Tomorrow Jay would get his honors and make a speech. I decided we wouldn't do any more drinking till it was all over; just the one I needed now to pick me up. Jay's voice said, "Save one for baby." (I wish the dialogue were better—deeper—as in a Henry James novel. But it was just two people talking. Nobody talks like H. J.)

"Look, Jay, tomorrow—"

> " *'Tomorrow, and tomorrow, and tomorrow,*
> *Creeps in this petty pace from day to day,*
> *To the last syllable of recorded time . . .'* "

At least he knew the best old quotes. "You have to be sober when you get your degree."

> " *'And all our yesterdays have lighted fools*
> *The way to dusty death. Out, out, brief candle!'* "

I divided what was left of the Jack Daniels between us (who can stand up against Shakespeare quotes?) and went into the bathroom with the idea of brushing my teeth and finding something for a blinding headache. Artie Makay (pronounced Mak-eye) was in there (surprise) soiled, smeared in his own vomit. Fortunately he was naked (stripped), sitting on the edge of the john. He moaned as he saw me and hunted for his eyeglasses (lost?). They were on the floor and I handed them to him. "What happened to you, Artie?"

"I've let the administration down. Badly, I fear."

"No, you just got drunk at the Red Lion keeping Jay from drinking."

> " *'Life's but a walking shadow, a poor player,*
> *That struts and frets his hour upon the stage,*
> *And then is heard no more . . .'* "

Artie said sadly, his nose wrinkled—he smelled: "It was my first big chance, Mr. Kite. Publicitywise, I mean. And I muffed it. I lost Mr. Tjaden. He was carried off somewhere drunk and disorderly."

"Now, Artie, your memory is much worse than mine. He walked off with Mrs. Smith, our class widow. Don't cry. Goddamn it, I hate to see a grown man cry. And *where* are your clothes?"

Artie had one of those thin white boy's bodies even at thirty, that look indecent because they seem to be made to be hidden from all but scoutmasters. He cupped his privates shyly. "I don't know where my apparel is. When we left the Cowley Bar later, these fellows, Class of '46, tried to debag me and throw me in the fountain. I suppose they went too far."

> " *'. . . it is a tale*
> *Told by an idiot, full of sound and fury,*
> *Signifying nothing. . . .'* Hey, Jocko! You talking to yourself?"

"Jay's in bed. Send somebody to your room for new clothes. Meanwhile put on my bathrobe."

"The disgrace, the revolting aspects of it all." (There was a sticky

352

mess on his chest.) "The failure," said Artie in my bathrobe (after using a towel). "I mean this was my chance. Publicity has been let down."

"Cheer up, Artie, and get the hell out of the bathroom. I need it. I'll try and have Jay pose for some pictures in East Pompton: Local Boy Returns to Old Home Town. Okay? Setting for his novel *Fragments from Carthage* . . . you know, that sort of thing?"

"If you only would." (The smile of a flogged schoolboy.)

"Now go get a message off for some clothes and keep Jay away from any more alcohol and Mrs. Smith. Oh, we need a car, say around noon?"

"Around noon? Can do." Artie blinked behind his glasses, rolled up the sleeves of the robe (too long for him) and went out of the bathroom. I committed the morning indecencies and tried to remember the night. The cocktail party had been pretty good; Class of '16 held up pretty well, what was left of it; the drink was pretty fair, the fight fair. The TV man, hair cut *en brosse,* had said, "You, Tjaden, and Faulkner are the best we have." Jay had agreed and said, "But I only admit Faulkner, nobody else around." I think it was talk of a group of writers, all named Mule or Mailer, Roth or Gold, or so it seemed to me, that got Jay upset, and the TV man said Jay's reputation was made by *not* writing. Jay resented that and then the feathers and glasses started flying and the TV man was on his head and ass down the steps. Jay tried to call Oxford, Mississippi (to tell William Faulkner what had happened). The large plump widow, Gondril Smith, whose husband had been Class of '16 ("was his third wife—he died in *these* arms") told Jay she had heard "Faulkner— I'm not sure— is dead." Jay said that was too damn bad, and he and Gondril Smith went to the bar and had some drinks (in honor of a great writer so lately dead). Gondril was in her forties and tight in her girdle, but a damn good head in drink. (Artie said to me, "I mean Balzac says a woman is at her best in her later years; the best parts wrinkle last.")

I had to agree with him there (no names, however), and after that the drinking got stronger and the dinner at the Red Lion was a shambles. But Jay and Gondril Smith and Artie and I didn't stay because somebody said there was a big shindig at the Anthony estate where the swans used to be and the flat-chested debutantes of 1914–1915 used to walk in their pleated skirts (get kissed in the

353

grape arbor). But the Anthony estate was long gone; only a row of grills and bars, ranch house style, stood there now, so we had either the wrong information or the wrong address, or the wrong decade. Jay cursed them with the shattered majesty of a Lear.

I did manage to lock Gondril Smith in a phone booth and get Jay back to the motel, and that was that. . . .

I came out of the bathroom, and Jay and Artie were seated at a little wheeled-in table drinking orange juice (looking at buttered toast but not eating). I pulled up a chair and poured black coffee. We all looked ludicrous, Jay's eyes hooded like a sick hawk's (birds were once reptiles).

"They say this doesn't help. But it's hot."

Jay picked up and looked at a copy of the *Princeton News* that had come with the breakfast table. "I'm going back to Italy. The hell with the honors. Artie, find out when Alitalia has a plane leaving."

Artie choked on his coffee, sputtered, "But, *but,* Mr. Tjaden—"

I said, "Jay, we can't let Artie down. He has a job to do and we've snafued it."

Artie nodded and grabbed at a bit of toast (nibbled on it). "I've got you a car and driver. Be outside at one o'clock."

"What time is it now?" Jay asked. "Anybody see a big plump broad? Somehow I scent a woman on my clothes."

Artie looked over at my grandfather's watch, still attached to the chain in my waistcoat. "Eleven-thirty-six. If you'll shower and shave . . . you'll have time for the auto trip."

Jay went over to the bed and lay down (strong premonition of death). "I learned how to do without all that showering and shaving most of the time when I had to in Italy. Wake me at one."

I waved Artie off when he wanted to protest. He went out into the hall to await a messenger with some clothes.

"Bill, I'm sorry for poor Artie. He's one of those doers, pushers, explainers. Meeting all over America. They have always existed. But in the past Emerson, William James, Darrow mocked them, laughed at them. Now the nation is on its racing toes, driving itself hard, and if you protest, someone will say, That's the way the cookie crumbles, that's the way the prune wrinkles."

"Go to sleep, Jay."

There was a honking outside the window and I looked out at a Cadillac as long as a tapeworm. Our car was on time. I got Jay—

354

protesting he couldn't face his father in this condition—down to the street. Gondril Smith sat behind the wheel of the car, smiling at us . . . blond long hair, plump overcurved body in green silk. "I heard you needed a car so I volunteered. I said, Take little old me."

"Thank you, darling," said Jay, grasping her gloved hand. "If we leave now we can get rid of Artie."

"Why not, Jaysie?" Gondril smiled at Jay, and Jay patted her jeweled wrist. I got into the back and he sat in front next to the widow and we started off with no sign of Artie. The car was one of those monsters of the period with a cruel set of tail fins, spurred like a Gothic instrument of torture, pronged with sword shapes as seen on the chariots of the Assyrians. The hood was in the abstract form of a shark's head set with chrome teeth.

Jay said, "The Cadillac is something to seat a dead tribal leader in and bury, car and all, in some tomb."

Gondril beamed on Jay and flung back her long blond hair flying in the wind.

Jay said, "Stop at the supermarket, darling. I need cigarettes."

"I've got some, Jaysie."

"Ha. Not my brand." Jay got out and walked across the supermarket blacktop strip toward the beehive of activity in the red-and-gold market.

"He's pretty remarkable at his age," said Gondril, inspecting her lipstick in the rearview mirror.

"Don't trust him. Never trust a writer, Mrs. Smith. It's a tortuous road to Eros."

"Huh—who's Eric? Jaysie reminds me of my brother Georgie. I adored Georgie. He died in Pasadena, you know. Buried in Forest Lawn. I cried for a week."

I was still hung over and I said it was a fine place for a burial. Jay came out carrying a brown paper bag, got into the car and patted Gondril's plump but finely formed knee.

"Drive on. I can face extinction now."

"How you talk."

Jay put the bunched open end of the paper bag to his mouth and I knew he had a fifth of whiskey there. He passed it back to me. I said, "Neither of us is getting tanked, Jay. You have a speech to make tomorrow and a degree to get."

355

Jay cuddled Gondril's thigh. "Listen to the rinky-dink square."

I took one long sip of foul whiskey, or rather alcohol-flavored whiskey. I swallowed, opened the window and threw bag and bottle out into a field. "That's all for today."

Jay shrugged his shoulders, but I suspected he was crafty enough to have an extra bottle someplace in one of the inner pockets of his jacket—one of those sports jackets made originally with poacher's bags.

Gondril drove well, and while she drove she told us the story of her life, her various married lives, divorces, her widowhood residence in Cleveland ("dull, my dears, from Dullsville"), and her income which came from turpentine, sulphur and shrimp boats. Jay said it was the modern way; a princess no longer came with a noseful of rubies and diamonds, elephants, and a train of jackasses bearing spices and mandrake.

I looked at Jay in the mirror reflection—was he drunk or maudlin?

"I don't know the road, Bill, to East Pompton any more. Perhaps this shark chariot does; it's on an eight-lane highway west. Ha, the trees had to be sacrificed for great factories making moon missiles, atom bomb parts, rocket shapes, jet planes. And laboratories, darling, whose miserable secrets one could only guess at."

The landscape was laid out flat, lying like a Mondrian painting, slicing off hills, bulldozing away trees, brooks and landmarks. Jay held Gondril's neck in a handful of fingers. "It's the world of George Orwell, all held together by highways, freeways, throughways, that turn and twist around each other with off and on ramps like concrete snakes screwing. Cloverleaves and overpasses, tunnels. I've seen it all before in some of the old films: *Metropolis, Shape of Things to Come,* dreadful motion pictures, darling, that tried to show the mechanical world of the future. We have been trapped. Here are those screenplays redone for earnest."

Gondril said, "Don't use words like screwing, Jaysie. You're too fine a man for vulgarity."

It was a shock seeing a land where we had fished and hunted, flown kites, played ball, picnicked, bicycled on country lanes—all done away with.

Jay leaned his head on Gondril's shoulder. "It's a mad world, Gondril, burning up its resources to go plunging, damn fools, into space."

"Mr. Smith said it was good for the economy, Jaysie. Gives jobs.

Pays dividends. This car is paid for by my stock in Dyno-Hifly Missiles. You've got to get with it, Jaysie, or be left behind."

"You're so right," said Jay, sinking back on his spine and closing his eyes. "Bill, we've got to get with it."

I said I was sorry I had thrown away the bottle. We drove down quickly to a great overpass and down a roller coaster of a wing of cloverleaf and were shot out onto a side road of merely six lanes, and before us (like the towers of a new Camelot) was what had once been East Pompton. Plastic plants rimmed it, huge hangars of an airfield, the snouts of control towers, and rows of military jets like lean bees jockeying on the ground. Armed sentries stood in de Chirico helmets at gates, and beyond what had been Miller's Brook was a mass of sculpture made of radar forms twisting and turning like mobiles over a naked hill where oak and walnut once had grown.

Royal Street was widened, landmarks gone; parking meters stood like rows of space robots facing new façades of glass and plastic and blind windows worked into walls.

"Royal Street," I said. "Gondril, drive with care."

"The British, darling, in their defeat at Trenton came this way in the dark, and at Princeton Washington defeated them and they moved through these streets toward New Brunswick, a rearguard action. Dead Hessians in the hedges and redcoats frozen stiff found in the spring, what the wolves had left. You can still see the cannonball holes in the old houses."

"*What* old houses?" asked Gondril, slowing down for a row of traffic lights. "It's a good thing the redcoats got out of here before this traffic took over."

"Turn left for Frenchman Street," I said. "It's not so busy."

I was wrong. The old mansions were gone, all the Victorian beauties, the solid General Grants, the Stanford White marble Italian villas. All impractical specimens destined for extinction, but so comfortable, so well made—so personal to their owners' tastes. It was all apartment houses. "Cheek by jowl," said Jay. "We should have known, of course. All those brain types, the executives, scientists, chemists, experts, German *Wunderkinder* we brought over to live here. They drain the nation dry and exist in style. Look at the sonsofbitches' houses, all glass and modern piano-box bad taste. No ornaments, no decor, just blind walls with blind eyes. And imagine the people in them, Gondril. Shot into their anthills, their hives, by the five o'clock traffic, by herd instinct. Fed by frozen TV dinners, air-

357

conditioned, Ex-Laxed, tranquilized, Benzedrined, fucking on Hollywood king-sized beds with built-in TV, radio, hot and cold contraceptives. Breeding more little swine in their own image so they can overrun the universe."

"You said a word I dislike, Jaysie. I'm not a lousy puritan, you know, and I don't hold to outworn morals. But the word fuck, frankly, I don't think should be used between men and women."

"You do fuck, don't you, Gondril?"

"That's beside the point. My husband and I always called it—you can smile—lovee activity."

"I salute you both. Why should I smile?"

We were near the corner of my grandfather's house on Frenchman Street. I should not have come. The old house was gone, just as Harry was gone and my grandfather and grandmother were gone. A huge shopping-center service station, all under a suspended roof, a free-flow roof, was there, held up by four huge pylons. It covered acres of concrete which had sealed off all the earth that had held the house and grounds. Shops, rows of gasoline pumps, a tunnel of chain-hauled car wash, rows of robots selling Cola, hot soup, postage stamps, prepacked paper towels and something modestly nominated the Female Hygenia Kit.

"Pull up," I said. "I have to buy something." I was shaky, and as I put a foot down where the side porch had once been, the chain-hung swing where Jay and I as boys had smoked my grandfather's H. Upmann cigars, I felt the earth shudder and my skin creep; there were spasms of peristalsis. I cried out. Jay said, "They didn't have to do it for this, Bill. Not for money and plastics and moon bombs and outer-space shit. If they'd done it to build schools and idiot children's homes, or better, all right, all right. But not for *this*. *Dio te salve, Maria,* may dogs mate on their graves." He was wrong, of course. Life insurance and rise in property values had replaced the local belief in Heaven.

A man in white with an admiral's cap and greasy hands at a pump said, "You want the Super, the Luxury or the Jetone?"

Jay said softly, "What about the Regular?"

The man looked at a thumbnail shaped like a small turtle. "We don't have no gasoline called Regular any more, mister."

I went into the shop that sold barbecues, pots, portable wine bins, canned king crab but had a sign reading: LIQUOR. I bought two fifths of Old Forester and a bottle of Black & White in the mood of Timon of Athens.

Jay was watching the row of autos creeping out of the car-wash tunnel. Negroes—my fine Billy Brunswick race—men and women in white rubber outfits—were swabbing, wiping and polishing. I got into the car and poured three paper cups half full of Old Forester. We sat sipping while our shark chariot was serviced by gas and air tubes and a crew of wipers and feelers of metal entrails. Jay held out his paper cup and said, "Let's us visit the underworld. It's always done when fates and furies send heroes on their way home; it gives them a look at what is below our world."

"Who went?" asked Gondril, shaky, and sweating under Jay's ardent attentions and movements.

"Orpheus among others, darling. Son of Apollo and Calliope—the first big-mouth wife. Orpheus played a good solid lyre and followed his dead wife Eurydice into the underworld by dazzling Pluto with a jam session. He was allowed to lead her back to life—provided he didn't look back."

"What, Jaysie, what happened?"

"He looked back. That always made no sense to me. Why look back? He had his chick again. Maybe if we all went down to the underworld we'd know why he looked back."

Gondril nodded and pursed her lips and let Jay's hand stay. "You mean go through the tunnel and get the car washed?"

"Yes."

"With us in it?"

I said, "It's against the rules."

"Rules, my dear Bill, are there to be craftily broken. How do you think this horrible town was built? Gondril, do you have a ten-dollar bill for Charon's attendant who will let us ride through Hades?"

Jay recited parts of the Orphikos Dionysus creed (in a translation) as we rode, all car windows closed, through the tunnel—clouds of soap and detergent, storms of water beating at us from all scientific directions, the tunnel lit by banks of tube lights. Cars like huge wet snails before us and cars behind us, all creeping up an incline and then down again, locked on a moving chain belt going at a steady three miles an hour.

From the sealed car we toasted the Brunswick families in their white rubber as they rubbed and hosed us. They waved to us and we lifted paper cups and sipped. I drank to cool off. Jay took a fresh drink. "Charon, the demon, with eyes of glowing coal, beckoning them, collects them all; smites with his oar whoever lingers. . . ." He beeped the horn, turned the lights off and on, turned up the radio. Majestically we rose out into the stab of sunlight, dripping like a spouting whale from every metal deformed torture twist on our spurred tails, every shark's tooth in the hood. The radio was tuned in on some folk singers' hootenanny:

> Hand me down my walking cane,
> I'm gonna catch the midnight train.
>
> If I had listened to what you said,
> I'd be at home in my feather bed.
>
> If I should die in Tennessee,
> Just send my bones home C.O.D.
>
> But if I die in New York State,
> Just ship my body back by freight.
>
> Hand me down my walking cane,
> I'm gonna catch the midnight train.
>
> The devil chased me 'round a stump,
> I thought he'd catch me at every jump.
>
> Oh, hell is deep, and hell is wide,
> Ain't got no bottom, ain't got no side.

Gondril rearranged her green silk dress and bobbed her neck and torso in dignified amusement at our game. She seemed swollen with some placid expectancy—like a queen bee preparing to egg.

CHAPTER 36

THE OLD BURIAL GROUND of the New Brethren of Christ had been small, and hidden away on cheap, unpopular bottomland. For this reason it had escaped the fate of the richer, more fashionable graveyards and had survived. Survived as a weedy, neglected, sun-tormented place. The cocoons and nets of spiders and moths were hanging from bullbrier and hardy roses grown wild, with thorns like barbwire.

Leaving the car, we walked along a grown-over path—gravel long since washed out. Gondril insisted on coming with us. The fence of wooden palings was down, and a very black crow rose from a patch of yellow weeds. Jay pointed at it: "Dostoevski's non-stinking monk."

I followed him and Gondril through the pungent weeds, the smell of rotting wood, the hum of insects. Some of the gravestones had been overturned; an old pint flask, its glass become pale purple by sunlight, lay across the path. There were no stone angels, no great lumps of granite or marble, no bleeding hearts, saints or *putti*. The New Brethren of Christ lay buried under soft brown stone slabs. Weather wore them down quickly, seeming to soften bereavement and excruciating loss.

We came in the dry June midday to a mound on which wild daisies spilling egg-yolk pollen and small blue flowers grew. The gravestone was tilted, and in the midst of all the neglect the grave seemed to suggest a catatonic state rather than death. It was the Bishop's grave. Jay brushed aside the vines to expose, as spiders scurried to other darkness, the stone with the name *Tjaden,* and a few faint lines of text under it:

> *Shall mortal man be more just than God?*
> *Shall a man be more pure than his maker?*

"What's that?" Gondril asked, dusting her dress and her gloved hands one against the other.

"The Book of Job. 'And so they sat down with him upon the ground seven days and seven nights, and none spake a word unto him: for they saw that his grief was very great.' Those Old Testament hipsters could really write."

I asked, "Why do the New Brethren neglect the place like this?"

"There are no more New Brethren here. Missiles, plastics, atoms drove them off." Jay was staring at the grave. "It wasn't a fancy religion, didn't dress itself up. Its mistake was taking the words of Christ seriously and leaving out the robes, candles, fancy Latin, easy answers, ritual punishments, confessions. It didn't have a chance when the Bishop died. Did you bring the bottles?"

I said I had. We sat on rank grass and the three of us all got a bit crocked. Being out in the hot sun didn't help. We had been sipping and drinking steadily since leaving Princeton, and since the journey through the car-wash Hades we had been buying fresh supplies. I had carried a cardboard carton marked LUX YOURSELF TO BEAUTY. In it I had collected at a shop sandwiches, garlic pickles, an assortment of bourbon, Scotch, and—for Gondril, who had mentioned her preference for it—a bottle labeled "Royal Romanoff Vodka," and in the Cyrillic alphabet: *My vashi druz'ya!*

"We could," I said, "go down by the river and wade barefoot."

Jay shook his head. "It's most likely a public sludge recovery plant or paved over for a highway." He held up a paper cup and I filled all around. Gondril nuzzled against him. "It's a mad day, Jaysie. Is it always like this with you? Picnicking on your father's grave?"

"Graveside? Ha . . . I'm an old man, Gondril. I want to stay with him a little bit before I go off and die myself."

She kissed Jay's cheek. "You're not old, not to me."

"That's because you have a rich, romantic inside—like good chocolates—otherwise after three husbands you'd give up."

I put sandwiches—corned beef, tuna, peanut-butter-and-jelly— onto paper plates, gave out paper napkins, sipped whiskey and bit a moon-shaped section out of a corned-beef-on-rye. We sat chewing, drinking, while the wind came to stir the weeds and coarse grass. A one-eyed cat with mottled white fur ran across the path and seemed to object with a mew of apprehension to our being there. Graveyards give me a heightened sensitivity. I felt the Bishop near us, mocking me. (A cat is the accepted shape of ghostly communication in all occult circles.)

Jay took a swallow, threw away the empty cup, and pushed his face toward Gondril, who was reclining in the weeds by his side, burrs on her green silk, runs in her sheer stockings. "It's a sort of sacred moment, Gondril. Hereabouts Bill and I were kids, adolescents, now just crocks of store whiskey. We are youth gone, feeding and guzzling, soon to be acting at love."

"Jaysie, don't talk as if I'm fifty or anything like that."

"Darling, you're a fine figure of a bag of woman. But me, I feel harmonious connections of memory, where only the past seems adequate. Ha, you, too, Bill?"

"I'm not as drunk as you are."

"The hell you're not. Even Gondril is looped here on paths where

362

nothing began but many things ended." Jay held up a fresh paper cup of Old Forester. "O, Father, I salute you, sir. You had a great talent for intimacy. Now grieved and decrepit, your son has come to say goodbye. I can't join you because I don't believe as you did—forgive my belch; I'm very drunk—in an expectancy of something on the other side of the gravestone." He pinched Gondril. "But I've brought you, sir, a fine plump heifer to sacrifice on your grave."

"Really, Jaysie, really . . . if you don't respect me, think of . . . of . . . .well, there are Christians buried here."

Jay sighed, made a kissing sound, put his hands between her nylon-clad legs.

"No, no, not here . . . I'd die of shame."

I said, "She's right. I wouldn't say this is paying the proper respect to the Bishop."

Jay grinned. "I find a Bunyanite when I thought of you, Bill, as a Voltairean. Not a fair trade, no, not at all. What do you say, Gondril, huh?"

"It's itchy on the weeds, and it's outdoors and broad daylight, and I'm a Lutheran and respect the dead."

We left the remains of the lunch to the ants and the grave mice, the empty bottles to the sun. We walked drunkenly, arms around each other, to the monster car parked on the dirt road.

Is there not an appointed time to man upon earth?
And are not his days also like the days of an hireling?

I had given up the idea of getting Jay back to Princeton. He was in no shape for tonight's reunion banquet of the Class of '16. But I hoped by morning he would be able to face the speech he had to make when he accepted the honorary degree.

Gondril was whispering she was "in love truly for the first time, really, for the first time in her life" and showing a proprietary jealousy about Jay as she confessed that the family gardener had deflowered her at the age of eight. Jay made her tell it all in detail and said she was stained with Lutheran conscience. I drove, for I didn't trust either of them. I didn't trust myself much, but if we got killed I wanted my death to be suicide by my own driving.

Gondril said that at college she had a lesbian experience with a gym teacher and two of her husbands had been indifferent performers of "lovee activity." Jay's head, wobbling on a thread, said it was all the goddamn orange juice and frozen TV dinners they ate in Cleveland. He added that he found her to the touch "pleasing as a melon," and he promised her great delights as soon as we took rooms at the Highway House. I didn't think he could or would; he was very drunk and looking very old. Age is intolerable when it takes no pride in itself. I felt sorry for Jay. He looked like a figure in one of those *quattrocento Last Judgments* one sees in Tuscan churches, faded, patched, a picture of the would-be sinner going wearily on his way to a dreary pleasure.

Only the rich look of the Detroit chariot got us admitted, baggage-less, shaky, to Highway House, an overmodern complex of buildings and dining rooms, bars, grills and service stations among pines and the last of the beetle-infested Jersey elms in their terminal illness.

We each took a room, and Jay managed to hold up a giggling Gondril, who said she lacked her overnight bag and nightie. I lay down on the bed smelling of just-gone occupants; the woman's hair, her personal self, the man's socks, his cheap cigars, the damp towels, the very patina of scents of all the hasty fornications going back since the place had been erected. I snorted, growled and fell away into a troubled sleep.

When I awoke it was a golden dusk with blue edges, like *crêpes* burning in brandy (a hell of a way to see things). I got to the phone by willpower and holding on, and called the Administration Building at Princeton and asked for Arthur Makay, "pronounced Mak-eye." Someone said he was in the club steam room and could not be called. I said they better haul his ass out of there and to the phone; it was beyond even life or death. The slightly Oxford voice said who was I really to take such a tone? I said bullshit really; if the college didn't want a snafu of its main commencement plans, they better get Artie to the mother-freying phone, and I'd hold on it if I didn't pass out. I sat on the edge of the bed, feeling very ill, my mouth tasting for some reason of jambalaya. There was about an inch of vodka left in the Czar's bottle and I had it. After a while Artie's voice, sucking, breathing, came to me over the phone.

"Now, Artie, don't get your bowels in an uproar. Tjaden is with me. Been laying flowers on his father's grave. Perfect son, fine gesture. No, didn't take any goddamn pictures for you. He's resting. Of course he's drunk. Worse, he's trying to lay Mrs. Smith. No, I can't tell you where. No, damn it, you want him there in the morning or don't you? I'm tired of playing nursemaid. Smith. S-m-i-t-h. It can't hurt unless it brings on a heart attack. Not her, *him*."

Artie said he was sorry, he was very sick himself, couldn't eat, could only sit on the john and pump bile, his whole life was a disaster. He was ruined. And there was a Fulbright he was *almost* promised. And now *this*. I told him to hold on for dear old Princeton. I would see it through. He could say Tjaden was visiting boyhood scenes getting material for his novel in progress, *Fragments from Carthage,* and if Artie played his cards right Jay might dedicate the book to him, which was better than a lousy Fulbright which gave you little more than some rights to buggery at Oxford or Cambridge, or was it the Sorbonne? Artie didn't know what to say, and so I told him to go back to the steam room and he'd see us in the morning.

I wondered what I was really going to do. Gondril was a fine woman but an emotional Cleveland matron, perhaps rich. She could be as full of sex as a sturgeon. Jay was a sick alcoholic—there was no doubt about it—and those scar tissues from old ulcer wounds could break open again in his animated carcass. And he was old. He was sixty-two, and looked older now that our drinking bout had broken him down and the sight of his father's grave had assaulted him in all its neglect. He was something my Calvinist reticence wanted to avoid talking too firmly to.

I had to do something. Yet what the hell was he really to me in his present image? I had not seen him for many years. This wasn't by a long shot the golden boy I had been young with, had all the crazy fun of the East Pompton years with; and even that was lost, a town wiped out by a monster called progress. There was a terrible incompatibility between the ideal image I had built up (Jay) and the reality (Jay). A writer who had little popular acceptance, a novelist who had hardly finished one book and couldn't finish the second. A man who had traded on his genius (if it was genius), who enjoyed in some perverse way sinking into a debilitating stagnation. Our lives had all gone so quickly, a chimeric dream of mercurial vacillation. La Stein had said to me once, "I sometimes think only a life work has any meaning." The old kosher battle-ax, the big lez, was right, of course. We're nothing but what we leave behind, like the drunkard in the Ben Jonson poem ("a *crapula*")—that was us.

I would be trying (Duty's child) to get Jay sober in the morning for his honoring—but the image was shattered; he was just a sour-smelling old man, little different from me.

I went out on the balcony of my Highway House room. Below were faceless people gossiping in a twilight punctuated by glowing cigarette ends. I was aware of the natural sounds of reality—a car starting, a record playing Richard Strauss whining to its end, the flush of plumbing—and the smell of coffee, the actually pleasant scent of a far-off skunk (which close up is not so pleasant). Night hid the intrinsically hideous mass the country around East Pompton had become. The old things had been annihilated by bland tolerance, by greed and power struggles, but basic life was going on all around me. The functions of sexual organs, urinary, propagative, erotic or ama-tive, were audible through thin walls. Poker players and dice shooters called for room service. I absorbed the clink of Ping-Pong paddles in the patio, the woodsmoke mixed with burning beef fat signaling the big steaks on the charcoal grills. And I knew God flowed over all— for I now sensed God as a fluid (and not a solid).

I turned from my philosophical brinkmanship back indoors. No, not Sodom and Gomorrah, no Roman hetaerae (Faustina, Poly-xena), I was among the citizens of the republic, digging the jive, making out, being very shoe, very camp. I *only* was really old *old,* the adrenalin flowing sluggish, and what was I doing here with all this nauseating crap of a Princeton class reunion? I hadn't even thought enough of the joint to graduate.

Someone was in my room. It was Jay, standing just inside the door, in his soiled underwear—just shorts, his socks, full of lint, fallen down around his ankles. He was holding the empty vodka bottle and looking over his shoulder at me, nodding diagonally like a monk.

I said, "Nothing left."

"Call room service."

"You have to be in shape."

"The kid's last fight, ha?" He sat down on the bed. His ribs stuck out, his chest had fallen in, he was round-shouldered, scarred, fish-belly white, the muscles of his calves seemed atrophied. "Listen, chum, you have to do me a big favor."

I shook my head. "I have to get you to bed for the last time."

366

"That's just it, Bill. I've been trying to get to bed with Gondril and listen—I'm ashamed to say it."

"You couldn't get your pecker up?"

"Ha, Jocko, you've been there too. Never mind. I've got to lay her or I'll develop another block—sexual, not literary, worse. I'm in love. I want to ejaculate for her. Make the scene."

"That's sex, Jay. Love is an emotion you feel."

"Don't hand me that." He wiped his face with his hands. "Look, Bill, it's a symbolic deed I need. She's in 6-C, the door is open. She's crocked but she keeps asking for lovee, Jaysie, lovee."

"Revolting."

"Sure it is, Bill, to somebody like you, not in love. But I find it affecting. She's alive, she's warm, she's wonderfully made for all the fat. Bill, you go give her a bang by proxy for me. She'll never know the difference, she's that boozed, and I'll not get blocked there too. She'll be ever so grateful, and I'll be fine in a day or so—I know it."

"Since when are you screwing with my cock? You're drunk, Jay. She's drunk. I'm drunk myself. Let's all just sleep."

He stood up, desperate, ridiculous, despair on his face. "Some lousy, inadequate friend. Carried you from since we were kids. I ask you *what?* A few gestures, a little contact with something that isn't anything but pleasure, a soporific effect. You querulous swine, you're crucifying me into permanent impotence. Go on, go! Room 6-C."

I said, "Jay, when you're sober you'll be revolted at what you suggest."

"You're not going to do it?"

"No, I'm not."

"Well, I'm not going to Princeton in the morning. How's that?"

"I don't give a shit any more."

"I suppose you think you're seeing the lath-behind-the-plaster in Eliot Tjaden? A phony in everything, even in the genitalia? Besides, you couldn't anyway. You lost it—that's why Pages brushed you off." He made a priestly gesture of blessing. *"Ne nous laissez pas succomber à la tentation."*

I thumbed my nose. "Jay, you're wearing your halo around your balls."

He turned in the doorway, ridiculous in his shorts, floppy socks. "This is the end of the friendship, Bill Kite. And over *what?* A little

367

exercise. All I asked was a gesture any man would execute for a friend."

"Sorry, Jay, it had to be like this."

"Not much of a tag line, is it, to a lifetime of what?" He stood there, his hand on the doorknob, a patch of rash visible over his left kidney, his hand scratching it, unaware it was scratching, and he said, "No?"

"No, Jay. Why don't you just tell her you did? She'll never know."

"Christ, that's a rotten thing to suggest."

"You too might think so in the morning. See?"

"No, no see," he said as he went out, still scratching.

I closed the door and said to nothing but the door, "Goodbye, Jay." It seemed a goofy way to part, and for such a comic, melancholy reason. I just hoped the day's dispositions wouldn't bring night's bad dreams.

I lay down without undressing. To understand without knowing each other—that is modern companionship. That is Jay and myself. Between us now the process of a final mortality is at work. The female pudendum, called jelly-roll and hog-eye by Billy Brunswick (so long ago), had done us in. Only the moment is true—*tick-tock,* and that one is gone, another gone, another gone . . . another. . . .

Still on the bed . . . moment by moment ticking away. Poor Jay; children and artists never lose some of their innocence. Still, we had once had it: the precious and the incommunicable. I turned my head and looked at the phone. I could still call him, I could change my mind. I didn't have papal infallibility, and Gondril was only . . . But I just lay staring at the ceiling. I lay in a carapace of hurt esteem, anger and pride.

Eliot Tjaden did not make the commencement speech that year at Princeton; he wasn't awarded the honory degree of Doctor of Arts and Letters. At seven the next morning (the desk clerk of Highway House had told me) Jay and Gondril Smith left in the spiny Cadillac for Cleveland. I never saw Jay again.

EDITOR'S NOTE: William Kite was not accurate about the awarding of the honorary degree. The East Pompton *Home News* of June 15, 1956, carried the following item:

NATIVE SON HONORED AT PRINCETON . . .
ILLNESS PREVENTS ELIOT TJADEN FROM RECEIVING
HONORARY DEGREE IN PERSON

The major commencement speech that was to be made by the noted modern author who grew up in our town, Eliot Tjaden, Class of 1916, was given instead by Senator Volney K. Perrigan. A recurring illness prevented Mr. Tjaden from attending, the University announced. The honorary degree was accepted for him by John Lawrence, acting secretary of the American Academy of Arts and Letters, and will be forwarded to him.

If Eliot Tjaden actually did accompany Mrs. Smith to Cleveland, it was not a visit of any length, for six months later in Florence, Italy, suffering from ulcers, he was admitted to the private Boboli Hospital on the Via Tornabuoni. The Writers League of America was appealed to to pay his hospital bills as he was reported "to be alone, and completely destitute. . . ."

I have been unable to trace any Gondril Smith, and William Kite most likely used a fictitious name for the woman involved. No one named Gondril Smith is listed in the city directories of Cleveland or its surrounding countryside. No dead Smith was a member of the Class of 1916.

William Kite gives no indication of his own activities from this period until 1962, when he again takes up his story in the next section. He had been doing, as he said, some work for publishers, reading French and Italian novels and reporting on their suitability for the American reader in translation. But after 1956 he does not seem to have continued such work. One major publisher (who wants his name withheld) wrote me—in part—the following letter, on my inquiring into the matter:

I do not think William Kite was capable of much serious reading after 1956 when he filed his last report with us on some European novels. The report was badly confused and in part made no sense. It was not so much that he had been drinking, but rather that he seemed senile and perhaps had had a small stroke. He could not remember names and places when I last spoke to him, and if he did, he became overtalkative, repeating something he had already told me again and again. However, I do remember several clear periods of brilliant conversation lasting hours, when he just sat in my office, drinking and talking about the changes that had happened in America, going off into some scandalous stories about some very important world figures he had known. Those details of his stories that I have been able to check seem to bear out his versions. He could be very witty, ironic and biting, but also lyric, and perhaps for modern tastes in rare moments overripe.

I would say that I last saw him at his worst, when he was still in

369

shock from a fearful bender after the affair of Eliot Tjaden's degree at Princeton. William Kite is supposed to have gone into a sanitarium for some months and come out in much better condition. I have no idea how he lived; he was desperate and several times tried to get our firm to advance him small sums on a book he said he was working on. I regret to say—it makes us appear such beasts—that the policy of our firm is such that we could not give him an advance without at least seeing part of a publishable manuscript.

If the Kite texts you are editing show any merit, we would be happy to consider them with a view to publication.

Cordially, etc. . . .

An unrelated note in pencil in the Kite manuscript: *"Manger de la vache enragée*—having a lean time of it . . . a sense of malaise. Have talked to some publisher, a Levantine reptile of a fellow, partner of a Yankee dog molester, who boozed me but didn't offer a red cent in eating money and in the end practically kicked me out on my ass."

370

BOOK NINE

FROM WILLIAM KITE'S POCKET NOTEBOOK

Whence did all that fury come?
From empty tomb or Virgin womb?
Saint Joseph thought the world would melt
But liked the way his finger smelt.
                                              —W. B. YEATS

The true Christian will always offer a drowning
man a cup of water.   —W. K.

Old men grow harder to please as they grow
more unpleasing.   —MONTAIGNE

CHAPTER 37

NOW

THE PAST DIES, Jay once wrote, yet is continuous—the best bony parts of it survive, the soft perishable stuff sluffs off. I have, perhaps, failed to materialize fully the reality in my life; I must go back and reread what I have written to see how much of what I have put down is of my fantasies rather than of myself and my world. Is the *I* here *now?* And the *now*—is that *I?* I remember talking to Thomas Mann one night in Zurich, and his saying, with that gray German seriousness of his, sleek with the power of being so right that often stains his work, "Only where the 'I' is a problem is there any sense in writing."

So I do have an excuse for going on. I feel like Mann's hero von Aschenbach in *Death in Venice;* I sense my isolation and yet dependence on others to whom I'm only an object in the landscape. And I, too, am I approaching death? Hardly unlikely unless the rules have been changed or the process improved for a more dignified exit. In the late afternoon before the Samuel Pfaelzers' cocktail hour there is a period of reflective melancholy, but at such a time I am at ease with my mortal limitations, the shoulder-shrugging acceptance of an unfulfilled life. I am beyond desolate grief, viciousness and certainly sensuality (except as a spectator sport). Only retrospect is left . . . and the two daily martinis, my crystal ball, into which I shall gaze for the density of life. While with some delicately apprehensive glance I look slyly about me at the other house guests this weekend and wonder *why* are we *here,* am *I* the *I,* are *you* the *you?* But conversation is never to be put to any serious use at these times. That is Rule One. No response to our *tristesse.* (The vermouth-tasting olives, Jay once said, are our stations of the cross, our *via*

373

dolorosa.) We are not really involved; that is Rule Two. I am working on Rule Three, a scheme that will do away with any reason for going on with this task of writing: *Experience and a fairly long life aren't any help.*

I can hear them moving below toward the terrace. It must be near five o'clock.

EDITOR'S NOTE: In the following section, as it is nearly contemporary with the present and for reasons to be made clear later, I have changed names in two instances. Both Bantley and Santa Madre are such fictions. The entire section (in several versions) is written in pencil and very difficult to transcribe. Dr. Morgan Gulick of the Johns Hopkins department of pathology, to whom I showed the original pages, suggests they have the appearance of a man writing with difficulty after a heart attack or a stroke.

1962

WHAT BROUGHT ME BACK TO LIFE was the death of Eliot Tjaden in Rome, at the bungling hands of Italian surgeons who operated on him in August, 1961, for a perforated ulcer. The obituaries were amazingly lengthy, almost with a Talmudic salute to greatness, and treated him as one of the two giants (the other being Faulkner) of American writing in the twentieth century. Some of the facts were wrong and often superficial. The newsmagazines wrote pure fiction, and the *Saturday Review* seemed edited down from a more vigorous text on the perspective of the tossed-away years. But in the main Jay had a great send-off. And there were demands for me as a lecturer on "A Key to *Stone Sunlight* and *Fragments from Carthage.*" Not from the ladies' clubs, the popular forums fed on hairy fried-chicken and iron green-peas, but from certain colleges given to such courses as The Europe of Gertrude Stein and Eliot Tjaden, or The American Writer in Exile, James to Tjaden. That sort of thing. It was badly done but it meant survival. And transportation, hotel and board, a lot of drinking afterward with men in worn tweeds with pipes, women in Capri pants, carrying copies of *Naked Lunch* often under the impression Jay had written it under a pen name.

The jet that took me to California the first week in May flew high,

374

nearly silently, smoothly, nimbly, hardly like the crates we flew in 1916 reeking of fuel oil, shaking and easy to destroy with a Lewis gun. In this jet age traveling by air was no longer flying; it was commercial transport. I was in San Francisco before I knew it. The steep hills were not my destination; I went onward in a two-motored job I didn't trust—did its motors consist of wound-up rubber bands? —that took me down the coast to Santa Madre, a rich man's graveyard with the dead mostly unburied, sitting in villas, modern ranch houses facing the Pacific . . . palm trees, lofting blue distances . . . where nearly everyone was very old, fingers twitching spasmodically, served by youth. "They have everything but good taste," Jay used to say, "so they become art collectors." Proud in reaction, given to the milder arts of string quartets, croquet and enemas. There was a huge new, ugly, red-tiled college on the edge of this place, a state university, no better or worse than most, a factory actually. Here thousands every year hurried through the courses, lockstepped to a degree, and went out to face the savage sunlight with clear-eyed mediocrity. If there was a distinguished name on the faculty I had not heard it. Still, I was promised two hundred dollars, room, food, and transportation back East all for taking part in some round-table discussions. (The professors all have little beards, and scratch their balls in their baggy tweeds when no one is looking, and there is always one who has a transistor radio and listens with an earphone to the Dodgers game—the Pop Art ploy). The rest are usually crack-ups like me, with bad kidneys, gout, blurred eyesight, or Stone Age dentistry. Some were once mentioned in *Transition* or *Hound and Horn;* others either wrote a book, diddled some canvas, or got into an out-of-print reference book. We'd stir stale facts, mumble, relight our pipes, look over the chicks and the beats asking about Beckett and Ionesco (and I decided in the words of someone I once knew: the world is going to hell in a hack). The only thing worse to me was the Writers' Conferences, those dishonest gatherings of second-rate hacks that attacked Scotty or Ernest and insisted American writing by Poe, Melville, Twain, was sly homosexuality. God save me from the American college brainstorming and the "higher minds." Better the bond salesman, the political fat cat, the real estate shark, the usual low-level standard product. . . .

I'm rambling. (I notice it.) I must watch that. Of late I enjoy my prejudices too much. . . . I arrived in Santa Madre at five in the afternoon. I had a room reserved at the Pineknot Inn. I got out the phone book and looked up an address.

I walked down the main street—parking meters, traffic lights that said DONT WALK, Hawaiian sport shirts, purple bougainvillea, jungle shorts, wide straw hats, green and bister shadows, and lots of shops selling Japanese ceramic trash and Natural Organic Foods. The place I was looking for had a small window trimmed in black and gold, a sign reading BANTLEY'S ANTIQUES FOR THE SPECIAL FEW. Some rotting medieval church pews were in the window with red leather buckets off Admiral Nelson's H.M.S. *Victory,* several T'ang horses battered enough to be the real thing. I went in. A Tibetan monk's bell made soft tinkling sounds. The air was conditioned and I coughed. The place was dimly lit, oak-paneled; several heavy drawers and chests of inlaid wood stood about—one used to see them in Vienna whorehouses in the '20s—and objects I could hardly guess the function of. Some oil paintings, black with age and varnish, showed dimly the bottoms of Christ children in the arms of Marys.

A young Negro girl, pale lemon, with hair dyed red and set high, came toward me on fine legs. Her accent was very Rex Harrison British. I said I'd like to see Mrs. Bantley and I said I didn't have an appointment, and when the girl said, "Really, now, you'll have to call," I said, "Get your cotton-picking ass in there and tell Mrs. Bantley it's Bill Kite."

I stood in the citron-green light, leaning on my cane, staring at some stone lambs from a primitive back-country graveyard. The girl was back and said (swinging her Billy Brunswick can—oh, his people had made it!) I was to follow her, and I did—to a fumed oak door, and she opened it and I went in. It was a small office, crowded by ancient tables and chairs and objects that gave off the smell of mothballs, lavender, crushed rose petals, cat pee and furniture wax. A large woman, very wide, very big, her hair a red mop redder than the girl's, sat behind a small colonial desk. She was smoking a little black cigarette and drinking something that smelled of gin out of a tall glass. The female gargantua's voice was harsh, hard, booming.

"God! Think of you still around and kicking!"

"I am. So are you."

"Ha!" She took a drink, puffed smoke, mashed out the cigarette in a silver Louis XIV inkpot. "Ha! The only way they'll kill *me* is beat me to death. Sit down, sit down."

The beauty was still there but raddled, weathered. The sun and coastal winds, and the gin, had worked on it. There wasn't much left, just the dark luminous eyes of a Caravaggio—bloodshot. I sat down in an uncomfortable chair.

"I'm here to talk about Jay at the college."

"So the paper said. Want a booze?"

"Yes, Pages."

"It's gin."

"That's fine."

She poured me a shot from a container of cut glass. I lifted the glass and took a draw. She toasted me back laughing. It was amazing how large she had become. Not fat, just huge, wide, as if released and grown a bit too wild.

"I figured I'd see you, Bill. You look like hell, a down-at-heels Silenus."

"I've been pretty sick. Had a bad attack of shingles. Funny-sounding thing but cruel. Very painful. Unbearable at times. Drink the only thing for it."

"You've let yourself go, sweet."

"You've held up fine. Very fine." I lied with a voice that was like an oboe coughing.

"Sure I have. But then I was always a hearty gal. I didn't go all the way as most of you did. I walk two miles a day. I sleep eight hours a night. And I spit in the eye of the world."

"I bet you do. Life is remorseless but not disapproving, Pages."

"Nobody has called me that since old Bantley died. We were married for eighteen years. He handled my aunt's estate for me when she died. Well, he was good company and a gentleman. An ingrained moral sense. Knew how to respect a woman."

"Not like us, Pages?"

"No, not like you bastards. You talking today?"

"No, tomorrow."

"Then you can have another drink."

"Thanks."

We sat sipping among Regency and Italianate trash, and she lit another cigarette and I relit my pipe. I suppose it was shock, just as I

377

must have been a physical shock to her. I had expected not reality but the woman I had last seen in 1945: still slim, fashionable, neatly combed, proudly and lightly walking over the earth. A tight coercive personality, skin clear, pearly; and now there was only this giantess spreading over a big chair and grinning at me as she drank.

"Go ahead, say it, sweet. You've just discovered we all grow old at the same time. All wreck ourselves on obligations and risks. Bantley, he liked me as I was . . ."

"Was he good to you?"

"The best, Bill, the best. The only man I ever was really sure of myself with. Fully released to endure life."

"That's damn unkind."

"Listen, boychik" (echoes of Tony!). "We're too old to horseshit each other with denials and penitence. All of you—Jay, Tony, you—what did you know of seeing a woman? Just your own fun slap-and-tickle, your damn male egos pounding something into a mattress and talking of art and literature. Bantley didn't have anything else, just me. Bantley took care of me, not the way you think—I lost interest in that, the thread-and-needle game—but for what a woman wants: comfort, love, affection, a base, a home. The human proportion not lost or blurred. Bantley, he—"

"Did he have a first name?"

"Bantley? Sure he did. What the hell was it? Kelton."

"Not much better. I'm pleased you had a good marriage."

She slapped the table with a ham of a hand. Laughed very loudly. There was a sculptured flow to her like an avalanche. "Ha, you're being ironic now. The hell with you, then. You still don't understand. A woman wants more than art and talk about art and dirty corners of hotel rooms, and the unwashed smell of genius."

"They're not all gamy."

"Enough are, sweet, enough. Here, give me your glass. Woman is woman and not a fake man. Woman is roots, and you can have the masterpieces. Burn them all. You, Jay, Tony—what the hell did you all want in life?"

"They wanted fame, money. I wanted to be where things happened."

"Well, they got it. Glory, money, a good look. So? Tony salting his bones in some sea bottom, for all his hunger, all his grabbing. And Jay, poor bastard, all those dirty hungry years in crummy cafés, all that scribbling, scribbling—for what? To spoil a lot of paper that college snobs have festivals for? So now he's gone and the fame is here. Can he taste it, enjoy it, wear it, screw it?"

"No, Pages, he can't. But aren't you pleased you knew him?"

"No. I wanted life you didn't print or hang on museum walls . . . fun, crazy parties . . . and I wanted babies. I wanted to have smelly, stinky wet babies. I wanted to see them grow up, cause me trouble, give me heartbreak; that's what children are for—to make life real. So instead I got laid by genius, and a dozen versions of myself were put down in his books, and *all* lies."

"Jay wasn't very good with women characters. Tony gave you the parties, the fast cars, the fun."

"He gave me his bourgeois Jew sickness. The desire to prove oneself, swallow things, own things. He couldn't rest, couldn't light. No, in the end he was worse than Jay. And *you*—" She waved me off with a ferocity of gesture, a bafflement of pity.

"We can skip *that*," I said.

There was a tap on the door and the girl came in. "I'm closing up, Mrs. Bantley. It's five-thirty."

"You do that, Drusilla."

The girl came over and kissed Pages's cheek with a respectful yet ostentatious gesture, and got a pat on the tail. The girl looked at me with that mean hateful look I've seen in a million Negro eyes—a look subservient to terror—and she went out on very slim legs.

"She's a lippy victim but very bright and good for the trade. My customers feel an exquisite guilt in front of her."

"Does she have to have red hair?"

"It's a mockery of us. Drusilla is a Phi Beta Kappa and is writing a thesis on the malevolence in James Baldwin's prose. I asked her if she was appointed to cut my throat when the Negro revolution takes over here, and she said . . . know what she said?"

"What?" I asked as Pages went into a gale of laughter.

"She said, no, that was the job of Hank Penrose, the Negro ceramic designer. Gives you something to live for, doesn't it?"

I said it did.

"Where did we fail you, Pages?"

"You didn't see I wasn't very bright, and I didn't care for what kept you busy. You didn't live." Pages put away the glass bottle and stood up. She was even more immense standing. "I didn't care for what you all had, really. And you couldn't come down to my level. I didn't want much, and you, none of you, cared to find me out. It's a great world, sweet."

"I've always felt that. I'm pleased you were happy with Bantley. Could we have dinner?"

"No, I have to drive down to L.A. tonight and sell a lot of crap to some golden ghetto down there, called Krousdale or something. All the bad taste of the world rolled in money and fried in the sun."

"Some other time . . ."

"I'm glad you caught me before I left." Pages held out a hand and I took it. She had quite a grip.

"You're strong."

"We're the last of the mob, Bill. Charlie gone, Jay, Tony, Gertrude, Scotty, Ernest—how did you like *his* last caper?"

"He always feared natural death. Loved to destroy the undulation of all breathing creatures, himself included. He shouldn't ever have been given a gun."

"Yes. Well, Bill, I have to hurry and change. You look ghastly. Here, try these, have all the A, B, C, B–12, and other vitamins you need. I thrive on them."

She tossed me a small bottle half full of yellow pills. I caught it and I said, "Do I get a kiss too?"

It was like touching your lips to a saddle. Outside I threw the little bottle into a bed of cyclamen flowers.

EDITOR'S NOTE: The above section of the manuscript presented several serious problems. First of all, it is one of those parts of which I wrote in the beginning: There are several versions; in this case four, two of them incomplete. All four differ somewhat, but I have tried to compile one version that puts together what they all have in common as to the story they tell and what they say, though the dialogue differs somewhat. There is a deceptive immediacy and spontaneity here. And more.

There is a patness, a summing up in the episode that worried and puzzled me from the start, an incongruity and mystification of pattern. It too perfectly capped the events in William Kite's manuscript. I have now come to the conclusion that the entire episode of the meeting is an invention, a sort of hallucinatory fiction with which William Kite, perhaps subconsciously, brings the image of Pages to a grotesque end in his memory, a sort of pathological elaboration—even a subconscious revenge.

I base my theory on the following. William Kite was not in Santa Madre

380

at the time he mentioned but two weeks later—when he did appear at the college for three days. A letter I wrote to Mrs. Bantley produce~~ the answer that she was not Nora Pages (she did not write that she had *never* been) and that, as she remembered, she was in New Orleans at an antique show at the time of the college event. Two other letters of mine to Mrs. Bantley for further details have remained unanswered.

So I include the best version of the event I could get out of the various drafts and leave it at that. I doubt if the difference between reality and fantasy was often too clear at this time to William Kite. He was a sick man, and must have known he had little time left. It may have amused him to project a version that was what he ironically wanted to exist, even if only on paper, rather than to leave merely a blank.

The following fragments seem to indicate that William Kite no longer had the strength to continue his narration, or that he had written as much as he cared to put down. He had, it would appear, tried to sum up in a kind of philosophy personal to himself.

Living is a lonely job—contemplation can make us essentially solitaries . . . the inner life lost to the outer crowds. Yet relationship is blood and bile—it feeds and enriches, gives to specks of inner illumination the bomb bursts of ecstasy. One can avoid a terrifying sense of the arctic, a universal emptiness, spiritual burial, the spearing to death of passion by just touching someone. It's enough.

No fashionable despair, no entire disillusionment eaten whole like cloying pie. There are fabulous presences all around us in the dancing dust. A shadow is not mere change—a life full of shadows becomes form and content. Illusions may be empty, but the world is not weightless—we can build a scale to put it on.

The more we see of life the more we are aware of its frailty, its transience—shifting, dissolving, changing. These unresolved discords are the few captured visions of experience.

We must try to plunge into insoluble mystery, try to pierce deeper but seek no explanation of the enigma—for the Absolute has been shattered. Enjoy the surface touch, the warmth of its beauty; and perhaps suddenly fragments of it will explain themselves, beg you to understand, roll at your feet like puppies, little riddles of the universe damping your floor as they bark out their small secrets.

Taste is perhaps the only morality. Then there are the people who prefer sensation to thought. The art of the inner eye is open to the

381

solar system. "The world is one great thought and I am thinking it."
(John Kemble)

If God is, then the solid objects of this world can become an
illusion; the starting point onward. The saint avoids life and the wise
man avoids saints. As the years go, the risks we take cost less.

In love there are ideas that set off emotional charges which liberate
the gases of passion. But most emotions are a little tragedy that
culminate in no catastrophe.

Love is a peculiarly virulent infection. To observe it without harm
one must stand at an angle to society and not defend one's position.
Love exists because men want to live twice; once alone, again with
another body.

Some pray for a release from amorous desire like a liberation from
an insane and cruel master.

The metaphysical aspects of life appear simple; you can't talk of
black without referring to white. . . . So most people want only to
stay alive, but the individual wants to live.

As Clemenceau said of Pétain—so can it be said of mass man—
"He is immortal. He has no heart, no brain, and no guts. How can a
man like that die?"

Few can accept the law of Karma and causation—cause and
sequence. The Atman who has neither form nor limit, who is
infinite—exhaling and inhaling—no repulsion and no attraction, the
nirvana of self-realization . . . and nothing. It is handing back life on
a platter and saying, "No, thank you—I can't face it today."

"The bulk of the People consist, in a Manner, wholly of Discoverers, Witnesses, Informers, Accusers, Prosecutors, Evidences,
Swearers, together with their several and subservient subaltern Instruments." (Swift)

For the alcoholic the easy solace of the bottle dissolves hard values
into digestible skepticism, and merges into an affected stoicism that
clothes a weary despair.

Drink is a clumsy audacity that hides a wary reticence and taut
nerves. It can come round to Baudelaire's *"Il a crée un nouveau*

382

frisson," the shakes at the daily horror of just existing. Yet under every snow lies a summer. . . .

EDITOR'S NOTE: Here follow two pages of indecipherable material in scrawling, formless scribbling that suggests an attack of some sort, physical or alcoholic in nature. These are followed by the last two legible items in the manuscript. The second is a newspaper clipping pasted down at the end of the page. I have been unable to identify the paper or the date.

I am responsible to all of life; all people are themselves responsible to bear the ideal of each great idea. So every great idea bears the ideals of all men.

We are easily seduced by personal fame or desire, too much in anger at our boredoms, too readily knocked off our trollies by emotional vagaries; still we remain in the end human beings. For the end to everything is our forgiveness.

There was a roll of thunder and a great voice spoke out in the sky. "This is God speaking. God speaking. I have dreadful news for you. The end of the world is at hand. The end of the world is at hand. . . . This is a recording."